THE CALL OF CRIMSON

MORGANA BLACK

Cover design and chapter headers by Selkkie Design
Hardcover artwork by Zoë J. Osik
Map artwork by Mytinybookshelfs
Editing by Samantha Swart
Proofreading and formatting by M.A. Kilpatrick

Paperback 979-8-9911585-9-6
Hardcover 979-8-9911585-8-9

Black Dahlia Publishing

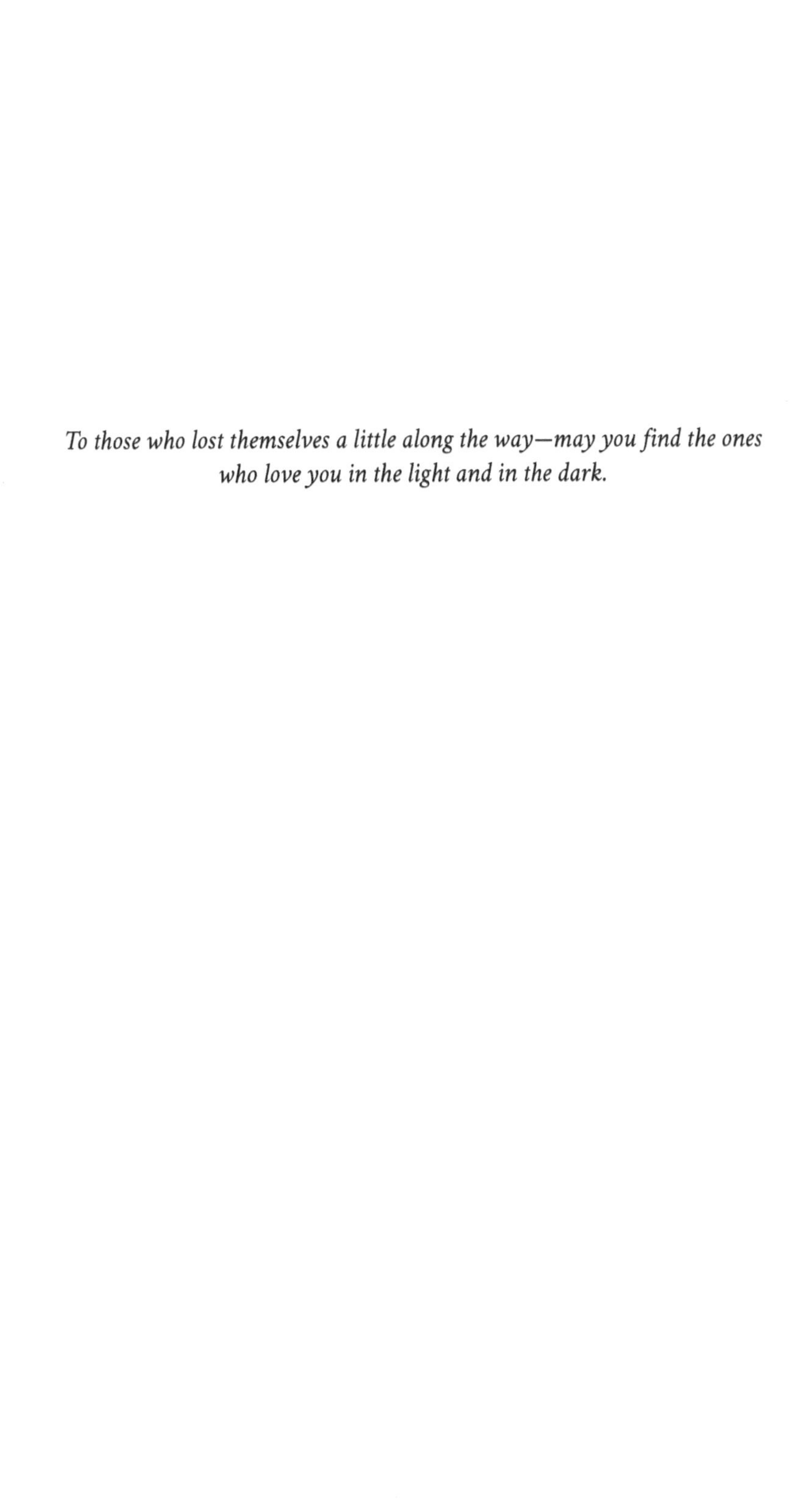

To those who lost themselves a little along the way—may you find the ones who love you in the light and in the dark.

A NOTE FROM THE AUTHOR

Dear Reader,

I believe in transparency and protecting your mental health. This is a dark fantasy romance and contains a lot of dark subject matter. I have done my best to compile any triggers, but I'm human, so I apologize if any were missed. This book contains graphic sexual content, explicit language, death (both off and on page), physical and mental abuse by a parent (in the past), psuedo-family love interest, poisoning, representations of grief, violence, attempted murder, drinking, breath play, blood play, knife play, and bodily fluids.

If you have any questions, please do not hesitate to contact me at MORGANA@AUTHORMORGANABLACK.COM.

ALSO BY MORGANA BLACK

The Crimson and Shadows Series

The Sorrow of Shadows (Book 1)

The Call of Crimson (Book 2)

THE CALL OF CRIMSON PLAYLIST

Do you love an immersive reading experience? The Call of Crimson playlist has songs curated specifically for each chapter, including the prologue and epilogue.

https://open.spotify.com/playlist/4XqSaz4mlzN0NPzPB7tKZz?si=MoE74QgbQE-cLhA75bOKwg

MAGIC SYSTEM

HEMONIA

Anything related to the physical body/energy

- Blood manipulation
- Life/death touch
- Energy siphoning
- Healers

KAMINARI

Anything related to the weather

- Lightning
- Storms
- Elementals (earth, fire, air, water, metals)

ANIMA

Anything related to the soul/mind

- Empaths
- Reading memories

- Sensing intentions/lie detection
- Coercion

VIZIE

Anything related to sight

- Visions
- Illusions
- Dream walking/manipulation
- Astral projection

MADILIM

- Light manipulation
- Shadow manipulation

TIERNA
TÓIN

SKERRY
MELORIA
LENNOX
CAEDEL
ELENTIA
DAREST
CIYORIA
PRUDIA
INASVINE
AMALA
PELANOR
TRIA
ANDHULL
RIMOR

LAST TIME ON CRIMSON & SHADOWS...

Hello sweethearts, Elijah here. Breyla's insisting that we need a recap of our previous shit show—I mean story—to remind everyone what the hell happened.

Our last adventure began with the untimely (and suspicious) death of King Raynor. That's not nearly enough drama for Breyla to come home and see me, but the ghost of her dead father sure did the trick! When she arrived home, it was to the announcement of her mother's betrothal to her long-time nemesis, Lord Aurelius. She's never gotten along with him (don't ask me why, I've never understood her hatred for him), but it didn't help that he's also her late father's adopted brother. Can you say daddy issues?

Weeks pass, and nothing happens until one night we're playing cards and getting wine drunk in Breyla's room. Well, I'm playing cards, she's mostly getting drunk. Eventually, we pass out, and she's woken up by her father's ghost. He tells her he was murdered. *le gasp* He claims it was none other than... HIS BROTHER. Weirdly enough, his ghost appears to Aurelius, claiming that he was murdered by Lord Seamus. Strange that not many people caught that or questioned the ghost at this point. Anyway, it sets the Breyla and Aurelius on a collision course in their quests to avenge Raynor's murder.

Breyla pretends to be drunk and mad with grief for a while—that was interesting. Lord Aurelius uses his Hemonia Gift to see right through the bullshit and tries to call her on it. They butt heads for a while until Aurelius pulls rank on Breyla. He commands her second and third-in-command to return to the capital, thus pissing her off and forcing her to show her true colors to him. This is also the part where Aurelius uses his Gift to calm her temper in the middle of a fight, then shows her *exactly* what he can do with his power *wink wink.*

Things get complicated when people start trying to kill them both. Someone poisons Aurelius' eggs, but a maid ends up dead instead. Then someone drugs Breyla's wine and attacks her in her sleep. Aurelius finds Breyla and sends her maid, Lyla, to fetch the court physician. Instead, she comes back with Lady Ophelia who, as it turns out, can heal people? The castle spent years believing she was magicless, turns out she's scary powerful.

But in a hot way.

We weren't totally sure if we could trust Ophelia before this, but we definitely were now. Aurelius and Breyla reluctantly agree to become allies since someone is obviously coming for them both. The enemy of my enemy is my friend, or something like that.

Right after that, someone slits Commander Nolan's throat, and everyone is devastated. He was like a second father to Breyla and well-loved by all. After his funeral, Aurelius corners Breyla and makes it clear he thinks it's stupid to invite Prince Ayden II of Prudia (the enemy kingdom) to the castle—something Breyla has already done by this point.

Breyla dispatches Julian to follow Lord Seamus because he's acting suspicious, and nobody likes him. As she's working out some frustration, Aurelius shows up and helps her work out a different type of frustration (these two really could not be more obvious), and he leaves her pantless in the middle of the woods.

I find it hilarious when she has to come to me for help, but she disagrees. We have a little heart-to-heart where I tell her she's being ridiculous, then send her on her merry way the next morning. Tensions are already high between Breyla and Aurelius when Ayden shows up to court just hours later. Kind of weird how quickly he arrives.

We know things are getting out of hand when someone sends Breyla a box with Julian's head in it. Frankly, I think I forgot how to breathe.

The next day, Aurelius finds Breyla planning an engagement ball for her mother and him. He tells her she needs to actually grieve, and they have a big emotional blow-out where we learn that Breyla's slipping control over her shadows is related to her compartmentalization of her emotions.

We have a ball, Breyla wears a fancy dress, but all I can look at is Ophelia. Breyla and Aurelius end up banging—finally—and all is right for about thirty seconds. Breyla has a dream where she's doing the deed with Ayden, and we learn about his ability to infiltrate and manipulate dreams.

Breyla gets insecure about the fact that she's sleeping with her mother's fiancé, so he exposes their relationship to Genevieve to prove a point. She's weirdly relieved but tells them they still need to keep it quiet.

The two lust-birds embark on a journey to recover Julian's body and make a stop at her grandparents' estate, where she gets a peek at Aurelius' childhood with her father. They meet a feisty female along the way, named Nameah, whom Breyla takes a liking to. She leads them to Julian's body, where they are attacked by a strange enemy. Nameah is cut with a poisoned blade, and they have to rush back to Ciyoria in hopes that Ophelia can heal her, since Aurelius isn't able to stop the poison.

While they're gone, I get some steamy time with that stunning female, Ophelia, and let Jade punch me in the face. When Aurelius and Breyla return, we discover that not even Ophelia can heal the poison, leaving Nameah to die tragically.

After Julian's and Nameah's funeral, our little group gathers to discuss what comes next. Ophelia and I break into her father's study and find incriminating evidence while Breyla goes searching for answers in town. She finds an entire family (remember that maid that died from eating Aurelius' eggs? Yeah, her family didn't leave town like everyone thought), slaughtered in their beds. This leads her to confront her old flame, the King of the Midnight Brotherhood, the local mercenary group.

Cillian insists he didn't have anything to do with it, but it might be the work of rogue mercenaries.

Lastly, Breyla breaks into the room of Prince Ayden and finds letters linking him to Lord Seamus' treachery. Which is not surprising, considering he's had it out for her since King Raynor killed his father in battle several years ago.

Everything goes to shit when Breyla decides to expose Ayden and Seamus at dinner that night. Ayden goes peacefully, which is suspicious, but we're more concerned with Lord Seamus. He's livid and throwing accusations at his daughter, Ophelia. He hurls a poisoned blade at her, but Layne steps in front of her, taking the hit himself. He dies in her arms, and Ophelia snaps. Exposing her power to the entire room, she literally sucks the life out of her father and drops his withered corpse on the floor before passing out. Gods, she's beautiful.

To make matters worse, Queen Genevieve decides now is the best time to admit that *she* is the one who murdered Raynor. But before we can ask any questions, she drinks poisoned wine.

As we're all reeling from what's just happened, Ayden reenters the room with a slow clap. Turns out he had nothing to do with any of the deaths he was accused of, but it seems like he knows who does. It's all overshadowed by his confession that Aurelius is his brother and Breyla is his fiancée.

We're left with a lot more questions, but that brings us to now. Now, it's time to get some answers.

PROLOGUE

Flames lick at my skin, their heat singeing my fingers as I stare at Rimor burning to the ground. Though it's midday, the smoke has eclipsed the sun entirely, casting darkness over the land. Fighting a scream, I clench my fist and cast my eyes down. The castle crumbles before me, and there's nothing I can do to stop it. My Gifts can't save them. All I can do is watch.

Blood streams through the cobblestones of the street below, staining them with the life force of the innocents slaughtered today. If there was anything left in my stomach, I'm sure it would have come up by now. The screams of those who escaped the massacre echo in the distance as they flee the flames. I sob, knowing their fate will be no different than those already dead. The fire was meant to drive them from the castle walls to the waiting soldiers outside of Ciyoria—and it has done just that.

My sword clatters against the cobblestone as it slips from my hand. I was never the target. This was all a punishment for failing to heed their warnings.

All for love.

I did this for love, and the price was my soul.

My vision blurs, and suddenly I'm somewhere different. I'm naked, lying in a bed, staring into hazel eyes. Never had I expected to care for him, but I do. With my entire being, I love this male. He's holding me close, a hand trailing down my side as he stares into my eyes. Silk sheets cling to our damp, exhausted bodies, and he presses a tender kiss to my lips.

"We need to get out of bed, my love. There are people waiting to speak with us."

"Fuck them. I'm staying right where I belong—buried between My Queen's thighs. They don't need us, anyway."

His normally warm, deep voice is glacial and foreign. It's everything he isn't.

My brow furrows. "You don't mean that. Our people rely on us."

He trails kisses down my throat, mumbling, "I do mean it. Enough talking, wife. The next sound out of your lips will be my name as I eat my breakfast."

My lips part to protest, but true to his word, the next thing out of my mouth is his name as he does exactly what he promised.

The scene changes again.

I'm staring at raven hair and grey eyes. An inexplicable knowing washes over me, something whispering that this female walks the line between life and death. She gazes into the dark eyes of the male embracing her, smiles lighting both of their faces. A crown of gold studded with black jewels adorns his head; a matching, more petite version sits on hers. He leans in and kisses her, and the scene fades.

Hazel eyes stare up at me, the green in them glowing brighter from the sheer disbelief and betrayal carving across his features. Tears stream down my cheeks as I stare at the male I swore to love forever. He's held immobile by the vines wrapped around his wrists. His eyes fix on me, begging for an explanation for the blade of ice that hovers against his throat. I owe him this.

"I've been keeping secrets, my love," I whisper.

"Whatever it is, we can work through it together," he says softly. His eyes are clear for the first time in weeks. Whatever darkness was tainting his mind has no hold on him for now.

"No, we can't. Not this time." I choke on a sob. "Something has infected your mind, and there is no cure."

My husband's soul is pure and noble. The most honorable male I have ever known.

"I know, darling. I can feel it too. But I don't know what it is."

"I can't name it, but the visions are clear on where this ends."

He looks at me in confusion. "Visions?"

"They started last year," I admit. I had told no one. It's unheard of for someone to develop a new Gift this far into life. I'm unsure what it means, but I believe it to be both a blessing and a curse from the gods.

"And what do they say?" he asks, face falling.

"I have a choice. I can allow the madness to continue, and Rimor will fall —you will be the death of our kingdom and people. Or I can end it now and save them," I whisper through the tears that pour freely now. "All it will cost is my heart and soul." My chest heaves as I stare into the eyes of my best friend, my soul mate, my lover, and my king.

"You swore an oath to this kingdom and our people before you ever swore yourself to me. I expect you to uphold that oath, no matter the cost."

His words shouldn't surprise me, but they do.

"My love?" I question, unsure how he expects that of me.

"I have one request."

"Anything," I breathe.

"Release your vines. Let me hold my wife in my last moments. Grant me that. Please."

A sob rattles me as I loosen the vines. His arms wrap around me, pulling me tightly into his chest. His fingers weave into my golden tresses, rubbing soothing circles into my skin.

"I love you, Genevieve. I have from the very first moment I laid eyes on you. Through every fight, every sadness, every difficult decision, every moment of joy, and everything in between," his voice trembles as he recites our wedding vows, "I have loved you in this lifetime and I'll love you through the next. Until the very end"

"I love you, Raynor. Through this lifetime and whatever comes after," The words shake from my lips, "Until the very end."

He reaches for my hand, his fingers gently wrapping around my wrist. "Form another ice dagger. Make it thinner, but sharp."

I do as he says, crafting a dagger barely wider than a needle. He lifts it, positioning it at his ear.

For a moment, I hesitate. The overwhelming desire to call for my fire and melt the weapon nearly wins. This isn't right, and I grapple with how I'm supposed to see this through.

These hands have soothed every hurt, mended broken furniture, and created the greatest pleasure. They held me when Breyla's delivery stretched into a twenty-seven-hour ordeal, massaging every muscle to help me relax. And when I wanted to give up, they refused to let me fall. Then they held our baby girl as she came screaming into this world.

My heart cannot reconcile those hands with the ones from my visions— the ones that take the lives of thousands.

"Right here, darling. Make it quick. No one will suspect anything." His deep timbre breaks through the fog, bringing me back to this moment.

"What do I tell our daughter?" My lips tremble, the thought of keeping this from Breyla nearly as painful as what I'm about to do.

"When she's ready... you'll tell her the truth. And that I love her—that I am proud of her. Tell her I'm so very sorry."

"I will tell her, my love. When she's ready."

"Gen, the council will force you to remarry to maintain the throne."

"I know," I whisper. "I don't want to think about that right now."

"It has to be Aurelius," he says definitively. "I trust no one else with my kingdom or my wife."

"I couldn't possibly marry—"

"You can and you will. You must survive this."

I meet his hazel eyes one last time and whisper, "Until the very end."

"Until the very end," he echoes as I slip the blade into his head.

It only takes moments for the light to fade from his eyes.

His body goes limp in my arms.

And my heart dies in that bed with him.

CHAPTER ONE

BREYLA

After death, when the heart has ceased beating, the body will occasionally continue breathing. The chest rises and falls for several minutes after the heart has stopped, making it appear as though the deceased is still alive. It doesn't always happen, but the first time you witness it is one of the most morbidly intriguing experiences.

It's the postmortem motions of my mother's chest that I see every time I close my eyes. The way her blue eyes glazed over and dimmed. The life leaving her, despite the rhythmic rise and fall of her chest for several long, tormenting minutes.

Dead bodies aren't foreign to me, but nothing could prepare me for holding my mother as she passed from this world. The sorrow of losing my father had clung to me, my shadows feeling the heavy weight of my pain, but nothing compares to watching the light fade from her eyes as Aurelius stopped her heart. The same poison that claimed Nameah and Layne claimed her, too.

And I wish it had taken me with her.

That was two days ago. I think. I haven't really slept, but judging by the number of meals left at my door, two days feels right.

I see no one, speak to no one.

I simply exist.

The soft patter of rain against my window is the only thing keeping me grounded as my mind drifts to memories of her.

"Come on, Breyla. It is time to meet your uncle," Mother called from the doorway.

I had known Father's younger brother was coming to live at the palace for weeks. Father said it was because he required more training than Grandpa or Grandma could give him. I didn't really care why. I only cared that their attention would be on him instead of me.

"I do not wish to meet my uncle," I said with a pout.

"And I do not care what you wish. You are eight and will do as you're told for once." An exasperated sigh left my mother's lips as she took in the state of me. "Are there twigs in your hair?"

"Probably," I said, fingers feeling through the tangled mess of red curls.

"But why are there twigs in your hair?" she asked, trying to pick them out and comb out my tangles.

I opened my mouth to respond, but she cut me off. "You know what? I don't want to know. This has Elijah's name written all over it. Let's just get them out so your uncle doesn't think you're a heathen the first time he meets you." Her tone shifted from frustrated to playful as she tickled my sides and made me giggle.

"But I am a heathen!" I protested as my giggling subsided.

"Yes, but we don't have to let him know that," she teased, pulling me into a hug as she combed out the last of the tangles.

"Mother, is Aurelius going to stay here for a while?" I asked nervously.

"Yes. He needs your father's help and training."

"But what about me?"

My eyes cast downward, insecurity filling me. What if I weren't as powerful as Aurelius when my powers manifested? Would they still care about me?

Her face softened. "Aurelius being here changes nothing for you. You will always be our number one priority, my love."

I try to smile at the memory, but I can't will the muscles in my cheeks to obey.

A knock rattles my door, but I don't bother to respond. A few moments pass before I feel the brush of a familiar Gift press gently against my mental barriers.

"Go away, Elijah."

Again, his Gift nudges me. I sigh, knowing he won't leave me alone. He could break down the door if he wished, but he would choose to be persistent to the point of annoyance first.

With a resigned sigh, I drop the barrier and let him in.

"Open the door, B." His voice is somber, but hopeful. This is the first I've let anyone in since my mother died.

He's standing just outside the door, speaking out loud so I'll hear. We can't communicate telepathically through his Gift, but I can see and hear what he does when we're connected. As much as I want solitude, his presence in my mind is a soothing balm to my aching soul.

Still seated by the window, I use magic to unlock the door. The handle turns, the door slowly creaking open. It clicks shut behind him, and his cinnamon chocolate scent invades my space, wrapping me in a blanket of familiarity.

"Have you eaten?" His voice is closer than I expected—he's right behind me.

"You know the answer to that question." I turn to look him over.

His dark blond curls are loose, hanging down past his shoulders, tangled and unkempt. Dark circles frame his warm brown eyes that take in my appearance. He nods—not in acceptance but understanding.

"When was the last time you slept?"

A humorless laugh escapes me. "I haven't."

"B—"

"What do you see when you close your eyes at night?"

He laces his fingers with mine, and I let him pull me into his chest. "I see Julian's smile. I see Jade on her knees before his funeral pyre, wholly consumed by the grief of losing her other half." His voice trembles. "I see Ophelia—the way she broke watching Layne die, knowing there was nothing she could do. I see her... never mind."

"I see the light fade from my mother's eyes. Her chest still moves, and it looks like she's still breathing, but I know she's gone. Yet, I hope that maybe I'm wrong. I see it *every single time* I close my eyes, Elijah. And if I manage to sleep, I'm forced to relive her dying in my arms. Over and over. I wake up screaming and alone. So no, I haven't slept."

"You wouldn't have to wake up alone if you let me stay. Or if you let him in."

"I have no desire to see Aurelius ever again," I spit, the memory of his betrayal flooding back with venom.

"You knew."

My eyes locked on Aurelius', heat rising in my chest.

"Princess—"

"Don't fucking call me that. You knew!" I shouted angrily at him.

He reached out a hand for me, but I recoiled at his touch, wanting nothing from him except the truth.

"I knew about your betrothal to Prince Ayden," he admitted, shame and resignation warring in his eyes.

Good.

He should be ashamed.

"And he's your brother," I hissed, lip curling in disgust.

"I didn't—"

"I want nothing from you, Aurelius. Go fuck yourself."

It shattered something inside me to utter those words. He had spent weeks earning my trust, winning my affection despite our sordid history—only to keep life-altering secrets from me.

Betrayal churned in my gut, warring with everything I felt for him.

"He's been a total disaster without you," Elijah murmurs, running a hand up and down my back in quiet comfort.

"He's not my problem."

"I know you feel that way now, B—but he's your heart. And you're his."

"He's my nothing. He betrayed me, kept secrets, and broke my trust."

Elijah sighs and gently guides me away from the window toward my bed. "If I recall, there was another male you swore the same thing about. And yet, he managed to win your trust back, eventually."

"I never felt for Cillian the way I did for Aurelius, E."

"You loved Cillian. Maybe not to the extent that you love Aurelius, but it was real."

I stiffen, furrowing my brow. "I don't love Aurelius."

He sits on my bed, bringing me with him and cocooning us in the heavy quilt.

"Who are you trying to convince—me or yourself?"

I sit with the silence for a while before muttering, "Yes."

Elijah's voice is hesitant as he suggests, "You know… Ayden could help with the nightmares."

"He's keeping more secrets than Aurelius—which is not a surprise since they're brothers—but I don't trust him anywhere near my mind."

"You'll have to trust him eventually. He's your fiancée."

"For now. I'll figure out how to get out of that arrangement."

"Of that, I have no doubt. But I have a feeling he's not your enemy." Something in the curious way he says that snags my attention.

"He sure as hell seems like my enemy right now," I say through a yawn. My body finally relaxes in his arms. I take a deep breath, finding peace in his embrace. Slowly, my eyes drift shut, and sleep finds me for the first time in days.

I wake to furious brown eyes glowing in the moonlight.

Aurelius.

Crimson specks dance in his irises, and his chest heaves like he's been pacing.

Elijah's arm is still curled tightly around me, his soft snores the only sound in the room.

My mind races, searching for clues to why he's here. I had made it clear—repeatedly—that I wanted nothing to do with him.

"Breyla, please. Hear me out—"

"I have no desire to listen to more of your lies, Aurelius. My father signed a marriage contract with Prince Ayden behind my back—but you *knew."*

"Yes, but I—"

"You what? Not only did you know about it, you were the one who facilitated the match on his behalf. You had every opportunity to tell me, yet you said nothing. Instead, you just fucked me and filled my head with pretty words," I snarled, turning on my heel to leave him with his lies.

The memory of our last encounter leaves my blood boiling. Not wishing to engage with him, I flip him my middle finger and mouth *get fucked.*

His hand darts out, catching the offending finger. In an unexpect-edly gentle move, he raises my fingers to his mouth and kisses them. I pull back, my emotions warring inside me. Anger and betrayal are at the forefront, but warmth fills my chest at his touch, leaving me confused. I latch onto the anger and let it drive me.

"I said get fucked." Shadows twist around his throat, constricting at my command. Aurelius drops to his knees, putting us at eye level. "Don't make me say it again," I seethe in his ear.

The shadows around his throat do nothing to stop the rest of him as he yanks me from Elijah's grasp, pinning me beneath him. "Gladly, Princess," he growls, voice rough with restraint. "Just open those pretty thighs so I can taste what's mine."

He gasps the words as the shadows continue to squeeze—but they don't stop him fast enough.

Elijah jolts awake. A protective snarl spills from his lips as he shoves Aurelius off me and onto the floor. His fist collides with Aure-lius' temple in the next breath.

"Elijah!" I shout, trying to stop the chaos.

The distraction is enough for Aurelius to retaliate. He rolls them over, landing a vicious punch to Elijah's cheek.

Blood splatters my floor, the crunch of bone reverberating through the room. Hard pants and a pained groan fill the space as I scream at them both to stop. Both too lost to the adrenaline, they ignore my shouts of protest as they trade hits back and forth.

It continues for what feels like hours—but is really only moments —until the door bursts open.

An irate Ayden glares at us all. The look is not one I have ever seen him with, and it doesn't suit his beautiful face.

"Perfect," I groan. "Just what I need right now."

It takes Ayden less than a second to assess the situation. With barely contained fury, he strides across the room and hauls Aurelius off Elijah, throwing him hard against the wall.

Aurelius hits with a grunt, blood smearing his lip as he sneers, "This doesn't concern you, Prince."

"I think you'll find it does, Prince," Ayden sneers right back.

Prince.

It hadn't even registered that Ayden's revelation about their familial relation meant that Aurelius is a prince.

I kneel, inspecting Elijah's face for injuries. He'll have a gnarly black eye—and his nose is definitely broken.

Grasping my hand, he smiles softly. "I'm fine, B. I've had worse—from you, if we're being honest." He winks.

"Breyla, darling," Ayden drawls. "Do you care to explain what's going on here?"

"Not particularly, darling," I reply mockingly.

"Humor me."

"Just know Aurelius got exactly what he deserved."

"He punched me first," Aurelius snarls, throwing his hands in the air.

"I said what I said," I snap.

Ayden lets out an exasperated sigh, rubbing his temples.

Unable to let it lie, Elijah adds, "I woke up to Breyla pinned beneath Aurelius as he whispered something about tasting what was his. The shadows around his neck made it pretty clear she was distressed."

Ayden's nostrils flare.

"You're not helping, Eli," I sigh.

He shrugs and pushes himself off the floor.

"Elijah, thank you for elaborating," Ayden says, voice tight. "Please return to your own chambers. I can take it from here."

His eyes dart to mine, but he doesn't move. "I'll leave when Breyla dismisses me."

"I'm fine, Elijah. You can leave. Thank you for staying with me."

With a nod and kiss to my temple, he leaves me with Aurelius and Ayden.

The two males face each other, and for the first time, I *really* see them. The resemblance is undeniable. Same strong jaw line, same height, same dark eyes and hair—though Aurelius' features are just a touch darker. Even their scents carry that same blend of spice and earth.

How had I not noticed it before?

"Aurelius," Ayden says coldly, "let me be clear—Breyla is *not* yours. She is *my* fiancée. And I believe she's made her feelings about you perfectly clear."

Possessive fury sparks in Aurelius' gaze. "Fiancée, or not, she will never be yours. She may be displeased with me now, but it will forever be my name on her lips."

I glare at him, willing my eyes to burn him where he stands. "Well, right now the only thing my lips are saying is fuck off."

Reluctantly, Aurelius turns and walks out—but not without pausing in the doorway a moment too long.

I turn my glare to Ayden. "That means you, too, asshole."

In true Ayden fashion, he ignores me and asks, "Care to tell me why Elijah was sleeping in your bed?" His tone is curious but not angry

"How many times must I explain this?" I groan. "Elijah is like a brother to me. Our bond runs deep, but it's never been romantic."

"And do you often share a bed with him?"

I hesitate just a moment before answering honestly, "On occasion. Tonight, he was helping me sleep. His presence calms me. Something I've needed lately." I try to explain without leaving myself exposed. Trust is not something I will give out easily again, and Ayden has not earned it.

His eyes roam over me—not sexually, but like he's taking stock. Assessing damage. "Tell me why you need help sleeping," he says. "What troubles you?"

"I..." the words catch in my throat. I contemplate how much I really want him to know.

"I can't sleep because every time I close my eyes, I see her die. Over and over again. It's all I see—and it torments me."

"Let me help you."

In my grief, I had forgotten about his Vizie Gift as a dream weaver.

My hackles rise, and I narrow my eyes at him. "Why should I trust you?"

"Did you know I was there when my father took his last breath?" Ayden asks in lieu of answering my question.

"I didn't."

I had been young when Ayden's father was bested by my own on the battlefield. The details were never disclosed to me, but I hadn't known Ayden was at that battle. "I didn't realize you were present that day."

"I wasn't," Ayden explains, a sad smile curling his lips. "He didn't die on the battlefield."

"Oh, I had assumed his death was…" My voice trails off, tongue stumbling over the right word for this situation.

"Quick?" Ayden offers, a dark brow arching.

I nod.

"His death took days as he slowly succumbed to not just blood loss, but infection."

I want to give him an empathetic apology, but something tells me it will fall short coming from the daughter of the male responsible for his father's death. As much as it pains me that he lost his father, I don't regret it—I can't. It meant that my own came home that day.

"Could a physician or healer not have saved him?" I wonder.

His shoulders drop. "There were none available to reach him in time."

"Oh."

His eyes go distant in quiet contemplation. "The point is," he says, shaking himself out of the memory. "He arrived home the day before he died, delirious with pain. I never left his side, holding him until he took his last breath."

"Ayden," I breathe, unsure what to say.

He saves me from having to figure it out when he continues, "I watched him die—for nearly twenty-four hours straight—knowing there was nothing I could do to stop it. And for six months straight, I relived it every night in my dreams."

"Six months?" I ask, utter disbelief and horror tinging my words.

He nods solemnly. "The only difference between you and me, love?" He laughs, the sound a dry, humorless thing that sends goosebumps down my spine. "I didn't have anyone to save me from my nightmares. Dream weavers can't alter their own dreams."

"What a cruel trick the gods have played on you."

"I blame Marynx," he chuckles.

"The god of chaos?"

He shrugs, a smirk tugging at the corner of his mouth. "Just seems like something chaos would delight in. Give someone the Gift of meddling or easing dreams, only to balance it by not allowing them to meddle in their own.

"Are you sure you don't mean Saelem? It seems way more in line with something the god of mischief would enjoy."

"Nah, I doubt it. Saelem may be a trickster, but he's not intentionally cruel."

"I think all the gods have a cruelty to them—even if it's small," I muse.

"Perhaps you're right, but I digress," he says, brushing a lock of hair behind my ear. "I know you don't believe me, but I am not your villain, Breyla. I don't wish to see you in pain."

"Pain is all I know right now." The words spill out before I can stop them.

"Then allow me to help," he pleads again, "I would have given anything to make the dreams stop after my father died. Please trust I'm just trying to spare you from that pain."

After a long moment, my shoulders sag. I nod.

Taking me by the hand, he leads me back to bed. I crawl in and stare up at him, waiting to feel the gentle caress of his Gift. He leans down and presses a kiss to my temple. The subtle touch of his magic caresses my mind, and I lower my mental shields to let it in.

"Was that completely necessary?"

"The kiss?" He smirks and glances toward the door. "Not even a little. But Aurelius is still watching from the hall. And I do love pissing him off."

"Fucking territorial male bullshit," I groan as something crashes against the other side of my wall in Aurelius' room.

"Good night, Breyla," he says with a chuckle, and slips out.

With the touch of his magic, it takes only moments for sleep to claim me again.

CHAPTER TWO

BREYLA

"**A**re you ready?" Elijah asks, though no one answers.

Aurelius, Ayden, Jade, and Ophelia gather in a circle around us. Ayden had dragged me from my room this morning for what he called a "family meeting" regarding the night of my mother's death. It was awfully presumptuous, considering I barely knew him, and Aurelius was hardly someone I felt a familial connection to. They were the only true family in the room, a fact that Aurelius did not enjoy me pointing out.

Despite my distrust, I wanted answers. I didn't mind gathering everyone with Ayden since I hadn't given him a chance to explain his involvement or what he did—or didn't—know.

Elijah revealed that in her final moments, my mother had shared a flood of memories with him. Until now, I hadn't been ready to face them. In truth, I'm still not, but Ayden didn't give me a choice. He carried me out against my will, despite the punches I threw at his kidneys.

I sit curled in an oversized armchair, Ophelia beside me. The two of us choose the furthest spot from every male in the room, which seems like the safest course after last night.

"How are you?" I ask Ophelia, ignoring Elijah's question.

"I'm…here." Her voice cracks. She looks as shattered as I feel.

"He's just… gone. Layne was the only family I truly cared about, who cared about me. And it doesn't feel real. It's like I'm walking through a dream, just waiting to wake up and find that none of this ever happened."

I take her hand in my own. "I know exactly what you mean."

Her head drops to my shoulder, her body trembling as a single tear slips down her cheek.

"My mother once told me that there are two types of family—the kind we are born into and the kind we choose. They're different, but both beautiful. I need you to know, you're part of my chosen family, Ophelia. We aren't alone in this world."

She gently squeezes my hand. "I choose you, too, Breyla."

I glance back toward Elijah. Ayden and Aurelius flank him, leaning against the wall with arms crossed. Aurelius glares daggers at Ayden, who wears his usual permanent smirk.

Ayden waves a hand for him to start. "Elijah, the floor is yours."

Elijah swallows slowly, his jaw clenching as he heaves a deep breath in, then finally out. His eyes glaze over as he searches for the words he wants to say. "In her final moments, the queen shared memories that answer a lot of our questions. I won't lie, some of them are difficult to watch, so I'll spare you those for now."

I cut in, choking on the question that's haunted me since the night she died, "Why did she kill my father?"

"The short answer—she had no choice." Elijah pauses. "And… he asked her to."

Bile pools in the back of my throat, the hot acidic burn making me choke back tears. "Wh-what?"

Elijah waits a beat, then asks gently, "Were you aware your mother had a Vizie Gift?"

"No, she didn't. I would have known."

He turns to Aurelius, whose face is, shockingly, ashen with disbelief. "She never mentioned anything like that to me."

"She had visions," Elijah says. "One, in particular, that came to her again and again. It never changed. Just grew worse each time."

He holds out his hands. One by one, we reach for him.

When we're all connected, he lets the memory play.

Flames crawl up the walls of the castle, engulfing Ciyoria. Smoke blackens the sky, swallowing the sun, and casting a dark glow over the land.

Queen Genevieve stands alone as the castle crumbles around her. The sword slips from her hand, clattering to the cobblestones, the sound dull compared to the scream tearing from her throat.

Streams of blood run through the cobblestone street, staining it with the lives of the innocents slaughtered here today. The people flee the flames right into the waiting line of enemy soldiers. Those that were not claimed by the fire die at the end of a sword. All innocent, but all slaughtered.

"I told you our people didn't need us, my love."

My father appears behind her, a wicked smile on his face. His eyes are cold and hard, devoid of any compassion or life.

"You vowed to protect them!" she screams, fury and sorrow in every word. "Instead, you butchered them!"

"It is time this kingdom paid for its sins," he replies. "Change is here, My Queen."

The vision ends.

My chest tightens, and the tears I've been holding back fall freely.

"That's what she saw?" I whisper.

"Every night. For nearly a year," Elijah confirms.

"That… explains a lot," Aurelius whispers, his voice cracking. His eyes meet mine for a heartbeat, then dart away.

My mind frantically tries to connect the dots. The pieces are all there, yet somehow not fitting. "You said he asked her to kill him?"

Elijah nods, swallowing hard. "The night he died, she confronted him. He admitted something had a grip on his mind, but he didn't know what it was. He told her she'd made a vow to the kingdom before she'd ever made one to him." Elijah's voice catches. "And he said he expected her to uphold that vow."

His face twists with emotion, his eyes watering as he forces out the answers. His parents had died when he was young, and mine took him in. They were as much his family as they were mine.

My mother was clever, passing along her memories at the last moment, ensuring we wouldn't be left without answers. But she was also unintentionally cruel, forcing the male she loved as a son to endure the heartbreak behind those answers.

"But… my father would never," I say, struggling to form words.

"I think I can answer this one," Ayden interjects.

"If you're going to spout some bullshit about how he would do something like that because he killed your father, then I don't—"

"Stop talking, Breyla." Ayden's voice is low and sharp. "Just let me fucking explain."

I glare at him but fall silent.

"Those letters you stole, the ones you used to condemn me, they weren't the only ones. And they weren't meant for *me*. Lord Seamus was communicating with someone in Tierna. I believe there was another traitor amongst your court."

My heart lurches. "Who?"

Ayden narrows his eyes. "Use that sharp brain of yours, General. Who's been missing since the moment your mother died?"

The grief turns to guilt as I contemplate the question. Since my mother's death, I had been neglectfully absent. Glancing around the room, I try to read the faces of my companions. "I-I don't know. I haven't left my chambers until now."

"We haven't been able to locate Lord Craylor," Jade offers.

Gratitude for her flares in my chest.

"I've never trusted him," I say with disgust.

"Your mother didn't trust him either," Elijah adds quietly. "In the months leading up to his death, your father met with Lord Craylor often. And always alone. I remember him making several questionable decisions, skipping council input entirely. I'd bet Craylor was somehow connected to the corruption in the king's mind."

Ayden cuts in, voice smooth and inquisitive. "Tell me, darling— what was Lord Craylor's Gift? Why was he chosen as the court's spymaster?"

He's fishing. I know it. But I play along.

"He always knew everything. Court gossip, military secrets, foreign whispers—he had information no one should've had. But I guess that's not strange for a spymaster."

"Yes, but what was his actual *Gift?*"

Realization hits me, and I grow pale. "I don't actually know."

Ayden scans the group. "Does anyone here know?"

Everyone shakes their head.

"How is it possible that no one knows what the *spymaster's* Gift is?" I ask.

"Because his Gift is unlike any you've ever seen before," Ayden answers.

"Explain," I demand, voice sharp.

Ayden smirks. "Simple, darling—he's Fae."

The room erupts. Voices rise in a cacophony of disbelief, anger, and confusion.

"Silence, all of you," Jade snaps. Her compulsion Gift rolls through the room like a wave, dousing the noise. She nods to me. "Go ahead, Breyla."

"How is that possible?" I ask Ayden. "The Fae have been gone for nearly a millennium."

He raises a brow. "Have they?"

"I know cryptic is kind of your personality, Ayden, but just give us a straight answer," Aurelius grunts.

"There's not enough time for an entire history lesson, but the short story is that most of the Fae are gone from this land, but not all. No one alive has seen one in Rimor, so you wouldn't know if they stood right in front of you."

"At least that was *sort of* an answer," I say sarcastically.

"She is beautiful, brother. The glimmer in his eyes tells me that Ayden is trying to provoke Aurelius. "But I really don't understand how that temper of yours ever tolerated her attitude. You two make *zero* sense together."

"We make perfect sense. Would you like a demonstration of how well we work together?"

Innuendo and seduction drip off Aurelius' tongue as his eyes meet mine, heat flaring in the crimson pieces of his dark irises.

"Maybe later," Ayden winks.

I groan, throwing my head back in frustration. "What have I gotten myself into?"

"I don't know," Jade muses, "but I wouldn't complain if I were stuck in the middle of it."

I blink at her, startled—and relieved. Her humor is returning.

"Oh, so watching is fine, but sharing is off limits?" Ophelia tosses in.

My eyes dart between them. "Neither of you is helping the situation."

"No," Elijah chimes in with a grin, "but they *are* making it more entertaining."

"I hate you all," I sigh. "Every one of you."

"Liar," Aurelius challenges, eyebrow cocked.

I ignore him and fix my gaze on Ayden. "Since we're all here—how exactly are you and Aurelius brothers, and no one knew?"

"I should clarify," Ayden says smoothly. "We're half-brothers. We share a father, but my mother will undoubtedly despise you now that she knows."

My eyes cut to Aurelius, hurt clear in my tone as I ask, "And you've kept *that* to yourself for how long, exactly?"

His glare snaps to Ayden. "I've known exactly as long as you have, Princess."

"Like I'd believe *anything* you say after everything else you've kept from me."

Ayden steps in, voice softening slightly. "Easy there, darling. He didn't know. Not about this. He didn't know he was the bastard prince of Prudia. Outside of this room, only a handful of people know the truth."

My anger deflates. Slightly.

So he hadn't lied about that. He was just as in the dark as I'd been.

"Well, I can see keeping secrets is a family trait."

Ayden chuckles darkly. "Oh, you have no idea."

"So, who is his mother?" Ophelia asks.

Ayden's face hardens, his lips forming a thin line. "That's a story for another time, I'm afraid."

Sensing we weren't going to get much more from him on the topic, I pivot. "Fine, tell me more about the marriage contract you signed with my father."

"I was wondering when you'd get around to that." Ayden's lips tilt in a mischievous smirk. "Honestly, I'm surprised you didn't ask Aurelius—he was there for the entire negotiation."

A low growl emanates from Aurelius as I level a glare at Ayden. I had already known that, but he was clearly up to something. "I'm not sure which one of us you're trying to rile now, but stop it."

"Such a perceptive female, you are," Ayden purrs. "I do admire that."

Shadows form in my palm, dark tendrils shaping into a dagger. "I'm about to be a violent female."

Out of the corner of my eye, I see Aurelius's expression shift—his eyes brighten, lips curling into a smug smile.

I narrow my gaze at both of them. "Unbelievable."

Ayden sighs, mumbling something about how I'm no fun. Finally, Aurelius speaks.

"Your father came to me just over a year ago and told me he wanted peace between Prudia and Rimor. I didn't know he planned to offer your hand to Ayden to achieve that peace."

Ayden looks like he has something to say, but wisely keeps his mouth shut.

"Not that you would have cared," I bite out.

"That's not fair, Princess."

"Life isn't fair, Aurelius. For any of us." I turn my attention back to Ayden. "Keep talking."

"The terms were simple. We would marry within a year of the agreement being finalized. That happened in June—so the clock's ticking. Our marriage ends the conflict between Prudia and Rimor."

"That's too simple. What else does it say?"

Ayden chuckles. "Clever girl."

The way he says those two words tickle the back of my mind, but I ignore it. For now.

"It also states that should either of us assume our thrones before the year is up, the agreement—in this instance, our nuptials—would take effect immediately."

"Well, it's a good thing that we're both still just prince and princess," I say, crossing my arms.

"Are we?" Ayden quirks a brow at me.

The room falls dead silent.

I scan each face, every one of them avoiding my gaze.

"Breyla," Ophelia says gently, "you may not have been coronated yet... but the throne is yours now."

My chest tightens as my jaw drops open at the gravity of what that means.

If I'm crowned, I become Ayden's wife. Immediately.

If I delay, leaving the throne empty, I buy myself time.

Eight months.

But at the cost of my kingdom's stability.

"So, My Queen," Ayden says smoothly, his smile unapologetically smug, "how does a winter wedding sound?"

The words hit their mark.

Aurelius snarls and lunges, slamming his brother to the ground.

They crash to the floor, fists already flying.

"Do you want me to step in?" Elijah asks, watching them roll across the floor, trading punches.

"I say let them work their differences out," Jade replies with a shrug.

"Maybe without shirts," Ophelia adds.

Clearly caught off guard by Ophelia's unusually bold commentary, Elijah turns to study her like he's trying to solve a puzzle. "That's enough of that," he says, scooping her into his arms.

As he walks toward the door, he tosses over his shoulder, "Good luck," and carries her out, her laughter trailing behind him.

Jade raises an eyebrow in silent question.

I don't even hesitate. "I don't give a fuck what either of these idiots do. Let them fight it out, for all I care." I shrug, pulling myself from the chair and leaving to find somewhere else to be. Somewhere with wine, hopefully.

Hopefully a *lot* of it.

CHAPTER THREE

AURELIUS

The scent of ale and incense hits me the moment I step inside. To call this a tavern would be only partially correct. Sure, it offers drinks, but its main source of income comes from the males and females who offer to provide far more than conversation. If the rumors were to be believed, the Midnight Brotherhood also operates out of the rooms on the top floor.

Here, one could find someone to warm their bed, dispose of their enemy, or, like me, simply fill their cup.

Bodies drape across chairs and cushions in various states of undress and sobriety. I pay them little mind as I weave through them in my journey to the bar.

Taking a seat, I motion toward the male I assume is the barkeep. Red hair, a jagged scar above his right eye, he's tall and sturdier than someone who works a bar has any right to be. A rag in one hand, glass in the other, he doesn't seem like someone who should be working here, but who am I to question?

"What'll it be?" he asks, voice low and melodic, with a lilt I can't quite place.

"Rum."

"And will you be drinking alone?"

He's asking if I'm looking to have other thirsts satiated.

"No," a familiar voice answers. "He'll be drinking with me, Cillian." Elijah settles into the seat beside me.

Cillian raises a brow, but without a word, drops a bottle of rum and two glasses in front of us. As he closes the space between us, I catch a whiff of his scent, which is strangely familiar. I can't place it, but I know I've encountered it before.

"Who gave you the black eye, Elijah? Been a long time since I've seen anyone best you." Cillian says, gesturing to the bruising beneath Elijah's left eye—the one I gave him last night.

So they know each other, but how? His name scratches at something in the back of my mind.

Elijah flashes a half-smile and tilts his head toward me. "That would be courtesy of Lord Aurelius, here."

Cillian stiffens, but his pulse remains steady as his eyes narrow. "You know we don't allow violence in here," he says coolly. "I suggest you take your business elsewhere."

"Relax, Cillian. It was a misunderstanding. We have no violent intentions here," Elijah reassures him, already pouring himself a generous measure of rum.

I take the bottle from him, pouring myself double the amount. The spiced liquor burns and warms as it makes its way down my throat, and I let out a sigh of relief.

"Knowing you," Cillian muses, pouring his own drink, "you probably deserved it. What did you do? Sleep with his female?"

"Do you really think so little of me?" Elijah scoffs.

"No, I just know you. Wouldn't be the first time you had a misunderstanding of that nature."

"You wound me," Elijah grins, then shrugs. "But yes and no to your question. I was sleeping with his *female*... just not like you're insinuating."

"What other kind of sleeping is there?"

"It was Breyla," he says simply. "So yes, it really was just sleeping."

Cillian's eyes spark in understanding. He knows her.

"And for the record," I cut in, finishing my glass, "he threw the first punch."

Cillian's eyes rake over me, slowly, deliberately. When he reaches mine, he smirks. "So, you're the one who makes her shadows sing," he says it matter-of-factly, like he already knows who I am.

My spine stiffens.

"I told him that I had found the one who makes my shadows sing and my heart beat faster." Breyla had said those exact words the night she came back covered in the smell of others. The night before everything had shattered.

"You," I growl, realizing precisely who this male is.

He smirks at me, all smug confidence. "Cillian. King of the Midnight Brotherhood. At your service."

So this is him.

This is the only male who might have once held a piece of Breyla's heart. Even if I know it's no longer his, the anger flares hot in my chest.

I feel the glass in my hand crack beneath the force of my grip.

"Aurelius," Elijah says calmly, "I assure you that is not a fight you want to pick."

"Or do," Cillian offers, arms folding as he leans back against the wall. "It's been a while since anyone was bold enough to challenge me directly. I'm sure after all your recent transgressions, it would send Breyla running right back into my arms. I did tell her I would be waiting when you inevitably fucked up."

I snarl, but before I can reply, Elijah snaps, "For fucks sake. Cillian, I would also suggest not provoking Aurelius. Can you just return to whatever it is you normally do? You're not a fucking barkeep. And I would like to drink in peace."

"Very well." Cillian downs his drink and pushes off the wall. "Breyla knows how to find me when the time comes. Good seeing you, Elijah. Don't be a stranger."

He winks at me before striding out, and I swear it takes everything in me not to go after him.

Elijah turns to me, serious now. "What's going on with you, Aurelius?"

"What do you mean?" I ask, pouring another drink.

"You're normally the level-headed one. Possessive, sure, but you normally talk Breyla off the ledge instead of flying off it yourself. That's the third fight you've picked in as many days."

I let out a deep sigh, contemplating whether I really want to have this conversation with him of all people. The alcohol swimming through my veins makes it a fight I lose.

"I can't believe I'm having this conversation with you." I throw back the remainder of my rum, swallowing hard. "I'm confused. I've felt nothing but anger since that night. Anger that Gen kept everything from me. I'm angry at her for dying, and at Ayden for revealing the truth the way he did—or that he feels like he has some claim to Breyla. Anger at Breyla for punishing me and refusing me a chance to make it right. But mostly, I'm angry at myself for not being able to save them or see Lord Seamus' betrayal. Just so much anger."

Elijah waits patiently for me to finish my explanation before speaking. "You're not just angry, Aurelius. You're grieving."

The realization slams into me, and my shoulders slump.

The heaviness in my chest—the weight I've carried since that night—finally has a name.

"Why does this feel so much heavier?" I ask quietly. "I grieved Raynor, but this… this feels unbearable."

"I'm no expert," Elijah replies, taking a long swig of rum straight from the bottle, "but I think watching someone you care about die is probably more traumatic than just hearing about it. And grief compounds. With each death, we feel the previous losses all over again. We're forced to relive that loss again in addition to the new one. Grief does not get easier or go away. We simply learn to live with it better each day."

"For someone who claims not to be an expert, you certainly sound like one." I pull the bottle from his hands and take a swig myself, the burn grounding me for a moment. "Where does such wisdom come from?"

He meets my gaze, eyes somber. "I lost them, too, you know."

"I know."

"But do you?" His voice softens. "Raynor and Genevieve were the only parents I ever really knew. I may not share their blood, but they never made me feel like I was anything less than family. I have burned two sets of parents in my life. Not to mention one of my closest friends and lovers."

Our eyes meet, and an understanding passes between us. "You're right, Elijah," I admit. "In my grief, I have become selfish and blind to the pain in those around me. You wear it so well, but I can't pretend to know exactly how you feel."

"I don't fault you for how you grieve or what you do not understand.

We sit in silence for a while before I finally work up the nerve to say, "I envy you, Elijah."

His brow furrows. "Whatever for?"

"The way you know Breyla so well. You make her laugh when she should be crying. You push her buttons and somehow avoid her wrath. And when she's hurting… it's you she turns to. You seem to know what she needs before she does. She needs you, in the way I want her to need me."

And maybe, in the way I need her, too.

"I've had years of knowing her. This connection didn't happen overnight. But it's also not one-sided. She lets me in because I let her in. As much as she needs me, I need her, too. Open yourself up to her," he says encouragingly. A look I can't decipher flashes across his face, expression turning solemn. "She needs you, too. As much as she denies it, she's going to need you even more in the coming months."

The way he says it fills me with an inexplicable sense of dread.

"What aren't you telling me?" I narrow my eyes at him.

"That's a story for another day," he says, brushing me off. Before I can push, he changes the subject. "Why are you here exactly? Luella's not enough for you?"

"This wasn't my first choice," I grunt. "Luella took one look at the bruises from you and Ayden and shoved me right out the door."

Elijah laughs, a full-bodied sound that fills the room. "I knew Luella didn't tolerate violence, but damn. I don't think I've ever seen her kick someone out for having a black eye. Serves you right for being such an ass lately."

"Probably," I shrug, not bothering to deny it. "But what brings you out here?"

"Cillian and I go back. Sometimes I pay him a visit to make sure I stay on his good side."

"He's not *that* intimidating," I scoff.

"Don't let him hear you say that," Elijah says, taking another swig. Wiping extra liquid off his lips, he asks, "Do you remember that trick Breyla used to pull on you?"

"Which one?" I raise a brow.

"The one where she would create a shadow blindfold and make you walk into walls."

I groan. "Ah, yes. Such a neat *trick*. My nose is still crooked from the worst of those encounters."

Elijah grins. "Who do you think taught her that?"

My eyebrows shoot up. "Cillian has shadows?"

"Not exactly. He possesses a Madilim Gift, yes. But not shadows. He's got at least one other Gift, but the bastard never would tell me what it was."

"He can bend light?"

Elijah nods. "He's incredibly skilled. He can make himself damn near invisible, even in broad daylight. I've seen him slaughter three men in under a minute, completely undetected. So yes, he *is* that intimidating."

"Fair enough. I'll do my best to stay out of his path."

Elijah chuckles. "Good luck with that now that he knows who you are to Breyla."

"Great," I grumble.

We sit in silence for a few more minutes before Elijah speaks again, his voice quieter now. "I know Genevieve kept things from us —from you. But I just thought you should know she didn't do it lightly. I believe she was genuinely trying to protect us. All of us."

Pain tightens my chest, leaving me gasping for breath. "I expected nothing less from her. Still doesn't make it any easier."

"No," Elijah agrees, his voice cracking. "But you needed to hear that. She loved us all so much..." his voice trails off, tears filling his eyes.

"I see so much of Raynor in Breyla. But it's Genevieve's capacity to love... that's the best trait she passed down to her daughter."

"Have you told her that?"

"No," I admit.

"Perhaps you should."

"You're probably right, but that would require her agreeing to talk to me without hatred and bitterness lacing every word."

"You'll get there. Just keep trying."

"How long did it take Cillian to gain her forgiveness?"

Elijah grimaces. "Three years."

I take another swig of rum at the thought of waiting three years to gain my little demon's trust back.

"Fuck."

CHAPTER FOUR

BREYLA

Another day, another funeral pyre. I've lit so many in such a short time. Now, I was preparing to light another.

A soft knock pulls me from my thoughts, the door creaking open.

"Can I help you dress?" Ophelia asks softly. She's dressed in a black, long-sleeved, velvet gown. Her raven strands hang in loose curls around her face, bouncing slightly with each step.

I nod, and the door clicks shut behind her.

"I don't know what to wear," I admit as she joins me at the wardrobe. A black silk robe is all that covers me as I stare into the oak armoire, overflowing with options that all feel wrong.

"Why wouldn't you wear your leathers as you did for the others?"

"We wear leathers for fallen soldiers. I was acting as the General then." I pause, voice cracking. "My mother was not a soldier. And I'm not just attending as a general today. I-I'm…" I choke on the words my mouth refuses to utter.

Ophelia, ever perceptive, nods in understanding. "So what are you feeling?"

I know she's referring to clothes, but the truth escapes me. "I feel broken. Weak."

Her expression hardens. She turns me to face her, her storm-gray eyes searching mine. "You are not broken, Breyla. Nor are you weak; never have been."

Her bottom lip quivers as tears pool in the corner of her eyes. The words are as much for her as they are for me.

"I'm sorry, O," I whisper. "Somehow I manage to forget I'm not the only one saying goodbye today."

I pull her into a tight embrace. She melts into me, and for several long moments, we hold one another. Two females fighting to hold back the tide of grief.

Then, gently pulling away, she wipes her eyes. "Okay. Let's find you something that shows them all you're *not* broken."

"Mother would have wanted me to wear a dress. I hate dresses." I run my fingers along a few options, none of them appropriate for a funeral.

Ophelia stops in her perusal, her eyes widening. "This one. It's exactly what you need today."

She pulls the garment out for me to examine and my eyes rove over the unfamiliar item. "I don't recognize this. It's not one I've ever worn before."

It's black with a fitted corset top, modest V-neckline, thick straps, but no sleeves. Running my fingers down it, I realize the material isn't one that is typically used for dresses; it's eerily similar to those used for fighting leathers. It's softer, but it's not silk or wool. The real draw of this dress is the hemline, though. It falls long in the back but tapers up and cuts just above the knees in the front. Deep crimson satin lines the inside of the skirt.

"It was made for you. It had to be."

"Help me put it on." I untie the robe, letting it fall to the floor at my feet.

The dress slips on with ease, perfectly hugging every curve. Ophelia's adept hands quickly lace the bodice, and I savor the feeling of the material on my skin. It provides the familiar comfort of my leathers but satisfies the image I need to portray. The higher hem in the front still allows me the freedom to move about should a threat arise.

"You were meant to wear this dress, Breyla."

I pull my thigh holster on, slipping a dagger in. The level of the gown hits perfectly to keep it hidden. "Whoever made this dress clearly knew who they were creating it for." Ophelia hands me the slim dagger I frequently keep in the front of my bodice, and I slip it into place. I'm stunned to find a pocket sewn into the lining, a perfect fit for the blade.

Taking a seat in front of my vanity, I let Ophelia brush out my gold-streaked copper tresses. In a matter of minutes, she has it tamed into soft waves that frame my pale face. She completes the look by placing the usual gold and ruby crown atop my head.

Laying a petite hand on my shoulder, she leans down and meets my eyes in the mirror. "We've got this, Your Majesty."

I lay my hand on hers and muster a smile. "Yes, we do."

Elijah's eyes widen when he takes us in. "Is it in poor taste to whistle at my two favorite females looking as beautiful as you do for a funeral?"

"Probably, but I would expect nothing less from you," I tease. For just a moment, Elijah's humor breaks through the fog of grief that hangs low over me. He's always had a way of making me laugh when I shouldn't.

We're standing at the castle door, watching as people gather round the pyres. He pulls each of us into him, laying a kiss on our cheeks.

Ophelia lets out a giggle as he kisses down her neck playfully. He whispers something I can't hear that has her blushing.

"Well, in that case. You both look absolutely devastating." He gives us a smile I know is hiding his own pain.

The three of us stand arm in arm, watching the crowd gather for the funerals today.

"We're all three orphans now," I point out.

"No, we're not," Elijah says confidently. "Because we still have each other. Our parents may be gone, but with you around, I never feel alone."

My heart swells at the outpouring of love I feel from him. "I love you, E."

"I love you too, B," he says, squeezing both of us tighter.

We make the short walk out to the courtyard, where it feels like the whole kingdom awaits.

I come to a stop in front of my mother's pyre, her preserved body lying atop the wood, giving the illusion that she's simply sleeping and not dead. My mind plays tricks on me, and I swear her chest moves. I'm reminded of the scene that haunts me every time I shut my eyes—

the steady rise and fall of her cooling body. Shaking my head, I blink several times to clear the image.

Elijah and Ophelia stand to my right, closer to Layne's pyre. Lord Seamus' pyre is further down, but no one gathers round it. His burning is simply because that's how we dispose of the dead. He will receive no final words, no honors, no recognition at all for the male who was the death of so many innocents.

To my left stands Prince Ayden, Aurelius lingering closely next to him, a look of pure annoyance on his face.

Ayden leans in and murmurs, "The combined colors of House Mordet and House Rozaria look so natural on you, darling."

"Did you know there is a spider native to Lennox that is all black except for a red diamond on its back?" My question has Ayden tilting his head, eyebrow cocked.

"It's one of the deadliest creatures in existence. But it's not just their venom that makes it so. The females are known for killing the males after they've mated. They're beautifully lethal little things."

My words leave him silent, and Aurelius' lips tilt in a subtle smirk next to us. I make eye contact with him, and his eyes trail up and down my body.

"It's often the most beautiful creatures that are the most danger-ous," Aurelius says, his eyes full of heat.

I break eye contact before it can go any further, turning my attention to the crowd gathered.

Clearing my throat, I deliver what I hope is the last eulogy I'll have to give for a very long time.

"Thank you all for being here. I must be honest and say I am so godsdamned tired of giving eulogies." That gains me a few chuckles, but more gasps.

"How do you really summarize someone's life or what they meant to you in just a few minutes? I don't really think you can. But I'm willing to give it another try." Elijah squeezes my hand reassuringly. "Today we bid farewell to Queen Genevieve Rozaria, but to many of us, to me, she was so much more than her title. She was mother, protector, and friend.

My hands tremble, and it's a fight to keep my voice steady as I continue. "I have never known another soul as fiercely loyal as she was. She loved this kingdom and all its inhabitants. Until the very end, she always did her best to put her people first. I never imagined I would lose both my parents so early in life, but I take solace knowing they both lived lives filled with love, and joy, and passion. My hope would be that I could someday live a life like they had—and that I can one day live up to the example they set for me."

"From your first breath until your very last, may the gods grant you peace."

The crowd murmurs my words back to me, and I retreat a step.

Ophelia comes forward, taking a deep breath. Having not known Layne well, I offered her the option to deliver his final words. She had accepted, despite being nervous about speaking in front of that many people.

"My brother, Layne, was the only family I had who really cared for me. He was my best friend, and I don't know how I'm supposed to do this without him." She twists her fingers, rubbing her palms softly. "Before Layne's Gift manifested, anyone could have told you that he would have the Empathi Gift. He was one of the most caring and compassionate individuals I have ever met, but he excelled at knowing exactly what a person would need before they even knew it themselves. He was always bringing me trinkets and gifts from his travels, and he always knew when I needed him."

Ophelia smiles softly, her eyes distant as if lost in memory. "I'm sorry, I'm rambling. I say that all to try and explain what a genuine and kind soul the world is now missing. It will never feel complete without you, brother. I'll meet you in Amara," she finishes, a morose look in her eyes.

I take a step forward, unlit torch in hand. Turning, I gasp at the realization that I was looking for my mother to light the torch. For years, her magic was all I'd needed to light the pyres. And now I have no one—just a useless, unlit piece of wood.

My chest tightens, and my eyes sting as I fight back the tears and the reality of the situation.

I look around, catching both Aurelius' and Ayden's eyes as I start to panic. "I don't—"

"I've got you, Princess," Lord Jaeson says quietly, his hand on my shoulder. With sure hands, he reaches out and calls on his Kaminari Gift to light my torch.

"Thank you," I whisper as he falls back into the crowd.

I reach my torch out to light the ones held by Aurelius, Elijah, and Ophelia. Together, Aurelius and I light my mother's pyre as Elijah and Ophelia light Layne's. As the wood begins to catch, I pass my torch to a guard with instructions to light Seamus' pyre.

For the first time, I am the one to start the traditional Rimorian death hymn. Ophelia joins me a heartbeat later, and together we cry out our grief.

> *May the mother keep you close*
> *And the father protect you now*
> *The tears that once were shed*
> *Make the flowers grow*
> *When the night is darkest*
> *And the sun has ceased its shining*
> *May you remember*
> *My love for you is eternal*
> *From your first breath*
> *Until your very last*
> *May the gods grant you peace*

As we approach the second round, I hear the voices of Elijah and Aurelius join us. By the third, the entire crowd is singing. Voices echo around us, being heard from miles away, as a kingdom laments the loss of its queen.

I don't remember losing the battle to stand, but I find myself on my knees. Sobs wrack through me as I let the hot tears freely flow. That chasm left by my father and Julian—the one I felt begin to scab over—is ripped wide open again. Not only do I feel the loss of my mother, but it's like I'm reliving the loss of each one that went before her. My body shakes as the immense weight of grief threatens to overtake me.

Elijah's warm hand takes mine, gripping it tightly. I thread my fingers through his, squeezing as we both cry over the mother we've lost. His other arm is wrapped tightly around Ophelia as she cries into his chest.

The familiar scent of warm spices and bergamot envelops me as Aurelius wraps his arms around me. For the time being, I forget I'm angry, let go of the betrayal I felt from his secret keeping, and just let him comfort me. I take pleasure in the familiarity of his embrace, savoring the way his arms still feel like home.

"It wasn't supposed to be this way," I say through gasping sobs.

"I know, Princess." His voice cracks, and I notice the tears streaming down his cheeks for the first time.

"I-I was s-so cruel to her before s-she died." My sobs are so violent they cause me to stutter through my words. "She d-didn't deserve that, a-and I never fixed things."

There are no words that will make this better, so instead, Aurelius pulls me into his lap, cradling me against him and rocking me gently. I gasp, my lungs desperate to take in the oxygen I can't seem to inhale.

"Shhh," Aurelius coos. "I need you to breathe, Breyla."

Another pained sob leaves me as I try to tell him I can't, but no words come out.

"I'm going to help you," he says as I feel his Hemonia Gift gently seep into my body, winding its way around my heart. He slows my pulse just enough to make breathing possible again.

Tears still stream down my face, but I take a deep breath, sighing in relief as my burning lungs calm. His fingers wind through my hair, gently massaging my scalp, helping me to relax.

"I'm not ready for this, Aurelius," I confess.

"No one ever is. You figure it out as you go."

I turn to meet his eyes, getting lost in the crimson flecks that seem to shine brighter through the tears. "I'm not her. How am I supposed to live up to her on my own? I can't even keep my people safe as General, and now I'm expected to lead a kingdom. I don't know how to do this—and she understood that! Why else would she fight so hard to stay on the throne?"

Just like that, all my silent doubts and insecurities come to light. His eyes soften at my admission. I don't want his pity, so I turn away, struggling to break from his hold.

Using his thumb and forefinger, he grasps my chin and turns my face back to his."Look at me," he demands, tightening his grip. "Your mother did not fight to keep you off the throne because she found you lacking."

"How do you—"

"She knew you did not want to rule." The muscle in his jaw ticks as he contemplates his next words, "More than that, I believe she knew what would happen should you take the throne." His eyes dart briefly to Ayden and back to me.

"She knew about the marriage contract?" I ask in disbelief.

"She never explicitly said so, but I suspect that she did."

Just like that, my anger returns, melding with my grief in a potent mixture. I force my way out of Aurelius' arms, much to his protest. I did not care, though. The anger was too consuming for me to feel anything else.

"Here, drink this," Elijah says, shoving a goblet into my hands.

Ophelia, Elijah, and I sat in a circle on the library floor. There was no warrior's celebration of life following the service for my mother and Layne, but Elijah had decided we needed something extra to get through the day.

"What is it?" I ask, sniffing the concoction.

"Does it matter?" He cocks his head and takes a drink from his own goblet.

"I guess not," I say, shrugging my shoulders. The drink burns going down. Whatever it is, it's strong. It warms me, my face flushing from the mix of spirits.

"Do you remember the time we both broke our arm?" Elijah asks.

"Of course, how could I forget?" I smile as the memory greets me.

"Eli, I'm bored," I complained.

"Aren't you supposed to be working on your arithmetic?"

"Why do you think I'm bored?" I scoffed.

"Where is the tutor?" Elijah asked, his innocent eyes trying to figure it out.

"She quit, and Mother has yet to find a new one. Turns out she's deathly afraid of spiders. Who knew?" I asked, a mischievous grin stretching across my face.

"Wait, you didn't..." His eyebrows rose as the pieces clicked into place.

"Create tiny shadow spiders and chase her around the castle with them? Of course not." Sarcasm dripped from my tone as I batted my eyes in faux innocence. My Madilim Gift had manifested just months prior, and forming small shapes was the extent of my control.

Elijah let out a full belly laugh, causing me to join in. After a few minutes, he managed to regain his composure. "Come on, I have an idea."

He led me through the castle, carefully avoiding anyone who would bust us and report back to Mother or Father. We ended up on part of the castle roof overlooking the back of the grounds. It was only one story up, but looking over the edge, I could see it was a significant drop to the ground.

"What are we doing?"

He pulled me to the edge, allowing me to see a nearby tree and a small pond just beyond it. "You see that branch?"

"Yeah?"

"I bet we could jump from the edge of the roof, catch the limb, and use it to swing us into the pond."

"If you wanted to go swimming, why didn't we just go to the stream?"

"Because this is significantly more fun," he said, as if it were obvious.

"How far is the drop if we miss?" I asked, trying to calculate our chance of injury.

"If you're too scared, just say so, B."

"Definitely not," I protested, crossing my arms.

"Then stop overthinking it, and just jump with me."

"Fine. Together, then?"

"Together," he agreed, taking my hand.

With a running start, we jumped from the edge of the roof towards the tree branch. To my surprise, we easily caught the limb, but to my horror, we had gravely miscalculated the distance from the tree to the pond.

Knowing our only chance of reaching the water is if we use the momentum from our first jump, I let go and prayed that I hit the pond. I screamed, arms flailing as I realized I wasn't going to make it.

"Oof," I moaned in pain as my body hit the muddy embankment. Elijah let out a pained grunt next to me.

Our legs had managed to hit the water, but we hadn't made it far enough, leaving our upper halves lying in the mud surrounding the pond.

"You fucker," I groaned at Eli. "I landed on my arm."

"Shut up, so did I."

Using my opposite arm, I shifted myself into a sitting position, hissing at the pain it caused me.

"I think it's—"

"Breyla!" my mother's annoyed voice rang out behind us.

"Oh, shit," Elijah whispered.

"Oh, shit, is right," Mother snapped. "What were you two thinking?"

The pain throbbing through my arm overrode my common sense as I answered her, "Uh... that we would be able to swing from the tree branch and reach the pond."

Her nostrils flared at my smart mouth. "You are intelligent enough to know better. You two aren't even supposed to be out here right now."

"Yeah, I'm starting to think you shouldn't have scared off the tutor. Obviously, our arithmetic could use some help," Elijah unhelpfully added.

"Obviously. Do I even need to say what comes next?" Mother raised an irritated brow at us.

"We're confined to our quarters?" I guessed.

"And that's just the start," she confirmed.

"I can't believe she refused to summon a healer," Elijah says. She had allowed the castle physician to set the bones and give us mild sedatives, but it took weeks for the bones to mend themselves.

"We learned our lesson, though, didn't we?"

"Debatable," Elijah says with a chuckle. "You know, my arm still aches with the first snow each year?"

"Mine does too!" I laugh heartily with him. As soon as it comes, it's replaced with guilt.

"It feels wrong to laugh…" I trail off, not completely sure I meant to say the words aloud.

"Yeah, I know," Ophelia agrees, Elijah nodding with her.

"But I don't think—no, I know they wouldn't want us to feel that way," Elijah adds.

"Doesn't make it any easier," I say as I throw back the remainder of my drink. My head swims, skin buzzing from whatever Elijah put in this.

The anger from earlier still simmers just below the surface. The alcohol helps numb the pain, but it just makes me want to feel something else. All I've felt for days is pain, grief, anger, and guilt.

"If you'll excuse me. I think I need to turn in before I do something reckless." I stand, swaying slightly as I feel the alcohol's full effects.

"Don't do anything I wouldn't do," Elijah calls.

"That doesn't give me many limitations, E."

"Then, don't do anything I wouldn't do!" Ophelia chimes in.

"That I can work with," I say with a chuckle, saluting them both as I exit the library.

Stumbling towards my chambers, I realize Elijah had made the drinks much stronger than I originally thought. I have surpassed tipsy and gone straight to drunk.

"You okay, darling?" Ayden's baritone voice drawls, sending shivers up my spine. I hadn't noticed him exiting his chambers until I stood just a few feet from him.

The anger bubbles close to the surface, and I decide I'm not playing nice tonight. "Not in the least, Prince." Before I can stop myself, I'm closing the distance between us and shoving myself into his space. "But that tends to happen when you lose both your parents in a matter of weeks and find out you're engaged and everyone knew, but kept it from you."

"Still angry, I see." He smirks at me, pushing off the wall and slowly backing me against the opposite side of the hall. "Good, I like my fianceé with a little fire in her veins."

He leans an arm against the wall, effectively caging me in. "Yeah, well, I'd like my fiancé to be someone I actually know."

"Someone who isn't full of secrets," I add. His woodsy citrus scent overwhelms my senses, and I catch myself wondering, once again, how I was so blind to not notice how similar it is to Aurelius' before now.

"Oh yeah? Someone like my brother?" Ayden challenges, a twinkle in his eye. "I may have secrets, love, but I do nothing without reason. As for wanting to know your fiancé—give me the time of day and I'll let you get to know every part of me." He smirks, knowing his twisted words have hit their mark.

The barely audible sound of a door creaking open catches my attention, then I feel it—feel *him*. Aurelius is watching this display, and my anger spikes. I remember I'm mad at both these males, and I want them to hurt like I'm hurting.

"No, not him," I snarl, curling my fist into his shirt, and pulling his lips into mine. Our kiss is all teeth and tongues, and I pour every emotion I'm feeling into it.

His hand threads through my hair, deepening the kiss, as he pulls my leg up and nestles himself against my core. Fingers trail the bare flesh of my thigh, leaving me desperate to feel more.

Aurelius' patience snaps, and I hear the door swing wide open. I throw up a wall of shadows, holding him in his chambers. Flipping him off, I wrap my hand around Ayden's neck, trying to deepen the kiss.

Much to my disappointment, Ayden breaks away, leaving me breathing heavily as I search his eyes for answers.

"How much have you had to drink, Breyla?"

"Enough to know I want this and not regret it tomorrow."

"She's drunk," Aurelius snarls.

"Thank you, *Breyla*," Ayden says sarcastically to Aurelius, before turning his gaze back to me. He drops my leg, straightening my disheveled dress and stepping back. "As much as I would love to repay my brother for his earlier kindness and fuck you in front of him—that won't be happening tonight."

"I told you I want this," I repeat.

"Right. You want *this*—not me. You want to drown your pain with a warm body? Fine, but that won't be me. Especially not when you're doing this to hurt him and not because you genuinely want *me*. When that changes, you know where to find me, *My Queen*."

Ayden places a soft kiss on my forehead and steps back to his side of the hallway. "Goodnight, darling," he says, disappearing into his room, the lock clicking shut behind him.

Aurelius manages to break through the wall of shadow surrounding his room and storms towards me.

"Leave me alone, Aurelius," I say defeatedly, turning towards my door.

"You know I can't do that, Princess," he says lowly as he grabs me by the waist, pulling my back to his front. His other hand wraps around my throat. The grip is possessive, but he doesn't apply any pressure.

"Listen closely, little demon. I know you're hurting, that you're mad at me right now. But mark my words, I will earn my way back into your bed and your heart." I stiffen at his words, but he continues, "And when I do, I will remember this little display. You'll regret playing with fire."

His words are a promise, but one I didn't need. I had already played with fire and been burned. The pain of his flame was a constant companion at this point.

I say nothing, and he releases me, pushing me into my chambers. The door closes behind me, and I quickly strip out of my dress, leaving it forgotten on the floor.

Naked, hurting, aroused, and angry, I fall into bed. I'm met with vivid dreams of my mother's death.

The next afternoon, I'm hiding in the private sitting room my mother favored. When I was young, I would find her here anytime she needed solitude. Even now, I swear I feel her presence in the room.

"We need to talk," Elijah says, breaking me out of the stupor currently consuming me.

"About?" I ask, curling my feet under me to make room on the chaise.

Taking the space next to me, he wraps his arm around my shoulders and pulls me into his heat. "Look, B," he starts, his tone something I don't care for. "This is going to hurt, but there are some things your mother wanted you to see."

"I'm not ready, Eli," I protest, nuzzling my head into his chest.

"I know," he whispers, "and I'm sorry. But we don't have the liberty of waiting for you to be ready."

I look up at him, studying the serious set of his brows. It's an expression I rarely see on him—one I know I should heed.

"Okay." My voice is more broken than I ever imagined it could be.

"Okay," he agrees, laying a hand to my temple.

I close my eyes, letting the subtle warmth of his Gift wash over me as the memory unfolds.

"She's perfect, my love," Raynor smiles, holding a squirming baby—me— in his arms. She's tiny and pink, a wild mess of red curls framing her face.

"I highly doubt that after what she just put me through," my mother sighs. "Twenty-seven hours of labor would suggest she's stubborn and head- strong, not perfect."

She looks exhausted, sweat soaking every inch of her, blonde hair plas- tered to her reddened face.

With a wide grin, my father sits on the bed next to her, handing the bundle back to my mother. "She is half you, and you are perfect."

"She is also half you," my mother teases.

"Are you suggesting I am not perfect?"

She scoffs. "I know better."

"Be that as it may," Raynor smiles, pressing a kiss to her forehead. "To me, you are both still perfect. I love you both so much."

The scene changes.

"You're going to refuse Lennox's offer?" Lord Seamus asks.

"Of course I am," my father replies.

"As your advisor, I must insist you reconsider. Having Lennox as an ally would put an end to our war with Prudia."

My father sighs, annoyance etched in the laugh lines that bracket his mouth. "I do not care. I will not betroth Breyla to their prince at just six years old."

Lennox had offered to aid us in exchange for my hand in marriage? This was the first I had heard about this proposal.

"We wish for Breyla to have a say in whom she marries," my mother adds, lacing her fingers with Father's.

"Royalty is never afforded such liberties, Your Majesty," Lord Seamus argues. "You, yourself, were promised at twelve," he says, this time to Mother.

"Yes, and while we were blessed in that match... we find the practice barbaric and will not subject our daughter to the same." My father's tone leaves no room for argument. Conversation over.

A new memory.

"How was your meeting with Lord Craylor?" Mother asks as Father enters their chambers. She sits in front of her vanity, thick robe draped over her thin shoulders, running a comb through her waves.

Exhaustion carves lines through his typically jovial face. Something heavy is weighing on him, but all he says is, "It was fine."

"Has he heard any whisperings from Prudia? Their silence unsettles me."

"Nothing, My Queen," he replies, slowly beginning to shed his weapons and outer clothes.

Mother, clearly not satisfied with his clipped answers, pushes, "What are we to do about Prudia and Prince Ayden II?"

Something unrecognizable crosses my father's face, leaving it cold and harsh as he barks, "We are to do nothing, Genevieve. I am working on a plan to ally Rimor with Prudia and end the bloodshed."

I had never—in all my years—heard my father address my mother in such a tone. And apparently, neither had she.

She flinches, her aqua eyes flaring wide in disbelief. Then hurt.

"Ally with Prudia?" she breathes. *"I can imagine no world where the prince would agree to any terms you propose. He is too embittered."*

"I wasn't the one who proposed them," he answers flatly.

"And what are his requests?"

"None of your concern."

"Raynor, tell me you didn't..." Fear and concern cover my mother's face, her mouth hanging open as she stares at him.

"I haven't done anything. Yet. But I will do what I deem necessary to secure peace."

"But at what cost?"

"Enough, wife."

"What have you done, Raynor?" A stray tear rolls down her porcelain cheek.

"I said enough," he roars, his fist landing so heavy on the desk that the wood shudders beneath it.

My father was not a violent male. Whoever this is… it's not him.

Tears stream down Mother's face, her body trembling. Not out of fear, but out of anger, I realize.

"You will not speak to me that way," she says calmly. Too calmly.

Something shifts in my father's eyes, the mist lifting from his mind just briefly enough for him to understand his mistake.

"I will stay in the queen's chambers tonight. When you come to your senses, you know where to find me."

I had never known my parents to sleep in private rooms. It was something other royals did—but not them.

"Genevieve, wait," my father calls after her.

Without saying another word, my mother unleashes her Kaminari Gift, freezing his boots to the floor.

Message received.

A half dozen more memories flash by, all of similar encounters. My father growing distant, cold, and borderline cruel. His warm hazel eyes fading and dimming with each passing memory.

I watch the father I had loved all my life transform into someone I didn't recognize.

And in the process, I watch my mother love him despite it all. Never leaving his side, never giving up.

I see the first instance of her Visions manifesting and the sheer panic and confusion it left with her.

Every instance of the vision becomes more vivid, greater detail revealed as time progresses.

My gut churns, nausea growing as I watch my people being slaughtered on repeat.

How did this not drive her mad?

Finally, we land on the one memory I've been dreading above all others—the night of my father's death.

It happens just as Elijah had conveyed. The scene unfolds with my mother leaning over my father in bed, an ice blade poised against his neck.

There's no anger in him. He doesn't even fight her. Betrayal and confusion fill his eyes as he tries to understand why the love of his life is poised to kill him.

I hear everything from their mouths—the truth of what led to this moment and how much it's breaking them both.

It's breaking me, too.

My attention snaps to Mother when she asks, *"What do I tell our daughter?"*

"When she's ready... you tell her the truth. And you tell her that I love her—that I am proud of her. Tell her I'm so very sorry."

He's sorry? Sorry for what?

My mind screams at me to find out what he meant. But my heart's caught up in his last confession. What I wouldn't give to have had this conversation in person with him—to hear him tell me he loves me so I can say it back.

"I will tell her, my love. When she's ready."

"Gen, the council will force you to remarry to maintain the throne."

"I know," she whispers. "I don't want to think about that right now."

"It has to be Aurelius," he says definitively. "I trust no one else with my kingdom or my wife."

"I couldn't possibly marry—"

"You can and you will. And just know that I forgive you. However you choose to survive this, I understand."

She stares into his eyes for the final time and says, "Until the very end."

"Until the very end," he echoes as she slides the blade into his skull.

The exit from the memory sequence is violent, leaving me gasping for breath as I sob into Elijah's chest.

"Until the very end," I softly utter my father's dying words.

"Until the very end," Elijah echoes.

I can't stop the torrent of tears that erupt from my eyes, burning a path down my cheeks.

"I've got you, B," Elijah reassures, squeezing me tighter. He rubs gentle circles into my scalp, while I tremble against him. Gasping, sobbing, pants are all I can manage, the room blurring around me.

I feel his chest shake against me, his own tears flowing freely as we mourn together.

He pulls me into his lap, and I bury my head into the crook of his neck. I wind my arms around his neck and let it all go.

"They loved you, too," I choke out, needing him to know I recognize his pain.

"I know they did," he whispers. "There were memories shared just for me."

"Good," I murmur. "I love you, E."

"I love you too, B."

CHAPTER FIVE

Sipping on warm tea, I stare out the castle window. I suppress a yawn, forcing another drink of the spiced liquid down. Today was not the day I could afford to be tired or inattentive; it was the first council meeting since Queen Genevieve's death. The lack of sleep was catching up with me, though. Last night had been a breaking point for me.

"Aurelius, why are you pounding on my door in the middle of the night?" Ayden asked through a yawn.

"Do you not hear her screams?" I asked, running a hand through my shoulder-length black locks.

"Of course, I hear them. The whole castle hears them, brother."

"You can stop them. Why don't you?" My tone bordered on pleading, and I hated that I had to ask this male for anything, especially when it came to her.

"Don't you think I would if I were able?" He glared at me, folding his arms across his chest. "My gift requires touch, and if you hadn't noticed, I can't get in her room." He waved his hands at the shadows forming a barrier around the door.

"You can't get through?"

He rolled his eyes, walking to her door and demonstrating how his hands hit a barrier anytime he reached for the handle.

"They must be reacting to whatever's in her dreams," I mused. "I wonder..." My voice trailed off.

Reaching for the door, I'm surprised to find my hand passes straight through.

"Interesting," Ayden said, his face hardening. "It would appear that her subconscious still trusts you, despite her conscious self wanting nothing to do with you."

"She may be in denial about what she wants for now, but I assure you that's only temporary," I grit out, jaw clenching.

"For all our sakes, I hope you're wrong."

I twisted the handle and pushed open her door, letting us both into her room.

Pale moonlight highlighted Breyla's tear-streaked face as she thrashed in bed. Even in pain, she was beautiful. Sitting on the edge of her bed, I placed a gentle hand on her cheek. Though her whimpers continued, her body immediately stilled at my touch.

"Come on, prick. Work your magic," I said reluctantly.

If you would just let me stay with you, I could chase away those nightmares, little demon. *I think to myself.*

Ayden knelt next to the bed, placing a hand on the top of her head, gently stroking her hair. A soft amber glow trickled from his fingers to her temples, and she finally ceased crying, her breathing returning to normal.

"I can't believe I'm saying this, but thank you." I continued stroking her cheek. She shifted slightly closer to me in her sleep, and I mourned the lack of her regular presence next to me in bed.

"I've told her this, but you never have to thank me for this. Whether you believe it or not, I am not your enemy, Aurelius."

"Your actions make that hard to believe."

He nodded in understanding. "I get that, but someday you will believe me."

I shake myself out of the memory, trying to force down more of the now tepid tea.

"I'm not sure even a whole pot of tea would help overcome three days of not sleeping, brother," Ayden says, taking a seat next to me at the table.

I grunt in agreement before snapping, "Stop calling me that."

"Testy this morning, are we?"

"We may share blood, but my brother is dead. You have not

earned the title, and you only use it to elicit reactions out of Breyla and me."

"Well, I can see it's certainly working," he says with a smirk as he sips on a fresh cup of tea.

"I'm not dignifying that with a response," I mutter.

"You just did."

"I can see you're taking your role as annoying little brother seriously," Breyla comments, taking a seat on the other side of Ayden.

I scowl at her choice of seating, but bite my tongue.

"You mean *younger* brother. I assure you, there is nothing little about me."

My eyes roll at his attempt to banter with her. We are evenly matched in nearly every aspect, but he has a solid twenty pounds of muscle on me. It wasn't much, but we had proven nearly identical in strength in our last brawl on the library floor.

"Perhaps you and Breyla should compare notes on how to best be the annoying younger sibling," I say sarcastically.

Ayden raises a dark brow. "But Breyla is an only child."

"Yes, but she's always perfectly embodied the traits of a youngest child. Not sure where she learned it from, but she excels at it."

"Most would call that being a brat," Ayden says.

"For two males who would like to be on my good side, you sure are doing a terrible job of acting it," Breyla says, then throws a biscuit at Ayden's head. It hits him square in the jaw, but doesn't faze him.

I see the food coming at my head and catch it before it makes impact. Taking a bite, I say, "I see we've moved from throwing knives to breakfast pastries. And why would I lie when that was what got me in trouble in the first place? I thought you wanted the truth; the truth is, you are a brat. Always have been."

She glares at me before spitting, "If I'm such a brat, then why did you pursue me so ruthlessly?"

I resist the urge to tell her she hasn't seen ruthless yet and settle on, "I never said I didn't like you being a brat."

Red creeps across her cheeks, and she turns back to her breakfast. Ayden sighs and returns to his own food before muttering, "Today should be entertaining."

"Someone pour me a drink," Ayden mumbles, rubbing his temples. Turning to me, he asks, "Are they always like this?"

Breyla had spent the last twenty minutes arguing with most of the members of her council. The only two that seemed exempt were Elijah and Ophelia, who had taken her late father's place on the council. "Breyla threw a dagger at Lord Seamus in the last council meeting, so yes. At least, if she's involved. Subtle isn't her style."

"All I'm asking," Lady Daphne starts, "is how you plan to take the throne here in Rimor, maintain your position as General, *and* marry Prince Ayden. You are talented, but last I knew you couldn't occupy three places at once, Your Majesty."

"And there is the line of succession to consider," Lord Rion unhelpfully adds. "This kingdom is in a precarious situation, and whether you like it or not, it is vital to establish an heir as soon as possible."

Breyla's jaw ticks as she shoves to her feet. I watch carefully as her shadows swirl and begin to form in her palm. Realizing the mistake she's about to make, I swiftly stand behind her to quietly whisper, "I would advise you to put that shadow blade away." Gently, I caress her wrist, urging her to recall the shadows. After a moment, she acquiesces, shrugging off my touch.

"Fuck your line of succession," she snarls at Lord Rion.

Elijah stands, placing a placating hand over Breyla's. "We're talking in circles. B, take a deep breath."

And because it's Elijah, she complies immediately.

Her willing obedience to him was something that once bothered me, even driving me to the point of jealousy. And while I was still envious of how well he knew her, perhaps even better than she knew herself, I was no longer envious of his position in her life. He held a place that was meant solely for him, and it was undeniably different than mine or anyone else's.

Ayden studies them, his gaze sharp and contemplative. "He has impressive sway over her."

"It's as infuriating as it is impressive," I grumble.

Ayden stands, leaning against the table. "At the risk of starting another fight, perhaps I can put this matter to bed. Breyla will not be coronated as the Queen of Rimor, nor will she be acting as General."

"Excuse me?" she asks in disbelief.

Ignoring her outburst, Ayden continues, "Per the marriage contract, you will be accompanying me back to Prudia, where you will be crowned queen once we are wed. When it comes to heirs, our firstborn will inherit the kingdom of Prudia, and any others will be in line for Rimor. So, I suggest you shift your focus to choosing a suitable regent to lead in your absence."

I expect chaos to erupt, but am instead met with stunned silence.

Breyla shakes herself out of her surprise and narrows her eyes at Ayden. "Absolutely not. There's no way I'm agreeing to that."

"I'm sorry, darling, but it was already agreed to. You can check the contract, as it's all clearly spelled out there. Aurelius was there for the drafting of it, so I'm sure he can confirm what I'm telling you."

Breyla's angry eyes turn in my direction. I utter the words that will damn me further, "He speaks the truth, Princess."

Her shoulders momentarily sag in defeat, but not before determination lights her emerald eyes. "I should like to read the contract. Since I am apparently the only one affected by this agreement who has not yet seen it." Bitterness fills her tone, but it's overshadowed by the authority in her demand.

"Very well," Ayden agrees. "We'll be leaving in two days. Oh, and Prince Aurelius will be joining us."

Breyla's startled eyes find mine, then shoot to Ayden. "Wait, what? Why?"

I try not to cringe at the tone of her voice.

"Well, firstly, he is being recognized as a Prince of Prudia, much to my mother's dismay. But secondly, we both know if I tried to leave him here, he would just find a way to follow. I'm just saving us all the trouble."

Breyla sighs, resigned to her fate for now. "Commander Jade will replace me as General of the Rimorian army."

"As you wish, Your Majesty," Jade says, bowing her head. "I'm honored."

Breyla turns regretful eyes to Elijah and Ophelia. "I wish—"

"I know you would if you could, Breyla." Elijah cuts her off, knowing what she's trying to say before she says it.

"Lord Elijah and Lady Ophelia will rule in my stead."

Ophelia's eyes widen at the unexpected appointment.

Lady Daphne chokes on her drink and sputters, "You're putting the traitor's daughter in charge of the kingdom?"

Breyla's shadows lash out, wrapping around Lady Daphne's throat. "Do not forget your place, Lady Daphne. Ophelia was the one responsible for uncovering the damming evidence against Seamus, as well as ending his pathetic life before he could claim more innocents."

Lady Daphne swallows hard and nods. "My sincerest apologies. I won't make the mistake again."

Breyla releases the shadows' hold, recalling them into her. "We are done here. You are dismissed."

The council room empties, leaving me alone with Breyla.

"Is there something I can help you with, Prince Aurelius?" She spits out my title, like it tastes vile on her tongue.

"Let me explain."

"Explain what, Aurelius?" Breyla rubs at her temples. "I do not care, nor do I want to hear more excuses for why you lied to me. Repeatedly."

"Regardless, I wish to tell you the full story."

She bristles, eyes full of distrust. "Well, it is unfortunate then that I do not wish to hear it. The simple fact of the matter is, I do not trust what you have to say. You had numerous opportunities to inform me of any number of things, yet you didn't. You were so busy fucking me, you apparently forgot how words work."

"So, we're back to this, then?"

"Back to what?"

"The hot and cold act—where you pretend you aren't a hypocrite for refusing to hear my truth, while simultaneously punishing me for not telling you everything. I may be a selfish bastard for wanting to keep you to myself, but at least I'm willing to face the truth. Fuck you, Breyla. At least I can own my feelings."

A pained look crosses her face but disappears in an instant, replaced by fury burning in her emerald eyes as her fist clenches at her side.

Had I gone too far? Perhaps. But the fact that she hadn't punched me was confirmation that my words were accurate, even if they were harsh.

This was not how I saw this conversation playing out, but I no longer care. I storm out of the council room, needing to distance myself from the female who infuriates me beyond belief.

CHAPTER SIX

BREYLA

The stone floor is cool to the touch as my bare feet pad along the throne room floor. Shadows fall along the walls, wrapping around every curve and distorting my view. Strong, defined, bare thighs are spread wide on the seat.

Darkness obscures my vision, only pieces of the male are visible to me. Chills erupt along my spine as a hand trails up his thigh. The shadows shift, revealing his cock standing fully at attention between his muscular thighs.

He's hard—rock solid with a bead of arousal glistening on the head of his cock.

My mouth dries, my tongue darting out along my bottom lip as I watch his hand grasp his length. He squeezes the base, pumping himself in slow, deliberate strokes.

He chuckles softly, the shadows shifting to reveal a gold crown with black jewels on his head.

With his free hand, he curls his fingers, beckoning me toward him.

I bite my bottom lip as my feet move forward of their own volition. Somewhere along the way, I come to the conclusion this must be Aurelius, his still-obscured features are enough to convince me. As I reach the throne, I decide I must be dreaming because I'm not angry at him—I'm desperate for him.

If this is a dream, it doesn't matter. I can let myself feel the damning pleasure he never fails to deliver.

His hand continues pumping his cock, thumb rolling over the tip in slow, tantalizing motions.

Using his free hand, he palms me just below my ass, pulling me forward onto the throne. I land straddling him and realize for the first time that I'm naked.

Rough fingers trail the skin of my thigh, drawing invisible patterns on my heated flesh.

My core clenches, and I rock against his leg, letting him feel the wetness pooling at my center.

"I want you inside me," I whimper with another roll of my hips.

I reach through the shadows still obscuring his face, willing them to move. They don't respond.

He pumps himself faster, a lustful groan escaping his mouth. His other hand grasps my hip, urging me to move higher up his lap toward his waiting cock.

I lift up, aligning my center over his weeping length. A frustrated sigh leaves my lips when he keeps me hovering above him.

"I said I want you, Aurelius," I whisper.

He rubs the head of his cock through the wetness pooling at my center, taunting me with what I'm so desperate to feel right now.

The shadows move again as he leans forward, trailing aggressive kisses along my throat. His lips reach my ear, and he purrs, "You said my name wrong, My Queen."

Recognition hits me as my body flies backward off his lap. I land on the throne room floor, staring into Ayden's unobscured face in horror.

I narrow my eyes, anger flaring in the pit of my stomach. "Fuck you, Ayden."

"Do you want to, love?" he asks, his hand still stroking down his length. "You were dripping for me."

"That wasn't for you," I seethe. "I thought you were Aurelius."

"Did you now?" His honeyed eyes blaze, roaming my exposed form from head to toe. "What was your excuse for the hallway incident?"

"Is that what this is about?"

"That is precisely what this is about, love. Consider us even." He disappears, the dream fading into blackness.

Two days pass too quickly.

I thought that saying goodbye to Elijah, Ophelia, and Jade would be the hardest part. But leaving my kingdom behind was proving to be even worse. Rimor was my home, and I did not want to leave it.

Trunks had been packed and loaded into the carriages. All the belongings I cared to bring were shoved into wooden boxes, ready to take me to my new life. It had taken such drastic turns in the last few months, I could hardly believe this was happening.

"Remind me again why we must leave so soon?" I ask Ayden. It had been an annoying task to avoid him since his walk through my dream, but I couldn't stand to look him in the face after. Even now, I shift uncomfortably under his intense gaze.

"Time isn't on our side," he replies, voice cool and rehearsed. "Though fall has just arrived here, winter comes earlier, and harsher, in Prudia. With a party this size, we'll need at least a week to reach the castle. I'd rather not be caught in the first frost."

His answer is logical and rehearsed. And I don't believe it.

"Have you said your farewells?" he asks.

I nod. We said them last night, and I made it clear I didn't want them there for the send-off.

"Having them here would make it feel more… permanent. I'll see them again. Once I figure out how to dissolve this godsdamned marriage contract." I would make no attempt at hiding my intentions with Ayden.

"Will I be dragging you kicking and screaming down the aisle, love?" He teases.

"You can count on it."

One side of his lips quirk as he rubs his chin. "Funny. That's not quite how I remember it the other night. It was *you* who dragged me into that kiss, was it not?"

I stare at him, not an ounce of shame in me. "If you want a reaction from me, you'll have to try harder."

I swing up onto Luna's saddle, checking my satchel one last time.

Aurelius rides up beside me, astride his horse, Crea. "Don't encourage him. He'll only try harder."

I had avoided him since the council meeting, still hurt by his words about being a hypocrite. My feelings on his presence with us are conflicting. I still felt the sting of his betrayal, even more so each time I discovered there was something else he knew about this betrothal. But a part of me that I want to ignore is grateful to have a piece of home coming with me.

"Are you sure you don't want to travel in the carriage?" Ayden offers for the third time today.

His normally unruly curls are tamed back today, sunlight highlighting the deep brown color that sets him apart from Aurelius' black locks. My eyes sweep his form, prior embarrassment still threatening to make an appearance. I really do not want to admit how good he looks in riding leathers, but the truth is undeniable.

The male is devastatingly handsome.

"Worried I might run off on you?" I tease.

"To be frank—yes."

"My natural response typically involves fighting, not running," I say with a wink, not wanting him to know I couldn't handle being trapped between him and Aurelius for even an hour, let alone a week. "I'd be more worried about me throwing knives if I were you. I could use some target practice."

Ayden's personal guards tense, hands drifting to their swords at my empty threat.

Ryder and Zion step in behind me, blades already half-drawn.

Ayden sighs, shaking his head. "Stand down. I can handle my fianceé and anything she might throw at me."

"Are you three quite done with whatever this is?" Ayden's cousin, Lady Charlotte, asks. Her long blonde locks are braided down the center of her back, the tip nearly reaching her waist. While she isn't dressed in leathers like us, she is dressed to ride, white blouse tucked into the waistband of fitted pants, riding boots, and a cloak. I'm surprised she isn't opting for the carriage, given her usual polished demeanor.

"Yes, we should be on our way." Ayden looks to the sky as if he is expecting bad weather. "We have a lot of ground to cover if we want to make it to the inn by nightfall."

And with that, we're off.

We make good time, traveling a straight six hours without stopping. It would have gone faster without the carriage and full entourage, but still, I can't complain. By late afternoon, we reach the forested area that separates Ciyoria and the outskirts of Caedel.

Caedel marked the border between Prudia and Rimor, often housing citizens of both kingdoms, though it was technically in Rimor. Despite any conflict between our countries, the people here always lived in harmony, making the area a neutral territory of sorts. It was one of Rimor's largest cities, the surrounding farms responsible for supplying a majority of the capital's grain and textiles. It would be the last city we'd see before crossing into Prudia.

The shade here is dense and damp, a welcome relief after the heat of the sun. We call a rest to feed and water the horses.

I sit with my back against a tree, a canteen of blessedly cold water in hand, thanks to a guard with the Kaminari Gift. The magic-chilled drink soothes my dry throat.

"Here. Eat this." Ayden commands, holding out a piece of bread and a handful of berries.

I take the food without a fight, shoving it into my mouth. "We should reach Caedel in the next few hours."

A twig snaps behind me, and my head snaps around to find the source. I sit at the outskirts of the group, so there's no one behind me. "What was that?" I ask quietly.

Ayden scans the trees. "I don't see anything."

In the distance, I catch sight of the faintest irregularity in the shadows. It's too dark, unnatural.

"There's something there," I say, rising to get a better look.

"What's wrong?" Aurelius asks, coming up behind me.

"There's someone out there," I say with certainty.

"I don't see anyone."

The shadow moves, and I catch a flicker of red. Drawing a dagger, I take off after the moving shadow.

"Breyla, wait!" Aurelius calls.

I ignore him, trusting my intuition instead. Both males follow, but

I pay them no mind. Someone is watching us, and I want to know who.

I move swiftly through the underbrush, dodging and weaving around low-hanging limbs and large roots. Flashes of black and glimmers of red evade me as I push my muscles to carry me faster. Finally, I close some of the distance between us, enough to get a better view of who I'm pursuing.

I nearly gasp as the features come into view, and it's none other than Lord Craylor, the former spymaster who had been missing since my mother's death. Why he's following us in a forest, I have no idea, but I have questions.

"Breyla, stop!" Aurelius roars as he crashes into me, taking me to the ground. Our tangled bodies meet the densely packed earth, the scent of dirt filling my nostrils as I turn my face to him.

"Get off me," I demand, struggling beneath him. He wrestles me to my back, my hands pinned between his thighs and my body. "Lord Craylor was watching us, and now he's getting away.

Aurelius' chest heaves, his dark waves falling in his eyes as he stares me down. "There's no one here except us. Whatever you saw, it wasn't real."

Fury burns in my veins, and I manage to free an arm from beneath me, reaching around to slap him across the cheek. The crack echoes through the trees.

"Fuck you," I seethe. "I know what I saw! He was right there, and you let him get away. The male responsible for my mother's murder, and you let him escape."

He catches my wrist, pinning it beside my head. He leans in until his breath grazes my lips. "No one is there, Princess."

Heart pounding, body pressed tightly against his, adrenaline coursing through my veins, the anger turns to something worse—lust. I see the moment Aurelius' keen senses pick up on the smell of my arousal, his eyes darkening and nostrils flaring.

"I hate you," I say, narrowing my eyes at him. They dart to his lips, just inches from mine, then back to his eyes.

His gaze drops to my mouth. "Say it again like you mean it," he growls.

He hardens against me, and my core clenches. "I. Hate. You." It comes out like a whisper, and I know I'm done for.

He rolls his hips into me, and a breathy moan breaks free of my lips. Using his free hand, he reaches down to the front of my leathers, shoving his hand in. "Tell me, Breyla—am I going to find this cunt dripping for the male you claim to hate so much?"

The wetness pools between my thighs, and I know the undeniable truth. Even if I hate this male, my body still begs for him, and that makes me all the angrier.

"Fuck you."

He shoves two fingers inside me, and they meet no resistance as I whimper, clenching around him.

"I think you want me to. This delicious cunt is begging to be filled; begging for *me* to fill it." He pumps his fingers in and out, curling them in a come-hither motion that has me arching my back into his touch.

"If you're going to fuck me, Aurelius, fuck me like you mean it," I demand.

His lips crash into mine, punishing me with every stroke of his tongue. He wastes no time, unbuttoning and sharply yanking my pants down as far as my riding boots will allow.

He breaks our kiss, flipping me over so my ass is in the air. I hiss as I feel the sharp sting of his palm on my bare flesh. Wrapping my braid around his fist, he uses it as leverage to pull me flush against his chest.

I feel the tip of his cock align with my center and gasp. "This means nothing. It's purely physical, nothing more."

"Sure, Princess," he growls, biting down on the spot where my neck meets my shoulder. "But let's get one thing straight—you will not come until I say so and not without my name on those pretty lips."

Before I can respond, he thrusts in deep, taking me completely in one stroke.

I bite my lip, trying to adjust to his size all at once. Despite how wet I am, there's still a sting from the sudden intrusion. He fills me in the most glorious way, but it's a lot to take all at once.

He yanks my head back further, claiming my mouth while his other hand finds my clit.. My tongue parts his lips, meeting his own and deepening the kiss. He circles my clit as he fucks me with long, punishing strokes.

The pace he sets is relentless, and I can't contain the sounds his pleasure elicits. I moan loudly, demanding, "More."

"Say my name," he growls as he fucks me harder. His cock hits that glorious spot inside me, sending shivers down my spine as my core tightens around him.

"No," I gasp as his fingers increase in pace and pressure against my clit. I push my hips back, meeting him thrust for thrust.

He growls, biting down on my bottom lip. "This cunt belongs to me and you know it."

I feel my inner walls tighten, a warmth building low in my belly. "I still fucking hate you," I reply, unsure if it's a moan or growl that accompanies the words.

Right at the edge of orgasm, it recedes. The throbbing in my clit dulls.

"Hate me all you want, little demon," Aurelius pants, his thrusts growing erratic, "but you will scream my name if you want to come."

My nipples tighten, sensation becoming intense as if someone were pinching them. He keeps me on that precipice until I decide it's not worth fighting anymore, and moan, "Aurelius, please."

"Good girl," he whispers, releasing his Gift's hold on me. The orgasm crashes through me, and this time, I scream his name as he continues to fuck me through wave after wave of utter blissful destruction.

A second later, he follows, spilling inside me with a low, guttural growl.

We collapse into silence, both of us gasping for air. He presses kisses along my neck, withdrawing with care, his come slipping down my thighs.

Fingers trail through the mess he left, and he smirks as he shoves it back inside. I fight a groan at the barbaric and possessive need he has when it comes to me. Lacking water and with no way to clean me, he pulls my pants back into place, trapping the sticky mess in my undergarments. He wipes one hand on his own tunic before dragging both to my hips, where they linger.

"Did you enjoy the show, brother?" he calls out casually.

My head whips around to where Aurelius is looking; horror tinged with intrigue swirls through my gut, the dream still fresh in my mind.

Ayden steps out from behind a tree, his expression unreadable.

I should be furious right now, but I'm too caught up in post-orgasmic bliss to care. Instead, I ask, "How long were you watching?"

"From the very start, Princess." Aurelius pulls me to my feet, dusting the dirt and twigs from me.

"And you knew he was there," I say incredulously, "but you just fucked me anyway?"

"I had to show the prince just how well we work together," Aurelius says, referencing their argument from several days ago.

"And you let him?" I cock a brow at Ayden.

"I—"

"Yes," Aurelius interrupts smoothly, "Because as much as you crave being watched, Ayden enjoys watching."

"Fuck," Ayden finally says. He refuses to meet my gaze, finding a patch of dirt rather interesting right now.

"Is that so?" I tilt my head, looking Ayden up and down. My eyes lock on the outline of his very obvious erection.

"Yes," he admits, finally meeting my eyes once more.

"Intriguing," I say, brushing past both of them on my way back to the group.

Charlotte gives me a strange look when I make it back. I didn't bother to brush off the twigs or grass on my clothing, and I'm positive my braid was disheveled from being wrapped around Aurelius' fist.

When it all clicks for her, the look shifts to a knowing one. "Well, I can see the prince found you," she snickers. "Have a nice moment with him?"

Internally, I'm laughing because I know she's referring to Ayden when she says prince. Aurelius hasn't been formally recognized as such, and Ayden only calls him that to provoke him. It seems Charlotte is trying to do the same to me now.

"Oh yes," I saw sweetly. "The prince definitely found me. My moment with him was most... pleasurable." The word rolls off my tongue, intentionally drawn out. "But, you already know how pleasurable time with him can be."

I watch her features shift to confusion first, then realization as she pieces together that I'm referring to our shared history, Aurelius, and not her cousin Ayden.

The males join us a second later as Charlotte's face heats. "But you're engaged to my cousin!" she hisses.

I chuckle. "I was, in fact, aware of that." I cock an eyebrow at her when Ayden shoots me a look I can't read. "Speaking of cousins, if you're Ayden's cousin, does that also make you Aurelius' cousin?"

Her face heats, but it's Ayden that answers, "No. Charlotte is my cousin through my mother. Thank the gods, Aurelius and I don't share her."

I mount Luna, tone airy. "Oh, well, at least there's that."

Charlotte curls her lip in disgust. "Says the female who fucked her mother's fiancé."

I shrug. "You left out *my* father's adopted brother. If you're going to insult me, at least get all the facts."

"Breyla," Aurelius says. His tone is meant to chastise me, but I also see the amusement he's trying to hide in the slight curl of his lips.

"What? She started it."

I know I'm being childish, but I also know it drives them all crazy. And they all deserved that as far as I am concerned.

Aurelius reins in his horse. "I'm finishing it. Charlotte, stay out of it."

She rolls her eyes, turning away from me and leading her horse to the front of the group.

Ayden comes to a stop next to me, leaning over to whisper, "Despite how much I may have enjoyed your display in the woods, I would very much urge you not to flaunt your previous relations with Aurelius. I know you do not want this marriage, but could you at least grant me that respect?"

I flush slightly at the realization of just how disrespectful my actions were. I wouldn't ever apologize for fucking Aurelius, but I could be discreet. "Don't worry, it was a one-time thing."

"We'll see about that."

Turning to Aurelius, I snap, "No, we won't."

He raises a brow. "We won't what?"

"You just said…"

Ayden cocks a brow at me. "He didn't say anything, love."

I sigh. "Never mind, then. Let's go."

The setting sun bleeds orange and red across the sky as we reach the outskirts of Caedel. Despite the... *detour*, we've made good time.

The inn sits on the eastern edge of town, its stone exterior modest but well-maintained.

"Wait here," Ayden instructs, dismounting and heading inside.

We all dismount, seeing to the horses and unloading what supplies we need. I'm feeding Luna an apple when he reemerges several minutes later. He distributes keys to several people in our party, but stops when he gets to Aurelius and me.

"There was a bit of a mix-up with the inn." He grins, not looking the least bit upset as he says, "All they had was one single and one double bed left."

"Aurelius, you'll take the single." He holds the key out to Aurelius, who shoots him a menacing look.

I let out a low, unamused laugh, snatching the key from Ayden's outstretched hand. "Not a chance, pretty boy."

"You're not sleeping alone, Princess." Aurelius snatches it right back, holding it just above his head.

I step into his space, annoyed, reaching for the key he's now holding high above my head. "Give me one good reason why not."

He shares a look with his brother, a silent conversation seeming to take place between them.

"You scream at night," Aurelius finally says.

"We need everyone well-rested," Ayden adds. "And no one will get that if you're keeping them up."

I narrow my eyes. "So? What does not sleeping alone have to do with that?"

Ayden takes a deep breath. "I can keep your nightmares at bay. I have been for several nights now."

"You—what?" I stutter.

"Before you get mad at him," Aurelius cuts in, "I asked him to."

"That's not your job," I snap.

"It took three sleepless nights for me to break down and ask him for help. It was that or sleep with you, myself. I figured that was what you would prefer."

"As much as I hate to admit this," Ayden says, "he's telling the truth. The only times you stop screaming are when you're with him… or if I pull you out of the dreams."

I turn their words over, trying to figure out which was the better option. I both missed and enjoyed the nights spent sleeping next to

Aurelius, but my emotions were a mess, and I couldn't handle being that close to him again. His rough fucking earlier was primal, passionate, and a physical release I needed. But something felt infinitely more intimate about letting him sleep next to me again.

I cross my arms, looking between them. "I still don't understand why I need to sleep with either of you. Ayden, you can just tuck me in, work your magic, and I'll be fine through the night."

They both look like they want to argue, but I don't give them the chance. Using my shadows, I tug the key out of Aurelius' hand, dropping it in my own. I grab my pack and leave to find my room.

I deposit my pack in my room, snickering at the thought of Aurelius and Ayden having to share one bed. While I didn't want to sleep with either of them, part of me also just wanted to punish them for my own entertainment.

When I make it downstairs, the rest of our party has gathered around the tables, steaming food in front of them. My mouth waters at the savory aroma. I haven't eaten a substantial meal since breakfast, and I just now realize how hungry I really am. My stomach growls, alerting the others to that fact.

Ayden pulls out the chair beside him, and I sit. I reach for the bowl of shepherd's pie in front of me, only to have my wrist slapped by Aurelius. He swaps our bowls. The one he had is completely deconstructed, with all the carrots picked out and pushed to the side.

Emotions war in my chest. I haven't been able to look at carrots since his attempted murder, given their resemblance to the water hemlock that was used as poison. He can't stand them either, but he took the time to remove them for me before starting on his own. I want to be angry with him, but he makes it so damn hard when he does things like this.

I meet his gaze, smiling softly. "Thank you."

"Eat," he grunts, already picking through his new bowl.

I resist the urge to groan as I take the first bite. Mutton, rich gravy, and potatoes delight my taste buds. I shovel several spoonfuls into my mouth, then wash them down with a swig of ale.

"I had no idea I was this hungry," I mumble around another bite.

"Well," Ayden says, smirking, "I'm sure you worked up an appetite after your little run in the woods."

I choke around the food, coughing and trying to dislodge the meat now lodged in my throat.

Aurelius rubs circles on my back, helping me through the coughing fit. He's sporting a smug look as he casually takes a bite of his food.

"You're both asshats," I grumble.

The rest of the meal passes quickly, and I let out a satiated sigh as I finish the hearty meal.

Ayden rises. "We should all get to bed. There are no inns for the remainder of our journey. This will be the last time we'll have beds until we reach Prudia."

When I reach my room, I eagerly open my pack, looking for my night clothes. I sift through everything, dumping it all on the bed, only to find them missing. I didn't even pack regular tunics, just my leathers.

I head over to the room next to mine and knock. Ayden opens after a minute, wearing only his sleep pants slung low on his hips. Just past him, I can see Aurelius dressed similarly. My mind goes blank as I try to remember what I came here for.

"Ready to be *tucked into bed*?" Ayden says with a chuckle.

My eyes trace the deep V lines that both males are displaying. My mouth goes dry as I try to form words. "Erm, no."

"Eyes are up here, love." Ayden winks.

"Breyla, is there something else you need?" Aurelius asks, bringing my attention to him.

"Uh, yes." I force my eyes to stay trained on his. "I seem to have packed my tunics and sleep clothes in the trunks. Um... could I maybe—"

"Here," Ayden says, handing me a spare tunic at the same time as Aurelius holds out his.

Ayden's face hardens when I reach past him to take Aurelius'.

"Sorry, Prince," I say, shrugging. "It's nothing personal. He burned the last male's shirt I wore that wasn't his."

"And I would do it again."

"Brute," Ayden grumbles.

"Can you do the thing now?" I ask.

Ayden reaches a hand to my cheek, stroking it softly, as he leans in and kisses my forehead. I feel the warm essence of his magic wrap around me, seeping into my mind.

A soft growl rumbles from Aurelius, and Ayden steps back, a shit-eating grin on his face.

"Good night, boys. Sleep well," I say, backing out of their room.

I slip back into my own and lock the door behind me. Sleep claims me within moments of my head hitting the pillow.

CHAPTER SEVEN

Warm sun beats down on my skin as the crashing waves build a symphony of peace. The sand is soft, but stickier than I expect. It squishes between the toes of my bare feet, and I take a deep breath. Turquoise waters stretch as far as the eye can see.

"Come on, Ophelia." Layne smiles, beckoning me closer with a wave of his hand. "We didn't travel all the way to Amara for you to stand on the shore."

Amara. This was to be our grand adventure—the one he had promised me all those years ago. Just the two of us, seeing the world, starting with the glittering beaches of Amara.

"I'm coming! I was just taking it all in," I reply, making my way to the water's edge. "Is it cold?"

"No, the water is perfect. Come on in."

"But I can't swim well," I argue, suddenly very nervous about this.

"I've got you, Ophelia. I'll always have you."

Of course, he will. Layne is the one person I trust most in this world. He's never let me down. I take a hesitant step into the ocean and am pleasantly surprised at the warmth of the water. Growing more confident, I take another step, then another, until it's up to my waist.

"That's it, O. You've got this. Come to me."

He's only a few feet away, the water up to his chest. I take a few more steps and I'm right in front of him. The water reaches my chin now and I can barely touch. I feel panic rising in me, my arms searching for him under the water.

"You're okay, Ophelia. Just breathe."

The air is heavy, humid. It feels like I'm sucking in water, not oxygen. "I'm trying, but I can't feel the bottom, Layne."

"Do you trust me?"

"Of course."

"Take my hand," he says, finally offering me something to hold onto.

I do as he says, feeling instant relief at the contact.

"Now, lean back and let your body float to the top."

I look at him skeptically.

"Just do it, O. Trust me," he urges again.

Steeling myself, I do as he says. My head tips back and my body follows, leaving me floating on the surface of the water. I turn my head to look at him, a bright smile on both our faces.

"See, Ophelia. I told you—"

"Dammit, Ophelia, breathe!"

"—I would take care of you. Always."

My chest tightens looking at him. He's vibrant, so full of life. My one constant in this world.

"I swear to the gods, Ophelia. If you don't breathe, I will find a way—"

My lungs burn and spasm as I cough, water spilling out of my mouth. I try to breathe in, but the air just irritates my lungs further, and the coughing continues. Slowly, I open my eyes to find Jade staring down at me.

Concern is etched on her face, but it's followed by relief when our eyes finally meet. Taking a look around me, I find that I'm lying on the bank of the river that runs behind the palace. I'm fully clothed and soaking wet.

"What happened?" I croak.

"I don't know, Ophelia, you tell me. I came out here for some solitude and found you floating in the river, face down, not breathing."

I sit up cautiously, trying to piece it together. "I... I don't know how I got here."

"What's the last thing you remember?"

"Going to bed last night. I dreamt about Layne. We were swimming in Amara." A sob catches in my throat, and my chest tightens. "Oh gods, he's dead," I whisper.

Immediately, I want to go back to the dream, to where my brother is still alive. Logically, I know he's dead, but every day I have to wake up and be reminded of that fact. We burned him next to the queen and my bastard of a father, but I still have to adjust to my new reality each time I open my eyes.

My tears have been frequent since his death, but they never seem to run dry. Even now, they pool in my eyes, threatening to run over. "He's gone, Jade. And I feel like he took part of me with him when he left."

"That's because he did." She drops to the ground next to me and picks at the sparse grass that grows around the river.

"Does it ever lessen?" I whisper. "This feeling of missing part of myself?"

"It hasn't for me." She stares ahead, lost in thought. "But being broken doesn't mean we're any less. Sometimes, the defect is greater than the entire. We just have to learn to live with that."

"Does the pain ever go away?"

"No, you merely get better at carrying it." Jade pauses, her voice softer now. "I wish I had hope to give you, but things don't really get easier; you just learn to live with them better. The female I was with Julian is dead. I'm still figuring out who I am now, and you will, too. But it takes time."

"It should have been me, Jade. That blade was meant for me." The guilt bleeds through every syllable.

"There isn't a day that goes by that I don't think the same about Julian. I would switch places with him in a heartbeat. But we can't. So we live, for them, until it's time to see them again."

I nod. "Layne would want me to live."

"As would Julian. So we will. Just promise me something."

"What's that?"

"No more late-night swims alone."

Her tone is serious, but I can't help the laughter that bursts out of me. "I'll do my best. I did tell you I had no idea how I got here."

"I'd hate to be the one to tell Elijah you died. Maybe you should just have him tie you down at night to keep you in place. Kinky fucker would enjoy it."

I flush at the thought of Elijah tying me down. "I, uh—"

"Oh!" Jade's eyes widen. "You haven't fucked yet, have you?"

"No," I groan. "He's more than happy to, uh—take care of me. But every time we get close, something gets in the way."

"Oh, babe," Jade grins. "You are in for the ride of your life."

"Wait—" my eyes widen. "You and Elijah…"

Jade laughs, throwing her head back. "Oh yes. But it's old news. There's never been anything except the physical between us."

"But he and Julian—I got the impression they were also lovers."

"They were," she confirms, her smirk deepening as the blush rises on my cheeks.

"So, you both slept with him?"

"I mean, not at the same time. That would be gross." Jade shudders at the thought.

"This is not how I thought this conversation would go."

Jade laughs again, her entire body shaking. "Come on, babe. Let's get you back to the castle and out of those wet clothes."

The trek back is quiet, a comfortable silence settling over us. The sun's risen higher now, and the castle bustles with mid-morning activity, staff hurrying to and from tasks, the weight of our world temporarily distant.

"Elijah!" Jade calls as we turn down the east wing toward my chambers.

He looks up, blond brow arched in confusion. The corner of his mouth quirks in a half-smile, dimple peeking out as he asks, "Why are you both wet?"

"Keep an eye on this female of yours—apparently she sleepwalks."

"Oh?" His brown eyes sparkle with mischief. "I guess I'll have to keep her in my bed, then." He loops an arm around my waist, pulling me into his embrace.

"I don't think you'll hear any protests from her," Jade says with a smirk.

"That's not necessary." I blush, embarrassment and something else flooding my veins. "I've never done that before. I'm sure it won't happen again."

His gaze roams over my wet body, taking careful note of everything he sees. "Care to explain what exactly happened?"

"I–I don't know, exactly." My eyes drop to the floor. "I was dreaming of Layne. We were swimming in Amara. Next thing I know, I'm puking up water, and Jade is yelling at me."

"She was floating in the river, not responsive. I don't know how long she was out there." Jade fills in the gaps, finishing the story. "I'm just glad I found her when I did."

"I am as well." Appreciation flashes across Elijah's face. "Thank you, Jade."

Elijah leans in and kisses me, soft and slow, and I part my lips for more before he pulls away. "You smell like river water," he teases. "Let's get you bathed, doll."

Internally, I groan, but nod in agreement. I really do stink.

"Take care of her, E," Jade says, her tone turned serious. "I'm leaving tomorrow and won't be here to save your damsel next time."

"So soon?" I ask, surprised.

"Breyla left me in charge of the army in her absence. I received a report this morning that attacks on the border are increasing. We're losing soldiers to an enemy we didn't know existed."

"I don't understand."

"Before they left, Ayden confirmed that most of the attacks weren't coming from Prudia. With the alliance and marriage contract, it wouldn't serve him to provoke conflict. So that means someone else is behind them, and we don't know who."

"That's… concerning," I say, but it feels like a weak word.

"That's an understatement," Jade scoffs. "Good luck running Rimor, though. I'm sure you two will manage. I'll keep you apprised of what I learn, Elijah."

"I'll miss you," Elijah says evenly. "Stay safe, Jade."

A sadness that I don't understand fills his eyes and words.

I squeeze his hand in silent reassurance before throwing my arms around Jade. "Thank you, Jade."

I know it's a silly sentiment, given her position, but I can't stomach the thought of losing another person.

"You're welcome, Ophelia." She hugs me back, and I wrinkle my nose at her matching river water scent.

Jade tilts her head, dark eyes calculating as she nods. "You too, E."

Her silver-white braids swing as she walks away, leaving wet footprints in her wake.

"Okay, bath time," Elijah declares.

Before I can protest, he scoops me up and tosses me over his shoulder. I let out a laugh that echoes through the corridor as he carries me the rest of the way to my room.

CHAPTER EIGHT

BREYLA

Ayden tends to the low-burning fire with a stick while people make their beds on the grass. We had crossed the border into Prudia two days ago and would reach the capital, Elentia, by nightfall tomorrow.

"I'll take first watch," Ayden says, and no one protests. Three days of riding and sleeping on the ground had taken their toll. Everyone's quiet as we make camp in an open field on the fourth night. Silently, we eat roasted rabbit and the last of the crusty bread we brought from Rimor.

I bend forward, trying to rub the stiffness from my legs. Riding hard with minimal breaks has left me sore and cramping.

Ayden smirks at my discomfort. "The carriage offer still stands if you'd like a break from riding."

"I might take you up on that. Luna would appreciate it, I'm sure."

I sigh, giving up on stretching the muscles in favor of sleep. The stars twinkle brightly overhead as a crisp autumn breeze rolls through. Shivering, I pull the blanket higher around my shoulders.

Several minutes later, soft snores sound around me. Despite my body crying for sleep, my brain is wide awake with thoughts of what will happen when we arrive tomorrow plaguing me.

We haven't spoken about it, but I wonder how long Ayden will wait before forcing me down the aisle. I truly need to look at that godsdamned contract—there *has* to be a loophole somewhere.

Unable to quiet my thoughts, I toss and turn.

Ayden adds a log to the fire, prodding it until the flames catch. "Trouble sleeping, darling?"

The flames lick at my skin, their heat just close enough to be comfortable. "I'm just anxious."

"Don't tell me you're actually getting excited to marry me, Princess."

"Don't get ahead of yourself, Prince."

"I know this isn't what you wanted. Believe me, it's never what I pictured for myself, but trust me when I say I did it for a very good reason."

"You must know I never wanted war with Prudia. It didn't require a marriage to ensure peace between us."

"I know, Princess." His voice is withdrawn, perhaps even regretful. "I did it to protect my people, and yours."

"You speak in riddles."

"Just trust I know what I'm doing."

"Aurelius once said the same thing to me when I confronted him about secrets," I say sadly. "You see where that got me."

"I don't intend to hurt you."

"I'm sure he didn't intend to, either." I yawn, blinking back years. "Doesn't change the fact that he did."

"How long are you going to punish him for that?"

The question catches me off guard. "Why would you care about me forgiving him? I would think you'd want that wedge between us."

"Breyla, you may be my betrothed, but I know you care for him. Just because I don't want you in his bed, doesn't mean I want you to hate him."

I mull over his words for a few moments before responding. "I don't hate him. Not really."

"Obviously," he teases, "I'm pretty sure you just have a thing for hate sex."

"Whatever," I say, rolling away from him.

"Good night, Breyla."

"Good night, Ayden."

Finally, sleep claims me.

The next morning, Ayden, Aurelius, and I all opt to take a carriage for the final stretch. Charlotte, Ryder, Zion, and the others trail behind us on horseback. To pass the time, Ayden insists we play two truths and a lie.

All our games are rooted in worship. Our gods and goddesses believe that respect for them should be freely given from a place of joy and reverence. Most gods and goddesses have one they favor, many of them responsible for the creation of their game. This happens to be attributed to Saelem, the god of mischief.

Ayden is bound and determined to find a way to get past Aurelius' Gift.

Aurelius crosses his arms, narrowing his eyes. "I'm telling you there's no way to lie to me."

"And I'm telling you there's always a way," Ayden argues.

"Fine. Go again. I'll prove you wrong once more."

"I can't stand green beans," Ayden starts, lifting a finger for each one. "I once lost a bet to my friend Malcolm, and he made me wear my sister's corset to a ball. And... I've been known to dabble in the occasional threesome."

"The threesome checks out with your fondness for watching," I say, my eyes assessing his frame in an attempt to picture him in a corset.

"You wore your sister's corset to a ball?" Aurelius asks, confirming the green beans was the lie.

"Ugh, yes. And let's just say I have immense respect for the ladies who wear those cages you call clothing."

I let out a chuckle, agreeing with him completely. "Why do you think I wear my leathers all the time?"

"I just thought it was because they were practical and made you look intimidating."

"I *am* intimidating," I say firmly.

Aurelius smirks. "Of course you are, Princess."

It makes me want to punch him.

"Aurelius, your turn."

"Fine. I used to give other males erections when they pissed me off as a boy. I find ducks adorable. The quickest I've ever brought a female to orgasm was forty-eight seconds."

I blush thinking about the last one. He had never brought me to orgasm that quickly, preferring to drag out my pleasure as long as possible, but I think about what it would be like for him to try.

"Her blush makes me think the last one is the truth," Ayden muses, "Although you do look like the type of male who would like cute little ducks."

"It's the ducks, right?" I guess, trying to recover.

"Nope." Aurelius grins. "I find them quite precious. I once tried to keep one as a pet."

"So, you're telling me," Ayden says, eyes lighting up, "that you have the ability to give males spontaneous erections—and you never once used that Gift to torment them?"

"I haven't. But don't tempt me. I'm not above that."

The carriage comes to a halt, and a knock sounds outside the carriage before a gruff voice calls out, "We're about to enter the city, Prince."

"Ah, that's my queue," Ayden sighs. "I'll be entering on horseback to greet my people. It is probably best you two remain inside until we reach the castle." With a sharp tug, he swings open the carriage door and disappears into the outside light.

The carriage lurches forward, my stomach going with it. Apprehension churns inside me, and I wish, for the hundredth time, that I were back in Rimor.

Aurelius shifts beside me, his voice low and teasing. "Your turn, Princess."

"Why would we continue playing? You've already proven it's impossible to get past your Gift."

"Because I love the way those pretty lies sound coming from your lips," he drawls, leaning back with that infuriating smirk. "Humor me."

"Fine," I sigh. "I hate you. I'm not wearing any underwear. My favorite dessert is apple pie."

He chuckles, deep and melodic. "That's not how the game works, little demon. It's two *truths* and a lie, not two lies. But it does things to me knowing you're sitting three feet away, not wearing any underwear."

"I don't know what you're talking about. There were two truths."

His gaze heats, crimson flecks sparking in his dark irises. "Then come over here and show me how much you hate me," he taunts. "Make me believe it."

"I suppose I have nothing better to do."

I rise slowly, dragging my blade from its sheath as I step between his spread legs. His eyes don't leave mine as I lift the dagger and press it to the side of his throat.

The crazy bastard grins. "I could do it," I whisper, the tip biting into the skin just enough of draw a drop of blood. "I could slide this blade straight across your neck and end both our suffering."

His pulse flutters against the edge of my blade, steady and unbothered. "I have no doubt you could, little demon. But you won't."

I press the blade harder, watching the blood trickle down his throat. "And why is that?"

"Because I know you better than you want to admit," he says confidently. In a move I wasn't expecting, he seizes my wrist, spinning me around and pulling me into his lap. I land straddling his thighs, heart thundering in my chest.

"You don't want to admit that your feelings for me haven't changed. There's betrayal and hurt layered over them that you're holding onto so tightly, but underneath it, you still want me. You crave me."

"If I crave you, it's only that I crave what you can do to me physically. You have no right to my emotions."

"I can smell it on you, you know. How much you desire me. If I were to slip my hand," his voice trails off as he reaches a hand to the front of my leathers. "I know what I would find."

My core clenches around nothing at his words. "You might know my body, but anyone can figure that out. You aren't the only one capable of arousing me."

"But I will be the only one to satiate that arousal," he snarls low in my ear.

I shouldn't be excited by that, but I am.

"I decide who touches me," I growl.

He chuckles, but it's menacing. "Test me on this, I dare you."

"I fucking hate you," I whisper.

One of his hands plunges beneath my leathers, swiping through the wetness dripping down my thighs. "Liar."

He lifts me from his lap just enough to tug down my pants, leaving them pooled around my ankles. I hear him unbutton his own, letting his throbbing cock spring free.

"Sit," he demands, pulling my hips back so I'm hovering just above him.

"Don't tell me what to do."

He just chuckles that same low, menacing sound before burying himself to the hilt in one hard stroke.

"Fuck," I moan. "I so fucking hate you."

"Let me feel your hate, Princess." He keeps one hand on my hip while the other wraps around my throat, squeezing just enough to heighten my arousal without cutting off airflow.

I'm panting from how full I feel in this position. Taking him without any warmup was a feat in itself, but at this angle, it was almost too much. I rock my hips, urging the muscles to relax around him.

He thrusts up into me, and I nearly cry from the sensation. His cock perfectly hits that magical spot deep inside me with every thrust. With his hand still on my hip, he urges me to keep moving.

When I set a steady rhythm, he groans low and whispers, "Gods, Princess. You're gripping my cock so hard. Your hate feels so divine."

With each roll of my hips, he hits that spot that makes me see stars. I whimper, feeling my orgasm build.

I hear voices outside the carriage. They're muffled, but I catch snippets of different people welcoming the prince home. "We're close, Aurelius."

"I'm not done with you yet," he grunts, taking his hand from my throat and gripping my other hip. "They can wait."

He stops my hips from rolling and lifts me, slamming me back down on him with force.

I whisper his name as he repeats this motion over and over. He pauses for just a moment as he runs his left hand through my pussy, gathering the wetness pooled there. A moment later, I feel his finger massage the tight puckered hole of my ass before it slips in.

I thought this would be painful, but I was so wrong. There's a slight burn, but it quickly disappears as he works in and out, fucking my ass with his finger while his cock fills my pussy. His movements are filled with possession so overwhelming, I can't help but shudder.

Once I'm thoroughly acclimated, he resumes his thrusts, bouncing me on his lap as he fucks both my holes. It's simultaneously too much and not enough.

He pounds into me at a punishing pace that has me mewling. "Please. Fuck, I need more."

"My greedy little demon," he purrs in my ear before working another finger inside my ass.

I shudder, dangerously close to unraveling. "Make me come," I demand, already tipping forward into the storm of it.

He doesn't hesitate. His thrusts grow erratic, relentless, until my body clamps down, and I have no choice but to fall. He covers my mouth with one hand as I scream his name into his palm, the sound swallowed by the velvet-dark confines of the carriage.

Pleasure crests in wave after wave, soaking the space between us, seeping into everything. My breath stutters, thighs trembling from the aftershock.

"Gods, Princess," Aurelius groans. "That was fucking sexy. I can't wait to wear your scent. Now I'm going to fill you with *my* cum as we enter your fiancé's kingdom. When you step foot into his palace, it'll be my seed spilling down your thighs."

His feral possessive words spark something volatile inside me. Uninhibited whimpers fall from my lips before he spills himself with one final thrust.

I collapse against his chest, the warmth of release slipping between us, his hands smoothing my hair back as the carriage begins to slow. My breath catches in my throat as I slide off his lap, limbs still loose with afterglow.

"Forty-eight seconds?" I pant. "Was that really true?"

He laughs as he buttons his own pants. Before I have mine back in place, he flips us so I'm sitting on the bench, looking into his devious, dark eyes.

"How about I just show you, hm? I'd say we have a couple of minutes before that carriage door opens. Maybe less."

He doesn't give me a chance to respond before he shoves two fingers on his right hand into my pussy, curling them forward. I feel his Gift work at full capacity as pleasure and blood flow immediately build around my clit. His fingers continue curling inside of me as his thumb finds my clit.

Sweet relief washes through me at his touch, and I hiss as his teeth find the spot between my neck and shoulder. He bites down, sucking the skin into his warm mouth. The combined sensation has me racing toward a second climax.

In and out, his fingers pump, curling every single stroke. His thumb circles my clit faster as his Gift continues coursing through me, heightening my pleasure. Then he mutters the words that are my complete undoing, "Be my good little whore, General, and come on my fingers."

My orgasm explodes through me, my back arching off the seat, legs trembling. I suck in a deep breath, trying to bring myself down from the high his touch created. Euphoria ebbs through me as I feel him pull my pants back into place.

He traces my lips with the fingers he just used to fuck me, then slips them in my mouth. "Suck."

I oblige, running my tongue over his fingers and savoring the salty, tangy flavor of our combined releases. Just then, the carriage door flies open, revealing an irritated Prince Ayden.

"Are you two fucking kidding me right now?" His angry amber eyes dart between us.

"No, we just *finished* fucking," Aurelius says easily, smirking. "Sorry you missed the show."

I move toward the door, but Ayden stops me. Heated eyes take me in as he scans every inch. "Princess," he says, quiet and firm, "you are going to play along with what comes next. Aurelius, you are going to restrain yourself and let it happen. There are eyes watching. Am I absolutely clear?"

I nod in understanding, wondering what comes next.

"Aurelius," Ayden growls, "I need confirmation."

After a few moments, Aurelius begrudgingly responds, "Fine. I won't react."

Ayden's shoulders sag in relief. "Sorry about this, love."

He pulls me from the carriage and into his arms in one smooth motion, one hand wrapped low on my back, the other threading into my hair. His lips find mine in a searing kiss. Using his grip on my hair, he tilts my head back and uses the new angle to take the kiss even deeper.

I play along, just like he demanded, letting my tongue meet his as my hand grips the back of his shirt tightly. He breaks our kiss, trailing his lips down my neck to the same place Aurelius had just bit. The flesh there is tender, and I realize Aurelius must have left a mark. Ayden covers the spot with his mouth, sucking it with fervor.

A soft, breathy whimper escapes me at the sensation, and I feel my body responding to his touch. It's nothing like the passion Aurelius ignites within me, but it's responding all the same.

"Brother, are you done attacking your fiancée's neck? I would like to meet her." A sensuous alto voice says, breaking the trance we were in. It carries the same familiar accent that Ayden speaks with, and I find myself wanting to hear her sing.

Ayden releases my neck and disentangles his fingers from my hair. He does his best to straighten my curls and clothing before turning to face the female.

When he steps aside, my eyes find a female who I have no doubt is Ayden's sister, Rowina. Dark brown curls bounce as she turns her head, amber eyes to match his stare back at me. She's shorter than me, but not by much. Round hips and a generous bust give her curves similar to my own. She's not toned like I am, but she's not delicate, either.

"Oh my brother." She cocks her head, a wicked grin spreading across her face. I take a step forward to introduce myself, but she beats me to it, pulling my hand up to her mouth and placing a gentle kiss across my knuckles. "She is far too beautiful for you. I should like to keep her for myself."

Rowina's behavior is strange, especially for a female. I do not know what to make of her words. Aurelius and Ayden come to stand behind me, and Rowina directs her attention to Aurelius.

"Well, well," the female muses. "If it isn't our other brother. I can't believe I never saw the resemblance. It seems obvious now."

"Pleasure to see you again, Princess Rowina." It sounds like anything but a pleasure.

Ayden steps in. "Ro, please, give them some space."

Rowina takes a step back at the behest of her brother.

"Mother will be pleased to have you home. In your absence, she has attempted to match me with three different suitors. You'd think she'd have figured it out by now, but she always seems surprised when they all leave with no intention of returning."

"You have mastered the art of scaring away males, dear sister. But you're rambling; we can catch up later."

"Fine," she says with a pout. "I shall go fetch some whiskey from the kitchens. Gods know you'll need it after they meet Mother. She's in a mood."

"She's in a mood because you put her in a mood," Ayden levels her with a knowing look.

"It's not intentional," she says, then mumbles, "most of the time."

"Go. I will see you later."

She turns and strides away, throwing a "Good luck!" over her shoulder as she disappears into the castle.

"What was all that about?" I ask after she's out of earshot.

"Which part?" Ayden asks, amused.

"All of it, really. But the part about the suitors?"

They both laugh, apparently knowing something I don't. "Let's just say Ro is capable of pleasuring females better than most of the males our mother keeps throwing at her."

"She still hasn't figured that out?" Aurelius asks. "I picked up on that my first visit here."

Ayden shrugs. "I'm pretty sure she's just in denial. Ro does not try to hide it at all."

"Would she care if your sister did not marry a male?" I ask.

"I do not believe she would love her any less, but I do not know how accepting she would be," Ayden explains, "My mother is fixated on ensuring the Mordet line continues. I think she would only have a hard time accepting that Rowina will most likely not bear her any grandchildren."

"What a ridiculous thing to be caught up on," I say, mostly to myself.

"Yes, well, prepare yourself," he warns, casting me a knowing look. "It likely won't take her long to push you for heirs."

I roll my eyes. "Fantastic."

Aurelius remains suspiciously silent and well-behaved as we make our way through the castle gates.

Aurelius walks ahead, but not before brushing close, his voice a soft whisper just for me. "Forty-two seconds."

CHAPTER NINE

BREYLA

We enter the grand hall of the castle, and I'm struck by the most unexpected, yet tasteful, opulence. Where I imagined all black velvet and gold accents to mirror the colors of House Mordet, I instead see something warmer and welcoming.

Open windows framed by black drapes flood the room with soft, golden light. The white marble floors gleam, subtle hints of black and gold streaking through it. The rays catch gold in the marble, creating a soft, ethereal sparkle.

I'm accustomed to the stone floors and walls of Rimor. It was dark and sometimes cold, but it was home.

Two thrones with curved golden frames and black cushioned seats sit low on the dais. The larger of the two remains empty, waiting for Prince Ayden to claim his birthright. On the other is a female who is nothing short of breathtaking.

Piercing amber eyes framed by dark lashes assess me the moment they lock with mine. Long raven hair flows down her back, landing in loose curls. A petite gold and black crown sits upon her brow, and a modest black dress made of silk hugs every curve of her body. High cheekbones, skin the color of moonlight, and rosy lips round out the

Queen's features. I don't need to see a portrait of the late king to know that Ayden and Rowina's beauty comes from their mother.

Her gaze is calculating but not cruel. That is, until it's turned on Aurelius. Gold eyes turn cold as they narrow on the male beside me.

Our party halts before the dais, waiting on bated breath for the queen to speak. As she lays eyes on her son, they light up and fill with warmth.

"My son." She smiles, and it reaches her eyes. She quickly rises from the throne and closes the distance between them, wrapping her petite arms around his large frame.

"Hello, Mother," Ayden greets her, wrapping his arms around her in return. Seeing their embrace makes my heart ache. What I wouldn't give for just one more hug like that with my mother.

Stepping back, the queen pats Ayden's cheek, her gaze roving over him with a mixture of pride and calculation.. "It is good to have you home. Your journey was uneventful, I trust?"

"We are here safe, are we not?" Ayden responds without really answering.

"Indeed," she hums in agreement, glancing at me for the first time with expectation.

Ayden clears his throat, stepping back and reaching a hand around my back. He gently guides me forward to face her.

"May I introduce you to my fiancée, Princess Breyla Rozaria. Breyla, this is my mother, Queen Josephina Mordet."

"Hello, dear," Queen Josephina says, making no move towards me.

"Queen Josephina," I greet, tipping my head just slightly enough to be polite while acknowledging that I didn't view her as higher in position. I may not have been crowned before leaving Rimor, but that made me no less a queen.

And her equal.

Her eyes inspect every inch of me, weighing and measuring the female set to marry her son and take her place as queen. "You are beautiful," she says at last.

"I am also smart," I add, voice cool. "And rather impressive with a sword."

A faint tightening at the corner of her mouth. "I'm sure those traits will also be valuable in producing heirs."

"Mother," Ayden warns. "You have just met. Can you please not thrust your talk of heirs on her yet?"

Ignoring her son's outburst, she continues, "Did you not allow her to change out of her travel leathers before arriving?"

Not liking being spoken about rather than spoken to, I interject, "She prefers leathers, actually."

The queen's face contorts into something between horror and confusion. Rowina stifles a laugh somewhere behind me as her mother's dark eyebrows nearly reach her hairline.

Ayden's face lights in amusement, but he remains quiet.

After a few minutes of stunned silence, Queen Josephina finally speaks, "The ladies of this court do not parade themselves in the clothes of males."

My fingers curl into the palms of my hands as I feel anger flaring inside me. "With all due respect, Your Majesty, I am a queen in my own right and general of the Rimorian army," I start, fighting to keep my tone even. "I will *not* be told what to wear. I will parade myself through this court naked as the day I was born, if I so please."

Amusement fills the faces of everyone around me except the queen. Her face darkens as she spits the next words at me, "A would-be queen without a crown and a former general. I will not relinquish my throne to a female so improper and uncouth."

A full belly laugh erupts at the notion of me on her throne. "Did you truly not know the female your son bargained for? This is me, Queen Josephina." I throw my arms wide and give her a slight mocking bow. "I am rough, loud, foul-mouthed, strong-willed, hate dresses, eat what I please, bed whom I please, and make no apologies for any of it. I will not change for you, and I do not want your gods-damned throne."

The queen rears back as if I had assaulted her with more than just my truth. "If this is how you were raised, it is no wonder your kingdom is in the state that it is."

Her words are venomous and vile. They sting like I've been slapped. It was one thing to attack my person. I harbor no regrets and make no apologies for the female that I am. In fact, it's something I usually take pride in. But insulting my country and my parents is taking it too far.

A look passes her face that tells me she knows it was too far, but her pride will never allow her to admit it.

"Yes, well, perhaps you should have left me there," I say quietly. The rage inside me turns sour and cold. "I never asked to be here."

"You're royalty, dear." The queen frowns. "You aren't afforded choices like that."

I think her words are meant to sound like an apology, but all I hear is pity as a little more of my freedom is stripped away. A kernel of resentment grows for the prince who brought me here and the father who sentenced me to be his wife.

"Staff, please take my future daughter-in-law's trunks to the prince's rooms," Queen Josephina calls.

Before I can respond, my things are being taken out of the hall. "The prince's rooms? Do I not get chambers of my own?"

"You are to be wed. Why would you need chambers of your own?"

"So, you find females wearing pants improper," I snap, "but unwed couples sharing chambers is perfectly acceptable?"

A light chuckle sounds from her nearly perfect lips. "Of course it is improper, my dear. But Prudia needs heirs, and if you insist on *bedding whom you want*, I will do what I must to ensure that the heir is not some bastard."

At the word, her crystalline eyes cut sharply toward Aurelius, her meaning clear.

"Not the heir talk again, Mother," Ayden groans, even as Aurelius steps forward.

"If you have something to say to me, Your Majesty," Aurelius drawls, "just say it."

While I'm grateful the attention is off of me for the moment, I do not wish her cruelty turned on him, either.

"I will never understand why my son thought it wise to bring his father's bastard into this court," Queen Josephina says coolly, "but you are not welcome here, Aurelius."

"I have been unwanted in some fashion most of my life," Aurelius says nonchalantly. "Your sunny disposition was hardly something I counted on, nor do I care if you want me here." His smile sharpens, cruel and knowing. "But I am curious, is it me being a bastard or the shattered illusion of your not-so-perfect dead husband that bothers you more?"

"Watch your tongue, brother," Ayden warns. "I can still send you back to Rimor."

Aurelius raises his brow in challenge. "We both know you could never keep me there."

"Well, this has been delightful!" Rowina chimes in, her tone cheery and excited. "I don't care if you don't like Breyla and Aurelius, Mother. I quite enjoy them. I'm keeping them."

A smile lights Rowina's face as she takes her mother by the arm, leading her away from the rest of us. "Mother, I believe there was a suitor you wanted to speak to me about?"

We breathe a collective sigh of relief once the queen has left the room.

I startle when an unfamiliar deep voice speaks behind me, "Well, that show was worth the price of admission."

"Darian," Ayden greets warmly, his smile reaching his eyes.

A warm hand wraps around my own, and it's then that I realize I had grabbed my dagger.

"That's Darian Ashcroft," Aurelius says quietly, "Ayden's general. He's not a threat."

Returning my dagger to its sheath, I respond, "I'm not used to others being able to surprise me."

"That would be his Gift," Aurelius explains. He starts to say more, but is cut off when the new male turns his attention to us.

Deep blue eyes meet mine, assessing and weighing me where I stand. Brown locks frame his face. Sun-kissed skin and defined muscles tell of his time training outside. Much like me, he's dressed in leathers, and I count no less than five blades on him.

Ayden lays a hand on the male's shoulder, turning to look at me. "Princess Breyla, I'd like you to meet my general, Darian Ashcroft."

A maelstrom of emotions rises inside me as I assess the male. I should feel respect for the warrior in front of me, but we've been two warring countries for a very long time, so I also carry a large amount of grief for the Rimorian lives lost at his orders.

Tentatively, I reach out a hand in greeting. "It's a pleasure to meet you, General Darian."

He sneers, the act contorting his beautiful face into something ugly. His arms cross his broad chest as he blatantly ignores my outstretched hand.

"Let's not pretend to be things we're not, *General*." The way he says my title is full of mockery. Though we possess the same title, he holds no respect for me.

My hand drops at the same time as my jaw. I know I'm brash, but this male is just rude.

"Excuse me?" I nearly stutter, unsure how to respond.

"You heard me," Darain says before turning to Ayden. "Is your bride deaf as well as inept?"

The fury I felt with the queen returns in a heartbeat. With a snarl, I wrap my shadows around his throat, lifting him into the air. The position should cut off air flow, but the bastard is grinning.

Before my eyes, he vanishes from my hold, only to reappear behind me in an instant, cold steel pressing against my throat.

"I know how I became General," he murmurs, voice low against my ear. "I'm still trying to puzzle out how you did."

A sly smile curves my lips as two swords are leveled at Darian. His hand goes limp against my throat in a tell-tale sign of Aurelius' Gift seizing control of his body. Darian stiffens behind me, refusing to move as Ryder and Zion give him deadly looks for daring to threaten their princess.

"She earned it." Aurelius' voice is low and threatening as he approaches my side. "I suggest you remove your hands, General. I will not hesitate to end you if I feel she is in danger."

Ryder and Zion grunt in agreement, just as Ayden finally decides to step in.

"Easy now." Ayden shoots Darian a sharp look, commanding him to step down. "Darian wouldn't hurt my fiancé. I trust him with my life. This is simply a lapse in judgment."

Darian seems to battle with himself a moment longer before finally stepping back. Ryder and Zion reluctantly sheathe their swords.

Stepping away from Darian, I rub my neck where a drop of blood has run from where his dagger nicked me. "Call me inept one more time, General," I bare my teeth at him, growling, "and it won't be my bodyguards you'll have to deal with."

His jaw ticks, nostrils flaring, as he fights to keep his temper in check.

"Darian," Ayden says flatly, "find somewhere else to be until you can figure out how to control your temper."

"Gladly," Darian responds, storming in the other direction.

When I'm sure he's gone, I turn my anger on Ayden. "Seriously, Ayden? What the fuck. Is your entire kingdom this hospitable?"

He shrugs, a coy smile fighting the corners of his mouth. "No, those two are just the worst. I figured we might as well get it over with all at once."

"Some warning might have been nice." I level him with a glare.

"Where's the fun in that?" he says, winking as he grabs my elbow lightly. "Come on, I'll show you to your room. Aurelius knows where he's going."

He leads me out and toward the royal wing. I find that the surrounding halls are just as bright and welcoming as the rest of the castle to this point.

"What's Darian's problem with me?" I ask as we begin ascending a staircase in the west wing.

Ayden sighs. "Darian has his reasons. I'm not condoning his actions, but his story is his own. If you want to know, you'll have to ask him yourself."

"That's all you've got to say?" I bark a humorless laugh. "The male held a dagger to my throat, and your explanation is *ask him*? Unbelievable."

"Everyone has a right to their story, Breyla," he says without flinching. "And the right to choose who hears it.. Darian is one of my oldest friends, and I will not betray him. I'll just say… you two have more in common than you might think, but he does have his reasons for disliking you."

Seeing that I'm getting nowhere, I take a different approach. "How long has he been your general?"

"A little over a year," he replies. "And while we're on that topic—I ordered the attacks on your borders to stop before that."

"You—what?" His confession is so nonchalant, I almost think I misheard him. The revelation throws my world off-kilter.

"I had no desire to fight a war with Rimor. That ended with my father. I simply want my people to live in peace."

"How am I supposed to believe you, Ayden? I've been on the front. I've seen the attacks and the blood your soldiers spilled."

"We keep a few units on the borders," Ayden says carefully, "but only to maintain order. The soldiers you've been fighting? They aren't mine."

My head screams that he must be lying because who could possibly be behind this if not him? But my gut, damn it—it says he's telling the truth. "I would be a fool to trust you, Prince."

"You would be a fool to trust anyone entirely," he says with a small knowing smirk. "But you can trust me on this. We can get Aurelius to corroborate this with his Gift if you'd like."

The way he offers proof without hesitation tells me enough. I believe him about this, but I still don't trust him.

We round the corner into the royal wing, grand marble halls stretching ahead.

"This room you're taking me to better not be yours," I grumble.

"Well, the way I see it, you have two choices."

"Oh? What would those be?"

"Your trunks, and therefore your leathers, are already in my chambers. You can either sleep where you belong..." He steps closer, voice dropping, "Or you can take a room across the hall and be forced to rely on my mother's choice in wardrobe."

"So, I can sleep with you or be forced into dresses full-time?"

He nods, a playful smile tugging at the corner of his mouth.

"You find this amusing, Prince?"

"I find a lot of things you do amusing, Princess."

"This doesn't seem like much of a choice," I mumble, mulling over my options. The idea of being trapped in dresses made me shudder, but the thought of sleeping next to a male who wasn't Elijah or Aurelius made my skin crawl.

Elijah isn't here. I had no intention of letting Aurelius into my bed, so it looked like I would be sleeping alone.

"I'll take my chances with the dresses," I decide.

"Not the answer I was expecting," Ayden muses.

"You're a terrible fiancé, Ayden."

He stops in front of a door, pushing it open for me. "I could be a wonderful one, if you'd give me the chance, Breyla."

"I'm not interested in a fiancé," I retort.

"Not interested in a fiancé, or not interested in *me* as a fiancé?" he challenges.

"Sorry, pretty boy," I say with a mocking smile as I stride past him. "It's not you, it's me."

"You think I'm pretty?" Ayden gives me a wide grin.

"Is that all you heard?" I roll my eyes.

I move about the room, inspecting every corner in the bright, open space. Dark wood floors provide contrast to the white marble that comprises most of the castle. A white duvet covers the four-poster bed, a thick black fur at the foot. Dark furniture fills the space, giving it a homey, warm atmosphere.

"It's all I needed to hear," he teases.

Mindlessly, I thumb through the gowns in the armoire, my nose wrinkling in disgust at the pale silks and gold embroidery.

"Not that your ego needs it," I say, "but yes, you're gorgeous Ayden."

He leans casually against the doorframe. "You sure you don't want to stay with me?"

"Positive."

"Well, you know where your pants are... if you change your mind."

He winks and backs out of the room, leaving me to explore in peace.

CHAPTER TEN

OPHELIA

"You traitorous bitch," my father hisses.

There was a time when those words filled me with terror. Pain and fear were once my constant companions, but now I don't even bother to flinch.

"No, Father." The strength in my voice surprises even me. "You're the traitor, and I'm done living in fear of you."

Our matching gray eyes meet across the dinner table, and for the first time, we're truly seeing each other. I've known the depraved depths of his soul for years, but now he sees mine. I feel nothing but disdain for the male before me.

"You will pay for this!" he roars, lightning bursting from his hands. It slams into the guards beside him. They drop lifelessly to the floor. For that, I do feel remorseful. That fury was meant for me, but it claimed them instead.

Everyone in the room retreats a step from the lightning dancing along his fingers. I don't blame them. I've felt the sting of his Gift, and I don't wish it on another. They don't want to be his next target, but none of them are.

He and I have been approaching this confrontation for years—I only regret not facing him sooner. Maybe if I had, there wouldn't be nearly a dozen bodies in his wake.

I realize too late that though I am his next target, it wasn't his Gift he *intended to attack me with, it was a dagger hidden at his side. The metal flies through the air, end-over-end, headed directly for my chest.*

I possess no Gifts that could stop this knife, so I just stare at the end coming for me. It takes less than a heartbeat, though it feels like slow motion as I watch it happen.

The sharp metal pierces my flesh, burying itself deep in the center of my chest. I expect it to hurt, but I feel nothing.

My knees give out, Elijah catches me before I hit the floor. He lowers me, gently stroking my cheek as tears fill his panicked eyes.

I try to speak, but nothing comes out. My body feels cold and heavy as the noise around me fades. All I can hear are the rapidly slowing beats of my heart.

Elijah is mumbling something through his tears, but I can't make it out. Layne appears on my other side, his blue eyes telling me all the things I can't hear.

"Ophe..."

I think he's saying my name.

It's cold.

"Wake..."

Everything is so cold.

"...safe."

Blackness clings to the edges of my vision, slowly spreading until all I see are blue eyes.

"Ophelia, wake up!" Elijah's voice breaks through the dark. He shakes my shoulder roughly until my eyes finally fly open.

A pained cry erupts from my mouth as I jolt upright, my entire body trembling. My hands grasp at my sternum, searching out the scar—the wound—I know must be there.

It burns and aches, my eyes filling with tears at the sensation.

"Make it stop," I sob, rubbing my hands frantically over the center of my chest where the dagger landed. No matter how much I try to soothe the area, the pain persists.

He grips my face between both hands, thumbs rubbing softly along my temples and cheeks. "Make what stop?"

"The pain, Elijah," I cry, tears running down my cheeks as I beg, "Where he stabbed me, it hurts so bad. Please make it go away."

"Where *who* stabbed you?" Elijah asks, trying to piece together my sobs.

"M-my father," I stutter. My breathing is rapid now, my lungs struggling to take in the oxygen necessary to breathe.

Confusion crosses his handsome face, and then understanding follows it a moment later. "No one stabbed you." Pulling me into his chest, he rocks me back and forth. "You're safe, darling," he whispers, leaving gentle kisses on the top of my head.

The shock of his words startles me enough to still the tears. "What do y-you mean? I remember…"

"You were dreaming. That was all," he reassures me. "You're safe now. Breathe for me…"

I take a deep breath, inhaling the familiar cinnamon and chocolate scent of the male behind me. It settles me enough to gain control of myself. The pain ebbs, leaving me all together in a few breaths.

Looking around, I'm greeted by a foreign room. It's a bedroom, but that's all I know. "Where are we?" I ask after a few more minutes of deep breathing.

"We're in my chambers," he replies, his fingers still gently stroking my face.

"H-how did I get here?"

"I found you sleeping in the gardens," he says softly. "They're not far from my room, so I brought you here for safekeeping."

A few moments pass before I quietly admit, "I don't remember going to the gardens."

Elijah places another kiss on my hair. "What's the last thing you remember?"

"I remember eating dinner with you. The kitchens made my favorite fall soup, roasted butternut squash. I was so excited for it."

Elijah tenses before asking, "Is there anything else?"

"No, not that I can recall."

"Ophelia, that was *last night's* dinner. It's nearly time for dinner now."

"What have I been doing all day?" I ask, trying to process how I could have lost that much time.

"I don't know. I was holding court for most of it, so I hadn't seen you until I found you in the gardens."

"I didn't show up for court?" I ask in disbelief. That was one of the tasks Breyla entrusted to Elijah and me, one I desperately wanted to prove my worth for. I wouldn't have missed it for anything.

"No, you didn't. I figured you had overslept and didn't want to disturb you. I know you haven't been sleeping well."

That was putting it mildly. I had barely managed a few hours of sleep each night since my brother's death. It had only grown worse as the nightmares intensified.

"You're telling me I have nearly an entire day unaccounted for?"

"It would seem that way," he says, gently squeezing my shoulder.

I remain quiet, trying to make sense of the time I can't account for.

"Do you want to tell me about the dream?" Elijah asks after a moment.

"It was of… *that* night," I whisper. "Except Layne didn't die. The dagger hit me like it was supposed to. I died in your arms."

"But you didn't die. You're safe, darling," Elijah reassures me, but I still can't shake the phantom feel of that blade embedded in my chest.

"Elijah, I feel like I can't trust my own mind."

"You went through something traumatic. It inflicted wounds on a soul-deep level. Your mind, soul, and heart will take time to mend. You may not ever completely heal, but you will get better."

I contemplate his words and silently wonder how long it takes for a soul to heal.

Hours later, I find myself wandering the halls of the castle as the rest of the world sleeps. Having slept most of the day and losing nearly all the last twenty-four hours, I was restless.

Dressed in a white sleeping gown and wrapped in a thick wool robe, I silently glide down the dark hallway. The stones beneath my bare feet hold a chill that comes with the onset of the autumn season.

I nod to the few guards I pass, letting them know I'm alright. They pay me no attention as I turn down a dark passage. There are no windows lining this hall, no moonlight to light my way, and no lit sconces. I conjure a faerie light to follow along with me as I walk.

Since the entire castle now knows I hold a Gift, there's no point in hiding my magic. The only person I feared discovering it is dead, by my own hand.

No one will ever use me again.

Shadows flicker as I pass down the hall, the dim light bouncing off every stone that makes up the walls.

"Traitorous bitch..." a haunting voice whispers.

I come to an abrupt halt, my eyes darting around my surroundings in search of the voice.

Nothing.

I'm alone, but it doesn't feel that way.

I push forward, determined to get out of this passage. For several more minutes, all I hear is the soft pad of my feet against the stone floor.

"Stupid girl," the phantom voice hisses. I feel putrid breath against my ear, and a shiver wracks my spine, covering my flesh in goosebumps.

I flip around, hand raised and ready to attack whoever is behind me.

Again, there is no one.

Shoulders tense, I turn back in the direction I'm heading. I'm officially done with this hallway and whatever ghosts haunt it. My speed increases, bordering on running, as I search for the exit from this nightmare.

Spotting a heavy wooden door, at last, my brisk walk turns to a full-on run. I yank on the iron handle, praying for the door to swing open.

It doesn't budge.

I groan, tugging at it again with both hands. It creaks and moans, eventually budging an inch.

"Come on, open!" I shout at the stubborn thing.

An eerie sensation floods my body as I sense eyes on me. My throat constricts like there's a hand wrapped around it.

It squeezes, sharp nails digging into the flesh of my neck.

Finally, the door relents, a loud scraping groan echoing around the passageway as I pull it open.

Bursting through the now-open doorway, I suck down fresh night air as the choking sensation dissipates.

A cough rattles through my chest as I pull oxygen into my burning throat.

I pull the door shut behind me, but don't let it latch. I'd prefer to find a different way back, but don't want to risk being shut out if there isn't one.

Leaning against a wall, I inhale deeply, waiting for my breathing to return to normal. My eyes open wider as I take in the beautiful garden before me.

This isn't like the castle garden Elijah had found me asleep in. There were no neatly trimmed rose bushes or well-kept flowers with stepping stones between them. This was wild, and raw, and savage, and utterly breathtaking.

Moonflowers with creamy white petals opened to the light shining down on them. The scent of night-blooming jasmine catches my attention right before I find the pink and yellow blooms amongst the moonflowers. The combined fragrance soothes something inside of me.

A soft violet glow emanates from the center of star lilies scattered throughout the space. Unlike any other lily, the star lilies were said to be created by Revna, the goddess of night, as a gift to her children. They resembled any other lily under the sun, but at night, they let out a soft glow so her children could always find their way back to her when it was darkest. They bloomed year-round, never missing a night, no matter the weather.

All around me, the flowers grew wild, covering wherever they pleased. In the center of the space surrounding the tree was a clearing of grass where no flowers grew. A sense of deja vu crept through me, a memory I couldn't place.

"You always loved this garden as a little girl," a soft voice says.

Spinning, I come face to face with the blue eyes of my mother. Dark hair flows around her in waves.

Gods, she looks just like Layne.

"Mother?" I ask, taking in her features.

The deep blue of her irises sparkles in the moonlight. Her olive skin almost holding an ethereal glow.

"Yes, baby girl." She smiles, reaching a hand out to cup my cheek.

"What are you doing here?" I ask, laying my hand atop hers.

"A mother knows when something is troubling her child." She

gestures to the ground beneath the great tree. "Come, let's sit and talk."

We settle beneath it, our backs to the trunk, shoulders pressed together, as she laces her fingers through mine.

Her hand is small and delicate. She's petite, something she passed along to me, but not Layne. Everything else about her is a mirror image of my brother. Chestnut waves, piercing blue eyes, olive skin, it was like looking at a female version of him. My creamy skin is pale against hers as her thumb strokes mine in soothing circles.

"Tell me what weighs on you, my dear," she urges.

"I thought you knew what was on my mind."

"I said a mother knows *when* something is troubling her child, not *what* is troubling them. Mothers aren't actually mind readers."

"Are you sure?" I grin, nudging her gently.

"Yes, but the bit about us having eyes in the back of our heads to see everything you do—that one is definitely true," she teases back, drawing a soft laugh from both of us.

"Why does this place feel so familiar?" I ask, ignoring her request to unburden myself on her.

"I should think it would," she replies. "It's been many years since you last played here, but this was one of your favorite places as a child."

"What is it?"

"It is the private royal gardens." She looks around wistfully. "They were a sanctuary tended by King Raynor and Queen Genevieve. Given their shared affinity for earth, they spent much of their time here together. This is where they fell in love." She sighs as she says this, her eyes misting over at the memory.

"If it was so cherished, why does it look so abandoned?"

"It was maintained solely by the king and queen for the last two decades. They forbade anyone from tending to it, instead using it as an escape from the burdens of the crown. When the king died... a part of the queen did, too. No one has set foot in here since the king's mind started going." The smile fades, replaced with a sorrow I know too well.

"I feel like a part of me died with Layne," I admit. "He took a piece of not just my heart but my mind as well."

She leans in and presses a kiss to my hair. "I know, my love."

"When does it get better?"

"I don't know, sweetheart." She sighs deeply, rubbing small circles on the back of my hand. "There is no time limit on grief, no hand-book on how to handle trauma, no right or wrong way to do it. You heal in your own time, in your own way. It will happen piece by piece, and you'll take it one day at a time."

"I miss him."

"He misses you, too."

I blink through the burn in my eyes. "So, how is it I spent so much time here as a child if it's a private garden?"

"At one time, there were a lot of flowers here that held healing properties. I was permitted access to pick those needed in the salves and tonics the physicians use. You would follow me here every chance you got, playing amongst the flowers and climbing the tree. Sometimes you'd sneak out and come here on your own. I found you napping amongst the star lilies on more than one occasion."

"I—"

"Ophelia," a voice calls.

Elijah.

My eyes search him out before returning to my mother as realization dawns on me. "Mom, there's someone I'd like you to meet," I say excitedly.

"Oh? Is it a male?" She lifts a knowing brow at me.

"Yes," I confirm, my cheeks flaming. "A very special one."

She grins. "Well, don't leave me waiting. Go get him, Ophelia!"

I spring to my feet, a smile forming at the thought of introducing my mother to Elijah.

As I reach the door I entered through, Elijah is already standing there. His hair is sleep-tousled, curls falling around his face and brushing his shoulders.

Relaxed, uncaring, messy Elijah is my favorite.

He holds me easily as I throw myself into his arms.

"What are you doing out here, goddess?" he asks, kissing me softly.

"I couldn't sleep, so I went for a walk. Honestly, I'm not sure how I ended up here, but it felt like something was calling me." I glance back toward the garden. "Isn't it beautiful?"

"Yes, it's gorgeous. Breyla and I played here on occasion, but we were rarely allowed here, especially not unattended. It saddens me to see it in such a state of neglect."

"How'd you know to find me here? And why are you awake?"

"I couldn't sleep either, so I went to the kitchens for tea. On my way, I ran into a guard who mentioned seeing you wandering the halls. He was concerned because you were in corridors no one uses and was afraid you were sleepwalking and lost. I came to track you down just in case that was the case. I didn't want a repeat of the river." His voice turns serious, eyes full of concern. "Speaking of which, I think you should stay in my room from now on. I would sleep a lot better knowing you were safe and not sleepwalking off a cliff or something."

My chest warms at his concern and the thought of sharing a bed with him.

"No sleepwalking tonight," I assure him. Grabbing his hand, I tug him toward the center of the secret garden. "I have something I want to show you."

"What is it?" he asks as we climb through the overgrown flowers and vines that cover the garden floor.

"There's someone I want you to meet," I explain as we near the tree. "She's just on the other side of the tree."

"Oh? Who is she?"

"My mother," I say with a smile.

"What do you mean, Ophelia?" Elijah asks, confusion marring his brow.

"You'll love her, Eli. She's amazing," I reassure him, attempting to calm any potential anxiety over meeting my mother.

"I'm sure she was, but O—"

"Mother," I call out before he can finish his thought. We round the tree to where I had left her.

"Where'd she go?" I ask when I find the space vacant.

Elijah looks at me, gently puzzled. "Where'd *who* go?"

"My mother, Eli. I told you I wanted you to meet her," I say, growing frustrated and confused by the second. "She was just here talking to me."

"Ophelia, look at me," he commands, taking my face between his palms. He stares me in the eyes as he softly explains, "I don't know who you were talking to, but it wasn't your mother."

My brow furrows as I try to understand his meaning. Something tickles the back of my mind. A feeling of something I should know but have forgotten. "I think I would know my own mother, Elijah," I say with a slight amount of anger filling my tone.

"Of course you would know your mother, sweetheart, but it couldn't possibly be her." He swallows hard, pausing before he continues, "Your mother is dead. She's been dead for fifteen years."

Something cracks in my mind, reality breaking through as it comes back to me.

Memories of my mother's funeral pyre.

Ten-year-old me, clinging to Layne as her lifeless body burned.

My father refusing to sing her death hymn.

My father throwing a poisoned dagger at me, but hitting Layne instead.

Layne dying in my arms.

My father dying as I drained the life from his body.

The rush of satisfaction I felt as the light faded from his eyes.

Alone.

"She's dead," I croak, tears filling my eyes. "I felt her, Elijah. I felt her hold my hand and kiss my forehead." The words unravel into a sob, the betrayal of my own mind slicing deep.

"Shhh," he soothes, pulling me into his arms. "You're going to be okay. I promise you will."

I bury my face in his chest as sobs wrack my body. "I'm alone," I cry, my legs trembling beneath me.

Elijah holds my body tight to him, keeping me from collapsing, then slowly lowers us to the ground.

"You're not alone, you have me." He kisses the top of my head, one hand running soothing circles along my back. "You'll always have me."

I tilt my head back to look him in the eyes. "But how do I know you're real? How can I trust that this is real?"

"Listen to me, Ophelia, I'm here. I'm real." He grabs my hand and presses it to his chest. "Do you feel that? That's my heart, and it beats for you."

I nod, feeling the steady rhythm beneath my palm. I lift my hand to his cheek, letting my fingers trace the stubble along his jaw. It's rough, and I relish the prickle of it against my skin. *Real.*

"From now on, if you need someone to remind you what's real," he says, his voice fierce with devotion, "ask me. I'll always tell you what's real, Ophelia. I'll always lead you back home when you feel lost."

"Tell me something real, Eli."

"You're really beautiful," he murmurs, "How's that for truth?"

I laugh lightly, my tears slowing.

"Layne died?" I ask.

His face falls. "That's real."

"My father is dead?"

"Yes, baby. That's real, too."

Baby. I blush at the pet name, liking the way it sounds on his tongue.

His mouth lifts on one side, a cocky smirk playing at his lips. "You like that name?"

"Maybe a bit," I admit.

"Good."

"I killed my father?" I ask.

"Real. It was the most impressive and hottest thing I've ever witnessed."

"I think I should find that statement concerning."

"But you don't," he says with a grin. "He got what he deserved. I just hate that he hurt you."

"My mother was here tonight?"

His expression softens. "Not real, baby."

I let out a sad sigh, wanting to hold onto the false memory my mind had concocted.

"Tell me something else real."

Elijah hesitates for just a moment before replying, "I really want to kiss you right now."

"Then do it," I nearly beg, desperate for something solid, something *true.*

He leans in, his lips teasing mine as they brush lightly. They linger, never closing the distance fully. I feel his breath against my lips and lose my patience, slamming my lips against his.

He grunts softly as I take what I want from him, my lips moving against his before his control snaps. He meets my kiss, returning it severalfold and sucking my bottom lip into his mouth.

I part my lips, my tongue darting out in search of his. He relents, his mouth opening to me, tongue tangling with mine.

The kiss is passionate, holding all the emotion we feel for one another.

It feels *real*.

Breaking the kiss, I pull back. "I want to feel more," I pant. "Give me something real."

"Tell me what you want me to make you feel, darling."

"I want you to make me feel *everything*. I want all of you, Elijah."

Groaning, his head tilts back. "Dear gods, Ophelia. I need you to say it again so I know you're real."

I giggle, pressing a kiss to the exposed curve of his throat. "I want to feel *all of you*," I whisper in a tone I hope is seductive.

His eyes blaze. "Gods help me. Can I keep you forever?"

"We'll see," I say with a shrug. "Let me answer after you show me what all of you feels like."

The heated glare he gives me leaves my mouth dry.

"I'm going to be gentle with you tonight," he says, voice low and raw, "but keep running that mouth and see what happens. I will make you feel so good, Ophelia, but it's also going to hurt a little." He leans in, his lips grazing my ear. "I promise it will only last a moment."

"What if I don't want gentle?" I ask.

"Then I'll fuck you roughly tomorrow night, baby. But tonight, I'm not going to cause you any more pain than necessary. Now get on your knees."

His words and the way he says them send shivers up my spine. I can't help but obey when he speaks in that tone.

I crawl out of his lap, anticipation fueling every movement. Kneeling in front of him, I wait for him to make the next move.

He reaches out, pulling loose the sash keeping my robe in place. It falls open, revealing the sheer white nightgown beneath.

His eyes hungrily roam my body, my nipples hardening at the attention. He brushes his thumb along the hardened peaks, a soft gasp escaping my lips at the sensation.

Broad hands run along my shoulders, pushing the robe down and letting it drop to the ground behind me. Soft lips kiss the column of my neck as one hand grips my hip.

He peppers kisses along my throat, alternating soft bites in between. My fingers reach out, lacing through his dirty blond locks and tugging roughly, pulling his head back from my neck.

"Kiss me," I demand.

"Yes, ma'am." He chuckles, his lips crashing into mine.

There is nothing soft or teasing about his kiss. His lips open immediately to me, tongue seeking entrance into my mouth. I grant it, wrapping my tongue around his.

As he continues ravishing my mouth, his hand trails down to my center. Lifting my nightgown, his fingers run along my slit. He dances around where I want him, intentionally dragging out the torture.

An impatient whine has him smiling against my lips.

"Is something wrong?" he whispers, peppering kisses along my jaw.

"You're teasing me," I pant.

"Mmmm," he hums.

"Why?" I whine.

"Tell me, explicitly, what you want me to do."

"You and your damn words," I groan, rolling my hips against his hand, trying to move his fingers to where I want them.

He pulls back just slightly. "Hearing such dirty things come from such innocent lips drives me wild."

"Fucking fine," I relent. "Right now, I want you to use those fingers to destroy me. I want the pleasure your touch promises. Inside me is where they belong."

"Good girl," he praises. "Now, lie back, my dark goddess."

Eagerly, I do as he says, dropping to my back where my discarded robe is the only thing separating us from the garden floor.

"Spread your legs," he commands.

I spread them wide, bending at the knees.

"Fuck, you take my commands so well," he whispers, voice husky.

He kneels between my legs, his body hovering over me, before he pulls the nightdress down to expose my breasts.

Light kisses trail down the column of my neck as his hand traces circles on my inner thigh. When he reaches the apex, he continues his kisses downward to my chest.

Between each kiss, he murmurs words of praise.

"So."

Kiss.

"Fucking."

Kiss.

"Beautiful."

Kiss.

His lips close around my nipple, sucking it into his warm mouth right as his first finger enters me.

I moan at the relief of finally having him where I want him.

In and out, his finger thrusts slowly while his thumb rubs circles on my clit. He greedily sucks my nipple, nipping it. The combination of his fingers and teeth mix as pain and pleasure heighten my arousal, and another louder moan escapes my lips.

A second finger joins the first. He keeps up a delicious pace that has me rocking against his hand.

Heat builds in my core, spreading throughout my entire body. I'm trembling at his touch as he unravels every part of me.

"Gods, you're so wet for me already," he murmurs against my breast.

A third finger joins the others, stretching me to fit around them. There's a slight burn that quickly dissipates as he circles my clit faster.

What he does next leaves me teetering on the edge of destruction. His fingers curl, hitting a sensitive spot deep inside of me.

"I'm so close, Eli," I whisper, my body coiling tight.

"Don't you dare come, yet," he growls. "I want to taste your sweet pussy when you come for me."

His mouth leaves my nipple and travels down to my center.

He shoves his tongue straight against my clit, his fingers still curling inside me. He licks and sucks the sensitive flesh, circling his tongue around me in the same motion as his thumb.

"Elijah," I beg, not knowing what I'm begging for.

He presses his other hand down against my abdomen, the slight pressure increasing my arousal in a strange, though completely welcome, way. "Come for me, baby."

His words are my undoing, and I shatter around him as utter bliss rolls over me in waves.

A liquid gushes out of me, covering Elijah's face as he drinks it down.

He swallows, licking my center up and down until he's certain he's gotten every last drop of me.

My cheeks heat in embarrassment at what just happened.

"I-I don't know what just happened." My voice trembles, embarrassment tinged with pleasure as it pulses through my body.

Elijah chuckles darkly. "Exactly what I wanted to happen just happened. Don't you dare feel embarrassed by that. It's one of the sexiest things a female can do in bed."

"Really?"

"Really, really."

He lifts himself from between my legs, leaning in to kiss me.

I taste the remnants of my orgasm on his lips, and instead of embarrassment, I feel a flicker of satisfaction.

"I want to taste you next," I whisper as I trail my hands down to his hardened length.

I pull the sleep pants down, exposing his hard member. There's a drop of pre-come leaking from the tip that I'm dying to have on my tongue.

"You can taste me next round, doll," Elijah promises. "I'm too fucking desperate for you right now. I need to feel this sweet cunt wrapped around my cock."

I pout, and he bites down on my bottom lip in retaliation.

I hiss just as he releases his teeth, kneading the tender flesh with his tongue to lessen the sting.

My arousal builds again as I feel the tip of him press against me.

"I've done what I can to prepare you," he says, stroking my cheek. "But this next part is going to hurt. Trust me?"

"I trust you," I say, nodding.

He lines himself with my center, the tip of him pushing slowly into me.

It burns as I stretch around him. I thought three fingers had been a lot, but it turns out his dick is much thicker.

I hiss softly as he pushes in another inch. He stops there, waiting for me to adjust. A finger rubs slow circles on my clit, the pleasure providing relief and distraction from the pain.

"Take a deep breath, Ophelia," he commands.

I comply, breathing in deeply through the discomfort.

"I'm good," I reassure him.

"You're more than good, beautiful."

His finger continues rubbing circles along my clit, building the arousal and need for him to fill me completely.

"More," I whisper.

"I promise it hurts less if we just do it all at once from here."

I nod, and he kisses me deeply, swallowing my cries as he thrusts all the way in.

"Fuck," I whimper against his lips.

His fingers increase in tempo, the pleasure helping to lessen the pain.

"You did so good, baby. That's it, the hard part's done. Now let me make you feel good."

I nod, smiling at his praise.

Fully adjusted to him now, I take a deep breath.

He slides out, then back in, taking me in shallow thrusts. The tempo he sets is even and slow, moving in and out in measured strokes.

I moan softly as it builds more pleasure in me. The burn has subsided into a dull ache, which is overshadowed by the pleasure coursing through me.

"This feels so good," I admit, my voice breathy.

"It'll feel even better the next time," he promises.

"Who said there will be a next time?" I tease. "I still haven't decided if you get to keep me, yet."

"Oh, baby. You are playing with fire," he warns.

I flash him a devilish grin that morphs into a gasp as his thrusts turn more powerful and faster. My arms wrap around him, nails digging into his back through his tunic.

I grunt, frustration mounting at the clothing still on him.

"Skin," I moan. "I want to feel your skin against mine."

His thrusts halt briefly as he rips the offending clothing over his head, leaving him bare to me. Fingers grip the nightgown still bunched around my midsection. Instead of pulling it over my head, he rips straight through the center, leaving it lying in pieces on either side of me.

He runs his hand down my chest, feeling every curve and dimple in my flesh, before grasping my left knee and hitching it over his shoulder.

In and out he thrusts, his pelvis grinding against my clit in the most erotic sensation. The new angle allows him to hit something deeper, and I somehow feel even fuller than before.

What's happening between us right now isn't just sex, it's not fucking, it's something so deeply profound I don't have words for it.

Elijah has seen every part of me—worshipped every part of me. He's showing me what it feels like to be treasured and wanted.

He wants me.

He wanted me when I was powerless, overlooked, abused, and nothing.

He still wants me now that I am powerful, yet so broken and lost.

And I never wanted anything as viscerally as I want this male.

Pleasure courses through me as his pace continues while his lips lay tender kisses along the inside of my knee.

Goosebumps cover my skin at the surprising sensitivity of that spot. They only increase as his thumb rubs slow circles against my clit.

Elijah groans as my inner walls flutter around his length, clamping down as my pleasure grows.

"Goddess, if you keep squeezing me like that, this is going to end so much faster than I'm ready for."

His words spark arousal in me, and I intentionally clench around him. "I want you to come, Elijah."

His eyes flash. "When did you get such a filthy fucking mouth, Ophelia?"

"I blame you," I rasp. I'm so close to the edge, I can barely think. I need more of him. "Now give me what I fucking want."

"Not happening," he snarls. He drops my leg from his shoulder, grasping me by the hips, then flips us. Suddenly, I'm straddling him, his back to the ground, his eyes dark and burning beneath me.

I quirk a questioning brow at him, unsure of what to do.

"Ride me, Ophelia," he orders, voice thick with hunger. "Roll those beautiful hips and chase your pleasure. I want to see you shatter around my cock."

His hands grip my waist, guiding me in slow, grinding circles until I catch the rhythm.

I find I like this new position even more than the last and throw my head back, chasing every delicious ripple of sensation as I move over him.

Rolling my hips back and forth, my clit rubs against his pelvis in a motion that has me moaning in pleasure.

I'm right back on the edge of oblivion when Elijah begins to thrust up into me, perfectly syncing with my own movements.

It takes only a few more thrusts for me to shatter. This climax is more intense than the last, and I feel it in my entire body. Never-ending pleasure and warmth spread through me in rapid waves, leaving me gasping for air and darkness dancing as I fight to maintain consciousness.

I collapse onto Elijah, unable to sustain my own weight as the pleasure rolls through.

"Shhh, I've got you, darling," he hums, one hand smoothing down my back as I try to breathe again.

When I can finally speak, I lift myself off his chest to look him in the eyes. "Now are you going to give me your come or not?"

His nostrils flare at the taunt, something primal flashing in his eyes. He threads his fingers through the hair at the back of my head, yanking me to him forcefully.

Warm lips crash into mine, taking everything he wants from me as his thrusts start again. They're deep and hard, and he switches from worshipping to fucking me.

He's not gentle as he takes what he needs, leaving me gasping for breath.

He bites my bottom lip as he takes one final stroke before reaching his release. A deep groan vibrates through his chest, and I swallow the sound through our kiss.

"That was…" I pant.

"Fucking incredible," he finishes, breath still ragged. "You're incredible."

His hand strokes my cheek, then tucks a stray lock behind my ear.

I flash him a pleasure-drunk grin, a slight chuckle reaching my lips. "I guess you can keep me. That was… adequate."

A low growl erupts from him, and he slams his lips back into mine. The kiss is rough but brief. When he pulls back, he whispers, "You little shit."

I slide off him, and he pulls me down to his side so my head rests on his chest. Nuzzling my head into him, I breathe in deeply, savoring the smell of sweat mixed with his cinnamon and chocolate scent.

Something settles deep inside me as exhaustion washes over me. I yawn, snuggling closer to Elijah.

"You sleepy, goddess?"

"Extremely," I confirm, my eyes drifting shut.

He chuckles, the sound pure masculine satisfaction. "An *adequate* fuck will do that for you."

I yawn again. "I lied."

"Oh yeah?"

"You're way more than adequate. Let's do that again tomorrow."

His arm tightens around me, his voice a satisfied purr. "As you wish, goddess."

I drift off moments later, the sound of Elijah's heartbeat lulling me into a peaceful sleep.

CHAPTER ELEVEN

AURELIUS

I hardly rested in the night, kept so far from the spitfire who haunts my dreams.

Breyla spent months sleeping next door to me or even in my bed. Now, she was half a castle away, sleeping across the hall from Prince Ayden.

It's better than *in* his bed, I suppose.

Once the castle quieted, I gave in to the primal need to lay eyes on her.

Being the royal bastard afforded me some liberties, with apparently one of them being the ability to move throughout the castle with little resistance from the guards. I had no doubt my movements would be reported to Ayden, but I didn't give a fuck. I needed to see her.

My room was the same as I always occupied on visits to Prudia—in the guest wing, far away from the royal family.

It could be worse; they could have housed me with the staff.

When I reached the royal wing, I was filled with relief to find Breyla's stubbornness had won out. She was sleeping in a separate room from Ayden.

The relief was minuscule, though. Not having her near me is

torture. Hence, the two miserable hours of sleep I managed to find before the sun dragged its pale light across the sky.

Morning light spills through the window now, catching the subtle gold accents that adorn the room.

A light wood bed frame and black linen sheets made up the bed I had tossed and turned in all night. A black carpet covers the white tiled floor. A modest desk and armoire, complete with gold handles, stand in the corner. On the nightstand sat a golden candlestick, cooled wax spilling onto the wood below. The bathroom held the necessities but nothing more. That was what made up the space I was to call home.

I had never minded it before, but I hate it now.

A soft knock pulls me from my thoughts. When I open the door, I'm greeted by the honey-colored eyes of Rowina, my half-sister, apparently.

"Good morning," she chirps.

"Morning," I grunt, the *good* part yet to be determined.

"Mother has requested a formal family breakfast today."

"This ought to be interesting."

"That's what I said." She shoots me an impish grin. "But I enjoy interesting."

"You have the same skill for stirring up trouble as your brother."

"Runs in the family, I suppose," she confirms.

Rowina falls into step beside me as we head for the dining room. She's dressed in a deep purple gown that's understated but beautiful. It complements her hair and eyes perfectly.

Breyla would look devastating in that shade of purple. It wasn't one I had seen her wear, but there weren't many things that didn't look good on her—myself included.

Her gilded eyes narrow at me. "Why are you exuding lust right now, *brother?*"

Nearly all the Gifts of the Mordet line were mental strengths rather than physical. Apparently, I had forgotten she was an empath. "I was thinking of what Breyla would look like in that color," I reply, seeing no point in hiding it from her.

"Oh, thank the gods," she sighs in relief. "But by the gods, try to keep those thoughts contained."

"No promises." My brow quirks as we turn a corner. "Why did the queen send you to escort me to breakfast when she could have easily sent one of the staff?"

"Oh, that's really quite fun," she replies, a smirk forming on her lips. "Mother didn't send me. She actually doesn't care if you're there or not. Ayden sent me to fetch you. He doesn't trust you won't… get lost on your way to the table."

"Smart bastard." I chuckle darkly at her astute observation. "And what about you, little sister? Do you trust me?"

Her lips quirk as she mulls over my question. "I think that is a tricky question. Do I trust you implicitly? Absolutely not. I think anyone who trusts another soul implicitly is either foolish or arrogant."

I nod at her assessment, but she isn't finished.

"Do I trust you not to harm me or mine? I think so, as long as no one threatens what you care for. Do I trust you not to touch our brother's betrothed?" She laughs loudly before finishing, "You'd be an idiot to, but fuck no."

"You forget that before she was your brother's betrothed, she was *my* brother's daughter. That didn't stop me, so why would this?"

The question has her stopping in her tracks. Her previously jovial voice takes on a sharp edge as she replies, "Because there is much more at stake here than getting your dick wet, brother."

"Breyla is much more than a way to wet my dick." I meet her piercing eyes head-on, "I made a vow to destroy anything that tries to take her from me."

"And what if your lies are the thing taking her from you?"

"I stand by my vow," I say calmly. "If that makes me her villain, then so be it. At least I'm in the right kingdom. This family reeks of deceit."

Something flickers across Rowina's face. "You know nothing of this family," she whispers so quietly I nearly miss it, and we walk the rest of the way to breakfast in silence.

The breakfast table is large enough for the entire Mordet family, plus Charlotte, Breyla, and me. Queen Josephina sits at the head of the table, politely waiting for everyone to be present. To her right sits Ayden, and to her left is Rowina. I take my place next to Rowina, Charlie on my other side. Breyla sits directly across from me on Ayden's right.

Breyla fidgets, constantly readjusting her dress. The gold gown lifts her breasts as if they are a dish being offered for sampling—and gods, would I love to sample—but it clearly makes her uncomfortable.

My lust is dampened by sadness as I take in the color. Truth be told, it looks horrendous on her. Gold suited Genevieve, but Breyla belongs in dark colors. This is nothing more than a gilded cage meant to soften her edges.

Seeing her like this guts me in a way I didn't expect. It's like looking at a ghost—and for a moment, it's not Breyla I see, but Gen.

The words slip out before I can stop them. "You look like your mother in that dress, Princess."

Hurt and sorrow flash in her eyes as they hold mine. She says nothing, turning her gaze away from me to speak to Ayden.

I've said the wrong thing, and my gut twists. The resemblance is bittersweet, but the observation wasn't meant to inflict pain.

Warm breakfast pastries, smoked meats, fresh fruit, and potatoes are laid out in front of us, the aroma delighting my senses as I inhale deeply. I frown as a plate of eggs is served. Hushed conversation continues around me, Charlie and Rowina chatting about the weather. But all I can focus on is the eggs and the way they turn my stomach. Pushing the offending food from me, I make room for the smoked meats and potatoes instead, even opting for a pastry.

Anything but the eggs.

We're only a few bites into breakfast when Queen Josephina asks, "What colors shall your maidens wear for the wedding?"

Breyla chokes on her potatoes. "Pardon me, what?"

"Your attending maidens, at your wedding to the prince," the queen repeats, tone clipped. "What color will they wear?"

Clearing her throat, Breyla replies, "Firstly, I have no maidens. Secondly, I don't give a shit. They can go nude for all I'm concerned."

The queen's jaw tics, her pulse visibly fluttering in her throat.

"Of course you have maidens," she says coolly, gesturing to Rowina and Charlie. "They're sitting at this table."

I stifle laughter at the ensuing storm Breyla is about to release.

"Like hell," Breyla snaps. "Rowina, fine. But Lady Charlotte? Not a fucking chance. I couldn't care less if she's the prince's cousin or not."

"Lady Charlotte is a female of good moral standing and manners," Queen Josephina snaps back. "Something you could learn from."

"Lady Charlotte openly propositioned Aurelius in front of my mother while they were engaged." Breyla leans back, crossing her arms. "I may be foul-mouthed and ill-mannered, but she can claim no moral high ground over me."

I hide my smile behind a drink of tea while watching the chaos unfold. We had done far worse things together, but at least it was behind closed doors—mostly. You wouldn't hear me bringing that up, though.

"Alright, Mother," Ayden says placatingly. "Perhaps Breyla would like to choose her own maidens. It is *our* wedding, after all. Not yours."

"Maybe I'd like to choose my own husband, too," Breyla mutters, rolling her eyes.

"Unfortunately, that decision is no longer available, love," Ayden says, tone full of unbothered charm. "I suggest you enjoy the choices you do have."

Like hell, I think.

Breyla's emerald eyes flare, pinning me for the briefest moment before snapping back to Ayden.

"Perhaps I'll choose which side of your face looks better with a black eye," she grumbles.

Ayden only chuckles and keeps going, rattling off about wedding dates. "Would you prefer a winter wedding or a spring? Personally, I find a solstice wedding irresistibly romantic."

Anger boils beneath my skin, a dangerous growl rising from my throat.

Mine.

I recall Ayden's warning about there being more at stake here and keeping my feelings in check. The logical part of me is thrashing against the part of me that is entirely male. I'm not sure which is winning at the moment.

He rattles on about colors and a guest list, my temperature rising with each question.

Breyla's giving him grunts and one-word responses, but I can't see past my need to possess her and mark her as mine.

Finally, when I can rein it in no longer, I smirk, and retaliate the only way I can.

As Ayden stands to leave, his brow furrows. Conversation stops mid-sentence as he feels my Hemonia Gift being used against him.

He wraps his arms around his mother in a hug as I redirect blood flow from his brain to his dick, making him painfully hard.

"Darling, I think your sword might be on wrong," Josephina comments uncomfortably. "There's something poking me."

"Does the prince not know how to handle his sword?" I taunt, sipping my tea as if bored.

Ayden shoots a murderous look in my direction. I raise my cup in a mock-toast, a lazy smirk playing at my lips.

One point for me, brother.

CHAPTER TWELVE

BREYLA

"Where are we going?" I demand as a rather uncomfortable-looking prince drags me from the breakfast table.

We barely make it out of earshot before Ayden ushers me into a vacant sitting room and spins, pressing me against the nearest wall.

A soft gasp escapes me at the boldness.

One hand wraps around my throat, the other clamps tightly on my hip.

His hard body cages me in, his thumb tipping my face up toward his.

For a long moment, he just looks at me, something contemplative flickering in his amber eyes, then he lowers his lips to mine.

From previous experience, I knew Ayden kissed like he was consuming you, but this wasn't that. It was soft and warm yet lacking passion.

I don't return the kiss.

Ayden shifts, grinding against me gently—and gods, one of them must have blessed his bloodline, judging by what's rubbing against my stomach.

His kiss turns hungry, more insistent, while his hand travels up the curve of my waist, stopping just below my breast.

I mentally shake off the surprise of his sudden actions, annoyance flooding my veins.

Gathering shadows around us, I wind them slowly up his torso without him noticing.

He's so busy trying to kiss me, he doesn't feel the moment I use them to flip us—Ayden's back slamming into the wall with a dull *thud* as I wrench his dagger free from its sheath.

The blade presses against his throat as I give him a dark look.

His chest heaves, heated eyes registering the anger in mine.

"Care to tell me what's gotten into you?" It's a demand, despite my phrasing it as a question.

"Fucking Aurelius made me hard," he growls.

I arch a confused brow at him. "Come again?"

"That sounds bad." He winces, visibly regretting his choice of words.

"It certainly sounds scandalous," I agree. "It makes 'I fucked my mother's fiancé' sound slightly better, though."

"Breyla," Ayden warns, voice strained.

"Ayden," I mirror his tone right back.

He sighs heavily, deflating against the marble. "He used his Gift to make me rock hard while I was hugging my mother."

"Oh."

"Yeah."

"That's an interesting use of his Gift…" I snicker, not bothering to hide the smirk that lifts the corner of my lips. "When it isn't being used to torment you."

"Doesn't feel very fucking interesting right now." Ayden's head falls back, hitting the marble wall behind him. "I can't get it to go down."

"He's punishing you."

He groans louder. "I gathered that much."

"You probably just need to get further away from him. He's strong, but there is a limit to his reach."

"Yeah, that makes sense." He nods, messy brown curls shaking free and falling across his brow. "It feels like I lost all rationality when he redirected blood flow to my cock."

"He has that effect on people," I murmur. "Perhaps you shouldn't antagonize him as you do."

"And how exactly did I antagonize him this morning?"

I level him with a knowing look. "Let's not play dumb with one another."

"I blame the erection."

"You had your hands all over me and were planning our wedding in front of him."

"And? You're my betrothed, Breyla. That's what we're *supposed* to discuss."

"I'm only your betrothed because my father was obviously out of his mind before his death," I growl. My grip on his dagger tightens, the metal kissing his skin. "I want peace for Rimor. The only reason I'm here is because we can't risk war against Prudia over a broken marriage contract."

The admission of weakness makes bile rise in my throat. It burns, acidic and humiliating.

Despite the blade against his throat, Ayden lifts his hand, brushing my cheek with a gentleness I wasn't prepared for.

"I don't want to hurt you, Breyla," he says softly. "Or your kingdom."

"There you go doing it again."

He tilts his head to the side. "Doing what again?"

"Being genuine with me."

He smiles faintly. "Can you detect intention as well?"

"No," I reply. "But I'm very good at detecting bullshit."

Ayden shakes his head. "Such a beautiful mouth you have."

I shrug, unapologetic.

Confident now that I won't slit his throat, Ayden pushes off the wall, reclaiming his dagger from my hand.

"Come on, love. I'm taking you to the library."

I don't move.

Pressing the second dagger, the one he hadn't seen me draw, against his groin, I smile sweetly. "One last thing, Ayden."

"Yes, Princess?" he asks, voice suddenly careful.

"I decide who I share my body with. If you ever try that shit again, I'll castrate you."

His eyes widen as he glances down and sees the blade pressed lightly but unmistakably against him.

"This shouldn't be arousing," he says breathlessly.

Backing away from him, I roll my eyes. "What is wrong with you two?"

"You have no idea, love." He chuckles darkly, sheathing his dagger. "My mother once drunkenly confessed the story of Rowina's conception. She was furious with Father for something, and he tried to manipulate her feelings to calm her down. So she stabbed him in the thigh. Apparently, he found her fire more enticing than frightening. Despite the open wound, he took her right there on the floor."

"I didn't need to know that." I stare at him, appalled and amused in equal measure. "But that actually explains so much."

We both burst out laughing.

I drop the dagger from his groin, returning it to him, and follow as he leads me to the library. "Do you know who Aurelius' mother is?"

"In theory."

"Are you going to share that theory?"

He smirks. "Now, what would be the fun in that?"

"Do you answer everything with a question?"

He laughs, low and maddeningly smug. "Do you?"

"Infuriating male," I grumble under my breath.

"Here we are," Ayden announces as he pushes open the library doors with a flourish.

Stepping inside, I blink at the sheer size of it, endless rows of books tower up well above my head. Tall windows illuminate the space, casting a soft afternoon light on the leather-bound tomes that fill the shelves. It smells of parchment, the familiar scent grounding me.

"I think you'll find some of the answers you're looking for here," Ayden says.

"To which questions?"

He only shrugs, sliding his hands into his pockets like a male without a single care in the world.

"Not only are you infuriating, but you're also insufferable," I mutter.

He ignores my jab. "Rowina will join you shortly."

"And where exactly are you going?"

"Well, thanks to Aurelius, I have quite the situation to work through." He gives me a look that's pure sin. "Unless you wanted to help me with that?"

"Ew, Ayden," I groan. "I didn't need that picture in my head."

"Doing what?" he asks innocently. "Training with Darian?"

Despite myself, my cheeks flame in embarrassment. "Fuck off, Ayden."

"I'm trying, but your riveting conversation skills are keeping me here."

"Ugh," I say, throwing my arms into the air.

"If you need to work off any energy, feel free to join Darian and me for training later."

"Or don't," Darian adds, suddenly appearing behind Ayden, looking thoroughly displeased.

"Don't worry, *General*," I purr. "I prefer training with males who can actually challenge me."

The self-satisfied look on my face is wiped clean when Darian snaps, "Intellectually or physically? Actually, don't answer that. Neither is truly a challenge."

Before I realize it, a shadow dagger flies from my fingertips, aiming straight for his throat. It hits the library door behind him instead when he vanishes and reappears behind me, a hand wrapping around my throat.

I grin wickedly at the pressure. Not enough to truly hurt, just enough to set every nerve alight. Chuckling low, I whisper, "Harder, General."

An exaggerated moan leaves my lips, and I feel his body tense behind mine.

Darian jerks away from me like he's been burned, his hand flexing as if to shake off the feel of me. "*What is* wrong with you?"

"Call me stupid again," I drawl, "and I'll really show you."

"Noted," he grunts as he storms off, dragging a reluctantly amused Ayden with him.

I laugh, watching them disappear down the hall.

"Well, that's certainly one way to spar with Darian," Rowina says, rounding the corner into the library.

"I didn't see you there, Princess."

"I certainly took notice of you, *Princess*," she replies, her tone both flirtatious and irritated.

"Don't like me calling you Princess?" I tease.

"I don't like anyone calling me that."

"That makes two of us."

Rowina grins. "Unless you're moaning it when I'm between your thighs."

My cheeks flame, eyes going wide as her words paint a licentious picture in my mind.

"Don't worry." She winks. "I won't tell my brother about that arousal filling your veins right now."

"He already knows," Aurelius says from the library doorway.

Rowina rolls her eyes and flips open a book, mumbling, "I meant the other brother."

"And that's barely arousal," Aurelius adds smoothly. "It's more like… intrigue."

"How would you know?" Rowina retorts. "Are you suddenly an Empath as well?"

"No, Rowina," Aurelius chuckles. "I just know the princess' body better than anyone."

"Knew. You knew my body better than anyone," I spit. "You lost that privilege, my lord."

"On that note," Rowina chirps, clapping her book shut. "I'll be finding something to read on the other side of the library. Behave, you two."

She vanishes between the stacks, leaving me alone with the storm brewing behind Aurelius' black eyes.

The library door clicks shut behind him.

In three strides, he's in front of me, crowding me back against a heavy oak table, his hands braced on either side of me.

"I *know* your body, little demon," he whispers. "No one will ever make it sing the way I do. And if you think my brother can stop me from reminding you of that… you are mistaken."

"It's not Ayden keeping you from my heart," I reply, meeting his gaze. "It's your own lies and betrayal."

"Tell me how to earn your forgiveness," he breathes.

His words tempt me, something deep within me begging me to let him in. I could survive without his body.

I don't think I can survive without his soul.

"Even if I forgive you." My voice cracks. "It's my trust I don't know how to give you."

"It wouldn't have made a difference," he says, voice rough with regret.

"What wouldn't?"

"The marriage contract. Your father signed it over a year ago. Telling you wouldn't have changed that fact."

"You've known for *a year*," I choke. "A whole year?"

"Ayden hadn't signed it until just before your father's death," Aurelius continues, the look in his eyes telling me he wishes he didn't have to. "But I didn't know it was official until the night of that damn ball."

"But you suspected."

He rakes a hand through his hair. "Yes, I suspected."

"That's why you warned me away from him." My heart twists at the realization. "Why you fought so hard to keep him out of Rimor."

He grimaces. "It's part of it."

I give him a long, stern look.

He finally sighs. "Okay, it was most of it. He wasn't supposed to have you," Aurelius says, his voice breaking on the words. "*You were always supposed to be mine.* I'm a selfish bastard who wanted you all to myself, Breyla. What do you want me to say? I'm not sorry for it."

"I had the right to know," I snap, ignoring the storm of emotions his words stir in me.

"Perhaps," he allows. "But it wouldn't have changed anything. You'd still be betrothed to Ayden."

"I could have taken the situation into my own hands," I argue.

"How?"

"I could have taken the throne from my mother, annulled the agreement, and chosen my own match."

"There's a clause in the contract. If either of you ascended your throne, you would be married within a month." Aurelius exhales roughly, dropping his head. "Ayden made sure the agreement was ironclad—there is no loophole. Had you married another, you would have ignited a real war with Pruida."

His words snap something loose in my memory.

As the warm broth fills my belly, I hear my mother speak for the first time this evening. "So, Prince Ayden, when might we expect to hear of a coronation ball for yourself?" Her tone is polite and inquisitive, but I know she's probing for information.

The spymaster, Lord Craylor, sits several seats down from Charlotte, but I see his gaze snap to my mother at the question.

"Well, seeing as it requires that I take a queen before I can take the throne..." Ayden's voice trails off, "I imagine it will be about the same time Breyla takes her throne."

My hands curl into fists. "That snake," I hiss, anger rolling through me in waves.

"I told you to be wary of him," Aurelius mutters. "You just didn't listen."

"You still could have told me," I growl.

"And shatter what was between us?" he says softly. "No, I think not. I regret how I went about it, but I don't regret wanting you."

"I need time to process this, Aurelius," I say stiffly, shoving him away.

"Of course," he acquiesces, stepping back. His face is unreadable as he rounds the table behind me.

Rowina appears a moment later, dropping a heavy tome into my arms. "Here, I found you some light reading material."

"The Genealogy of House Mordet," I read aloud, brow arching. "Why are you giving me your family tree?"

"Thought you should know the family you're marrying into," she replies with a shrug, handing Aurelius a different tome.

"The History of Crimson," he reads, a puzzled look on his face.

"Enjoy," she sings before disappearing between the towering shelves.

I sink into a chair across from Aurelius, flipping open the heavy book.

"You know," I mutter, "it's a little ironic you're suddenly the most well-adjusted of your siblings."

Aurelius raises a brow at me. "Does that include your father?"

"I mean, he raised me—have you met me?"

"Touché," Aurelius chuckles, a rare lightness in his voice.

I leaf through pages, scanning centuries of names, physical descriptions, their Gifts, their deeds.

The Mordet family had ruled Prudia for more than fifteen hundred years. Very few had ever thought to challenge or unseat them. Formidable didn't begin to describe the family.

I'm not sure whether it's been minutes or hours that have passed when a name catches my attention.

Elythia.

A frustrated grunt escapes me as I try to recall why it feels familiar.

"Something interesting?" Aurelius asks.

"Just… a name. Elythia. I know it, but I can't place it."

"Perhaps you're thinking of Elentia—the capital?"

"Maybe that's it," I say, but I'm not convinced. "What have you learned?"

"Other than my sister needs better taste in books?" he deadpans.

We both laugh lightly.

"This reads like a history text," he explains, "but with sections on lore and the Hemophilia Gifts—well, just one of them, actually."

"Let me guess," I say, arching a brow. "Yours?"

He nods. "According to this, the ability to manipulate or control blood is incredibly rare, but it passes through bloodlines."

"That can't be." I frown. "Gifts aren't inherited."

"Not according to this. Have you noticed the Mordets all carry Gifts from the Anima and Vizie families?"

"The thought had occurred to me, but I wrote it off as a coincidence."

"Is it, though? Even I carry an Anima Gift. Does your book list Gifts?"

"It does," I confirm.

"What does it say King Ayden's Gift was?"

I flip forward, searching for the most recent history.

"King Ayden of Prudia carried the Anima Gift of Empathy and the Vizie Gift of Illusion," I state. "So if the book is telling the truth, then your Hemonia Gift was inherited from your mother, whomever she may be."

"It would seem so."

"Well, it can't be that hard to narrow down." My brow furrows. "Like you said, it's incredibly rare. We find a female with the same Gift, and that's her?"

"It's not that simple, Breyla," Aurelius sighs. "Have you met *anyone* else with my Gift?"

"No," I say automatically. I had never come across another soul with his Gift.

"Exactly," he says grimly. "I'm the only known blood wielder in all four kingdoms. I've checked."

I swallow hard. "So whoever your mother is…"

"She's either dead," he says bluntly, "or not from the four kingdoms."

Knowing that she had abandoned her son, I'm not sure which option I wish for more.

CHAPTER THIRTEEN

OPHELIA

"We should start at Luella's," I suggest, threading my fingers with Elijah's as we stroll out the castle gates. Guards flank us on either side, something I'm still getting used to. Growing up in the castle, I was accustomed to their presence, but being followed by them day and night was new—and irritating.

"I think that is an excellent idea." Elijah squeezes my hand, leading me toward her tavern. "She always has a good gauge on the general attitudes and outlooks of the people."

It had been a heavy burden adjusting to running a kingdom over the last several weeks. Burnt out and exhausted, we had decided last night that a break was needed. I had suggested a visit to the town might be a nice change from the castle walls, and Elijah had quickly agreed. This would allow us to connect with the people and get a more accurate feel for the state of Ciyoria.

Luella's tavern boasts its normal orderly and welcoming facade, complete with red painted shutters and the savory aroma wafting out of the open windows. We walk through the sturdy oak door of the tavern, the hinges creaking slightly as it closes.

The guards occupy a spot in the back corner, and I mumble, "How did Breyla deal with the constant companions?"

"She didn't," Elijah chuckles. "We were masters at evading our guards by the time we were fifteen. Once Raynor deemed us capable with a sword, Genevieve stopped fretting so much."

"They must have trusted their people greatly to keep their heir safe."

"I don't think it was so much trust in their people as it was exhaustion from fighting Breyla on the matter," Elijah explains, pulling out a stool at the bar for me. "Once she was appointed general, there was a condition that guards were required, but she was allowed to select them herself."

"Zion and Ryder?" I guess.

"Exactly," he says, sliding into the chair next to mine. "They trained with us, and outside of the twins, they were the only ones worth a damn. Plus, she actually liked them."

"Makes sense."

It's relatively quiet considering the time. I would have expected it to be packed with lunch patrons, but there are maybe half a dozen people in the establishment.

Luella turns the corner, appearing from the backroom. "What can I do you for, Lord Elijah?" Her curly brown hair is tied up in a knot atop her head, loose tendrils framing her almond-shaped eyes.

"Two of whatever your special is for the day, please." Elijah smiles, slinging an arm around my shoulders. "How are you Luella?"

"I wish I could say better, but we're surviving," Luella answers, as she slides two mugs of mead to us. "The special isn't anything particularly interesting today, by the way."

Elijah's brow furrows. "What do you mean by that?"

"It's just lamb stew, I've had to make a few substitutions for my normal—"

"No, I mean the part about you 'surviving.' What's going on?

"It's been slow. I'm having trouble getting in my normal products," she sighs, her shoulders sagging. "It comes in delayed or with significantly less than I ordered. I'm not sure what's going on with my suppliers, but all of them seem to be having issues."

"I'm sorry to hear that." My lips turn downward, mind racing to come up with a solution. "Is there anyone locally who can provide the same items?"

"Some of them, yes." She disappears around the corner, coming back with two steaming bowls in hand. "But not at the quantity or price that I'm accustomed to."

Once Elijah has begun eating, I spoon the hot broth into my mouth, only slightly flinching at the scalding liquid. I'm not sure what substitutions were made, but what I taste is delicious.

"I'm sorry, Luella," Elijah says sincerely. "That's a tricky situation. Please let me know if there's anything we can do."

"You're sweet, kid." She chuckles, patting his hand. "But as long as my spirits continue arriving, I'll manage. People sure do get grumpy when you take away their liquor."

Around a mouthful of stew, Elijah asks, "What can you tell us about the town? Anything we should know?"

Luella's face hardens, and she leans across the bar top, keeping her voice low as she says, "There's something strange happening."

I glance down, seeing that I've already finished the dish, and fight a flush of embarrassment. Clearing my throat, I ask, "How so?"

"I've never seen the people so spooked. I hear whispers that the gods have abandoned Rimor, with both the king and queen dying within a year, then Breyla being whisked off to our enemy. People are scared." Luella's eyes dart around the room before landing back on us. "I've noticed an influx of strangers. They keep to themselves, so I'm not sure if they're just from other towns or from somewhere further away."

"That is... unsettling," Elijah finally says after a few moments of silence.

"I agree," Luella says before clearing our empty bowls. "I'll let you know if I notice anything else, Lord Elijah."

Elijah stands, dropping several gold Remis on the counter. "Thank you, Luella."

We exit into the late afternoon sun, a new sense of unease filling me.

The cobblestone path turns to dirt as we leave the city center on our way to the outer ring. It's silent on our journey through the streets, eyes carefully taking us in as we navigate the narrow path. Dirt-covered children pass us, their tattered clothing barely clinging to too-thin frames. A girl with midnight eyes approaches me, mud caked on her bare feet, dark hair knotted and stringy. Her bones protrude in sharp angles, cheeks gaunt.

When was the last time this child ate?

"Are you the princess?" she asks.

"No, but I'm friends with her." I bend down to her height, taking her open hand in mine. "Where are your parents?"

"Dead," she says nonchalantly.

Perhaps I should be startled by the casual way she refers to death, but I'm not. The blunt tone that children carry was refreshing to me.

"Mine too," I say with a shrug.

Elijah crouches down to our level and asks, "Do you not live at the orphanage?"

"I did until the orphan mother left."

"She left?" I ask.

"Yeah, one day she was just gone. No one's seen her in..." She begins counting on her fingers. "Two weeks."

Elijah shoots me a worried look. "When was the last time you ate? Or any of the children from the orphanage, for that matter?"

"The pantry was bare the morning she left. Some people give us scraps, but we haven't had a meal since we saw her." She looks us up and down, then whispers, "Do you have any food?"

Elijah's face falls. "Not on me, but here," he says, pulling out his coin purse. He drops what's easily enough gold to feed her for weeks into her outstretched palm. "Take this to Luella's and tell her Lord Elijah sent you. Take whoever needs food with you and make sure they eat too. The castle will send someone to replace the orphan mother and make sure you're fed. I'm sorry we didn't know sooner."

Dull eyes sparkle at the thought of food, and she gives us a toothy grin. "Thank you, m'lord."

"You're most welcome," I say, mirroring her wide grin. "What's your name?"

"Leah."

"Be well, Leah." Elijah straightens as Leah dashes away in search of food.

Once she's out of earshot, I ask, "How is Luella going to feed them all?"

"I'll have extra food sent to her from the castle stores. It's just until we get someone in there to care for them."

"How did this escape our notice?" I say, my chest falling.

"I don't know," Elijah sighs. "But it begs the question of what else we're missing."

Our return walk to the castle is a somber affair, the heaviness we had tried to escape feeling more burdensome than before.

The last of the day's warmth beats down on me as the sun begins setting. Golden rays dance along my skin, casting shadows behind me. I sit on a blanket in the middle of the palace garden, admiring the beauty of the nature around me. Inhaling deeply, I take in the floral aroma and sigh. Peace settles over me. The irises, roses, and carnations reminding me of my mother.

"Would you like a bite, sweetheart?" Elijah asks, offering me a plate of chocolate cake.

"Is that a serious question?" I giggle, taking it from him.

Decadent, sweet, chocolate hits my taste buds, and I moan at the taste of heaven on my tongue. I try to chew slowly, to savor the delicacy, but I can't resist the call of the divine treat and shove bite after bite in my mouth.

"So. Good," I mumble around a mouthful of cake.

"Let me have a taste," Elijah begs.

Begrudgingly, I hold out a forkful for him.

He swats my hand away, wrapping his hand around the back of my head and leaning in close. "Not what I meant," he says with a devilish glint in his eyes.

Just before his lips meet mine, he shakes me instead.

"Ophelia, wake up," Elijah urges, and my eyes snap open.

I blink rapidly, trying to take in my surroundings.

"Where are we?" I ask, my eyes adjusting to the low light of the moon.

"You sleepwalked to the kitchen." Elijah casts a Faerie light, the soft glow illuminating the kitchen. "I thought you were awake at first and just hungry."

"I don't think I'm hungry," I say, laughing softly.

Elijah's eyes fall to my hands. "Are you sure about that?" I follow his gaze to find my hands fully covered in *chocolate cake.*

With a hysterical laugh, I say, "I was dreaming about eating chocolate cake."

Elijah chuckles, reaching for one of my hands. "It was when you began eating the cake with your hands that I realized you weren't awake."

I pull them out of the now destroyed dessert and pray this wasn't for something important. "We should probably clean this up."

He raises my hand to his lips, inspecting the frosting covering every finger. "We should," he says, a lascivious smile spreading the corners of his mouth. His wet tongue darts out, curling around my finger as he sucks the dessert off.

A sudden and violent heat sparks in my core. "Elijah," I whimper.

Sucking another finger into his mouth, he groans. Releasing my fingers, his voice is a husky rasp as he asks, "Yes, Ophelia?"

He lifts my other hand to his lips, his tongue darting out to swirl around two fingers. I lose whatever thought was plaguing me when he sucks and licks every speck of chocolate from my skin.

"Ophelia." My name is like a song on Elijah's lips as he drags a hand down the center of my chest. He lifts my nightgown, exposing my heated flesh to the chill night air.

"Hmmm?" I hum, unsure what he's asking.

"Arms up," he demands.

I comply, and the nightgown is removed from my body before being set behind me on the counter. His hands grasp my hips, squeezing tightly as I'm lifted onto the workspace. He pushes against my bare chest, urging me to lie back.

A wicked thought enters my mind when I catch sight of the chocolate next to us.

Instead, I reach for the cake, digging my fingers into the frosting. I smear the sugary substance over his chest, swirling a finger around his nipple.

His eyes heat as I lean in to lick it from his skin. My tongue traces the same path my fingers took, paying special attention to his collarbone and reveling in the wanton sounds coming from his lips. I lick around each nipple, sucking gently to ensure I've cleaned him thoroughly.

"Ophelia," he moans. "This was supposed to be my job."

"I made the mess," I argue, reaching a hand for the bulge between his thighs. "I should clean it."

He groans deeply when I wrap my messy hand around the hard length beneath his sleep pants. I pump him slowly, being sure to smear the frosting all over him. His mouth latches onto my throat, nipping and biting at the skin until I'm whimpering.

My pace quickens as I feel frosting cover my nipples, his fingers trailing down my abdomen.

"Fuck, baby," Elijah pants. "You're making such a mess."

"Then perhaps you should let me clean it," I suggest, my tone sultry, as I lean in to kiss him.

Dropping his sleep pants to the ground, he growls, "Lie back." This time, I comply, letting my back rest against the kitchen counter.

Elijah climbs onto the counter, straddling my chest. Stroking his cock, he grins. "Open those pretty little lips, baby."

I oblige, savoring his taste mixed with the chocolate cakes as he slides into my mouth. He stops halfway, letting me run my tongue along his shaft as I clean him.

He releases a guttural sound as he slides further into my mouth, close to bottoming out. I can breathe, but just barely. I hollow my cheeks, sucking hard as I work a hand under his shaft to grasp his balls.

The sounds he makes are wild and unrestrained, his hips jerking forward as he thrusts in and out of my mouth. From this angle, I have limited mobility, but I let him take his pleasure, my own arousal building at seeing him come undone.

"Fuck, Ophelia," Elijah whispers. "I'm going to come straight down that pretty throat if I don't stop now."

His hips falter, and I scowl as he attempts to pull out. I squeeze tightly on his balls, and he hisses. Lust-drunk eyes meet mine as he stops retreating and asks, "No? You want me to finish in your mouth?"

With the tip of his length still inside my mouth, I nod, bobbing my head forward to take him back in.

"You sure, beautiful?"

I roll my eyes, sucking hard on him until his eyes roll back. "I'll take that as a yes," he groans.

He thrusts back into my mouth fully, eliciting a gag when he hits the back of my throat. Tears pool in my eyes as he continues thrusting.

There's something serene about submitting to him, taking everything he gives, and being completely at his mercy. Everything quiets around me, the world makes a little more sense when I'm under his control.

His pace increases, and all I can do is let him use me to find his release. Warm salty seed fills my mouth, his cock pulsing as he empties himself into me. I swallow, the sweetness from the cake mingling with the slightly bitter taste of his come.

"Gods, you look beautiful swallowing my cock like that," Elijah purrs as his dick slides out of my mouth with a wet pop.

I suck in a breath, my chest heaving as he crawls off the counter. When I move to sit up, he pushes me back down.

With a sexy smirk, he rubs more cake across my body, covering my hips and pubic bone with frosting. He's careful not to spread any near my actual sex, but he covers just about everywhere else. "I'm not done cleaning up *my* mess."

My core heats as his lips move along the trail of chocolate, warm tongue darting out to clean every piece of the cake from my skin.

I gasp when his mouth meets my heated core, tongue flicking and swirling around that bundle of nerves.. Over and over, he laps at my sensitive flesh until I'm writhing beneath him.

He slides not one, but two fingers inside me. In and out he thrusts his hands, my hips leaving the counter as my back arches.

Elijah alternates sucking my clit with quick fluttering motions that leave me dizzy. Pleasure quickly builds, my core tightening as his fingers curl forward. The motion sends me straight over the edge, pleasure racing through every limb as I cry out his name.

He continues lapping at my core, drinking every drop of my release until I'm shaking beneath him.

"Enough," I beg, weakly shoving at his shoulder.

He pulls back, his lips quirking in a self-satisfied smirk. It quickly dissolves into laughter as he moves me upright.

"What's so funny?" I ask, searching for my clothing.

"We're terrible at cleaning," he says through his laughter.

I spot the nightgown, pulling it over my head. "Why do you say that?"

He grins sheepishly, reaching for one of the wild, stray locks that frame my face. "There's cake in your hair."

"Oh gods," I can't help the laughter that bursts from me, joining his. There's some on your shoulders."

"We should probably leave before we make a bigger mess for the kitchen staff," Elijah says, pulling his sleep pants back into place.

"Agreed," I say, giggling as I jump from the counter. I grab what remains of the cake and head for the door. "But I'm taking the evidence with us."

The sultry grin he gives me says he has no arguments with that.

CHAPTER FOURTEEN

The next two days pass in a similar manner—uncomfortable family breakfasts, bickering, endless library research, more awkward family meals, then bed.

After lunch on the second day, Queen Josephina requested I join her for tea and needlepoint.

I quite literally ran in the other direction.

By the third day, I'm itching to get out of the castle. I'm bored. I've read the entire Mordet family history twice over, and will do anything to avoid more "female bonding time" with Queen Josephina.

When Ayden offers to walk me to the library after breakfast, I fake a headache and tell him I'd rather rest.

He gives me a highly suspicious look but leaves for training with Darian.

I count to one hundred after his footsteps fade, just to be sure. Then, exhaling softly, I crack my door open and peek down the hall. Seeing it empty, I slip out, pulling the door shut behind me without letting it latch.

Quickly, I cross to Ayden's room. I tug at the handle but find it's locked.

Smirking, I pull shadows to my hand, forming a shadow key as I had so many times before.

"Silly male should have learned from the last time I broke into his room," I whisper.

I let the shadows seep into the lock, filling every crevice before hardening them into a solid form. A simple twist and the lock clicks open.

Smiling triumphantly, I push open the door and slip into his chambers.

His woodsy citrus scent fills the space.

I take in his quarters for a moment, admiring the display of opulence. Unlike the rest of the castle's gleaming marble and gold, his room is dark—dark wood floors, black velvet furnishings, rich black carpets. Gold accents glint on the bed's curtain ties and along the furniture's edges.

It's excessive and decadent, but it suits him perfectly.

Then I spot it. My trunk is tucked beside the bed. A shiver runs up my spine at the thought of getting out of dresses. "Oh, sweet pants."

I drop to my knees to open the chest just as the door slams shut behind me, the lock clicking into place.

"Well, fuck," I sigh defeatedly.

"If you wanted in my room, love," Ayden drawls, chuckling as he leans casually against the wall. "All you had to do was ask."

I scowl. "I want out of this dress, Ayden."

His amber eyes darken immediately, a sinful glint flashing there.

"Careful, love," he purrs. "That's beginning to sound like consent."

I roll my eyes. "What will it take for you to return my clothing?"

Ayden crosses the room, stopping inches from me. He tucks a loose curl behind my ear, tipping my face up to meet his. Calloused fingers lightly brush my bottom lip as he says, "Kiss me."

One kiss.

I could survive one kiss to get my belongings back.

I lean into him, our lips nearly brushing, his breath dusting across my mouth. At the last second, I turn my head and press a chaste kiss to his cheek.

He chuckles low in his throat. "Nice try, but not happening."

"You didn't specify where."

"Yet, I'm the one making the rules, and I say it wasn't good enough."

"You're an ass," I grumble, pushing away from him.

"If you would just give me a fighting chance, you would see I am so much more."

"I don't give chances to people who don't give me choices."

"We aren't afforded those choices, Breyla." His face tightens slightly. "We're royalty. With the crown comes obligations. We all make sacrifices."

"What sacrifices have you made, Ayden?" My tone is venomous, eyes hardening into a glare. "Because from where I'm standing, it looks like I've sacrificed plenty, but you get a wife and throne out of the deal."

"I've sacrificed more than you know," he whispers, something pained flickering through his eyes.

Feeling uncomfortable, I change topics. "Give me another deal."

"No."

"Why not?"

"Because I want a real chance."

"I don't know how!" I snap, frustration boiling over. "Letting people in isn't easy for me."

"You let Aurelius in," he counters.

"I didn't *let* Aurelius do anything," I retort. "He shoved his way in and took what he wanted. And look where that got me. Ayden, I've only ever cared for two males like that, and they both betrayed me in the end."

He studies me, quiet for a moment. "Yet you still care for him."

" I-I don't know what I feel for him," the lie rolls smoothly off my tongue.

Truthfully, I felt a lot of things for him—lust, betrayal, anger, confusion, and longing. I just wasn't sure which feeling was winning.

Ayden steps closer, his fingers once again finding my jaw.

"We would be so good together, Princess. I love how your mind works. I believe you'll make a formidable partner, and an even greater queen. You weren't just chosen to broker peace. You were chosen because you are *worthy* of standing beside me."

He lifts my chin, holding my gaze with devastating intensity. "I asked about you. I studied you in battle and watched you lead. I chose you for your passion, your bravery, your brilliance."

He leans closer, his breath brushing my skin. "And every night," he murmurs, his voice dark and silky, "I would worship you. I would make pleasure a religion—and you, my goddess."

The breath catches in my lungs. Warmth fills my chest when I realize how Ayden truly sees me.

Not just a pawn or peace offering. But as something desired and worthy.

"You certainly make a strong argument," I finally manage to say.

"And I'll keep making it until you give us a chance."

"I can't make you any promises, Ayden."

"All I ask is that you actually try."

A nod is all I can manage in response.

"Thank you," Ayden whispers.

I circle back to the thought that snagged in my mind. "You inquired about me?"

"Of course I did. I wanted some idea of who I was marrying."

My brow furrows. "But who did you ask?"

"Aurelius," he says, like it should have been obvious.

It should be, though. Aurelius was the royal emissary and had spent more time here than in any other kingdom.

"And he gave you a positive assessment of me?"

"Glowing, actually." Ayden rubs the back of his neck, a small smile tugging the corner of his lips. "He sounded rather fond of you, even if he was reluctant to speak about you at first."

"I don't understand." I shake my head, trying to piece together a puzzle that doesn't fit.. "Aurelius and I, until very recently, couldn't stand one another. We've *never* gotten along."

"For someone so intelligent," Ayden teases, "you're very oblivious."

I punch him in the shoulder, snorting. "I am not."

"But you are," he insists, smiling. "As much as it pains me to admit this to my fiancée, that male isn't just obsessed with you, Breyla. He's in love with you. I thought perhaps it was a lingering loyalty to your father at first... but after arriving in Rimor, it became painfully obvious"

Ayden runs his hand through his dark curls, mussing them into a charming, disheveled mess that, annoyingly, makes him look even more attractive.

"Then why would he treat me the way he did?" I ask, frustration creeping into my voice. "We've hated one another for *years*, Ayden."

"You were off-limits to him," Ayden says simply. "My guess? It was easier for him to keep you at arm's distance, to fight you, than to risk feeling more than he was allowed to. There is nothing more painful than having the object of your desire within reach, yet being unable to touch it."

"You sound like you speak from experience."

"Not me," he says with a shrug, pulling me closer, pressing his nose along the column of my neck, and inhaling deeply. "Someone I know."

"Get back or I'll punch you again," I warn, trying to shove him off.

"I do like it when you get violent." He chuckles, stepping back half a pace.. "But I have a better idea for how you can burn that violent energy."

"I'm not fucking you, Ayden," I deadpan.

"Get your mind out of the gutter, love. I wasn't even going there." He winks. "I meant training."

My face lights up, a grin stretching wide across my lips.

"That sounds like significantly more fun. Do I get pants?"

"Ah, no," he says, far too pleased with himself. "You'll have to train in that."

I glance down at the lavender dress that hugs every curve. This one doesn't lift my breasts as much as the others did, but the skirt is tight and leaves little room for movement. There is no way I can train in this.

Leaning down, I pull the hem up my leg to reveal the dagger sheathed against my thigh. Ayden's heated gaze tracks the movement, his eyes lingering far too long.

"Eyes are up here, Prince," I remind him sharply.

"So they are," he says, but makes no effort to move his gaze upward.

Rolling my eyes, I unsheathe the dagger. Using the tip, I hook his chin and tilt his face up to meet mine.

"Up here, asshole," I say pointedly.

He only shrugs, utterly unapologetic. "Not sorry."

"Whatever," I mutter, turning back to the task at hand.

I slide the dagger through the right side of the dress, cutting a slit all the way to the floor. The fabric tears easily, freeing my leg for movement.

I repeat the process on the left side, creating a crude but functional fighting skirt.

"If you didn't want me staring at your legs," Ayden says, voice roughened, "you probably shouldn't have exposed them to me so completely."

"That sounds like a you problem, Prince."

Fifteen minutes later, we stand outside the training grounds, the sounds of swords clashing and soldiers' grunts filling the air.

"You've got to be kidding me," Darian huffs when he sees me step up beside the prince.

Rowina watches from the other side of the training grounds, a curious look on her face as she sees me approach the ring.

"No jokes here, brother," Ayden says smoothly.

His navy eyes narrow in irritation. "I'm not training her, Ayden."

"Hey, asshole," I snap, crossing my arms. "In case you've forgotten, I am also a General. I don't need you to train me. I just need someone to spar with."

"Not happening," Darian bites out.

"And if your Prince demands it?" Ayden asks.

"Don't you dare try to pull rank on me," Darian growls, voice deadly. He rakes a hand through his chestnut hair, then points a finger at Ayden. "Not with this."

Ayden deflates slightly, shame flashing across his face. "You're right. I'm sorry, Darian. I shouldn't have said that."

"Look," I interject. "I don't want to spar with him. Darian probably isn't even capable of keeping up with me."

Darian scoffs. "I'm not dignifying that with a response."

"You technically just did," I smirk. "Regardless, I'll spar with literally anyone else."

Across the grounds, Aurelius's voice cuts through the noise. "Then spar with me, little demon."

Before I can respond, Ayden snarls, "Not fucking happening. You and I have things to work through, brother."

"Still mad you don't know how to handle your sword?" Aurelius smirks lazily.

"I can handle my *sword* just fine when I'm the one controlling it," Ayden growls, grabbing Aurelius by the arm and dragging him toward an empty ring.

"Ayden, I'm still not doing this!" Darian calls after him.

"You know she's too skilled for the others," Ayden throws over his shoulder.. "Just do it, and I'll make it up to you later."

Darian folds his arms. "How, exactly, are you planning to make it up to me?"

"What if I make it up to you?" Rowina asks, a sweet smile curling her lips.

Darian lifts a skeptical brow. "Are you finally going to get in this ring and let me train you?"

"Mmm, no. But what if I let you take me home for family dinner?"

"Fine," he finally relents, "but I'm not pulling my punches for her."

"Wouldn't expect you to," Ayden replies as he strips off his shirt, heading for Aurelius across the ring. Beside him, Aurelius pulls his own shirt free, leaving both males bare-chested under the late morning sun.

What a glorious sight that is, I think to myself, momentarily distracted.

Ayden may not be what my soul craves, but his body does something to me. He and Aurelius are the same height, but Ayden carries at least thirty more pounds of pure, defined muscle. I thoroughly enjoy every inch of Aurelius' lean, honed form, but Ayden?

Ayden is like reading the same book in a different, equally sinful language.

"You done ogling them, *General?*" Darian sneers.

I snap my attention back to him, only to find him shitless as well.

Fuck me, I think grimly. *Why did the asshole have to look so good without a shirt?*

Darian, like Ayden, is all carved muscle and brutal strength. But where Ayden and Aurelius's skin is kissed by the sun, Darian is fair like mepale and dusted with chestnut hair that trails down the hard vee of his hips. He's taller too, by at least half a foot, and solid as a wall.

Gods, what was wrong with me? Did I really find this male attractive?

Yeah, babe. Assholes are kind of your type, my inner voice supplies helpfully.

The inner voice had started sounding suspiciously like Elijah lately.

Not that asshole, I grumble inwardly.

"You done flirting with the princess?" I snap out loud, ignoring my traitorous brain.

"Are you going to fight me or just drool all day, *General?*" Every time Darian says my title, it holds more disdain than the last. It was really starting to piss me off.

"Let's go, *General,*" I retort with equal disdain.

"There are a couple of ground rules," he says as he paces into the ring. "One—you fight without your Gifts. You're only good as your powerless self."

"I can respect that," I say with a curt nod.

"Two—first to tap out, pass out, or exit the ring loses."

"Fair enough."

"Three—nothing else is off limits. Your enemy won't fight fair, so I don't train fair. There is no honor in dying because you played nice."

"I'm feeling an odd sense of respect for you and your rules. I don't like it."

"I swear to the gods, though—" His eyes narrow. "If you go for my cock, I'll make you fucking regret it. That's kind of an unspoken exception to the third rule."

"Males and their damn cocks." I roll my eyes. "You have nothing to worry about. I want to stay as far away as possible from your tiny appendage."

"Didn't feel that way when you rubbed your ass against it and moaned for me in the library."

"First off, I did not rub any—"

Punch.

His fist crashes into my gut before I can finish the sentence.

"Fuck," I wheeze, staggering.

I right myself just in time to dodge his second punch, snapping a kick into his chest. It doesn't land clean, sending a sharp spike of pain up my calf.

Darian stumbles but keeps his footing.

I rush him, throwing a right hook toward his nose.

He deflects it easily, countering with a brutal punch to my jaw. Pain explodes across my face, rattling my teeth.

Spitting blood onto the dirt, I glare murder at him.

"Come on, General," he taunts. "You fight like the spoiled brat you are."

With a growl, I launch myself at him, feinting high before slamming my body into his torso. He buckles under the momentum, and we crash to the ground hard, me landing on top.

Before he can react, I pull back my arm and drive my fist into his nose.

The victory is short-lived, though. Using his greater size, he bucks his hips and throws me off, rolling me beneath him. He pins my shoulders, pressing a forearm against my throat.

"Submit," he growls.

"Fuck you," I rasp, my vision darkening at the edges.

I need oxygen as badly as I need to win this match.

"No thanks," he smirks.

"Wasn't really an offer," I choke out.

With a sharp jab, I jam my fingers into the pressure point at his neck.

He jerks back with a grunt, loosening his hold just enough for me to shove him off.

Rolling free, I gasp for air, blood slicking my jaw, my chest heaving. I flip to my feet, dropping into a crouch.

Darian rises too, blood running freely down his face from his broken nose.

"What now?" he pants.

I grin, sharp and feral, beckoning him forward with a cocky two-finger wave. "Come on, General. Thought you said you weren't done yet."

"You haven't had enough?" he growls, circling me.

I mirror his steps, keeping him in front of me at all times. "I'll have had enough when you're flat on your back submitting to me."

"That will *never* happen," he promises.

We'll see.

He makes the first move, charging me.

I wait until he's almost on top of me, then pivot in a tight twirl. At the last second, I crouch low and sweep my leg in front of his feet.

Darian stumbles, arms flying out to balance himself, and I don't waste a breath.

I leap onto his back, my arm snapping around his throat. He thrashes violently, but I tighten my grip, locking my arm until it aches.

"Submit," I whisper in his ear.

He doesn't.

Of course he doesn't.

I hold tighter, feeling the muscles in his body tense, then slowly, alarmingly, go slack.

"Oh fuck," I breathe, realization dawning too late.

Gravity pulls us down hard, and this time it's my body that slams into the ground first. Pain sears through my spine, my grip loosening out of sheer instinct.

But before either of us can move—

Crack.

The sharp, sickening sound of breaking bone cuts through the courtyard, followed by Ayden's furious wail.

Our sparring forgotten, I scramble upright, just in time to see a castle guard hit the ground, lifeless, eyes staring blankly at the sky.

I bolt toward the commotion, finding Aurelius standing rigid as more guards rush to surround him.

"What did you do?" I whisper.

Aurelius meets my gaze with a terrifying calm. "What was necessary," he says, utterly emotionless.

I search his face, trying to discern what might be running through that mind of his.

Aurelius didn't kill without cause. But gods, what possible cause justified this?

"Why the fuck was this necessary?" Ayden roars.

"Yes," Darian growls. "Explain to me why murdering one of my guards was necessary."

Aurelius turns to Ayden and spits, "Would you have preferred a dead fiancée instead?"

Ayden's face darkens. "Guards, restrain Prince Aurelius and escort him to his chambers. He's confined there until further notice."

Guards immediately restrain Aurelius, but he doesn't fight them. He complies, letting them escort him inside the castle.

I crouch by the body at my feet. There's nothing remarkable about the fallen guard, but he was a person. Someone who lived and breathed. Someone who just died.

Gently, I close his vacant eyes.

Something glints at his belt. A knife, sleek and unfamiliar, unlike anything issued to Prudia's soldiers.

I slip it free, raising it to my nose. The horribly familiar metallic scent hits me like a blow.

"Ayden," I croak. "This is poisoned."

"Seven hells," he curses, moving to my side

"It's the same poison," I whisper numbly. "The one that killed Nameah, Layne, and my mother."

Memories crash over me—

Nameah's body limp in my arms.

Layne's blood staining my dress.

My mother's final breath.

My hand trembles violently. The knife slips from my fingers, clattering against the stones.

"Stay with me, love," Ayden murmurs, crouching in front of me, anchoring me with his steady hands.

"I-I'm sorry," I stammer, trying to shake myself out of the memories.

"It's okay, Breyla." His voice is low, firm. "I'm going to take you to your room now."

The walk back is a blur. I barely register the castle walls, the guards stationed outside my door, the heavy click of the lock behind me.

None of it matters.

Moving on instinct alone, I shove the dresser in front of the door. Only then do I exhale, sinking to the floor.

I don't bother undressing. Forming my shadows into jagged edges, I slice the cursed dress from my body, the fabric falling away in ribbons, blood welling where my shadows bite too deep.

I welcome the sting, letting it distract me from the emotional turmoil happening inside my own head.

Crawling into bed naked, I wrap the thick duvet around my trembling body.

And I cry.

Three shades of blue eyes stare back at me every time I shut my eyes. The glacial hue of my mother's, Layne's deep navy, and finally, Nameah's piercing blue irises.

Eyes that will never see again because of me.

Sobs rack my body as I let it all go. I hadn't thought of or cried for them in weeks. That guilt makes me cry harder.

Eventually, the grief drags me into a fitful, broken sleep.

When I awake, it's dark outside. I must have fallen asleep sometime around lunch, and now it looks to be well past dinner.

Ayden sits on the end of my bed, a plate of food in hand. "How are you?"

"What time is it?" I rasp, ignoring the question.

"Just past eight."

I nod numbly and reach for the plate.

He hands it over, watching silently as I devour the roast lamb, vegetables, and crusty bread.

"Aurelius?" I ask when I can finally speak.

"He's free," Ayden says. "I cleared him of any suspicion or wrongdoing."

I pause, fork halfway to my mouth. "What happened?"

Ayden sighs heavily, running a hand through his hair. "His Gift picked up on something off about that guard. Apparently, the guard intended to attack you with that poisoned blade you found. Aurelius acted before he had the chance."

I lower the plate to my lap, swallowing hard.

"We're still investigating," Ayden continues. "Looking into his family and belongings. We'll find whoever sent him."

"Good."

Silence stretches between us, heavy and brittle.

"Tell me what you're thinking, sweetheart," Ayden nearly begs.

"How did you get in here?" I ask instead, eyeing the dresser I shoved in front of the door.

"Darian assisted once I discovered your barricade."

"Of course he did," I mutter, dragging a hand through my tangled hair.

"What do you need?"

"Sleep," I say simply.

"Of course." Ayden rises, gathering the plate. He hesitates at the door.

"Ayden?" I call softly.

He turns. "Yes, Princess?"

"Can you... make the dreams stop?"

A soft smile curves his lips. "As you wish."

He leans down, brushing a kiss to my forehead. His fingers weave through my hair, and magic—warm and sure—settles deep into my bones, lulling me toward peace.

He moves the dresser against the wall and shuts the door quietly behind him.

I flick my wrist, sliding the lock back into place.

And finally, *finally*, I slip into a deep, dreamless sleep.

CHAPTER FIFTEEN

Ayden smiles the moment my door swings open. "Good morning, love."

I startle, eyeing him suspiciously. "Good morning, Prince."

"Are you wearing shoes?"

Winter hasn't arrived yet, but Ayden had been right about one thing– the chill settles in Prudia much earlier than it does in Rimor.

I lift the hem of my gown, displaying the only pair of flats the queen had deemed necessary for me.

"Unfortunately," I mutter, wishing the day were warm enough to go barefoot.

"Excellent," Ayden says, grinning. "We have a date this morning."

"We do?" I ask warily as he offers his arm, leading me away from the royal wing.

"I know this wasn't your choice, Breyla," he says, voice light yet sincere, "but I am intent on courting you properly. I want to show you exactly how wonderful your life with me could be."

"Your sincerity," I sigh, "makes it annoyingly difficult to keep hating you."

We reach the courtyard, the sun casting warm rays over the bustling staff as they go about their morning tasks. A few feet away, a black carriage with gold accents awaits us, the horses already harnessed.

Silently, I wish we were traveling on horseback instead.

"Come now, darling. You might not trust me, but you don't hate me," he teases.

I consider my words carefully as we climb into the carriage.

"No, Ayden, I don't hate *you*, but I despise what you and our betrothal represent."

"And what do I represent to you?" he asks, his tone losing some of its teasing edge.

"Chains," I reply without hesitation. "This betrothal... it's a cage."

A solemn look crosses his handsome face. "I never wish to chain you, Breyla. I only want to see you fly."

"I'm no bird, but if I were, consider my wings clipped."

The remainder of the ride unfolds in silence, heavy and unsettled.

We step into a bustling street, morning energy humming through the town. In front of us stands a modest building, its white façade softened by the wild riot of flowers spilling from every available space. A sign sways overhead that reads *Esme's Café*.

"I hope you're hungry, love." Ayden grins, holding the door open for me. "This is my favorite breakfast spot."

I shrug. "I could eat."

Inside, the warm scent of fresh bread, spices, and strong tea envelops me instantly. Ayden waves down the nearest server, a young female balancing several steaming plates. He deftly swipes a plate from her arm, setting it before a waiting patron. "It's a beautiful day, Violet. How are you?"

"We're busy today, Prince," she replies, not unkindly but clearly immune to his charm

"You're busy every day, love." He gives her a cheeky grin. "Do you have a table for your favorite patron?"

She rolls her eyes, shaking her head. "I don't know about favorite," she mumbles.

"You lie," he teases.

"And you flirt entirely too much," she retorts.

A sudden laugh bursts out of me before I can stop it. "She knows you well."

"I always have a table for our rakish prince," a new voice adds, the sound like a melody, yet somehow still rough. A tall, lithe woman with dark hair and darker eyes sweeps toward us, exuding a rough-edged warmth.

"Esme, darling," Ayden greets her with a dramatic flourish. "How lovely to see you."

"You don't need to flirt to get a table, Ayden," she says dryly, steering us toward a cozy corner. "I always keep one for you, and for your charming companion."

"Breyla Rozaria," I introduce myself before Ayden can speak, holding my hand out.

"Esme Calder. It's a pleasure." She pulls me into a quick, fierce hug instead of a handshake. "You must be the betrothed."

"Word travels quickly here," I say uncomfortably.

"The prince has a big mouth," Esme says with a wink, "He couldn't shut up about you. It was all he talked about for a month before he left to fetch you."

"Now you're embellishing," Ayden grumbles.

Esme gives me a conspiratorial wink as she fills our cups with steaming tea. "What can I get you?"

"The special," Ayden answers immediately. "And one of those," he adds, pointing to the enormous cinnamon roll Violet carries past.

Esme disappears, leaving us alone. I stare at the steam rising from the cup as I try to think of something to fill the silence.

"Ask me anything," Ayden says suddenly, watching me over the rim of his cup.

I raise a skeptical brow. "Anything?"

He nods. "This is your chance to get to know me. I'm an open book."

I lean back, pretending to consider. "Did you sleep with Violet?"

He smirks. "Would it make you jealous if I had?"

"Hardly," I scoff.

"No—" he starts.

"I find that hard to believe," I cut in.

"I slept with her sister," he finishes. "Twice."

"There it is," I say, laughing.

"And her brother," he adds shamelessly. "Three times."

"Not at the same time, I hope."

"Heavens, no," he exclaims, laughing. "I didn't even know they were related until much later. I went through some… dark times following my father's death. Liquor and warm bodies became a coping mechanism."

"That would explain why Violet is immune to your charm."

"Nah," Ayden says with a grin. "She's always been immune. Rowina's more her type."

"Ah," I say, understanding clicking into place.

Esme returns with our food, placing the dishes in front of us.

A rich, decadent scent rises from the plates. A poached egg glistens atop a fluffy biscuit layered with ham, all drenched in a creamy yellow sauce.

Beside it, the cinnamon roll towers, so thick with icing it's threatening to melt off the plate.

Ayden bats my fingers away from the sweet treat, leveling me with a stern look. "You have to try that first," he says, nudging the egg dish toward me.

"Fine." I roll my eyes, stabbing my fork into the egg.

When the first bite hits my tongue, I have to choke back a moan because, *holy hell, that's good.* The sauce on top is somehow creamy and tangy and perfectly balances the sweetness of the ham. Egg yolk spills, deepening the flavor profile of the dish.

"This is delicious," I mumble around a mouthful.

"It's my favorite for a reason," Ayden says smugly.

"Why don't you hire her to work for the castle?" I ask, going in for another bite. "I would eat this daily if I could."

"If you want it every day, I'll make that happen," he promises with a wink. "And to answer your question, I've tried. Sadly, she can't be bought."

"That is sad," I agree, taking another bite. The yolk dribbles down my chin, and I let out a soft groan of satisfaction.

Ayden reaches across the table, his thumb swiping up the golden trail before brushing lightly over my lower lip.

"You missed some," he says, bringing his thumb to his mouth to suck it clean.

"Do you flirt this way with all your conquests?" I blurt out.

Ayden's face turns uncharacteristically serious, almost heartbreakingly so. "You are *not* a conquest, Breyla. You are my future wife and queen."

"You didn't answer my question."

He exhales, defeated. "Only with the stubborn ones."

"And does it work?"

"Typically," he admits. "I'm not accustomed to having to try this hard if I'm being honest."

I shove the last bite of my dish into my mouth, savoring the tangy sauce as I lick it off my fork.

"Maybe you should try less."

His dark brow quirks in question. "You want me to try less to woo you?"

"If I must marry you, I want to know the real you, Ayden. I don't need over-the-top flirting, I need authenticity."

I don't know why I'm telling him how to win me. Maybe because something deep inside says he needs to hear it.

His brow furrows, expression shifting into something sincere. "I can respect that, but I don't think I can turn off the flirting entirely," he admits. "That's just part of my personality at this point."

I chuckle, tearing into the cinnamon roll and popping a piece in my mouth.

The spicy sweetness melts across my tongue, and an involuntary groan of satisfaction slips free.

"I think your eyes just rolled back into your head," Ayden teases, laughing boisterously.

I flip him off. "Is all the food here this good?"

"Pretty much, though her pancakes are only okay."

"I heard that, you liar," Esme calls from across the room.

I continue devouring the cinnamon roll as Ayden and Esme banter back and forth. Esme threatens to revoke his table privileges unless he takes it back.

I chuckle at how easily he rolls over and submits to her after that.

"So tell me," Ayden says as the laughter dies down. "How exactly did *Aurelius*, of all people, win your heart?"

I nearly choke on the last bite of the gooey delicacy. "You really want to know?"

"I may regret it," he says, grinning, "but yes."

I debate how much I really want to divulge about our relationship. It feels violating, in a sense, exposing that part of myself. But I told

Ayden I would give him a genuine chance, and if I'm expecting transparency from him, I know I must give a little in return.

"To start with," I say slowly, "Aurelius doesn't flirt. The closest he comes is whispering filthy things in my ear and throwing daggers."

"Dear gods," Ayden snorts. "Are you telling me fighting is your foreplay?"

I laugh, throwing my head back. "Something like that."

"If you want the truth, though," I continue, "Aurelius understands me. Better than most. He was there through the worst moments of my life, but he never coddled me. He knows when to push, when to call me on my bullshit, and when to pull me back from the edge."

Ayden nods, quiet now, truly listening.

"I can't tell you how he came to know all that, but he does. He's always been unapologetically himself and never shied away from what he wants. He never tried to overshadow me; he only ever made me stronger. Standing beside him felt like... standing taller."

"That's a lot to live up to."

"Perhaps it is, but I'll accept nothing less." I lower my voice. "He also broke my trust by keeping secrets, and I don't forgive easily."

"Did you ever consider," Ayden says carefully, "that maybe he had a good reason for keeping secrets?"

I let out a sharp, bitter laugh. "Sure, let's entertain that notion for a moment. Tell me, Ayden, what possible good reason could there be for hiding the marriage contract from me?"

Ayden shrugs, picking at the last of his food. "Perhaps he felt it wasn't his secret to share."

"Even if that were the case, which I don't believe it is, why continue pursuing me? Why care for me, fuck me, fill my head with pretty lies about how I was his, knowing none of it could last?"

"Fair point," he frowns. "That does seem rather cruel."

"Now you know," I say quietly. "How he won my heart... and how he lost it."

"I will be sure to learn from his mistakes," Ayden promises.

"Are we done here, Prince?" I ask, sharper than I intend. Pain and bitterness constrict my chest, wrapping tightly around my ribs.

"We're done with breakfast," he says, standing. "But we still have more to do today."

He leaves a generous pile of gold on the table, grabbing a pastry for Rowina on the way out.

The morning has mellowed into a golden afternoon, sun high and warm against my skin. I breathe deeply, curling my toes in my flats, longing to slip them off and feel the earth between my toes.

I'm about to do just that when the sharp crash of splintering wood rings out, and a feminine scream pierces the air.

My eyes lock with Ayden briefly before we both take off toward the sound of screaming. The scene that greets us is nothing short of horrific.

A young female lies pinned beneath a broken carriage, her thigh crushed, a massive chunk of wood driven deep into her muscle and bone.

Three males struggle to lift the carriage while she sobs in agony.

I don't even think, I just act.

My shadows surge under the carriage, pooling and solidifying, helping the males lift. As soon as the weight shifts, Ayden dives in, hauling the female free.

The moment her body clears, the wreckage crashes back down.

She's pale, too pale, her wide eyes fixated on the bloody stake jutting from her thigh. One of the males lunges for it, hands reaching to pull it free.

"Stop!" Ayden and I bark in unison.

He freezes, looking between us, confused and desperate.

"If you pull that out now, she'll bleed out in minutes," I explain, then turn to Ayden. "We need Aurelius, and a healer, preferably, but a castle physician if you don't have one."

He doesn't hesitate, spinning to bark orders to the nearest guard, who bolts off on horseback.

The female stares up at me, blinking slowly as the shock sets in. "Who are you?" she asks.

"My name is Breyla." I kneel beside her. "What's yours?"

"Rochelle." Her voice quivers. "Am I going to die?"

I thread my fingers through hers, squeezing them reassuringly. "Not today," I say with a soft smile.

"You're going to be okay," Ayden adds, gently brushing her sweat-drenched hair from her forehead.

Her eyes droop.

"We've got someone coming from the castle to help fix your leg," I reassure her. "You just need to stay awake until they get here, okay?"

"Okay," she whispers.

"Tell me about yourself, Rochelle," I suggest. "How old are you?"

"Thirty-two," she answers. Older than I expected, but still young.

"Well, you certainly age gracefully," Ayden murmurs. "I wouldn't have guessed you to be more than twenty-five."

For once, Ayden's subtle flirtations are just what is needed. A slight flush covers her cheeks.

"What do you do for a living?" I ask.

"I'm... a midwife," Rochelle replies, alarm flaring her eyes wide. "I was on my way to check on a mother... She's due any day... babe's in the wrong position."

"It's okay," I soothe, running a hand up and down her arm. "We'll get someone else to her."

"If you give me her name," Ayden says, voice low and steady, "I'll send the castle midwife to see to her personally."

Rochelle rattles off the name and address, and Ayden relays it swiftly to another guard.

"See?" I murmur. "Everything is going to be okay."

She nods weakly.

"Are you in pain?" I ask, scanning her for worsening signs of shock.

"Yes," she whimpers.

Her tanned skin is clammy, her body trembling, and I know the shock has fully set in. We need to move *fast*.

It feels like hours, but finally, Aurelius arrives, Rowina right behind him on horseback.

"Thank the gods he brought Ro," Ayden mutters, relief flashing across his face.

"What's the damage?" Aurelius asks.

"Crushed leg," I say, fast and grim. "Not sure if there are any breaks, but we can't move the wood. If we do, she'll bleed out. She's already in shock."

Rowina drops to the ground beside Rochelle, taking her hand and flashing her a warm, brilliant smile. "You have beautiful blue eyes, darling. Keep them on me, alright?"

Rochelle's trembling eases, her muscles relaxing under Rowina's Empath Gift.

Aurelius crouches next to Ayden, assessing the injury.

"Breyla, you apply pressure the second I pull it free. I can't clot it until the object is removed. Ayden, you carry her to the carriage and get her to the castle. My Gift won't hold indefinitely, so move fast."

We nod, falling into place.

Aurelius meets my eyes, counting down from three. When he hits one, he slides the wood free. I slam both palms onto Rochelle's thigh, trying to stem the flow of blood.

Her eyes widen, horror blooming across her face.

"Eyes on me," Rowina commands sharply, and Rochelle blinks up at her, breathing in shallow gasps.

Aurelius' Gift surges through the wound, slowly but surely, staunching the blood. By the time Rochelle's stable enough to move, she's concerningly pale.

Aurelius nods, and Ayden lifts her, bridal style, into his arms and climbs into the waiting carriage. It takes off for the palace, leaving Rowina, Aurelius, and me standing in the middle of the street, covered in blood.

The crowd falls quiet around us.

"Thank you, both." My voice is hoarse, exhaustion filling me in place of the quickly receding adrenaline.

"There's no need to thank us." Rowina lays a hand on my shoulder. "These are our people. It's our job to protect them."

A light touch taps my arm. I turn to find an elderly female and a boy holding towels and a pitcher of water.

"Let us wash your hands," the boy says.

We stretch out our arms, mine the worst by far. They pour water over them, scrubbing away all they can before toweling them dry. It's not perfect, but it's a hell of a lot better.

"Thank you," I murmur.

"No," she smiles. "Thank you. Rochelle is my niece, and you didn't have to save her."

"I would do it for anyone."

She studies me with eyes the same bright blue as Rochelle's and smiles. "I believe that, Your Highness."

"Please," I say, voice rough. "It's just Breyla."

"You have an uncommon soul, Breyla," she says, squeezing my hand.

"That she does," Aurelius says, sliding an arm around my shoulders.

Shrugging, I try to shake off Aurelius' hold, but his grip only tightens. "Thank you for your hospitality."

"We'll send word about Rochelle the moment we know more," Rowina promises.

"Thank you," the little boy says, flashing us a toothy grin.

Aurelius' arm stays firmly clamped around me as we reach the horses.

"Let me go," I hiss.

"No," he says flatly. "You're trembling. Your heart's all over the place, and you're dangerously close to passing out."

I glance down at my shaking hands and realize he's right.

"Oh," is all I manage to say as Aurelius lifts me onto the horse, then joins me a heartbeat later.

I lean forward, trying to escape his warmth, his solid presence.

Aurelius grunts, shifts the reins to one hand, and presses the other against my lower belly, pulling me back against him.

"Quit fighting me, you stubborn female," he growls. "I'm keeping you upright."

I sigh, but stop struggling. I'm too tired.

For a few minutes, the steady beat of the horse and the warmth of his chest at my back lull me.

Then discomfort creeps in. I shift in the saddle, trying to ease the cramp building in my hip.

"For the love of gods," Aurelius groans. "Quit moving. There's only so far I can push my restraint."

The unmistakable pressure against my lower back tells me I've already pushed him further than I intended. My core heats, irritation rising at my body's involuntary response.

I don't even try to fight the snark that fills my voice as I retort, "This saddle wasn't made for two people, Aurelius."

Aurelius tightens his grip, pressing firmly against my navel to hold me still.

"If you don't quit moving," he warns, voice low. "I'll have you riding something other than this horse by the time we reach the castle."

"Unless it's my own hand, I'm not interested," I deadpan.

He chuckles darkly, hot breath fanning my ear. "Your body, your *scent*, tells me otherwise."

"Maybe so," I snap. "But my heart and my mind are unequivocally clear. I may enjoy your body, Aurelius, but I certainly don't need you."

The rest of the ride is silent.

When we reach the castle gates, Ayden is waiting, tense and grim.

"How is she?" I ask before my feet even hit the ground.

"Stable. The physician is with her now until my healer can arrive. She'll survive."

Relief sags my shoulders. I let out a breath I didn't even know I was holding.

"Thank the gods."

Ayden catches me when I stumble, steadying me with his hands at my waist. "Easy, love."

"Sorry," I whisper. "Adrenaline crash."

"Let's get you a bath and some rest," Ayden makes a show of pressing a kiss to my hair as he leads me inside.

Later, clean and warm under heavy covers, Ayden sits beside my bed.

"I enjoyed today," he says softly, "despite how it turned out."

I smile despite myself. "I did too."

"Good." He smirks. "Rest up. There was something else I had planned for today, but you'll need your energy."

I narrow my eyes at him. "What is that?"

He just winks. "You'll just have to wait and see."

"Whatever." I yawn. "I'll find out sooner or later."

I don't even hear the door click closed before sleep claims me.

CHAPTER SIXTEEN

BREYLA

My shoulder pops as I throw it across my chest, stretching it out. I repeat the motion on the other side, then move to my legs. It's been too long since I felt the strain of a solid sparring session, and gods, I'm looking forward to it.

"Why the private training room, Ayden?" I ask, scanning the empty space. "Afraid to have your ass kicked in front of your soldiers?"

"Hardly, love," he says, mirroring my stretches. "I take my rare losses with grace and humility."

"Yes, because humble is the first word that comes to mind when I think of you."

"We're in this room because I wanted to ensure you had privacy," Ayden continues, rolling his head side to side until it pops loudly.

I stretch my arm up and behind my head, connecting it with my opposite hand behind my back. "Why would I need privacy? I spar all the time."

"Because we're not just sparring," he says easily, lunging forward to stretch his thighs. "I'm getting to know you."

I mimic him, arching a brow. "Oh?"

"Remember when I said you'd need your energy for what I had

planned the other day?" His grin is pure mischief. "This is what I actually had planned."

I think back to two days ago when Ayden had taken me to his favorite breakfast spot in Elentia. It had started with unexpected enjoyment and ended in near tragedy. Rochelle had lived, Ayden's healer reaching her in time to save her leg. She returned home to her family yesterday.

I snort. "Let me get this straight—you plan to court me by fighting me?"

He winks. "I want to see you in your element. I figured I could observe you where you're most comfortable and ask questions as we go."

"Alright, I'll play along. But I get to ask you questions as well," I demand, pointing a finger at him.

"Of course."

I fall into a defensive stance, weight on my toes, waiting for him to make the first move.

He strikes fast, a punch flying toward my chest. I deflect easily, spinning out of his reach and throwing a sharp jab at his shoulder.

"What's your favorite color?" he asks, catching my forearm before my punch can land.

I tear my arm free, dancing back. "Deep green."

"Not just green?"

"No." I lunge, throwing a punch that glances off his cheek. "Green like the color of pine needles."

He sucks in a breath, wiping a thumb across his lip. It comes away red, wet with the blood of a split lip.

I bite back a smirk. "What is your favorite color?"

"Navy blue—like the midnight sky on a full moon."

He sweeps his leg toward mine, aiming low. I barely leap clear, nearly losing my balance in the process.

Ayden seizes the opportunity, tackling me to the ground.

"What's your favorite food?" he asks as he wrestles my arms above my head, pinning me.

"Getting real deep now," I tease, twisting my hips. While he's distracted trying to control my hands, I wrap my legs around his hips and roll him beneath me. "Roasted lamb." I grin down at him. "But cheesecake is my weakness."

I don't waste time trying to pin him. It's pointless. Instead, I wrap a hand lightly around his throat, squeezing just enough to make him uncomfortable. "Are you more of an ass or tits kind of male?"

He laughs, even under the pressure of my hand. "I'm an equal opportunist."

His strength is infuriating—and wildly attractive. He grabs my hips, rolling me again.

Breathing heavily, he straddles me again. "What's your fondest memory?"

A dozen memories come to mind. Dancing in the rain with Elijah, training with Jade and Julian for the first time, my parents' faces when they made me general. But one memory settles over me like a warm blanket.

"Learning to dance." I smile fondly. "My parents hired an instructor, but I was awful at first. I wanted to quit. Until I snuck out of bed one night and caught them dancing by candlelight. There was no music, no audience. Just pure, unadulterated love between them. The way they twirled and laughed in that silent room..."

Ayden's expression softens, real affection gleaming in his amber eyes. "That sounds..."

"Magical," I finish for him. I smile, small and aching. "It absolutely was. I didn't just want to dance like that. I wanted to love like that."

His gaze sharpens, more serious now. "And have you?"

"Have I what?"

"Loved like that?"

My breath hitches, something tight swelling in my chest. I turn my head away, breaking eye contact. "No."

Warm fingers catch my chin, gently coaxing me back to face him. "Let me love you like that," he pleads, his thumb brushing tenderly across my cheek.

I close my eyes, swallowing down the knot in my throat. "I don't know if that's possible."

"I believe anything is possible."

I sigh. "What a sickeningly optimistic view."

He chuckles. "It's better than whatever viewpoint you seem to have."

"I'm pragmatic."

"It's depressing."

I roll my eyes, grateful for the shift in tone. "Alright, you win this match. Let's go again."

He grins, pulling me to my feet.

We reset, and this time, I land a clean hit to his left eye.

"Oh, that's going to bruise," I say delightedly. "How do you look in purple?"

"I look good in everything, love." He cocks an eyebrow. "I look especially good in nothing."

I snort, circling him. "What's your most embarrassing memory?"

As he opens his mouth, I dart forward and land a punch to his gut.

"Ompf." He doubles over slightly, gasping.

I follow with a quick roundhouse kick that nearly topples him.

"The first time I bedded someone," he manages between breaths, "I was so drunk, I didn't know who I had taken to my bed."

"That doesn't sound that bad."

"It was a stableboy with a wicked sense of humor," he continues. His fist connects with my gut, and I double over as the breath leaves my lungs. "The next morning, I couldn't remember what had happened. He wouldn't tell me which of us had..." He muses, grinning wickedly as I dissolve into laughter.

"Well," I manage between gasps, "at least you're an equal opportunist *and* a good sport."

"See?" he says, flashing a bright, cocky grin. "You understand me. I suspect you're already falling for my charms."

I shake my head, wiping tears of laughter from my eyes. "Not a chance, Prince."

But gods help me... for just a moment, it almost feels easy to imagine a world where I could.

"So you didn't know who'd taken it up the ass?" I offer sweetly.

"Such a crude mouth," Ayden chastises, amusement sparkling in his amber eyes. "But yes."

"Did you ever find out?"

"No," he laughs, the sound unbothered. "To this day, I have no idea. But he made sure the whole palace knew how long, or rather, how short, it lasted."

"You're quick to arrive? Never would've guessed that," I muse.

My foot lands square against his chest, sending him stumbling backward. He trips over his own feet, and I pounce, pinning him by the wrists.

"I'm anything but *quick to arrive* now, love," he purrs, looking altogether too pleased. "Would you like to find out just how long I can last?"

"Hmmm," I pretend to consider it, tapping my chin.. "No. Better save the disappointment for our wedding night."

"Such a cruel female," Ayden mutters, grinning despite himself. "Alright, you've won this one."

I release him, climbing to my feet with a satisfied hum. "Would you like me to kick your ass again, Your Highness?"

"I wouldn't mind another," he says with a lazy shrug, pushing himself upright.

We spar again, harder this time. I land several solid hits, but by the end, we're both panting, our movements slowing.

"What was your favorite game as a child?" he asks, dodging a sloppy jab.

"Hide and seek," I reply, landing a hit to his shoulder.

"You would favor the goddess of war and strategy, wouldn't you?"

I shrug. "My parents used to say they should have named me after Kraenta."

He catches me off guard with a fist to my cheek. I hiss, heat flaring under my skin.

Despite the throbbing, it's obvious he pulled that punch.

Ayden freezes instantly, guilt flashing across his face. "Are you alright?"

I wipe the back of my hand across my mouth, tasting blood, and scowl. "Afraid to hit a female, Prince?"

"I'm not taking it easy on you, Princess," he insists, his voice hardening.

I drop my stance, folding my arms. "You pulled your punch just now."

He mirrors me, arms crossed over his chest. "I'm not leaving my fiancée with a black eye."

"It wouldn't be my first."

"That doesn't mean I'll ever be responsible for giving you one." His tone is flat, final.

Part of me knows I should appreciate the care in his words, but it just pisses me off. I don't want to be protected. I want to be respected.

My fists clench, nails biting into my palms.

"What's the matter?" It's meant as a taunt, but bitterness leaks into my voice. "Afraid to leave a mark on a female?"

Ayden smirks, his eyes darkening.

Slowly, he backs me toward the wall. Bracing one arm beside my head, he leans in close and whispers, "I much prefer to leave my marks by other means."

His scent, woodsy citrus, and the faint salt of sweat wrap around me. I feel it like a physical touch, shivering down my spine.

Annoyed at my body's reaction, I bark a laugh and knee him in the groin. "No thanks, minute-male."

Ayden doubles over with a grunt. "Fucking dirty, Princess."

I shrug innocently. "Better luck next time, Prince," I call over my shoulder as I leave the training room.

All I can think about as I make the walk back to my room is how good a bath sounds. The sweat has begun to dry, and my cheek is warm and swelling from Ayden's hit. The burn in my muscles is a welcome relief, though. Endorphins flood my system from the workout, and I'm riding the high.

The castle corridors blur as I walk, staff and courtiers parting around me.

I barely register the voice that stops me.

"Princess Breyla, are you quite alright?" Queen Josephina's voice cuts through my haze.

I turn sharply. "Yes. Why wouldn't I be?"

"Ah, dear," She gestures delicately at her lower lip. "You do know you're bleeding, don't you?"

I swipe my tongue across my own and taste copper. "And you smell like sweat," Lady Charlotte adds, wrinkling her nose.

Curling my lips into a saccharine smile, faux kindness fills my voice as I say, "Oh, I had no idea, Charlotte." I press a hand to my heart, tipping my head in mock gratitude. "Thank you for pointing out to me what sweat smells like."

Charlotte rolls her eyes dramatically. "I'll never understand what Ayden sees in you."

"And I'll never understand what Aurelius sees, excuse me, what he *saw* in you," I reply without missing a beat.

Her cheeks flush an ugly shade of red, blue eyes narrowing as she fumbles to come up with an appropriate response.

"Ladies, let's not fight and insult one another." Queen Josephina places a hand on my shoulder, squeezing gently. "I need for us all to get along. We are to be family after all."

All the fight leaves my body; my desire to hurt Charlotte, verbally or otherwise, is gone in an instant.

"Very well," I relent. "I'll be off. I'm in need of a bath."

The queen's hand tightens on my arm. "Breyla, wait."

"Yes?"

"I would like you to join Charlotte and me for tea soon," she suggests, far too pleasantly. "Perhaps we could discuss plans for your nuptials over needlepoint?"

Pure terror flashes across my face.

"I, absolutely—" I begin to protest.

"I insist," the queen interrupts, her words firm as a familiar heaviness settles over me.

I want to resist and turn down her invitation, but I feel incapable of disobeying as I mumble, "As you wish."

The queen smiles softly. Charlotte smirks in triumph.

"Very well. I look forward to it," Queen Josephina says, releasing me.

The moment her hand falls away, the heaviness lifts, but the sour taste of it lingers.

Without another word, I whirl away.

Needlepoint? What did I just agree to?

I rush back to my chambers to avoid making any further unpleasant plans with people I don't care for.

If I hurry, I might just beat Ayden to his rooms. If I can slip past the guards unseen, I can break into his chambers and finally steal back my clothing.

As I turn the corner, I collide straight into a wall of solid muscle.

Aurelius.

"Whoa there, Princess." His hands close around my shoulders, steadying me before I topple over. "Why are you in such a hurry?"

The warmth of his hands feels good against my rapidly cooling skin. The sweat has dried, leaving me chilled thanks to the season's dropping temperature.

"I'm trying to avoid making questionable decisions," I mutter, my flesh pebbling beneath his touch, and I'm reminded of a sobering truth. "You happen to fall in that category as well, so if you'll excuse me."

I tug my shoulders free, moving to pass him. Before I can escape, his arm snakes around my waist, pulling me flush against his body, pinning me to the nearest wall.

I suck in a ragged breath.

Aurelius presses into me, his body a living furnace.

"Aurelius, please." I pray my restraint holds out, because right now I really want to keep savoring him.

His nose brushes my neck as he inhales deeply—and then he growls, low and furious. "You smell like *him.*"

"You mean I smell like my *betrothed,*" I correct, coldly.

He rears back enough for me to see the anger flashing in his eyes. "Why?"

"We sparred," I say simply, even though I owe him no explanation.

Dark eyes roam my body, searching for injuries. They land on my face, the swelling more prominent, a steady pulse beating in my cheek. He brushes his thumb over my split lip, then the mark just below my eye. "He marked you," Aurelius accuses, voice rough. "Hurt you."

"That is a typical hazard of sparring, Aurelius. Besides–" I lift my chin. "I got him far worse for pulling his punches."

His nostrils flare, fingers tightening around my throat. Not choking, just claiming. "I do not like his marks on your skin."

"What?" I shake my head. "It's only acceptable when it's you leaving them?"

His wicked smile sends a shiver through me. "My marks are different, little demon, and you know it."

His thigh presses between my legs, grinding slowly and deliberately against my core.

I gasp, clutching his tunic, my restraint slipping.

"Your marks mean nothing, Aurelius," I whisper, even as my body betrays me.

Aurelius' lips graze my ear. "Is that so? If they truly mean nothing, then perhaps I leave one—" His thumb strokes over the pulse at my throat. "—and we'll see just how meaningless your betrothed finds it?"

My heartbeat quickens. Heat pools in my core, thighs tightening instinctively around his leg as he rolls his hips ever so slightly. Chest heaving, I struggle to remember why this is a bad idea.

I hate him for knowing how to unravel me so easily.

Ice douses the heat between us by the sound of clicking heels a few feet away. Aurelius steps back just as a maid rounds the corner. She's one of Queen Josephina's. She nearly collides with him, cheeks pink as she drops into a quick curtsy.

There's nothing overtly damning about our position, but anyone with half a brain could sense the tension between us.

"Pardon me, My Prince," the maid says sweetly. "I did not see you there."

"That's quite all right, Nell. No harm done," Aurelius replies smoothly, straightening his tunic and patting her shoulder with calculated casualness.

She lingers, casting curious glances between us.

I clear my throat. "Is there something you need from one of us?"

Nell looks sheepishly at the floor. "I was fetching something for the queen, but I can't remember what it is now." She shuffles her feet. "I'll just be on my way."

She scurries off.

"On that note," I say, shoving off the wall, "I have a room to break into and clothing to steal."

"Let me help you," Aurelius calls as I move down the hallway.

"That's not necessary," I toss over my shoulder, forcing my pace faster to put as much distance as possible between myself and the disaster he represents.

If I hurry, I might even salvage my afternoon—retrieve my stolen clothing, drown myself in a bath, and pretend for just a few minutes that my heart isn't still trying to claw its way out of my chest.

CHAPTER SEVENTEEN

BREYLA

"**I** have a new book for you," Rowina says, dropping a heavy tome in front of me.

Aurelius had joined me this morning in the library, intent on sharing my space, regardless of my desire for the opposite. He sits across from me, lazily flipping through a book, its cover weathered and clearly well-read.

I had been reading through *The Genealogy of House Mordet* for a third time, trying to decipher if there was some hidden reason she had given it to me.

As far as I could tell, there wasn't.

"What's this?" I ask.

"It's the history of magic in the four kingdoms," Rowina explains.

I examine the title, flipping through a few pages. "These look like stories."

"What is history but a collection of stories?"

"No new reading assignment for me?" Aurelius teases.

"No," Rowina states, her tone cold. "Go find your own book, Prince."

It had been raining all morning, so Darian had canceled training, using the opportunity to check in with his troops stationed away from the capital.

Having nothing better to do, Ayden had joined us for library time.

"And what will you be reading today, Prince Ayden Liam Mordet II?" I ask, trying to keep the humor out of my voice.

His lip twitches at the use of his full name and title. "I see you've been paying attention to your reading."

"Well, what did you expect? You've left me with little else to do."

"If you're bored," Ayden purrs, "I can think of a few things to occupy your time." His sultry tone should make me weak in the knees, but I'd grown accustomed to the flirting and filthy words that seemed to be a part of all the Mordet children.

I was starting to wonder if dirty talk was a new category of magical Gifts that went unrecorded in history.

I yawn, the rain lulling me into a tired contentment. "No thanks."

I turn my attention back to the book in front of me, consuming the history I had already learned as an adolescent.

The Fall of Magic

When the Fae first arrived in the kingdoms of Prudia, Rimor, Lennox, and Meloria, their beauty was unlike anything the humans had ever seen. The Fae were quick to display their superiority and power through magical Gifts.

It was soon discovered that the Fae could choose to bless humans with a piece of their Gifts, allowing them to wield magic. Over the years, humans began developing more Fae-like qualities. Their lives extended, often lasting well into two centuries. They became more resilient, quicker to heal, and possessed keener senses.

The humans became less... human, but not quite Fae. Their lives and abilities still paled in comparison to those of the Fae.

When the first occurrence of a Fae and human mating surfaced, it shocked both races. No one thought it possible, but no one could deny the couple's bond.

Mating bonds were thought to be unique to Fae. No records existed of it occurring between humans prior to this.

Yet it was clear the mated pair, Elythia and Myer, felt the bond as deeply as any other had before them.

Where the Fae had difficulty conceiving previously, no such problem existed between Fae and human mates. Elysia and Myer welcomed their first children, a daughter they named Olivia and a son named Finn, within a year of their bond settling.

The family lived in peace and happiness in the kingdom of Rimor, where Myer served as the hand of King Grayson Rozaria. Queen Amantia had been blessed with the Gift of vision—the most unstable and unreliable of Gifts, even for the Fae.

Just after the twins' second birthday, the queen received a vision of what Olivia and Finn might one day become. It was a vision that frightened her enough that she shared it with her husband.

The laws of Rimor stated that anyone could challenge the ruling family for the throne if they believed themselves strong enough to take it. Though the royal heirs had been born with Gifts, the Queen's vision told a story of Olivia and Finn far surpassing them in magical strength.

Though nothing suggested that either child would challenge the king, the threat was too much for King Grayson to tolerate.

Without warning or explanation, the babes were slaughtered in their sleep.

Myer begged Elythia to flee to her homeland to protect herself and the life of their unborn child. He promised to follow as soon as he had ensured the safety of the rest of his family.

Reluctantly, Elythia agreed, leaving their home that day. But she didn't immediately leave the capital. Fearing for her mate's life, she watched from the shadows.

After warning his parents and siblings, urging them to leave the city, Myer confronted his king. Trust had existed between the two males until this point, so he believed he could approach him before leaving the country for good.

He was wrong.

Elythia watched from the shadows as the cruel king executed her mate, followed by his entire family.

Her sorrow-filled screams echoed through the castle as half of her soul was ripped from her body.

Broken by the loss of her mate and children, she let the kingdom feel her grief. For Elythia carried one of the rarest and most powerful Gifts amongst the Fae—the ability to wield blood. The call of crimson was too much for her to ignore, and she gave in to the bloodlust.

Every guard in the room dropped dead, their hearts having given out under the pressure of her magic.

While holding the queen in place, Elythia made her watch as she boiled her husband's blood, slowly cooking him from the inside.

It was a slow and excruciating way to die, but Elythia felt no remorse.

When the king lay dead, she turned to the queen.

"From one mother to another, you should have stayed silent. My family was innocent. Your vision was wrong; my children would have never challenged for your pathetic human throne. They had one awaiting them in Tierna. I should slaughter yours in front of you, but I won't."

The queen tried to thank Elythia for her mercy, but no words would escape her lips. With one final snap of her fingers, every blood vessel in the queen's body burst.

"Ayden," I say, my voice shaking.

"Yes, Breyla?"

"Why does your history tell a different story than Rimor's?"

This wasn't the history we'd been taught about Myer and Elythia. Theirs was a cautionary tale against those who wished to commit treason against the crown.

It wasn't *this*.

"That," he gestures to the book, "is the truth of magic in our four kingdoms."

"Why does it read more like a journal entry than a historical document?"

"Because it is a journal entry," Ayden says simply. "Elythia wrote that, and her daughter brought it here when she left Tierna."

"This isn't how it's told in Rimor," I whisper. Shame and sadness fill me thinking of what my ancestors had allegedly done.

Aurelius returns from his search, new book in hand. "Not how what's told?"

"Your grandmother's tragic origin story," Ayden explains.

"Excuse me?" I stutter, just as Aurelius says, "You know who she is?"

"Perhaps we should start over from the beginning," Ayden suggests.

He spends the next several minutes recounting the story I had just read. My stomach drops when he gets to the part about them murdering Olivia and Finn.

If the story were true, there is nothing I can use to justify my ancestors slaughtering innocent children just because they might one day be powerful enough to challenge the ruling family.

"Why should we believe you?" Aurelius finally asks.

"You would know if I'm lying, and you can tell I'm not right now."

"I know you believe this to be the truth, but that doesn't mean it actually happened. History can be altered."

"And it has," Ayden replies, rubbing his temple. "*Rimor's* history was altered. What reason would I have to fabricate this?"

"I don't know," Aurelius sneers. "I don't pretend to know your reason for a lot of the things you do."

"To the best of my knowledge, this is the factual account of what happened to Myer and Elythia nearly eight hundred years ago." Ayden sighs. "But it doesn't stop there."

"There's more to this horror story?"

I had taken countless lives, both on and off the battlefield. Never an innocent, never on purpose. The thought of murdering babes in their cribs has me stifling a sob.

"There are details I'm unclear of, but I am relatively certain that Elythia had another child with another Fae and that child grew up to be your mother, Aurelius."

"W-what?" Aurelius stammers.

I narrow my eyes. "Why would you say that?"

"Because it was the last thing our father confessed before he died." Ayden pauses, a heavy silence filling the room. "I had to put some things together, but that was the most obvious conclusion."

"It's not obvious to me, so explain how you came to that conclusion," Aurelius replies.

"Father admitted that he had created a child with a beautiful traveling female, but held regret that you had become lost to him. Shortly after finding out she was carrying you, she disappeared, leaving my father heartbroken."

"What was her name?" Aurelius breathes.

"He never told me," Ayden admits. "But he said she was the most beautiful female he had ever seen. Long, raven black hair, violet eyes that almost seemed to glow red when her emotions were high."

The red in Aurelius' irises always seemed to glow when he felt strongly about something, be it pleasure, fury, or joy.

"The most remarkable thing about her was that she carried the Hemonia gift, which—"

"Is incredibly rare and passed exclusively through bloodlines," I cut in, the pieces clicking together in my mind.

"*Clever girl.* There's that beautiful mind at work," Ayden praises, causing a slight growl from Aurelius. Ignoring him, he continues, "As far as I can tell, there is only *one* family line recorded to have the Hemonia Gift—Elythia's."

My attention snags on the way he purrs the words *clever girl.* There's something so familiar about it that I can't place.

Aurelius runs a hand through his hair, mussing the loose black waves around his face. "So, what? You're saying I'm *Fae?*"

"Half-Fae," Ayden corrects.

"I don't believe it," I whisper.

"No?" Ayden's brow quirks. "Think about it, love. Has Aurelius ever done something he shouldn't have been able to? Displayed stronger than possible Gifts or abilities?"

I bite my lower lip, hesitant to travel down this path. "He shredded through my leathers like they were made of paper."

Aurelius smirks at the memory. "I've always been strong."

"You smell and hear things that others don't," I add.

"Like what?" Rowina asks.

"Nothi—"

"I can smell when she's aroused," Aurelius says unashamedly.

I rub my temples to assuage the growing headache this male creates for me. "Among other things," I mumble, avoiding eye contact.

"Face it, brother, you are related to Elythia," Rowina says.

"But how do you know she's my grandmother?" Aurelius asks.

Ayden drums his fingers against the polished wood table. "Call it an educated guess."

A beat of silence passes.

My brow furrows, a memory of something I read resurfacing. "The third child?"

"Ah, not quite," he replies. "That child was also named Elythia, and she died in Prudia nearly four hundred years ago."

Confusion mars both my and Aurelius' faces.

Then I remember the book on the Mordet family lineage. "Her name was in The Genealogy of House Mordet."

"Yes," Ayden confirms. "Not much is known about her, other than at some point she returned from Tierna and ended up marrying the prince of Prudia, to then later become queen."

"So, then you two…" My eyes dart between Ayden and Rowina. "Are also part Fae."

Ayden nods. "Less so than Aurelius, but we do have Fae blood."

"How do you think we got to be so beautiful and charming?" Rowina asks, waggling her eyebrows.

"That explains so much." I laugh.

"Yet I still have so many questions," Aurelius says.

I page through Elythia's journal. "This altered history, is it why the Fae disappeared?"

"This is why Elythia left, but I do not believe that is why all Fae vanished," Ayden says, flipping the book in front of me to a new section. "If I had to guess, I would say it had more to do with this."

"The prophecy of crimson and shadows," I read aloud.

> *"Born of blood and bone*
> *A son of two kingdoms*
> *Forged of sorrow and shadow*
> *A daughter of secrets*
> *When two become one*
> *The flames will drown in salt*
> *The crimson prince and the queen of shadows will fall*
> *When the darkness comes*
> *The royal line will know her fury*
> *And the world will feel the sorrow of shadows"*

"The crimson prince and the queen of shadows will fall," Aurelius murmurs.

My stomach churns at the familiarity of those words. "That's the warning note that was left pinned to Julian's body."

"You're sure it was those exact words?" Ayden asks, his voice tightening.

The image of Julian's decaying body nailed to a cross was seared into my mind, etched there permanently, waiting for me behind every blink, every breath. "I'm sure."

Ayden remains quiet, but the look he gives me—sharp, calculating, deeply concerned—says more than words.

Later, when the others have long since left the library, Ayden grips my shoulders, leaning down so close I can feel the weight of his stare.

"Love, it's time for you and me to have a talk."

"I'm exhausted from talking, Ayden," I sigh, closing my book and pushing it away. My limbs feel heavy, my heart heavier.

"That's fine," he says, shoving an apple into my hands. "Eat and I'll talk while you listen."

Too tired to argue, I take a bite. The sweet, tart juice floods my mouth, and I nearly groan aloud at how good it tastes after hours of sitting still.

"Your second Gift is weak," Ayden blurts out.

I freeze, still mid-bite, leveling a glare at him over the apple.

"I don't—" I start, but he snorts, cutting me off.

"You can't deny it, darling. I assume it's not common knowledge, if your reaction is anything to go off."

My jaw tightens. "And what do you think this supposed second Gift is?"

"I caught your projection the day you ransacked my rooms for evidence." He leans back casually, like we're discussing the weather.

I try to play it off, taking another slow bite. "I don't know what you mean, Prince. I was in that room the entire time."

"No, you weren't." Ayden levels me with a serious look, daring me to challenge him. "Not really. One moment you were sitting at a table, then you were on the floor."

I sigh, knowing I've been caught. "What do you want, Ayden?"

"Answers."

"Fine." I set the apple down. "Outside of this room, only Elijah and Jade know about my Vizie Gift. I can astral project."

His eyes narrow slightly, thoughtful. "You're so talented with shadows. Why haven't you mastered this?"

"Insensitive, much?"

"You're not a sensitive female, love. Stop pretending my words hurt you."

Despite myself, I let out a short laugh. "The Gift came much later than my shadows. I was twenty-two. My only teacher was… my father."

The admission makes me feel weak.

"So why didn't he?" Ayden asks, brushing over the fact that I revealed a secret very few knew.

My father's Gifts were rare and kept hidden. His earth-wielding was common knowledge. What fewer knew about were his *other* abilities. One of them being astral projection. When he was betrothed to my mother, it caused quite the uproar amongst the nobility since almost none of them knew he even possessed a second Gift, let alone a third.

"He had started, but we had so little time to train, and it was never high on the priority list. Then he… died."

A long pause.

"I'm sorry, Breyla, but that's unacceptable," Ayden says softly, but firmly.

My eyes snap to his. "Excuse me?"

"I refuse to let you settle for less than your full potential."

"I have no one to help, Ayden."

"That's where you're wrong," he says, grinning now. "I can help you."

Suspicion floods me. "More secrets, Prince?"

He pulls me to my feet. "I'll show you mine if you show me yours."

"You can astral project?"

"Not exactly." He steps behind me, wrapping one arm lightly around my waist. "Close your eyes."

Against better judgment, I obey. "Now what?"

"You still feel me wrapped around you?"

"Yes."

"Good. Open your eyes."

When I do, he's standing in front of me *and* still wrapped around me from behind. I gasp, reaching out to touch his face and find he's solid.

"What is this?" I whisper.

"It's an illusion, darling." His form in front of me smirks, while the arm at my waist gives a playful squeeze.

"But you're solid," I sputter. "How?"

"Part Fae, remember? That makes me special."

I roll my eyes. "You're something alright."

"I'm being serious. Mine and Rowina's Gifts are stronger than most because of our blood. I can cast multiple illusions at once and control whether they are corporeal or not."

"Holy shit," I breathe.

"I thought you might say that."

"This is amazing, but how are you going to help me? They aren't the same Gift."

"No, they aren't the same," he agrees. "But they're similar enough that I can. And you need all the help you can get."

I shove my elbow into his stomach behind me, making him grunt. "Don't be rude. It's unbecoming of a prince."

"You are the definition of what is unbecoming for a princess," he retorts easily.

"Now you're just being crass."

"No, I'm being honest. Neither of us really cares what's unbecoming for our station, now do we?"

I huff a reluctant laugh. "I hate that we have anything in common."

"Stop lying, Princess." His illusion in front of me disappears, and he releases me, stepping away.

"So, how are you going to help me?"

"First, I'll train you how to recognize illusions."

"What are the signs?"

"There aren't any." Ayden smirks, his eyes dancing with delight.

I roll my eyes. "Well, that certainly makes things easier."

"It's more about feeling your environment, listening to your intuition and gut when they tell you something is off."

"I don't know if I trust my intuition right now."

"There's nothing wrong with your intuition, Breyla," Ayden says, tone firm. "The problem is you've been ignoring it."

I hate it, but I know he's right.

"My head says not to trust you, but my intuition disagrees."

"Good. Never blindly trust anyone." He grins. "You can trust me with this, though."

I hesitate, then nod. "Let's try, then. Give me an illusion and let me see if I can tell the difference."

"Close your eyes."

I comply, waiting for him to give me a signal to open them.

After a few moments, he says, "Open."

When I open them again, he holds two identical parchment rolls in each hand. I reach out and run my fingers over both. They feel identical, and I see no visible differences.

I'm at a loss and make a guess, grabbing the one in his right hand. "This one?" I ask.

"No," he says, and the illusion evaporates.

We try three more times, and I get one of them right, but it's pure luck, and he knows it. I have no idea which one is the illusion.

"Come on, Breyla," Ayden says, pushing. "I know you can do this."

I try again. I fail again.

"I'm exhausted," I groan, throwing my hands up. "This is pointless."

"No, this is not pointless. This is crucial."

"Why, though? Why is it so important for me to know this?" My gut is telling me there is something else going on, something he's not telling me.

"It could save your life someday."

"Whatever," I yawn. "I'm done for the night."

"Take this seriously," Ayden snaps, sharper than I've ever heard from him.

"I am taking this seriously!" I shout back. "But I'm exhausted and mentally depleted after everything. I've hit my limit today. "

"I'm sorry, love." His face softens, voice dropping. "That was a bit harsh of me. I understand you're tired, so we'll resume this in a few days."

"Thank you," I nod, half in apology. Another yawn escapes me.

"How about I make a deal with you?" he says suddenly.

I eye him curiously. "What kind of deal?"

"Starting tomorrow, I'll start using illusions around you. For every one you catch, you get a piece of your clothing back."

"Deal," I say immediately.

"I'm not done yet. Be careful how quickly you agree to things," he says, holding up his hand. "Think about all our encounters in the past. If you can correctly name all the times I used one around you, then I'll return your entire trunk."

"This seems like a pretty lucrative deal for me."

His eyes sparkle with mischievousness. "For every time you miss an illusion or are wrong, you owe me a kiss. On the lips, to be specific."

"I suddenly like this deal a lot less," I grunt.

"Your choice, Princess." He smirks. "Do you want your pants back?"

I hesitate for only a second. "My intuition says this is an incredibly bad idea."

"Are you going to start listening to it?" Ayden asks.

"Not on this," I sigh. "I hate these dresses and want my clothing back too damn bad. You have a deal."

He leans in closer, tilting my chin up to him. "You know, we typically seal deals in Prudia with a kiss."

I dodge out of range before he can try. "Not a chance, asshole. I'm going to bed," I call over my shoulder as I head for the door.

Behind me, his laughter follows.

CHAPTER EIGHTEEN

OPHELIA

My skin blisters and cracks as lightning races through my muscles, filling me with a familiar and bitter pain. A nauseatingly sweet scent permeates the air from the blackened flesh of my arms.

"You stupid, worthless female," my father hisses. "Layne was the only child worth anything, and now he's dead because of you."

I gasp, fighting to stay conscious through the pain. Words are impossible, so I let him rattle on.

"Layne's Gift was at least useful in negotiating trade and alliances. You can't even create a Faerie light," he sneers. "I could've at least used you to secure an alliance through marriage, but you had to go and give yourself to the court whore."

I can take his insults and attacks on me. But Elijah? No. He needs to leave Elijah out of it.

A surge of strength fills me, and I stand abruptly. My fingers wrap around his throat and begin squeezing.

The scene shifts.

My hand is no longer around my father's neck, but Layne's. His skin withers, going grey, the life draining out of him.

"No!" I shriek, realizing what I've done. I release my grip on his neck, and his body drops to the floor. Blank eyes stare up at me.

Knock.

"Lord Elijah," a muffled voice calls, dragging me out of my dream.

"Eli," I whisper, nudging his sleeping form behind me.

He nuzzles his face into the crook of my neck, tightening his arms around me.

Another knock, louder this time.

"Elijah, someone needs you," I say again, trying to pull his arm away.

"Oh yeah, baby?" he whispers, rolling his already hard length against my backside.

Warmth spreads through me at his arousal, lighting every nerve ending. "I'm not talking about me."

"Are you sure about that?" He runs a hand up my thigh to my center, his fingers trailing lightly over my sex. "I think if I dip my fingers into your pretty pussy I'll find it ready for me."

"Lord Elijah, this is urgent," the voice yells.

Groaning, Elijah pulls away and throws the blankets off. "Fuck Breyla for leaving us in charge. I never got woken up in the middle of the night before."

He pulls a robe and stalks toward the door. Before he opens it, he shoots me a look that promises this isn't over.

I bite my lip, shivers running through me at the silent vow in his eyes.

The door flies open, revealing a disheveled guard.

"What is it, Samson?" Elijah asks.

"General Jade just sent word. We're experiencing multiple attacks along the border."

"Which border?"

"All of them."

"Hold on," Elijah says, closing his eyes. His brow creases for a heartbeat before he opens them again, sharp and clear. "Say that again for me."

"Rimor is experiencing multiple attacks along each border right now," Samson repeats.

"How many casualties?" Elijah asks.

"Our best guess is several dozen so far, but it's hard to say for sure."

"Are any of those civilians?"

Samson swallows hard, his eyes dropping to the floor for a brief moment before shooting back to Elijah. "A few."

My heart sinks at the thought of innocent lives being lost.

"Send three hundred soldiers from the capital and divide them between each border," Elijah commands Samson.

"Yes, sir," Samson acknowledges. "And the refugees?"

"There are refugees?"

"General Jade evacuated Caedel after it began burning. The entire city will be here within the week."

"How many?"

"A thousand give or take."

"Dammit," Elijah sighs, rubbing his jaw. "When the staff wakes, call a meeting. Let them know what's happened and have them begin preparations. They'll need to ready all the guest wings and the main hall for the survivors. If that's not enough, we'll have to use the inns and the brothel."

"Understood. Thank you, Lord Elijah." Samson bows and leaves.

The door clicks shut softly, leaving us alone.

Elijah sighs and turns to me. "Fuck you, B. Tell Ayden I'll punch him in the godsdamned face for taking you from Rimor and leaving me to do this without you." He isn't talking to me, but Breyla, somehow. "I love you, though. Good night."

He shakes his head, refocusing his gaze on me.

"So where were we?" Elijah asks, prowling toward the bed, a hungry gleam in his eyes.

"Uh uh." I shake my head. "We're circling back to what I just saw you do."

"That party trick?" he asks, cocking his head slightly. "With those I have a strong connection, I can allow them to see through my eyes for short periods. It's one-way, so they can see and hear everything I do, but I can't hear or see anything from them. It's how I communicate with Breyla at a distance."

"Who knows you can do this?" I ask.

"Breyla and Jade. And now you," he says, climbing into bed and straddling my hips.

He leans down, brushing light kisses along my neck, rolling his hard length against my center.

A soft whimper escapes before I catch it. I lace my fingers through his hair, tugging him gently back.

"Elijah, why am I just now learning about this?" I don't bother hiding the hurt in my voice.

"I'm sorry, doll." His eyes shift from heated to regretful in an instant. "I didn't even think about it. I wasn't keeping it from you. I just use it so rarely that it didn't occur to me to tell you."

"I share everything with you, Eli. I just want to know you as you do me," I whisper.

"I know you do, and I cherish you for trusting me with that." He cups my chin, kissing me softly. "Do you want to see how I see you?"

My heart answers before my mouth does. "Yes."

"Close your eyes and trust me."

I shut my eyes, exhaling slowly.

"You'll feel a pressure inside your head—that's me. Don't fight it."

A moment later, a foreign but not unpleasant sensation brushes my mind, like a hand caressing my thoughts. I tense briefly, then relax into it.

"Good," he praises, his voice low. "It should feel gentle, like a soft nudge. Keep your eyes closed, but let me in."

The soft caress grows, and an image begins to form behind my closed eyelids.

Black hair that almost glows blue in the moonlight ripples out around me on the bed, flushed pink cheeks, pale skin, and peach lips. It's like looking into a mirror with my eyes closed.

It's me, as he sees me.

"Do you see how beautiful you are?" Elijah whispers.

"I don't know about beautiful," I murmur. "But I see myself."

"Let me show you some of my favorite ways I see you," Elijah says, his voice thick with emotion.

"Okay," I breathe, keeping my eyes closed.

The view shifts, the perspective sliding away from my face and slowly down my body.

"What are you doing, Eli?" My voice trembles with uncertainty.

"Showing you one of my favorite views," he says, and I can hear the grin in his voice.

The image lowers, down my stomach, hovering over my hips. My breath catches as I feel his hands push up the hem of my nightgown, baring me to him.

The fabric slides over my hips, leaving me exposed.

I glimpse my navel as he lays a kiss there, then trails them languidly down to my pelvis.

The soft, dark curls come into view right as I feel his fingers brush lazily along my inner thigh. My legs are sharply pushed apart as the perspective changes once again.

I'm staring directly at my own sex, something I've never seen before.

Liquid heat pools in my core. The sight is somehow both erotic and overwhelming.

"Do you see that pretty pink pussy, darling?" Elijah murmurs. "How it's already glistening for me?"

A soft moan escapes my throat at his filthy words.

"Use your words," he growls.

"I see it," I whisper.

"Good," he praises, voice low and rough. "You're about to see a whole lot more."

That's all the warning I get before he dives straight into my center, his tongue licking a firm line from my opening to my clit.

I whimper and write against his mouth.

From the vision in my mind, all I see are the soft folds of my body, flushed and glistening.

The sight is still undeniably arousing.

He slides two thick fingers inside me, curling them with deliberate precision, while his tongue flicks and sucks at my clit.

He devours me as if I am his last meal, savoring every inch of my tender, swollen need.

I cry out when he changes the rhythm, thrusting his fingers deeper, then curling them hard against that hidden place inside me. His tongue circles and presses, never letting up.

Pleasure builds sharp and fast, and then detonates.

"Fuck, Ophelia," Elijah groans. "I wish my Gift worked with taste, too. I need you to taste how sweet you are."

The view shifts again. He looks up at me from between my thighs, his lips shiny with my release.

His fingers gather my slickness and lift it to my mouth. "Open."

Without hesitation, I part my lips, letting him slide his fingers inside. I suck them hungrily, savoring the tangy sweetness of myself.

A groan rumbles from his chest, and the next moment, he thrusts into me with a single, deep stroke

"Elijah," I gasp, stretching to take him in.

"Yes, baby?" he murmurs, rocking into me in slow, rolling thrusts.

"More," I beg.

He chuckles, the sound deep and sensuous. "You're going to watch yourself as I fuck you now."

"Yes," I pant. "Please."

"If you open your eyes before I tell you," he whispers.

Thrust.

"I will blindfold you and bind your hands."

Thrust.

"Then I'll turn you over my knee and spank your perfect ass until it matches the flush of your cheeks."

My core clenches at the image his words paint.

"Fuck," he pants. "You like that, don't you?"

"I shouldn't," I gasp, feeling him rock deeper inside me.

Not with all the pain I'd been dealt at the hands of my father.

"It's okay to like pain with your pleasure," Elijah utters softly. "Take control over the pain you allow, turn it into something beautiful, and rename it."

I blindly reach for him, my hands finding his neck. I pull him down, crashing our mouths together.

The vision goes dark as he closes his eyes to kiss me, nothing but the heat of him, the fierce way he claims my mouth, filling my senses.

He nips my bottom lip, soothing it with his tongue. For every hurt, he chases it with pleasure.

He pulls back, the vision reappearing in my head as he opens his eyes.

"Tell me what you want," Elijah demands, before lowering his mouth to my breast and sucking through the thin fabric.

"I want what you wouldn't give me the first time," I rasp.

"And what was that?" he taunts, teeth scraping gently.

"I don't want you to make love to me, Elijah." I rock my hips, silently begging. "I want to feel what it's like to be fucked hard by you."

A low growl reverberates through his chest and out of his lips. "Be careful what you wish for, baby."

"I know what I want," I say.

With a rip of fabric, my nightgown tears down the middle, baring my breasts to his heated gaze.

He groans, rolling one nipple between his fingers while he sucks the other deep into his mouth, hips pistoning hard into me.

Each thrust slams into the deepest parts of me, leaving me breathless, gasping his name.

My nails scratch at his back as he drives harder, filling me to the hilt.

Pleasure coils low in my belly, sharp and hot and inevitable.

Elijah's hand finds my clit, circling in slow, punishing strokes, sending me hurtling toward the edge.

I cry out, begging him to stop because I feel I can't handle the pleasure.

"Do you really want me to stop, darling?" he pants against my ear. "The way your pussy is clenching my cock says otherwise."

"No," I whimper. "It just, it feels like too much."

"You just need release," Elijah purrs, his hips rolling against mine. "So come for me, baby."

He thrusts twice more before the unmistakable tingle creeps up my spine.

"Open your eyes," he commands, "and keep them on me."

I obey instinctively, and see it all. Through his gaze.

The way my gray eyes brighten to silver when I'm about to come. The way my body trembles, flushed pink, writhing for him

"There are those beautiful grays I adore," he hums.

He gives my clit a gentle pinch, sending me over the edge into beautiful oblivion.

My body arches off the bed, clenching and pulsing around him, my cry raw and hoarse as he drives me through every wave of pleasure.

Through his eyes, I see it all.

The beauty. The wildness. The sheer, breathtaking need.

He thrusts a few more times before he finds his release as well, spilling hot seed into me, a deep groan tearing from his lips.

The connection between us fades as we both fight to even our breathing.

"Do you see now?" he pants.

"See what?" I ask, still dazed.

"Why I'm obsessed with that sight," he says, flashing a cocky grin that softens his perfect features.

I sigh. "I admit… that was pretty amazing."

"You're amazing," he counters, voice low and sure.

When he pulls out, I whimper at the loss of him. A few minutes later, he returns from the bathing room with a damp cloth in hand.

Elijah tenderly wipes the mess from between my thighs, the care in his touch making my chest ache. Tossing the cloth aside, he pulls me up into a sitting position in bed.

"Time to get you dressed," he says lightly, retrieving a brush from somewhere nearby.

He runs it softly through my hair, taming the loose waves that tumble around my shoulders.

"It's going to be a long day, isn't it?" I ask.

"A very long day, indeed," he says, planting a soft kiss atop my head.

"Elijah, can you tell me why my tavern rooms are full of people from Pelanor?" Luella asks, her hands planted firmly on her hips. "And why I can't get any of my usual shipments from Lennox?"

We have been holding court all morning, listening to the citizens air their grievances and requests for the crown's support. Some issues are trivial, land disputes, bickering between merchants, but others are far more troubling.

More than one farmer has mentioned livestock disappearing, or worse, being slaughtered outright.

"Did any of your patrons mention why they were in Ciyoria?" Elijah asks, his face neutral.

But from my spot beside him, I can see the tension in the way his muscles pull tight beneath his tunic.

"They said their crops started failing a month ago," Luella explains. "Then they heard of attacks at the borders and decided it was safer to leave. Or something like that." She shrugs. "Hard to keep it all straight with no shipments arriving this week."

Elijah rubs his jaw, troubled. "I'll come speak with them myself," he promises. "What goods are you missing?"

"Port and mead mostly. I rely on Caedel for beef, so hopefully I'll still be able to feed my patrons," Luella answers.

My stomach clenches, the news from this morning flashing through my mind.

"Caedel is—" I start.

"If you do not receive the beef this week, please let me know," Elijah cuts in smoothly. "For now, you may see Lord Jaeson for access to the royal wine cellars. The vintages may not be as good as Lennox's, but they'll get you by."

Luella nods. "Thank you, Elijah," she says before heading off to find Lord Jaeson.

As soon as she's gone, I turn sharply to Elijah. "Why did you keep the truth from her?"

He leans in, his voice pitched low. "Sometimes it's better if they don't know everything. Yet."

"They *deserve* to know, Elijah," I argue, my voice edged with scorn.

"I'm not saying they don't." His eyes are heavy with exhaustion. "But when the refugees arrive, the truth will come out soon enough. There is no need to incite uncertainty early."

"They should feel uncertain," I snap.

"It's the crown's duty to shield them from unnecessary fear," he replies calmly.

"By lying?" I scoff. "What happens when the beef never arrives?"

Elijah shrugs helplessly. "Then we feed them from the castle stores."

"We'll need that for refugees," I argue. "This isn't sustainable."

Elijah reaches for my hand, squeezing it reassuringly. "I know. This isn't a perfect solution. It's a temporary one. We'll find better answers as we go."

"For the record, I don't agree with this tactic," I mutter.

"And that's fine, Ophelia," he says, lifting my hand to his lips. "I don't want you to blindly agree with me. But no disagreements in front of the people, okay?"

Silently, I nod and drop my hands into my lap.

Several grueling hours later, we finally reach the last petitioner. My back aches from sitting, and my stomach growls loudly enough that Elijah smothers a laugh behind his hand.

The doors open, and in strides a male I've never seen before.

He's tall, easily the tallest I've met, with cinnamon colored hair and sharp teal eyes that gleam like a polished blade. He looks... furious.

"Cillian?" Elijah says, clearly surprised.

The male crosses the floor to the dais in four long strides and tosses a sack at Elijah's feet.

"I'm not your fucking guard dog, E," he says, irritation rolling off him like smoke.

"Of course you're not," Elijah says mildly, bending to inspect the sack.

He opens it cautiously, swearing beneath his breath just as I catch a glimpse of the contents.

It's a head. There's a severed head inside the sack.

"What an odd gesture," I murmur dryly, turning my gaze to the stranger—Cillian, apparently. "Who was it?"

Those teal eyes lock onto mine, roving over me with sharp, almost unsettling interest.

"A half-cracked mercenary I found trying to extort villagers," he says simply. "The better question is, who are *you?*"

"Lady Ophelia Delencourt," Elijah answers for me, eyes narrowing on the male. "This is Cillian, the King of The Midnight Brotherhood."

The name has me craning my neck to stare between them.

My eyes flare wide. "The assassins?"

A low, wicked chuckle escapes Cillian. "We're mercenaries, beautiful."

"That sounds like a pretty way of saying you kill for coin."

"Is that not what your soldiers do?" he asks, raising a brow.

"That's different," I argue stiffly.

"Is it?" he counters.

"Cillian," Elijah interrupts before the debate can escalate. "You're not exactly known for charity work. Why intervene?"

"Call it boredom." Cillian shrugs, inspecting his nails.

Elijah sighs. "What do you want?"

"My normal fee is one thousand Remis," he says lazily. "Or..." His lips curve into a wicked grin. "I'll settle for taking Lady Ophelia to dinner."

Heat creeps up my neck, but I fight the blush.

Elijah is on his feet in an instant, stepping between us. "She's not some whore you can barter for."

"If I thought she was a whore, I would've asked to fuck her," Cillian keeps his voice maddeningly even. "So, what do you say, beautiful?" he adds, locking eyes with me.

I stroll down the dais, meeting them both with a slow smile. Giving Cillian an appraising once over, I raise a brow.

The male is beautiful, I'll give him that.

"Sorry, but Elijah already promised to feed me," I say, yanking Elijah down by the front of his tunic. Our lips crash together, and he kisses me with the kind of desperation that borders on feral.

To drive the point home, I run a hand down his chest and over the front of his trousers, feeling him harden under my touch.

A low, possessive growl rumbles from Elijah's chest as he catches my wrist and pins it against his chest.

Message received.

Breaking the kiss, I whisper against his lips, "Delicious."

"Behave," Elijah warns with a dark look, before turning back to Cillian. "Does that answer your question?

Cillian laughs, a deep and hearty sound. "Oh yes, but it also created several more. Unfortunately, there is still the matter of payment."

"Name something else," Elijah demands, his tone tight.

"How about a drink," Cillian suggests, "and a few truths?"

My brow furrows at the price he asks.

"In my line of work," Cillian continues, "secrets, information, and truths are worth just as much as gold."

"Fine," Elijah grunts. "But I'm going to need a lot more than one drink." Wrapping an arm around my waist, he tucks me into his side and leads us to the great hall's side door as he calls, "You coming, Cillian?"

Cillian catches up easily, even beating us to the door and pulling it open with a smirk.

I study him casually, noting the scar that bisects his brow. Somehow, it makes his striking eyes stand out even more. A light spattering of freckles dots the bridge of his nose, not quite as prominent as Breyla's but still unusual for this region. Other scars cover his arms, a physical representation of the life he leads. They do nothing to diminish his handsomeness.

"Where are we going?" I ask, as we wander the halls.

"I was thinking the library," Elijah replies.

I smile. "Fine by me."

On the way, we detour through the kitchen, commandeering wine and leftover dinner. By the time we reach the library, I'm nearly feral with hunger.

I attack the roast chicken, finishing it quickly, and take a long pull from my glass of wine.

"Gods who knew listening to people talk could make me so hungry," I say, wiping the wine from my lips.

Elijah bursts out into laughter, leaving both Cillian and me staring at him in confusion. When he finally catches his breath, he wheezes, "It's not court that made you so hungry, doll. It's what we did instead of breakfast this morning."

My cheeks flush. Did he really just suggest that having sex is what made me so ravenous?

"Oh, gods you're adorable." Elijah grins. "I really forget how innocent you still are."

Cillian chuckles, clearly enjoying my mortification.

"There's blood on my hands," I mumble, glaring at both of them. "So I'm not sure how innocent that makes me."

"Blood, you say?" Cillian asks, his interest clearly piqued.

"Restrain yourself," Elijah snaps, shooting Cillian a look. "It was justified, and no literal blood was spilled."

"It's best not to mention blood around this one," he adds, jerking his thumb at Cillian. "If you thought I was filthy in bed, you haven't seen this lunatic after a kill."

"Whatever," Cillian huffs. "Ruin my fun,"

Elijah refills his wineglass before turning serious. "Ask your questions, Cill."

"Why is Breyla in Prudia while Rimor crumbles?" Cillian demands bluntly.

"The late King Raynor signed a marriage agreement with Prince Ayden II before his death," Elijah explains. "The prince honored the contract and retrieved his bride, just as everything fell apart. She had no choice if she wanted to maintain peace between our two countries."

I continue sipping wine silently, letting the two males volley information back and forth.

"So it wasn't of her own desire, then," Cillian muses.

"Not even a little," I add, finishing my wine.

"And why," Cillian continues, "would the late king's brother accompany her?"

"There are two reasons," Elijah answers. "One, you know damn well he's her lover. Prince Ayden's no fool. He knew if he didn't bring Aurelius, the male would cause a much bigger scene trying to reach her."

"And the second reason?"

"Because Aurelius is Ayden's half-brother," Elijah sighs, taking another drink of his wine. "Technically, he's an heir to Prudia's throne, if the court acknowledges him."

Shock flashes across Cillian's face, but he masks it quickly.

"Breyla sure knows how to pick them," Cillian mutters, refilling both our glasses.

"What's your next question?" Elijah asks.

"If this marriage was to bring peace, why the fuck is Prudia attacking our western border?"

A muscle ticks in Elijah's jaw as he fights the urge to spill everything.

"We're not convinced it is Prudia," he finally says. "It wouldn't serve them to attack the kingdom they just allied with."

"Agreed," Cillian says, "but they should at least be helping defend it."

"You care an awful lot for someone who stands to profit from the situation," Elijah notes.

"I don't want to see Rimor fall," Cillian replies evenly. "Just because we fall on opposite sides of the law doesn't mean I don't care for this kingdom."

"Have you had your fill of truths for tonight?" I cut in, my head pleasantly buzzing from the wine.

Cillian smirks at me. "For now."

"Then let's have another and speak of lighter things," I suggest, tipping back my glass.

Elijah downs the rest of his glass. "That sounds like a great idea, doll."

Several drinks later, my head is swimming, and I lay it against Elijah's shoulder. The low rumble of his laughter vibrates against my cheek, and I smile. He pulls my head into his lap, his fingers stroking my hair with a comforting rhythm. The simple touch pulls me back to memories of my mother and Layne doing the same once upon a time.

Instead of sadness, a strange, peaceful warmth fills me.

I drift, half asleep, while the two men continue talking like old friends. It isn't until I hear Breyla's name that I rouse a little.

"You still love her, don't you?" Elijah asks.

A tense beat of silence. Then Cillian answers, voice rough, "I never stopped."

Elijah sighs. "But she did."

"Which she made abundantly clear the last time I saw her," Cillian admits, something broken threading through his tone.

"It was your own doing, you know that, right?" Elijah says, not unkindly.

"I've known that from the moment I lost her, Elijah," Cillian says softly. "Why do you think I put my blade through his throat?"

"I always suspected you were behind that," Elijah muses. "It never made sense how he was killed so easily in his own home."

"He deserved worse," Cillian mutters. "He forced me into this life. Forced me to lie to her."

"Males like us do dangerous things for those we care about."

"And you would too, if you knew the depth of what I felt for her," Cillian replies. "Maybe you already do."

Their conversation blurs as sleep finally claims me, but I still catch the last few lines.

"So, she's yours, then?" Cillian asks.

"She is," Elijah says. His voice is steady, but layered with emotions I can't quite untangle. "At least for..."

But I don't hear the end.
Darkness pulls me under.

CHAPTER NINETEEN

Deep, petrifying panic fills my veins, violently ripping me from sleep. My chest rises and falls in sharp, shallow bursts as I scan the room, searching for the source of the threat.

It's still dark outside. The soft moonlight filters through the single window, painting the stone walls in a pale glow.

My Hemonia Gift kicks in automatically, searching for any other heartbeats nearby.

Nothing.

No intruder, no danger I can see.

So why does my body feel strung tight, like a bow ready to snap?

Another wave of panic crashes into me, even stronger this time. It feels...foreign. My mind is calm, but my body is wound so tight it's painful.

I rub at my sternum, trying to settle the erratic thudding beneath my ribs. When that does nothing, I throw back the covers and stand. There'll be no sleeping until I figure this out.

I head into the halls, the castle eerily quiet at this hour.

Letting my steps guide me, I roam aimlessly at first, until a few turns bring me to the royal wing.

"Might as well get some reading in," I mutter, feigning casualness even though my feet are already steering me toward the library Breyla favors.

I don't get far.

Raised voices echo from further down the corridor, the sharp edge of distress cutting through the air.

Breyla.

Instinct overrides thought. I sprint toward the sound, every nightmare I've ever had of her bleeding out rushing back to the forefront of my mind.

The sight that greets me is vastly different, though.

I reach Ayden's door, cracked open and spilling warm light into the hallway. Expecting the worst, I push the door wide open.

Breyla stands pressed against Ayden, a shadow dagger poised at his throat.

Ayden, to his credit, looks concerned but not afraid. His body stays relaxed, nonthreatening, as if he knows she's not truly lost to the rage.

I remain silent, observing the interaction between the two people who don't seem to notice me.

"I need answers, Ayden," Breyla snarls, her voice trembling at the edges.

"And I would love to give them to you," Ayden replies, surprisingly calm. "But I don't know everything you're asking."

"Then you better start talking before I shove this dagger through your heart, Prince," Breyla threatens. "Peace be damned, I will do it."

There's fear beneath her fury—raw, shaking fear.

Ayden swallows. "I believe you mean that." His gaze flicks over Breyla's shoulder and finds me. "Aurelius is here now. He can tell you if I'm lying."

She doesn't move, her grip on the shadow dagger tightening.

Slowly, carefully, I step forward. I lay a gentle hand on her shoulder, feeling the tension vibrating through her skin.

"Lower the knife, little demon," I murmur close to her ear. "Killing the prince would cause a war none of us wants. Whatever he's done, we'll sort it out together."

For a long moment, she stays rigid. Then, blessedly, she softens under my hand.

"Please, love," Ayden says, voice low. "I'm not fighting you. Drop the dagger, and I'll answer anything you want to ask."

I move carefully, wrapping my hand around her wrist, applying just enough pressure to lower her arm. She lets me.

Ayden exhales deeply, relief flooding his face.

I could have locked her body in place with my Hemonia Gift if I had to. But I didn't want that.

I wanted her to choose mercy for herself.

"Good girl," I whisper into her hair.

Breyla rewards me with a sharp glare, but I'll take that over tears or regret any day.

"Talk to us, Princess," Ayden says, his tone softer now. "Tell me what you heard."

We move to the sitting area, the fire still crackling in the hearth. Ayden takes one chair. Breyla another. I sit next to her, close enough that I can feel the heat radiating from her body.

She doesn't waste time. "I received word from Elijah that Rimor is under attack at the border with *Prudia.*"

Ayden's brows knit together. "How did you receive word from Elijah in the middle of the night?"

"I'm the one asking questions," Breyla snarls.

Ayden lifts his hands in surrender. "My apologies. Let me start by assuring you, I did not order any attacks on Rimor."

Breyla flicks her eyes toward me.

"He's telling the truth," I confirm immediately.

"Was your general acting on his own?" she presses.

Pride burns in my chest. She caught the subtle distinction. He said *he* didn't order it, but that didn't mean Prudian soldiers weren't involved.

"I do not believe so," Ayden answers. "I can confirm with Darian, if you'd like. It will take a bit to reach him."

She nods. "I would like to hear it straight from his mouth."

"As you wish," Ayden replies. He closes his eyes, concentrating. A few heartbeats later, he opens them again. "He'll be here."

"How exactly are you contacting him without sending a messenger?" I ask, curiosity getting the better of me.

Before Ayden can respond, Breyla says flatly, "His second Gift is illusions. I imagine he sent one to Darian to summon him back."

That range is rather impressive. By my estimation, Darian is at least fifty miles out.

"Yes, that's exactly what I just did." Ayden exhales heavily. "Giving away all my secrets, love?"

Breyla shrugs, utterly unrepentant.

"Be careful sharing others' secrets," Ayden warns. "Especially when you have some of your own."

"You never swore me to secrecy, asshole."

"Something I'm regretting now," Ayden mutters.

He turns away, eyes distant as he continues his conversation with Darian.

"Don't leave me in the dark, Princess. Secrets got us into this mess," I lean over in my chair until I'm right next to her ear. "What did Ayden mean when he said you have some of your own?"

She shivers at the slight brush of my fingers along her skin as I trail them up her arm.

"*Your* secrets got us into this mess." Pulling away, she shoots me a venomous look that quickly fades to indifference. "Thank the gods I'm capable of learning from others' mistakes, so I'll tell you."

I don't bother telling her that it wasn't just my secrets, letting her continue instead.

"Ayden figured out my second Gift—astral projection."

I tilt my head, studying her and trying to come up with any instance where I had seen her use this ability. "How were you able to keep this from me?"

"Easily," she snorts. "I've never used it in front of you. Only Elijah and Jade have seen me, the others are dead."

"The others being your parents?"

Her eyes drop to the floor momentarily. "Yes."

"Why don't you use it?"

"Because I'm awful at it." She shrugs, the motion stiff. "There's really not much use for it."

My brow furrows. "I don't believe that. You had one of the best teachers available."

"Except I didn't," she sighs. "It didn't manifest until a few years ago."

"Ah," I say, all the pieces finally clicking together. "And what about the other secret?"

Her head tilts slightly, auburn brows raised in confusion. "What other secret?"

"The one that explains how you're talking to Elijah in the middle of the night from a kingdom away."

"Oh, that." She shrugs. "That's technically not *my* secret. Elijah has a secondary Gift that allows others to look through his eyes and hear through his ears."

That certainly explained a lot.

Ayden's attention shifts back to us, whatever conversation he was having clearly over.

"Do you know why Lennox and Meloria would be waging coordinated attacks on Rimor's northern and eastern borders?" Breyla asks.

"You're sure it was Lennox and Meloria?" I breathe, heart sinking in my chest.

"Rimor's borders were attacked simultaneously tonight. Caedel burns as we speak. Jade evacuated the city to protect…" her voice waivers, "the surviving citizens."

"There were casualties?" I ask, not really wanting the answer.

Her shoulders fall. "Yes."

Dread fills my veins. "Are there reports of attacks on Pelanor?"

"Not that I've heard."

Relief washes over me for my parents. "Thank the gods," I whisper.

Breyla turns her attention back to Ayden. "Answer the question."

"I have theories, but I don't know anything for sure."

"Truth," I say right as Breyla snaps, "Not good enough. I need real answers."

"I'm giving you the best I can," Ayden bites out. "My guess is someone either sees Rimor as a threat or a weakness they can exploit. It's no coincidence they attacked right after you left the country. There were traitors in your court, and they've probably been working with Lennox and Meloria."

"Are you suggesting Fae are behind this as well?" Breyla asks.

"If I were a betting male, I would say so."

Before Breyla can ask another question, Darian appears in the room.

He's dressed in full armor, blood splattered across the chest plate, hair disheveled, dripping in sweat.

"You called?" he grunts.

"Did you launch an attack on Caedel tonight?" Ayden asks.

"No, of course not," Darian grunts. "I've been too busy dealing with the attacks on our camps and outposts to launch unsanctioned missions."

"Truth," I confirm.

Darian's eyes heat, his rage palpable. "What the fuck is this?"

"Rimor's borders were attacked tonight," Ayden explains, "resulting in civilian death and a city burning to the ground."

"Why does that require my presence here?" His jaw ticks. "I have more important things to attend to."

"Breyla needed to hear from you directly that you weren't behind the death of her people," Ayden says.

Darian turns his furious gaze on Breyla. "Fuck you, *General*," he snarls. "There are people out there who need my help. I'm genuinely sorry your kingdom was attacked and that lives were lost. Trust me, I get that better than anyone in this room."

He stalks toward her, and Ayden intercepts him, holding a hand to his chest.

"But you could have just trusted your fucking fiancé when he said it wasn't us," Darian continues, voice dropping low. "Instead, you took me away from the dozens of soldiers dying slow, agonizing deaths from a poison we can't cure." Vitriol threads his tone, blue eyes burning into Breyla. "Our borders were attacked tonight as well, but I bet you didn't bother to ask about that."

Breyla looks like she's been slapped.

Every protective instinct roars at me to come to her defense. But that's not what she needs.

While Darian is livid, my Gift whispers that his intentions aren't dangerous. He's not going to hurt her—not physically, at least.

"How am I supposed to trust any of you when I've been lied to for *months?*" Breyla grits out.

A pang of guilt racks my chest, knowing I'm part of the reason she doesn't trust Ayden, part of why he pulled his general from the battlefield in the midst of an attack.

"I don't know about these fuckers," Darian growls. "And maybe it's because I have no interest in that cunt of yours, but I have no fucking reason to lie to you. I've been unequivocally clear on my feelings.

Everything I've told you is the truth, so don't try to pin your trust issues on me. Your father got you into this fucked up situation, maybe blame him. Or these two, I don't fucking care."

Darian's words hit her hard, I can see it in her eyes. She's fighting tears. What he said didn't just hurt; it eviscerated her. It cut deep because it's true.

And I'm complicit.

"Fuck you, Darian," Breyla seethes, her voice quieter than I've ever heard it.

"The feeling is mutual," he says, turning to Ayden. "Fuck you, too."

He vanishes in the next heartbeat.

Ayden sighs. "Are you happy now, Breyla?"

"No," she says, voice trembling.

"The poison he mentioned…" My voice trails off, unsure.

Ayden nods. "It's the same."

"Who is attacking you?" Breyla asks.

"There's only one group that uses that poison—the Fae."

My brows shoot up. "That poison comes from the Fae?"

"It does."

"Could they have been the ones responsible for the attack from your border?" Breyla asks.

"I can almost guarantee it, love." Ayden's face softens. "We would have known if another kingdom had invaded Prudia to get to Rimor. The Fae are slippery. They have magic stronger than you've ever seen."

"Why?" Breyla asks, her voice bordering on something that sounds dangerously close to hopeless. "What have we done to them?"

"I don't know," Ayden says, and for the first time tonight, I catch the lie in his answer.

I would confront him about it later. Right now, I don't think Breyla can handle another blow. This, combined with Darian's words, has shaken her in a way I've never seen.

She nods solemnly.

"Now, if you'll excuse me," Ayden says, pulling on a fresh tunic. "Today is going to be long. I need to wake Ro to prepare for the poison victims arriving later."

Breyla's eyes light up. "You have a way to treat them?"

"No, sweetheart." Ayden exhales, running a hand through his dark curls. "She's only going to ease their suffering while I figure out how to tell their families."

"Oh," she whispers, biting her cheek.

She's teetering on the edge of breaking.

"Come on, Princess." I brace my hand on the small of her back. "I'll take you back to your room so the prince can get ready for the day."

She doesn't fight me at all, letting me lead her back to her room.

Breyla's deathly quiet as the door clicks shut behind us.

"Are you okay, Breyla?" I ask hesitantly.

Cold, broken eyes lift to mine. "Why would I be okay?"

"Shit, you're right." I rub the back of my head, sighing at my own careless words. "I'm sorry, that was a stupid question."

"Why were you there tonight?"

"I couldn't sleep," I explain. "I was startled awake by a panic attack unlike anything I've ever felt. Then I heard your voice on my way to the library."

"Why were you having a panic attack?"

"I haven't figured that out, but it felt… unnatural. Foreign." I rub at the phantom pains in my chest. "Then I heard your distress, and all I could think about was the night I found you bleeding out. The panic that created, that was real, and it was terrifying."

She steps toward me. "I'm sorry you had to feel that."

The sincerity in her tone startles me. "I'm sorry that I'm part of the reason you feel like you can't trust anyone," I reply.

A weight lifts from my shoulders, the long overdue apology easing the tightness in my chest.

Something shifts in her, her eyes growing distant and lost. I can practically see her mind replaying Darian's barbed words.

Hesitantly, I reach for her. My body hums at the feel of her skin as I trail my fingertips along her jaw. Her emerald irises meet mine. I swear I forget how to breathe when her head leans softly into my touch.

Her lips form a hard line, the moment gone before I can truly savor it. She jerks her head back, stepping out of reach.

I could weep at the sudden loss of her warmth.

I'm seconds away from begging her to come back when she turns away.

"I need you to leave, Aurelius," is all she says before crawling into bed.

"Sleep well, Breyla," I say softly, my chest deflating at the distance she's putting between us again.

The moment I think we're making progress, she pulls back.

She says nothing, her silent dismissal landing like a slap to the face.

Not even two hours later, soldiers start appearing in groups at the castle gates. They're in various stages of decline from the poison tainting their blood. Some are walking and talking normally, but others are delirious with pain and hallucinations.

For those in the late stages, Rowina moves quickly to block their pain, ensuring the only thing they feel is peace as they transition from this life into the next.

Those in the early stages spend the day eating what they please, drinking, visiting with friends, and saying goodbye to their families.

Watching soldiers who were perfectly healthy just days ago say goodbye to their loved ones was cruel torture. Some of them will last all day.

I'm not sure which scenario is worse, being faced with a quick, painful end or a slow, drawn-out one.

Rowina is depleted, her eyes dull and glassy.

"Aurelius, I could use your Gift," she calls, tucking a loose strand of sweaty hair behind her ear. "I'm exhausted. There are a few that have requested you end it, rather than wait."

I nod. "Take me to them."

She leads me to a group of females, all in the end stages. Black lines creep through their skin as the poison inches its way to their hearts.

These aren't soldiers. "They're innocents," I breathe.

"There are always casualties in battle, brother," Rowina says sadly.

"Don't fret, Prince," one of the females says sweetly. "We stood between poisoned arrows and children. This was our choice."

"One we would make again," another says with a pained smile.

I nod, knowing I would do the same. "Who first?" I ask gently.

"Me, I suppose," the first female says. She's short with plenty of curves and mousy brown hair. Kind brown eyes crinkle at the corners when she smiles at me.

"What's your name?"

Their names will not be forgotten.

"Trixia," she says stiffly.

I take her small hand in mine. "It'll be painless, Trixia."

"Thank you," she sighs, relief washing through her as my Gift goes to work.

Her eyes flutter shut when I reach her heart. The blood flow ceases, her heart stopping slowly to give her the peaceful death she deserves.

The remaining two females sob in unison. Staring at your own mortality didn't make it easier to accept once it came.

Their grief would be short-lived.

I take the hand of the next female—she's older with a willowy frame, black hair, and green eyes.

"What do they call you?" I ask.

"My name is Mallory."

I squeeze her hand gently. "You're incredibly brave, Mallory."

"I know that, boy," she says, full of sass even at the hour of her death. "Now get to it. I have a husband waiting for me."

I chuckle lightly. "Yes, ma'am."

She closes her eyes before my Gift even begins its job. Within moments, her head rolls to the side as her heart makes its final beat.

Exhaling, I turn to the final female. I'm immediately thrown back in time as I take her in.

Strawberry blonde hair, sky blue eyes, tall and beautiful. Her resemblance to Genevieve is startling.

Before I can ask, she tells me, "My name is Jenny."

Something fractures in my chest.

This must be the gods playing a cruel joke.

"Hi, Jenny," I croak.

"I'm ready," she rasps painfully.

I take her hand. "Any last requests?"

"Actually, can you hold me?"

My heart sputters in my chest. I nod. "Of course."

Pulling the stranger who feels so familiar into my chest, I hold her tightly. She trembles slightly, so I rock her back and forth until her body calms.

"I wouldn't change anything," she admits quietly. "But I'm also afraid to die."

"That's normal, Jenny." I squeeze her arm in gentle reassurance. "I promise it won't hurt. It'll feel like falling asleep, slowly at first, then all at once."

"Thank you," Jenny whispers.

"From your first breath until your very last," I whisper the words from the death hymn, hoping they provide some modicum of peace as I let my Gift unfurl and wind through her blood. "May the gods grant you peace."

I find her heart, stopping the flow slowly at first. Her lids grow heavy, unconsciousness claiming her in the next moment. Then I stop it entirely, the last breath escaping her lips as her head droops against my chest.

I can't help but stroke the strawberry-blond tendrils around her face, still rocking her back and forth.

Memory crashes over me like an unwelcome house guest.

Blood dribbled down the corners of Gen's pale lips, the poisoned wine working too quickly. Blue eyes locked on Breyla.

"I love you, Mom," Breyla rasped. "I'm sorry I never said it enough."

"I love you, too," Genevieve told her daughter through a wheezing breath. "Your father and I are both so proud of you. Keep making us proud."

The blood dripped from every orifice now. Her time was coming to an end.

Those beautiful blues turned to me.

"I love you, too." Genevieve weakly gripped my tunic. "Take care of my daughter, or I'll find a way to haunt you."

Trembling, I stroked the hand clutched to my chest. "I love you, Gen. I'm sure you'll haunt me, regardless."

Gods, I almost wished she would. I felt my soul shatter, watching Gen die.

It's not time yet. That's what I wanted to scream. I wanted to demand she live, that this world was not ready for her to leave.

I wasn't ready for her to leave.

I had lost my brother, and now my best friend was dying in my arms.
It was more than I could bear.

The memory fades as reality comes back into view.

I'm still holding Jenny, her lifeless body growing cold in my arms.

Gently, I lay her on the ground to be collected with the others we will burn after this.

CHAPTER TWENTY

"You look morose," Aurelius comments, taking a sip of tea. The one small mercy I received this morning was that Queen Josephina didn't insist on a large family breakfast. It was just Ayden, Aurelius, and me gathered around the large oak table right now.

I pick at the tepid potatoes on my plate, wishing they were one of Esme's cinnamon rolls. "How observant of you," I mumble.

Ayden smirks behind his stack of missives, pretending to read while very clearly enjoying my misery.

The breakfast on his own plate had gone cold a while ago; the herbal tea in his cup was the only thing still warm. He's been done eating for half an hour but lingers at the table, no doubt savoring my impending doom.

"Feeling excited for your teatime with my mother and Charlotte?" Ayden asks, far too gleefully.

I shoot him a withering look, fighting the urge to flip him off. "I'm thrilled. Can't you tell?"

"You're having tea with the queen and Charlotte?" Aurelius asks, clear disbelief in his tone.

"And she's doing needlepoint," Ayden adds helpfully, like twisting the knife.

Aurelius' lips twitch, eyes wide. "Are you ill?"

"It wasn't my idea." I groan, my head thrown back. "I tried to decline… I just couldn't somehow."

Aurelius cocks his head, studying Ayden. "You didn't–?"

"Didn't what?" I ask sharply.

"Not another word," Ayden says, cutting him off. "If she didn't bother to ask, I'm not volunteering the information."

"What didn't I ask?" A knot of dread forms in my stomach.

Aurelius looks like he desperately wants to say more, but ultimately presses his lips together.

"Besides," Ayden drawls, "watching her pout is far too entertaining." He waves a dismissive hand. "Quit stalling and go meet them for tea."

Pushing my chair back with a loud scrape, I rise stiffly. "I hate you both," I announce pointedly.

"Liar," Aurelius says, smirking into his tea.

"Run along, love," Ayden teases.

For good measure, I flip them both off as I storm out of the room.

"Breyla, dear, your stitches aren't even," Queen Josephina says brightly, the cheeriness in her voice barely masking her disappointment.

I stare at the pathetic excuse for needlework in my lap. Three pricked fingers and not a damn thing to show for it.

Setting the embroidery aside, I reach for my tea, mercifully brewed from the spicy blend I favor. Whether it was coincidence or insider knowledge, I don't know. And I don't care. It's the only bright spot in this whole miserable affair.

"I'm afraid I'm quite dismal at needlepoint, Your Majesty," I say lightly.

"It's okay, I'm not that skilled with it either," Rowina offers kindly.

Her presence, at least, is a small mercy. I don't know her well or fully trust her, but compared to Charlotte's empty simpering, Rowina is a blessing.

"Nonsense, darling," the queen says, cutting her daughter off. "You are adequate, I made sure of that. Breyla, however, needs considerable improvement if she hopes to be a suitable bride for Ayden."

Perhaps I'll stab my finger again and bleed all over this damn thing. Let her see just how unsuitable I really am.

My grip tightens on the teacup until it nearly cracks.

"I believe there are more important qualities for a queen and wife than decorative stitching," I say smoothly. "Qualities Ayden and I agree are far more valuable."

The queen scoffs. "Such as?"

"The kingdom does not need a pretty face who excels in flattery and needlepoint. Prudia needs a queen who thinks. Someone who challenges Ayden, who makes him stronger."

"I highly doubt Ayden desires such a thing," she says dismissively.

I bite back a laugh. "Actually, Your Majesty, that is exactly what Ayden told me he wants in a queen. Don't you think he deserves what he wants?"

The queen's slowly slipping cheery disposition finally falters, the familiar disapproval visible in the thin line of her lips.

I sip my tea, victorious.

Finishing my cup, I pick up the needlepoint again, deciding it'll simply be initials on a handkerchief now.

Carefully, I thread the needle through the fabric in slow, even stitches.

"Perhaps we could discuss what you'd like for your wedding ceremony?" Rowina suggests, trying to steer the conversation away from open warfare.

"That sounds lovely," Charlotte adds. "What flowers are your favorite?"

"I rather like Oleander," I say nonchalantly.

The queen sputters. "Are you being serious?"

Laughing, I say, "Relax, Your Majesty. I was being facetious."

She visibly relaxes, and I lean in with a grin. "I actually prefer foxglove. The shape is just so unique."

The queen eyes me suspiciously, trying to determine if I'm joking again.

While oleander was well known for its ability to be fatal, not as many were aware that foxglove was also toxic if consumed. Neither was my favorite; truthfully, I wasn't sure I had a favorite, but I was quite enjoying watching the queen's reactions.

"So perhaps pink for your accent color?" Charlie suggests brightly.

"Absolutely not," I say firmly.

Her brows narrow in confusion. "But both flowers you mentioned are pink."

"I detest pink," I say. "While we're on the topic, I also hate yellow, and orange isn't my favorite."

"What colors do you like?" Rowina asks.

"Purple, red, dark green, any shade of blue, and black."

There's a beat of silence as they absorb that.

Then the queen, as if she's been waiting to pounce, asks casually, "Do you have any requests for who you would like present for the consummation?"

Surely I misheard her.

But then the needle bites deep into my finger, blood welling up and staining the handkerchief.

"Shit," I hiss, sucking the wounded finger into my mouth.

"Mother!" Rowina scolds, aghast. "That tradition hasn't been observed for hundreds of years."

"This is different," the queen argues. "For the sake of both king-doms, we must have confirmation that the union is true."

Bile rises in my throat.

I drop the bloodied needlepoint entirely, my hands trembling slightly. "There will be no one—" I start to say, my voice shaking with fury.

"Perhaps Aurelius?" the queen suggests, cutting me off. "He is your family, after all. Some familiarity might be comforting."

With a wicked grin, Charlie heartily agrees, "Yes, I think Aurelius would be a perfect choice."

For a breathless moment, I wonder if the queen somehow knows, if she suspects the true nature of my history with Aurelius.

Surely, if she did, she wouldn't be so casual. Would she?

"I have already been sold off like chattel, forced into a marriage I do not want," I bite out. "So help me, if you put *anyone* in that room, you will be hearing reports of how your son fucked his hand on his wedding night. I will not consent to bedding him under those circumstances, and he doesn't strike me as the type to violate a female."

By the end of my declaration, my voice is nearly shaking with fury, but the point is made.

At least, I hope it is.

"We'll see about that," the queen says dismissively, returning to her needlepoint.

I stare at her, speechless with rage.

"I'm quite tired," I say stiffly, dropping the blood-stained handkerchief onto the table without a second glance. "If you'll excuse me, I'm going to retire."

I don't wait for their farewells. I storm down the hall, my breathing choppy, thoughts fogging into a maelstrom of panic and rage.

Halfway down the corridor, I'm accosted by the scent of bergamot and spices. A smell that, despite my current animosity towards its source, still feels like home.

Without thinking, I throw myself into Aurelius' chest, burying my face against the solid warmth of him.

"Princess?" he asks, startled.

"I just need a moment," I mumble into his chest, fighting back tears.

His arms wrap around me without hesitation, holding me tightly, tenderly. "Tell me what's wrong," he murmurs against my hair.

"The queen..." I choke on the words. "She's insisting there be a witness for the consummation with Ayden," I explain, refusing to move from where I'm buried against his chest.

His whole body stiffens, his hold tightening almost painfully around me.

"That's an outdated tradition," he says flatly, though fury vibrates under every word.

"It gets worse," I whisper.

He pulls back just enough to tip my chin up, forcing me to meet his eyes. "How so?"

"She suggested you," I say softly. "She wants you to be the witness."

For a heartbeat, there's only silence. Then a low, lethal growl rips from his throat.

"Like hell," he snarls. "I would sooner kill the male that tries to fuck you in front of me."

"You can't say that, Aurelius," I whisper urgently. "That's treason."

He grips my chin between his thumb and forefinger, the crimson in his irises flaring brightly.

"I don't give a fuck, Princess," he says lowly. "I will gladly spill blood for you."

I try to pull away, desperate for space, but he doesn't let me go. His hands tighten around me like a cage.

"Aurelius," I say, pleading, "no one can take me from you. I'm not yours anymore."

I was growing tired of having this conversation with him.

He stares at me, reading the truth I can't bear to voice. He sees it, *feels* it, and the smug grin that curves his lips tells me he's won something, even if he's lost everything else.

"Then why," he breathes, low and dangerous, "is it still my arms you run to, hm?"

Because you're the only piece of home I have left.

But I don't dare voice that.

I don't need to, though. He reads it all over my face, a smug grin curling his lips.

"Oh, there you are, Aurelius," Charlie's saccharine voice cuts through the charged silence.

We both jump apart, springing to opposite sides of the hall.

Aurelius recovers first. "Were you looking for me?" he asks coolly.

Charlie steps closer, placing a hand on his chest. "I was, actually."

He calmly lifts her hand from his body and lets it fall. "What can I do for you?"

"I assume Breyla told you about the consummation?"

I look away, refusing to meet either of their eyes as I bite back my emotions.

"She did," Aurelius replies dryly.

"Well, the queen would like for you to be comfortable," Charlie says, grinning wickedly. "She's arranged for a special chair to be delivered. You'll have a perfect view, of course."

She laughs, as if this entire nightmare is some grand joke.

My face burns with the fury and horror I'm feeling, but Aurelius' expression doesn't flicker.

It remains neutral, no emotion giving away his inner turmoil. Until he speaks.

"Fuck off, Charlie," Aurelius says, shoving her aside.

He reaches for my hand, but it's too late.

I'm already running, the tears I swore I wouldn't shed, burning my vision as I flee down the hall.

CHAPTER TWENTY-ONE

Several days later, Ayden forces me into the library to start working on my astral projection. Poor weather had cancelled any outdoor plans, giving him the perfect opportunity to torture, I mean, train me.

"Try again," Ayden encourages.

I let out an exasperated sigh before closing my eyes, pulling my focus inward. It's easy enough to project my image, but making it believable? That's another matter entirely. If my physical body has to focus on anything else, my astral form flickers.

I manifest next to Ayden, visible and clear. He can see me, but if he were to touch me, his hand would pass right through. As far as I knew, there was no way around that with my Gift. While his illusions could take a corporeal form, mine would always remain intangible. A projection.

So, the trick was to make it so believable that no one questioned it. Maintain enough distance that no one could reach out and prove it false.

I circle him slowly, inspecting him from head to toe, waiting for his next instruction.

"Good," Ayden praises. "Now open your eyes. Walk to me."

I crack my physical eyes open, careful to hold onto the tether between myself and the projection.

It's dizzying, seeing through both forms at once, but I manage it.

Ayden smiles, slow and dazzling. He claps once, then leans into my space. "Very good. You're improving."

A second later, hot breath tickles the back of my neck. "Now tell me where you went wrong," he whispers.

I groan and let the projection collapse.

Spinning to face him, I scowl. "You fight dirty."

"So do our enemies, love." He smirks. "You owe me a kiss."

Begrudgingly, I lean forward and press a chaste kiss to his lips, the taste of smug satisfaction rolling off him.

Before I can pull away, Ayden's hand closes around my hip, deepening the kiss.

Jealousy and fury surge through me in an instant.

I shove him back, the low growl that escapes my throat shocking even me. "Watch yourself, Prince."

"Why would I do that? I do so love watching you lose our little deal."

He's grinning like the cat that got the cream. So self-satisfied it makes me want to punch him.

The jealousy and anger pumping through me feel foreign and disconnected, but I can't see clearly enough to understand why.

Instead, I make my first guess. "When I had you arrested in Rimor... you weren't really there, were you? That was an illusion."

"Very good, sweetheart," he hums. "That one is a bit easy, though."

"There's more," I state grimly.

"There is."

"Shit."

He only chuckles, completely unbothered. "Keep thinking on it. That clever mind will get there eventually."

"You're insufferable."

"You get used to it." He shrugs, his lips lifting at the corners. "Now, enjoy your library time. I have things to attend to for the autumn equinox ball."

He's barely gone two minutes before I feel Aurelius' presence, looming, watching. I sensed him lingering in the hall even while Ayden was here.

Now, he crosses the threshold without hesitation.

"Here to help me research?" I ask dryly.

"Oh, yes," he says, voice dark and bitter. "I've learned quite a bit already."

I quirk a brow. "Oh? And what wisdom have you gathered today?"

He strides toward me, doors slamming shut behind him with a wave of his hand. The lock clicks.

The air shifts, the space between us charged and electric.

"I learned that despite my numerous warnings, despite every reassurance I gave you, you still seem to think you're not mine. "

I open my mouth to snap back, but he barrels forward.

"I learned you've made a little deal with Ayden." His voice drips venom. "That involves you kissing him when you lose."

"Oh yeah?" I taunt, my blood still high from earlier.

"Yeah, Princess. I've learned plenty." His jaw ticks. "I've also learned that I'm not a patient male, and right now, I can't decide if I want to bend you over this table and remind you what the end of my patience looks like… or track down that arrogant prince and cut his tongue out."

His threat lands like a punch to my gut.

"Be impatient all you want." There's bite to my voice as I relay the harsh reality of our situation. "It won't change the fact that I'm not yours. The deals I make with my fiancé are none of your concern."

"That's where you're wrong," Aurelius growls. "The beast that lives within me demands I erase every trace of him on you. This isn't want anymore, Princess. It's need."

His fingers tangle in my hair, yanking my head back until I'm forced to look at him.

His eyes are barely brown, black swallowing the irises, flecked only by burning crimson.

"I *need* you right now, little demon. I'm done fucking waiting."

As hard as I fight it, I can't keep the moan from slipping through my lips as he uses the grip on my hair to drive my back into a table.

His lips claim mine in a kiss that's anything but gentle. It's savage and filled with every angry emotion that's festered between us.

"I'm so fucking angry right now," I hiss against his lips, "and I don't even know why."

His mouth moves down my throat, alternating between sharp bites and soothing kisses.

My mind screams that we need to stop, but my body refuses to listen. It's taking what it wants, what I've been denying it.

"Good," he snarls. "Now you know how I fucking feel."

His teeth scrape the tender spot where my neck meets my shoulder, and a helpless whimper tears from my throat.

"Bloody fucking hypocrite," I breathe. "You were engaged to my mother. How do you think I felt?"

He breaks the hold on my neck, abruptly flipping my body so I'm splayed out on a table with my back to him.

The skirts of my dress are shoved up, my bare sex exposed to him. A cool breeze pebbles my skin as he groans at the sight of me.

"I was only engaged to your mother to protect you and the kingdom," he grits out. "And now I'm here to watch you come undone."

A sharp slap lands on my ass, making me cry out.

Another.

Another.

Pain and pleasure twist deliciously together.

"How is this any different?" I gasp. "I'm not here by choice, Aurelius. This was decided for me, and you were there to see it happen."

I hear the rustle of his pants behind me, then he presses the thick head of his cock to my entrance, teasing me.

"Maybe not." His voice is a rumble of pure, vicious need. "But this? This is."

I tremble as he nudges the tip inside.

"Don't," I warn, but even I hear how weak my resolve is.

"Don't what, little demon?" he growls. "Don't fuck you until you remember you're mine?"

He slaps my ass again, making me clench around nothing, desperate for him to give me more than just the tip.

"Don't shove my cock so far in you that you scream my name for the entire castle to hear?" he taunts, voice rough.

Aurelius circles my clit with slow, deliberate strokes, coating his fingers in my liquid heat.

"You're already so fucking wet for me," he muses, almost in awe.

"Aurelius, please." I don't even know what I'm begging for anymore.

Begging him to stop.

Begging him to *break* me.

"Please, what?"

He swirls his fingers again, building the heat in my already throbbing center.

"I'm engaged, Aurelius. You know this is wrong." It's a last, feeble attempt at reason.

Instead of pulling away, he growls, and with one brutal thrust, sheathes himself inside me completely.

I gasp, my nails clawing at the table as I struggle to adjust. He was a lot even when I was warmed up, but with no preparation, I'm left feeling so full I might burst.

"Little demon," he grits out, "don't pretend that means anything to either of us. You're mine. And I'll keep reminding you until you remember."

He pulls back and thrusts harder.

A shrill laugh sounds from the hallway, and he stills, every muscle locked tight.

We're too far gone to stop.

Without hesitation, I throw a silencing bubble around us, Aurelius reinforcing the lock on the library door and levitating a heavy chair to jam it.

"I'm still so fucking mad at you," I growl, voice breaking around a moan as he pumps into me again.

"Good," he snarls, slapping my ass again. "You fuck like a wild animal when you're mad at me."

The pain from his palm, combined with the pleasure of his length stretching and filling me, creates an intoxicating, heady mix that I want to drown in.

He pulls out nearly to the tip, then slams back inside, forcing a strangled sound from my throat as my hips smack against the edge of the table.

His cock hits deep, leaving me breathless and panting for more. Bracing my hands against the table, I shove back. I'm grasping for some tiny shred of control but coming up short.

Aurelius grabs my inner thigh, hoisting my right leg onto the table, spreading me painfully wide.

"If you want control," he growls, "you'll have to fucking fight me for it."

I sob out a moan, nails digging grooves into the wood beneath my hands.

"You're going to leave bruises, asshole," I pant.

"Good," he says, thrusting harder. "Let them fucking see my marks so they know who owns you."

I moan loudly at his words, hating that his feral possessiveness still excites me.

With another punishing stroke, he continues, "Then I'll carve their eyes out for daring to look at what's mine."

"Aurelius—" I protest weakly, but it comes out more as a whimper than a warning.

He chuckles darkly, slamming into me again. "Yes, little demon?"

I call the shadows in the room to me, letting them slither over his skin in a sweet caress. They climb higher, reaching to explore every part of him.

Just as they reach his shoulders, I whisper, "And what will you do if I let them kiss me?"

A growl, deep and possessive, reverberates in his chest but is swiftly cut off by the shadows constricting around his neck like a noose.

He's ripped from inside me with a vicious growl, crashing onto the library floor.

He gasps for air, pinned by the shadows' hold on his throat, trying to reach me, but gasping for air as the shadows constrict around his flesh. They look beautiful against the deep sun-kissed tone of his skin.

Realizing he won't be able to move unless he chooses to fight back with his own Gift, he relents, letting his head rest against the floor as he stares up at me with murder and hunger in his glowing eyes.

"Well?" I purr, striding toward him. "What would you do? Because I made a deal with him, and if I don't figure his illusions out soon, I'm going to be kissing him a lot."

"You're playing with fucking fire, Breyla."

"Yes, but you like my flames," I smirk.

"I'll tell you after we're done here," Aurelius promises.

I stand over his body, my feet straddling his hips. Ravenous, lust-crazed eyes stare up at me, but there's something else there, too. Something akin to desperation.

"Tell me what you want." I lift my skirt up to my waist, exposing my dripping sex to him.

"Sit that pretty wet pussy down. *Now*," he demands.

With a devious grin, I acquiesce to his request. Mostly.

I take a step forward until my feet bracket his face, then drop to my knees, hovering right above his dark and sinful mouth.

"Breyla." My name is a strangled moan on his lips.

"You know damn well this is not what I meant," Aurelius says, his hands coming to grasp my thighs. His fingers clench down on the tender flesh as he draws in a long breath of my sex.

"Is it not? Instructions were unclear."

"You're hovering." I moan softly when his fingers bite into my thighs. "I. Said. Fucking. Sit."

The words are clipped and guttural, then he's pulling me down so my center comes crashing down onto his mouth.

His tongue cleaves in and out as I writhe against him, hips rolling in my attempt to take him deeper.

A thick finger gathers the arousal between my thighs before tracing a line back to my other hole. He rubs the tight muscles slowly as his tongue trails up to my clit, flicking back and forth quickly. With no warning, he buries a knuckle inside, drawing a sharp, surprised gasp from me.

"Aurelius," I hiss. "A little warning next time."

He pulls back, chuckling darkly. "How about this for a warning? The next time I take you—I'm taking you here, little demon."

My inner walls clench, tightening around his digit as he works it in and out.

"Fuck," I rasp, "you say such romantic things to me."

With a wicked grin, Aurelius returns to eating my cunt like he's starving, and I'm the only sustenance in sight.

I roll my hips, the movement driving me between his tongue and that sinful finger.

The burn quickly fades to warm pleasure, building deep in my core.

His tongue nips and sucks at my clit, driving me steadily higher towards release.

Shamelessly, I grind against his face, chasing my pleasure against his hot, wet mouth.

Despite being fully buried in my center, I swear I hear him whisper, *"Come on my face, little demon."*

Aurelius' teeth find my clit in the next heartbeat, shooting me straight into bliss. Pleasure detonates through every nerve ending, my vision blackening around the edges as I crash into release.

I slump forward on trembling arms, catching myself with a hand braced next to Aurelius' head.

Chest heaving, I whimper as the aftershocks roll through me, and still, Aurelius laps at me with unrelenting hunger.

On shaking legs, I finally wrench myself away.

There's a smug gleam in his dark eyes, the crimson flecks bright and burning.

He wraps his large hand around the column of my neck, his thumb tracing the line of my jaw, and yanks me down into a punishing kiss. I taste myself on his lips, the tangy sweetness eliciting an erotic sensation I can't refuse.

He pulls back, his voice a growl against my mouth, "Now, for the love of the gods, sit on my cock and ride me like a good girl."

I swing a leg over his hips, straddling him—*backward.* I grin to myself as I lower, his cock nudging my entrance.

Aurelius snarls, his body tensing beneath me.

"Turn around," he orders, voice lethal. "I want you looking at me as I fill that sweet, filthy cunt. I *will* see you as I bottom out and take you to heights no one else ever has—or ever will again."

"But I like the way you fill me from behind." I pout, sinking lower so just his tip presses inside me.

A shiver runs up my spine, and suddenly, my legs *lock*, refusing to obey my desire to move.

"I said—turn around," he hisses. "Or I will gladly *turn you myself.*"

The grip on my body slackens enough to allow movement, and with a sigh, I shift to face him.

"Happy?" I ask sweetly.

"Ecstat—"

He doesn't finish the word. I slam down onto him, burying him to the hilt in one brutal move.

We gasp in unison.

"Move those hips, Princess," he demands, voice strained.

I obey, rolling my hips in slow, deliberate figure eights.

Aurelius cups my breasts, rolling my nipples between his fingers, sending pleasure sparking through my core.

My pace quickens, need driving my every move.

I listen to the demands of my body, riding Aurelius harder and faster, then eventually switching to lifting myself up and slamming down onto him. The change leaves us both panting, desperate for more of the other.

Aurelius strains upward, trying to bring himself closer to my writhing body atop him. The shadows still woven around his neck keep him anchored.

I tighten their hold ever so slightly in warning. I will take what I want from him because I am in control now.

"Harder," he demands.

His words catch me by surprise. He likes it rough, but I never pictured it going this far.

I tighten the shadows more, and I swear I feel him harden further inside of me, his head thrown back in utter bliss.

Aurelius bucks up from below, driving into me with brutal force, and I barely have time to brace myself.

"Fuck," he rasps.

Worried he might pass out, I slacken the shadows' hold just enough for him to drag in air.

Heated eyes find mine instantly. "I didn't say stop," he growls. "Now fucking come for me before I lose all control."

I keep moving, swiveling my hips in such a way that my clit rubs against him, driving me to the precipice of another orgasm.

My shadows constrict around his throat once more, and his hand shoots up, wrapping around my own throat. He squeezes just enough to make my vision blur.

At the same time, his Hemonia Gift flares, sending a rush of blood straight to my sex and nipples, magnifying every ounce of sensation.

It pushes me right over the edge.

I cry out, clenching around him in a devastating orgasm as he shudders beneath me, pulsing deep inside.

Hot, wet release spills between us, and I collapse forward onto his chest, both of us panting like we've been fighting for our lives.

When we finally break apart, Aurelius's voice is low and smug as he purrs, "As I said—just like a wild animal."

Shaking my head at his antics, I roll off him, immediately mourning the loss of him inside me.

"Now," I rasp, "tell me what you'd do to someone who kissed me."

Aurelius' smile is slow, feral. "I would cut out his tongue and remove his eyes, then fuck you in front of him—"

"Oh, but we've already played that game, and the prince quite enjoys it," I interrupt to taunt him.

He grins wilder, lethal."—leaving him only his ears," he finishes. "So he can hear your pleasure but never witness it. Never taste it. Never *touch* it."

I turn my head to the side to study him. Sweat clings to his face, his dark locks drenched. Still burning with violent devotion.

"Gods, you say such depraved things," I finally say.

His hand slides up to tangle in my hair, pulling just enough to make me gasp.

"I'd do much more depraved things, little demon," he whispers, "if it meant keeping you mine."

It's a threat and a promise all at once.

It's a prayer.

And gods help me, I believe him.

CHAPTER TWENTY-TWO

AURELIUS

Crisp autumn air assaults my face as I watch the slow ascent of the sun.

In the weeks we've spent in Prudia, late summer has faded into autumn swifter than I remember. The green of the trees has surrendered to hues of red, orange, and gold. Mornings are brisk enough now that I favor a long-sleeved tunic and wool overcoat most days. Today is no exception.

I've been awake for hours, waiting for the sunrise, the bitter chill biting my cheeks.

Sleep has become an elusive mistress. Haunting dreams plague me night after night—vivid, almost familiar, yet I know I've never seen the places in my waking state.

Most nights, I find myself standing on the ocean shoreline, staring out at the sea. Salt from the water permeates the air, mixing with the scent of the wild forest behind me.

Sometimes, I find myself wandering through the dense trees, exploring the strange flora and fauna that run wild there. The area seems untouched, yet I can't shake the feeling of eyes on me.

There's a soft humming that makes my blood sing, tugging and pulling me toward... something.

Each time, I wake before I can find it.

Despite the lack of rest, my body is buzzing with unspent energy.

The moment the sun fully crests the horizon, I head out.

I have no patience today for libraries or dusty tomes. Not even with the memory of what happened between Breyla and me the last time we were there.

No, I didn't need her pliant body beneath me, no matter how tempting it might be. I needed to move, to sweat. I needed to train.

I make it to the training grounds in record time, surprised to find I'm not the first to arrive.

Breyla stands in the center of a ring, chest heaving, sweat gleaming along her flushed skin. Stray curls cling to her face, damp from exertion, her freckles standing out starkly in contrast.

Her sun-kissed copper curls are woven into a tight braid around her head, and I admire the way the gold shines in the early morning light. With the coming winter months, the gold will grow muted, and the red will deepen. In the summer, her hair favors her mother's coloring. But in the winter, her hair comes directly from Raynor's bloodline—a deep crimson flame.

Something reaches into my chest, squeezing gently around my heart. I'm not sure which color I wish to see more right now, both of them simultaneously opening and soothing wounds that Raynor and Gen's deaths caused. I love it and hate it in equal measure.

My lips curve in a half smile as I fight the urge to laugh at her attire for the day.

A simple black dress, the skirt pulled between her legs and tied to form loose, makeshift pant legs. I know with certainty that she was able to win back one pair of her leathers from Ayden in the last week. She had also worn those leathers, much to the queen's protest, every single day since then. At some point, she had to send them for laundering, and it appeared that day had come.

Brown leather boots stomp the earth beneath her feet, and I silently wonder where she procured them. For the first couple of weeks in Prudia, she had simply walked the castle barefoot rather than slip her feet into the dainty, uncomfortable flat shoes that most females favored.

No, my female would be in boots or nothing at all. Not that I minded.

"Are you just going to ogle me all day, or do you plan to fight?" Breyla asks, breaking me out of my trance.

"Is ogling you all day an option?" I quip back, a flirtatious smirk taking over my mouth.

"No."

She's in a mood.

I pull a sword from the rack of training weapons and step into the ring. "Were you just training with someone?"

There had been no one else in sight when I arrived, but the space had not begun filling with other soldiers as they started their mourning routines.

"Darian," she says curtly.

I give her an incredulous look. "Willingly?"

She shrugs. "He was the only available option."

"I meant on his part. He despises you."

"Astute observation skills. I couldn't tell," she deadpans, her emerald eyes rolling.

I narrow my gaze, daring her to do it again.

She catches herself, stiffening slightly, and wisely keeps her eyes locked on mine.

"I think he enjoys the opportunity to knock me on my ass," she says, starting to pace.

I match her step for step, circling warily.

"Someone bested Rimor's general?" I question, knowing I could probably best her if I wanted to, but not many others could say the same.

"Believe it or not, Aurelius, I'm not perfect," she says, her lips quirking. "Elijah often bests me. Cillian, too, though I haven't faced him in years. I'm skilled, but not invincible. Darian provides a real challenge for me on multiple levels. As he should."

Her self-awareness is refreshing.

"Care to add me to that short list of defeats?" I ask, twirling the sword in my hand.

"Please, My Lord," she says as she makes the first move, lunging for me. I easily block and spin to the left, bringing my own sword around in an arc that she dodges. "I have no doubt you are skilled, but you have spent far too long among courtiers and wielding your words rather than actual weapons."

"Foolish little demon," I chide, lunging another attack that she parries with ease.

Her brow quirks. "How so?"

We dance around each other, our swords clanging together in a series of attacks and blocks.

"You forget," I say, voice low and mocking. "I was trained by the same males who trained you. I've watched you fight for years. I know every move you'll make as well as you know mine."

"How cute," she coos, dodging my next swing. "Though some might say your obsessive tendencies are unsettling."

We fall into a brutal, beautiful rhythm, swords clashing again and again, neither gaining the upper hand for more than a few heartbeats.

"Obsessive tendencies," I snort. "Says the female who worships my cock like a zealot."

I smirk as her steps falter for just a moment, having been caught off guard by my comment.

It gives me the opening I need to slip past her defenses. I disarm her, sending her sword clattering across the ring.

"Bite your tongue," she hisses.

I wink. "I'd much rather you bite it for me."

A low snarl curls her lip as she continues circling me. She's unarmed and at a disadvantage, but that doesn't stop her.

I swing my blade in a wide arc, intent on making her yield. I crave her submission in bed as much as I do in battle. But I want to earn it, fight for it.

Breyla doesn't just dodge my attack; she dances from it, her back arching to avoid the blow. She crouches low, swiping her leg out and catching my own in its path.

I hit the ground, my back taking the brunt of the impact. She straddles me and pulls two daggers from gods know where, crossing them at my throat.

I hiss, realizing these weapons aren't blunted. The metal bites my skin, tiny droplets of blood pooling beneath the blades.

"It doesn't look like I'll be adding to my list of defeats today, darling," she purrs, smugness filling her tone and eyes.

A slow rolling clap echoes across the grounds.

"Well," Ayden drawls, approaching. "That was beautiful to witness. Watching her draw blood is quite… arousing."

A low growl escapes my curled lips and is answered by one from Ayden's. Our eyes lock over Breyla's shoulder, neither of us backing down.

Breyla lifts off me, turning toward Ayden. She opens her mouth to speak, but then hesitates.

Eyes sharp, she spins in a tight circle, scanning the courtyard. In one smooth motion, she hurls her dagger toward a tree at the ring's edge. It thuds into the trunk, just inches from a smiling Ayden.

The illusion in front of me fades as the real Ayden to our side chuckles.

"Your intuition is strengthening," he muses. "Pity. I was hungering for a good morning kiss."

"You can try again tomorrow, Prince." Breyla smirks. "I very much enjoy the look of disappointment when you lose."

"Hmmm," Ayden hums, undeterred. "Would you like to earn another pair of your leathers back?"

"Always." Breyla grins, the excitement flashing across her features too quickly for her to mask.

"I have a bonus offer for you today, love."

"What is that?" she asks, her curiosity piqued.

"You may make your usual guess," Ayden says, strolling closer. "But also, we have a council meeting after this for the autumn equinox ball. If you behave at the meeting, play nice with my mother, and truly make it seem you're smitten with me... I'll return your boots."

She crosses her arms. "I already have boots." She raises a foot to show off the brown leather.

"I see that," he says, unimpressed. "However, Rowina would like them back since they are her only pair. She said, and I quote, 'Tell your fiancée, if she wants me out of my clothes, she can remove them herself rather than stealing them.'"

So that's where she got them. I suppress a laugh.

"Fine," Breyla relents with a heavy sigh. "I'll play nice. But I want the boots up front."

"That's not how this works, sweetheart."

"It's that, or I show up to the meeting barefoot," she threatens sweetly. "Your choice, Prince."

"Very well." He lets out a heavy sigh. "Stop by my room before the meeting. What's your guess today?"

"Was Charlie actually coming onto Aurelius that first night at dinner?" Breyla asks.

"Is that your final answer?" Ayden asks, keeping his tone even.

"Yes," she confirms, her voice not convincing.

"Yes, my cousin Charlotte really is that bold. That was her touching and flirting with him that night. No pants for you today," Ayden says with a wicked gleam in his eyes. He enjoys this game they play entirely too much.

I chuckle when Breyla mumbles under her breath something about Charlotte being a heifer.

Maybe someday I'll mention that she resembles a salmon more than a cow. She was a distraction to pass the time in Prudia for me, but she lay in bed like a dying fish. Where Breyla was fire and passion, Charlie was cold detachment. I honestly don't miss her at all.

"How long do I have before the meeting?" Breyla asks.

"Half an hour," Ayden says.

"Then I should bathe and change," she sighs, retrieving her sword and tucking her real daggers back into the folds of her dress.

"Would you like me to escort you?" he offers to Breyla's retreating form.

"I haven't forgotten my way to my room, Prince," she says with a dismissive wave over her shoulder.

Ayden turns to me, serious once more. "You will be joining us at the meeting."

I arch a brow, unbothered. "Why?"

"Like it or not, you are an heir of this kingdom now," he says. "It's time you met the council as a prince, not a mere emissary."

"So, I shall play the role of bastard prince, then?" I ask coolly.

"Those are your words, brother. Not mine."

"Those are everyone's words, Ayden. I've always been a bastard of some sort. The difference was that my adoptive parents didn't care. They loved me regardless. Here, I'm barely tolerated."

The words sound harsh, but they're true. The title of bastard had never really bothered me. Feeling like a bad smell that everyone tries to pretend isn't in the room was what actually got under my skin.

Ayden doesn't flinch. He leans closer, lowering his voice. "I know we are at odds right now, but I don't just tolerate you. Despite the…" His lips twitch. "Female between us, I rather enjoy your company. I hope one day we may be more than brothers in name only."

I stare at him, conflicted.

Truthfully, the more I got to know the male outside of what he was to my little demon, the more I was coming around to the idea of him. But with a Breyla-shaped chasm between us, I could never see us moving past this point. I don't dare voice these things out loud, but just give him a slight nod.

"I'll see you at the meeting." Turning on my heel, I return to my chambers to bathe.

The meeting took place in the small council chamber, a room I had spent more time in than I cared for.

A long white oak table occupies the space with black cushioned seats surrounding it on every side. Windows line the opposite side of the room, their curtains pulled open to allow in the late morning sun.

Various council members occupy several seats, followed by the head of the castle staff, the captain of the guard, and several merchants from the town.

At the head of the table, Ayden sits in the chair reserved for the king. To his left is Queen Josephina. To his right is Breyla, her hand laced with his and a wide smile plastered on her face.

It wasn't the smile she made when laughing or the smile she gave Elijah when he managed to say something that caught her off guard. Nor was it the unguarded one she donned while dancing. It's the courtly, polished smile of a well-trained Princess. It was warm, but obligatory at its core.

But it's for Ayden.

And that alone was enough to make my blood heat and my jaw tighten.

Inhaling a deep breath, I slip into the seat between Rowina and Charlie.

"Thank you so much for deigning to join us," Queen Josephina says sardonically.

Her displeasure with my presence grows every day. It's a wonder she hasn't attempted to end me in my sleep.

I offer her a bored look. "It's not as if I was given a choice."

"That's enough," Ayden cuts in. "Let's begin."

"I think the first order of business should be deciding whether your engagement ball shall have a guest list," Charlie says sweetly, "or if we shall open the castle doors to all of Elentia to celebrate with you."

My mind stumbles over the words *engagement ball.*

Ayden had said this was an autumn equinox ball, but it sounded like there was far more going on here.

"I thought this was an autumn equinox ball?" Breyla questions before I get the chance to do anything rash, like call him a liar in front of this entire room.

"I did say that," Ayden confirms, shooting a sharp look at Charlie.

Judging by her poorly hidden smirk, she knew exactly what she was doing when she asked that question.

"It is both," the queen adds. "Certainly you must be excited! We should share the happy couple's joy with everyone. The doors will be open to all."

Breyla swallows hard, fighting back the normal sharp-tongued remark that would have come from her. Remembering her bargain with Ayden, she pastes a wide, glittering smile on her face and says sweetly, "Of course. It would be selfish to keep the joy to ourselves. All are welcome."

Playing into her farce, Ayden leans down and brushes a kiss to her cheek before turning his attention back to the council. "Then open it shall be," he agrees. He leans into her, whispering something inaudible.

It's too low for me to catch, but I sense the lie roll right off his tongue, whatever it is.

Several more matters are discussed as the minutes tick on. It's decided that it shall be a masquerade. There will be four courses of food, entertainers brought in from surrounding towns, and dancing, of course.

When they inform me I shall escort Charlotte, I suggest Rowina instead.

Predictably, I lose that battle.

The last matter of business is attire. Emery, a seamstress from town, steps forward. "I have brought the designs you requested for Princess Breyla, My Queen."

"Delightful," the queen replies. "Let's see them."

Emery pulls out the first dress, a black shimmering gown threaded with subtle gold overlays that shimmer in the light.

The moment I see it, I know it's her.

The next is a gold A-line ball gown. It's eye-catching, but doesn't hold a candle to the black.

"I think the gold would complement your hair so beautifully," the queen gushes.

"Thank you, Your Majesty," Breyla says dutifully, but it lacks enthusiasm.

"Well, go on then," Rowina encourages. "Try it on."

Reluctantly, Breyla stands, following the seamstress from the room.

A few silent moments pass before they return. A gasp leaves the queen at seeing Breyla in the gown. Meanwhile, my heart sinks.

Breyla is beautiful in whatever she wears, but in that gown, it's not her I see. Standing before me is Genevieve with auburn hair. Breyla's emerald eyes shift to sky blue, the freckles vanishing before my eyes.

"You look lovely tonight," I said, offering my arm as Gen greeted me outside the ballroom.

"Thank you, Aurelius." Her smile was soft, wistful, as she adjusted the collar of my shirt. "The red lining suits you. You belong in our colors."

I smirked, knowing the real reason I wore red. I couldn't outwardly claim Breyla, but the signs were there if you knew where to look.

"It should be a crime how good you look in gold," I teased.

"Stop flirting." She laughed, swatting my chest playfully.

"I'm just complimenting my queen. If I wanted to flirt, I'd be much more obvious about it," I said bluntly.

She rolled her eyes, but smiled. "Thank the gods for that."

Before the door opened, I pulled her into a hug. "You're the bravest female I know, Gen."

"I'm filled with terror and anxiety, Aurelius," she admitted softly.

"Bravery isn't the absence of fear—it's persevering despite it."

"I tire of persevering," she sighed.

"Then let me carry you for a while," I offered.

"It's a deal." She smiled half-heartedly.

"Are you ready to put on a show for your kingdom?"

"No, but let's give them one hell of a show anyway."

"That's the spirit."

I grasped her hand, leading her into the ballroom.

I blink rapidly, my focus returning to the present.

The blue of Gen's eyes fades back to green, the freckles dancing against Breyla's pale skin.

Suddenly, she doesn't look like Genevieve at all.

The gold washes her out even more, making her look sickly. The cut of the dress isn't flattering on her like it was on Gen's lean frame.

But the court swoons, praising her perfection.

Only I see the truth.

"Gold doesn't suit you," I say flatly.

The queen scoffs, offended by my assessment.

But Breyla, gods, she looks relieved.

"She looks stunning," Queen Josephina insists

"Perhaps I could try on the black," Breyla ventures carefully.

"Why would you?" the queen trills. "The gold is perfect. It will pair splendidly with Prince Ayden's attire."

"I really—" Breyla starts, hope lighting her voice.

Ayden squeezes her hand, cutting her off.

To the rest, it might look like reassurance, but I know it's to remind her of their bargain.

"—love the gold," Breyla grits out, a faux smile plastered on her face.

Watching Breyla bite her tongue and resist the urge to be her authentic self incites an anger and pain I didn't know I was capable of feeling.

This isn't about a dress.

It's about watching the brightest soul I've ever known dim herself for their convenience.

All over a fucking pair of boots.

Fuck this, I'll buy her all the boots she wants if it means she isn't forced to change herself to fit their desires.

"She's clearly uncomfortable in the gown," I grit out, fighting the growl clawing up my throat.

"Breyla can speak for herself," Ayden replies coolly, leveling me with a dark glare. "And her comfort is no longer any of your concern, Aurelius."

I turn to Breyla, silently hoping—no, begging—her to tell them all what she thinks of the dress.

"It's fine, Aurelius," Breyla says, her voice monotone. "The gold really is lovely."

Before I can do something I regret, I shove my chair back, the legs scraping hard against the floor.

"We aren't done here," Ayden calls.

"I am," I bite back, storming from the room.

The door slams behind me with a satisfying finality.

CHAPTER TWENTY-THREE

BREYLA

The day of the ball arrives, and I lock my door, refusing breakfast and company.

The emotions are overwhelming, and it feels like there's no one I'm allowed to share them with. I find myself wanting to confide in Rowina, but I don't know if I can trust her, and she just reminds me how much I miss Ophelia.

Ophelia prepared me for the last engagement ball.

This time, I'm on my own.

I could ask for help, but my emotions are all over the place, and I prefer the solitude. The only people's presence I crave, I can't have.

I stare at the new brown leather boots at the foot of my bed, the other source of my emotional turmoil.

After the planning meeting, I had reluctantly returned the pilfered boots to Rowina. Ayden had held up his end of the bargain and allowed me to keep my own boots, but when I returned to my room, there was a wrapped box waiting on my bed.

Inside, I found the new boots with a note, penned in Aurelius' perfect script: *Don't ever let them silence your voice.*

I find my resolve weakening day by day. I had been so angry, so sure I couldn't forgive him for the secrets, that I refused to hear when he tried to tell me his truth. Since we arrived in Prudia, he had spent so much energy trying to bridge the gap between us.

But now... now I realize it's past time I actually *hear* him.

Aurelius had never given me anything, not that I had expected him to. But the fact that the first thing he gifted me was something so meaningful and thoughtful has me more conflicted than ever.

It was a promise.

A reminder of who I am.

And the knowledge of what I could never have, not without burning everything to the ground.

I was engaged to his *brother*. Not that it was my choice, but I wouldn't start a war over this. I couldn't willingly put more of my people at risk over my own heart. It was selfish and short-sighted.

I just wish I saw another way.

It was already midday, and past time for me to get dressed. Guests would be arriving soon, and I needed to be ready.

Sighing, I opened the wardrobe to pull out the gown I was to wear. Only, I don't find it. Well, not all of it.

The gold ball gown hangs shredded and singed, the ends blackened as if they'd been held over a flame and allowed to burn just long enough to char the edges.

There was no way I could wear this now, and somehow, I know exactly who is responsible.

I pull out the ruined dress and toss it on the floor. Behind it hangs another gown with a note pinned to the bodice.

You're beautiful in whatever you wear, but gold really isn't your color. Wear this instead. Please.

The please was tacked on the end as if it were an afterthought to make it a request rather than a demand.

The dress it's pinned to is the first gown that the dressmaker showed me, the one I was too hesitant to fight for.

Aurelius had somehow seen how much I preferred the black and abhorred the gold. He had seen me and encouraged me to voice my feelings.

I feel another bit of ice melt from around my heart at the gesture.

A smile forms at the corner of my lips as I run my hand down the gown.

The fabric is a nude satin overlaid with layers of lace and tulle, the deep V-neckline edged in black lace. Gold leaves adorn the bodice of the dress and trail down the skirt to the floor, giving the appearance of autumn leaves falling against a night sky.

I slip into it easily, the silken material hugging my curves perfectly. Relief floods me, gratitude so fierce it leaves a lump in my throat.

I weave my hair into intricate braids, twisting them together in a low, neat bun with several loose curls framing my face.

My natural, bare face stares at me, mocking me for never learning how to apply makeup. What use was that skill on the battlefield? None whatsoever.

I slip on velvety, soft black flats, grateful that I wasn't expected to dance in heels. Boots would have been preferable, but they ruined the aesthetic and weren't as easy to dance in.

A knock rattles my door, startling me out of my thoughts. When I open it, I find Rowina looking disappointedly up at me on the other side.

"I said I didn't need help," I say before she can speak.

She pushes her way past me. "I didn't ask." Her keen eyes assess me, lingering on the dress. "What happened to the other gown?"

"An unfortunate encounter with your brother."

"I've never known Ayden to destroy a female's clothing," she hums, suspicion filling her tone.

I give her a small shrug. "I guess you don't know everything about your brother."

"You keep saying my brother." Her eyes narrow. "But not which one."

"Why are you here exactly?" I deflect, still unsure where my trust in her stands. "As you can see, I'm perfectly capable of dressing myself for the evening."

She snorts in disbelief. "I can see that. Was the natural look a fashion choice or a lack of knowledge?"

"A fashion choice," I say flatly.

"Liar."

"Rude," I scoff.

"Sit," she demands, pointing to the stool before the vanity.

I relent, falling ungracefully into the seat.

"Close your eyes."

I feign reluctance before finally obeying. Soft brushes glide across my lids, cool fingers lining my eyes with kohl. When I open them again, I barely recognize myself.

The reflection is me, but sharper. Bolder.

Brown and cream shadows smudge my eyelids, the black kohl winged softly at the corners.

"His outburst at the council meeting was inappropriate," Rowina says casually as she brushes color onto my cheeks, "but Aurelius was right."

"About?"

"The gown. The black really does look better on you. Gold doesn't suit your skin tone."

"As much as I'm loath to admit it, Aurelius is right about a lot of things."

She smirks. "Don't let him, or Ayden, hear you say that."

"I wouldn't dare. Their egos are far too fragile," I say with a giggle that she matches.

Rowina completes the look by applying a pale pink lip stain.

"There," she praises. "Now you are ready."

I stare at myself in the mirror. My eyes meet hers—a perfectly golden color that shines underneath dark lashes and the kohl rimming them.

Not a pawn. Not a girl in a gilded cage.

"You're dangerous like this," Rowina whispers, her voice a caress against my ear.

"I look presentable," I say lightly, breaking the spell.

"Presentable?" she scoffs. "Darling, you look good enough to eat."

I blush, breaking our eye contact.

"I love the shades of pink you turn for me," she whispers, leaning in to brush a kiss against my cheek. "Gods, I detest both of my brothers right now."

I dare to voice the question I'm not sure I want the answer to. "Why?"

Her answer is surprisingly sincere: "One because he's had you, and the other because he gets to keep you."

"Such a strange princess you are," I say, trying to shake myself out of the trance she has me in.

"The same has been said about you, Princess," she quips right back.

"Yes, but for very different reasons." I turn away from her, moving to stand.

Her hand catches my shoulder, holding me in place.

"If you let me in, if you *really* got to know me," Rowina says quietly, "I think you'd find we're not so different."

"I want to let you in," I admit, surprising even myself. "I just don't know if I can trust you."

"Do you trust Ayden?" she asks, her tone unreadable.

"Maybe with some things," I reply slowly. "But overall, no. I know he's hiding things."

"And yet," she presses, "you trusted Aurelius when he was hiding things from you."

The accusation stings more than I want to admit.

"I did," I say, but find it lacks some of the bitterness I was used to. "And it came back to hurt me. Hence the reason I'm more cautious with my trust now."

"And do you trust Aurelius?"

Her question lands with the weight of a boulder.

I hesitate before responding. "Yes."

Rowina nods, satisfied. "Did you ever stop to consider that the things they've kept from you weren't your burdens to bear? That maybe, *just maybe*, they kept them to protect you?"

"The thought had crossed my mind."

"You need to learn to trust even when you don't have the full story," Rowina says bluntly.

"I'm working on it," I admit softly.

"Forget what you think you know. Forget what you've been told about my brother, about our kingdom. What do his actions tell you?"

I frown, considering her words.

Ayden had arranged a marriage with me for the sake of peace between our kingdoms, but he had done it without my knowledge.

He had been moving pieces among my court, but in doing so, exposed a traitor behind so much tragedy.

When I had come onto him to drown my own pain and in an attempt to hurt Aurelius, Ayden had turned me down. I don't know many males who would have turned me down, regardless of my intentions.

His actions are a tapestry of manipulation and care so tightly interwoven that pulling one thread unravels the other.

"That's a complicated answer," I finally say.

"I think you'll surprise yourself when you figure out the answer." Rowina smiles.

She pulls a gold and black diadem from a small box I hadn't noticed, settling it into my braids.

It digs into the side of my head, slightly too small for me. While it matches my dress flawlessly, it doesn't feel natural to me. I long for the crimson jewels of my normal crown.

"One last thing," she says, retrieving another box.

Inside is a mask. Intricate gold filigree patterns twist together and overlay a soft black velvet to form a dainty covering.

I hold it to my face, feeling a part of me slipping away. The mask hides nothing—and yet it hides everything.

Rowina ties it in place, securing it with a few pins.

When I look in the mirror, I see myself, and yet, I don't recognize the reflection at all. This beautiful stranger isn't someone I know.

The knock comes a short while later.

When I open the door, Ayden greets me with a wide, easy smile. "I see Aurelius was correct about the dress," he says, offering me his arm.

"And how is that?" I ask, taking it.

"The black suits you far better," he admits sheepishly.

"I could have told you that. Why do you think I wear it so often?"

"I figured it was just your preference for leathers," he muses as he leads me down the marble-tiled hallway.

"You figured wrong," I say lightly. "My mother actually made me wear color the last time you escorted me to a ball."

He chuckles. "That does not surprise me in the least."

A sly grin plays at the corner of his lips before he comments, "And what I said about you at the last ball still stands."

"And what was that?" I ask as we slow to a stop just behind Aurelius and Charlotte.

Charlotte is dressed in a low-cut ball gown that starts as a deep red and gradually fades into a shimmering gold. Her shoulders are bare, but long sleeves cover her thin arms. Aurelius' arm is wrapped loosely around her lower back, brushing the exposed skin.

"The colors of House Mordet suit you beautifully," Ayden whispers against my ear. Then, softer, more wicked, "But you still look even better out of them, love."

"Ouch!" Charlotte gasps, stepping away from Aurelius.

I catch the angry red mark blooming on her porcelain skin where his hand must have gripped too tightly.

"Aw, Charlotte," I say sweetly. "It's such a shame you're so delicate. At least the mark blends in with the color of your beautiful dress."

She shoots me a seething look, but before she can respond, Aurelius pulls her forward as they're announced.

"That was rather cruel of you," Ayden comments.

"So is your constant taunting and using me to hurt your brother."

"Is that truly what you think?" He asks, face solemn. "That I'm trying to hurt Aurelius?"

"That is certainly how it appears, Ayden."

Ayden sighs. "Yes, I suppose it may appear that way," he admits. "But I'm not trying to hurt either of you, Breyla."

Before I can ask what he is trying to do, we're ushered forward.

The herald announces us. "Princess Breyla Rosaria, betrothed *of Prince Ayden*, future Queen of Prudia."

A wave of applause rises up to meet us.

The ballroom is filled with royals, nobles, and common folk alike, all masked and glittering under chandeliers of a thousand candles.

Ayden introduces me to what feels like half the kingdom, and I make an earnest effort at remembering their names. I'm not sure what good it will do since everyone here is masked. Though my mask may not be hiding my identity well, others certainly are.

I'm flooded with well-wishes for our marriage and questions on everything from the style of my dress to whether I'm looking forward to my first night with the prince. The last question leaves me momentarily floored, and thankfully, Ayden intervenes before I'm forced to answer.

Ayden, ever the savior, swoops in with an offered hand. "Shall we dance?"

"Please," I nearly beg.

Ayden sweeps me onto the floor in a traditional waltz.

I find the steps without thinking, grateful for something, *anything*, familiar.

"You look overwhelmed, love," he says, smiling softly.

I bite my lower lip. "Maybe just a bit."

"I thought you'd be accustomed to this."

"To which part?" I ask dryly. "Being engaged? Balls with nearly a thousand guests? Or the questions from strangers regarding your bedroom skills?"

Ayden nearly stumbles mid-step, laughing so hard he has to grip my waist tighter.

"Relax, darling," he chuckles. "We'll figure it out together. This is new for me as well."

"You mean to tell me your subjects don't normally inquire about your sex life?"

"Not typically, no." He grins. "I think they're just excited to have a new princess."

"They already have a princess," I point out.

"Yes, and they love Rowina dearly, but she will never rule. If she has her way, she'll never marry or bear children, either. *You*, Breyla, represent the future. They will adore you."

By the time the dance concludes, I feel the nerves settling.

I wrap my arms around him in an appreciative hug. "Thank you."

"It is always a pleasure to dance with you, Breyla." Ayden squeezes me gently before patting my shoulder.

"May I steal your partner?" A sultry voice asks.

Charlie.

"Gladly," I say, smiling as sweetly as I can manage.

Taking a step back, I let the shadows of the corner consume me as the next song begins.

Ayden sweeps Charlie through the room, and my eyes wander to the other dancing couples. I'm surprised to find Darian leading

Rowina in a graceful dance, her head thrown back in pure joy at something he says.

They fit together seamlessly, their moves practiced and fluid. Her smile is blinding, and the look he gives her is something I recognize. Yearning. Dancing with her is the most relaxed I've ever seen him. His navy eyes track her every movement in a deeply meaningful way. This male wants her.

I break my gaze, the moment feeling far too intimate for observation.

"Are you hiding, Princess?" Aurelius asks, startling me out of my silent perusal.

"No, I was hoping someone would find me," I say flatly. "That's why I cloaked myself in shadows in the corner of the room, after all."

Aurelius chuckles deeply, shaking his head. "I see that tongue is still sharp."

"I keep a whetstone by my bed to ensure it stays that way."

He laughs again, and I wonder if he may be drunk.

His eyes aren't on me, but Ayden. I track their movement, seeing a look of pure discomfort and horror on Ayden's face.

He's holding himself at an awkward distance from Charlie as they spin through the ballroom.

My eyes flick back to Aurelius. "Two questions for you."

"Hm?" Aurelius asks, his eyes finding mine.

"How did you find me in the shadows?"

"I've been watching your tricks for years. I know when something looks unnaturally dark," Aurelius explains. "Whether you're aware, or want to admit it or not, your shadows are quite fond of me."

I chuff in annoyance, displeased that my own Gift would betray me like that. "Why are you so... jovial? You've been watching Ayden the entire time you've been talking to me."

He grins, mischief sparkling in his eyes.

"You could say I've repaid Ayden's kindness with the compliment he gave you before entering."

I process his words, trying to recall what Ayden had said.

"The colors of house Mordet suit you beautifully... but you still look even better out of them, love."

Realization dawns on me, Ayden's stiff posture suddenly making sense. "You gave him a boner, didn't you?"

"I have no idea what you're talking about," Aurelius says innocently.

"Unbelievable," I murmur.

"Is it, though?"

I give a half-hearted laugh. "Not really."

He shrugs. "I learned my mischief from the best."

"My father?" I surmise.

"In a way, I suppose." Aurelius smirks. "But I was thinking of you, actually."

"I'm not sure if I should be flattered or insulted right now."

"Maybe a bit of both," he suggests.

Our eyes meet, and for a brief moment, the world stops spinning around us. The sound fades to silence, the guests disappear, and it's just us.

But then Ayden's voice startles me out of my stupor, bringing reality crashing down.

"Breyla?" he calls for me, his eyes passing over us as he searches the room.

Aurelius' hand wraps around me from behind, his arm snaking down and resting against my lower belly. Warmth pools in my core as his form presses firmly against me.

"He can't see us, Princess." His breath is hot against the shell of my ear. "Are you going to move your shadows and allow him a view?"

One hand trails lower as the other grasps my breast, kneading the flesh tenderly. Soft kisses pepper my jaw, his tongue trailing over my pulse point and swirling at the juncture where my neck meets my shoulder. A shudder wracks my body, goosebumps covering every inch of exposed skin.

Charlie's voice douses the flame when she calls, "Aurelius?"

With the moment gone, I push Aurelius away, a heavy sigh leaving his lips.

I straighten my dress, ensuring my hair is in place, before releasing the shadows.

"There you are," Ayden says, a smile lighting his handsome face.

"I just needed a moment of solitude," I explain, returning his smile.

"Now, shall we eat?"

I nod, allowing him to lead us to the table.

We take our seats near the head of the table, and I catch the queen's eye just briefly enough to tell me she is disappointed in my dress.

Though she says nothing, her displeasure is clear.

The first two courses pass quickly, the wine flowing freely and joyful chatter filling the space around me. By the third course, drunken laughter and light-hearted conversation are all I can hear.

"So, tell us, Prince Aurelius, might we be hearing of another royal engagement soon?" A lord whose name I do not remember asks.

I somehow manage to maintain my composure, something hot and bitter boiling inside me.

Aurelius does not. In a rare lapse of control, Aurelius chokes on his food, pure shock lining his features.

He wipes the errant crumbs from his lips with a gold napkin before responding. "I highly doubt there are any suitable matches for a bastard such as myself."

Charlotte leans over, clearing a bit of debris he had missed.

The move is so intimate that it makes me sick. I avert my eyes, clenching my fists beneath the table in an attempt to control my temper.

The lord chuckles. "It looks like there's a perfectly suitable match at your side right now."

I reach for my wine goblet, swallowing a generous amount to cool the rage pooling in my core.

"I don't—"

"Aurelius and I make a handsome couple, don't we?" Charlotte cuts in, a coy smile firmly in place as she leans in and kisses Aurelius.

Her delicate hand traces his jaw as my own burns.

"Princess Breyla," the queen gasps. "Are you quite alright?"

I glance down to find the crystal wine glass shattered, red wine mixing with the pooling blood and dripping onto the table.

Only then do I recognize the fire in my palm to be from a broken shard of glass lodged under my flesh.

I hiss, dropping the remaining pieces of the goblet, and push my chair back. Standing swiftly, I sputter, "I'm sorry, Your Majesty. I had a firmer grip than I realized. If you'll excuse me, I'm going to clean this."

Not waiting for her dismissal, I stand, hurriedly making my way out of the room and away from the eyes of a thousand people.

I find an empty room off the grand hall and slip inside.

As the door clicks shut, my entire body shudders as I lean my back against a wall.

The room is dark, so dark I can hardly make out what its purpose might be. Just as my eyes begin to adjust, light flares from the door opening.

It shuts, leaving us in the dark once more.

And somehow, I know without seeing, it's him.

"What do you want, Aurelius?" My voice is cold and flat, revealing none of the storm inside me.

"Are you okay?" He asks, reaching for me.

I see only the vague outline of him, but I feel his hands finding my face.

"My well-being is none of your concern," I respond, willing cold indifference into my tone.

"Horse shit," he hisses.

His breath dances across the skin of my cheek, telling me he's close enough to kiss.

A soft glow grows from the Faerie light he casts, bathing his features and the room in a soft amber hue.

He lifts my still-bleeding palm to his face, inspecting the gash.

"It's just a cut," I say, attempting to pull my hand from his grasp.

His eyes harden, connecting with mine as he tightens his hold on my wrist. "Quit moving, brat. There's still glass in your hand. It's embedded under the skin."

I feel the blood in my hand move in an unnatural pattern and understand he must be using his Gift to direct it. Two thin shards of glass work their way from under my skin, and I grunt at the sharp sting, but the relief is immediate.

"Thanks. Are we done here?" I ask, trying to free myself.

"No." His tone is harsh, but there's an undercurrent of something else—something desperate. "I can't heal it, but I forced it to clot. You won't bleed all over this gorgeous dress."

The anger eases just a bit at the reminder that he's the entire reason I have this dress.

"Thank you for the dress, Aurelius," I say quietly. "And for the boots."

He releases my hand at last, but doesn't step back.

"I hate agreeing with Ayden about anything," Aurelius says. "Especially about you. But he was right about one thing."

"And what's that?" My voice wavers.

He cups my cheek, his thumb brushing my skin. "You look unequivocally devastating in this dress, little demon."

My heart beats a little faster at his praise, but I'm swiftly reminded of Charlotte's words at dinner.

"Aurelius and I make a handsome couple, don't we?"

I pull away, crossing my arms. "You have an equally devastating partner waiting for you."

Aurelius' expression shifts, something dangerous flashes behind his eyes.

"So we're finally going to address your reaction out there?" He steps closer. "Good. Let's talk about it."

"There's nothing to discuss. I was distracted and clenched the glass too tightly." I divert my gaze from his, knowing the lie is showing on my face.

"Fucking hells, Breyla," Aurelius gasps. "Just admit it."

"Admit what?"

"That you don't hate me!" His voice is desperate, yet determined. "Admit that you feel *exactly* what I feel for you. Seeing Charlotte kiss me made you so irrationally angry that you shattered a goblet."

"There's nothing to admit," I whisper, still refusing to meet his eyes.

He catches my chin between his thumb and forefinger, forcing me to meet his gaze.

"Admit it," he growls. "Admit that you aren't as unaffected as you're pretending, that the sight of seeing someone else kiss me knots your stomach. Makes you want to murder them. Because that is exactly what I feel every time I'm forced to watch Ayden kiss you."

Something breaks inside me, the anger from earlier bubbling to the surface, accompanied by nausea.

"Fine," I hiss. "Watching that heifer trail her fingers over you fills me with fury. I wanted to shove my shadows down her dainty throat and watch her choke. I've never been jealous before, Aurelius. I don't understand why I want to break every bone in the hand she used to touch you!"

A small smirk plays at the corner of his lips. "I think you do understand, Princess."

"I assure you, I don't."

"Stop lying to me," he says, his voice low and guttural.

"What do you want me to say?"

He doesn't hesitate. "I want you to say that you feel even a fraction of the all-consuming love I feel for you!"

His words ring true, and I freeze.

No one had ever said those words to me, not like that.

Desperation floods his crimson-flecked eyes as the silence stretches between us. "Tell me he loves you."

I can hear the way his voice trembles, the words catching in his throat.

"He cares for me, Aurelius," is all I can manage, because I don't know the truth of Ayden's feelings. Even if I did, I wouldn't dare voice them. "He knows me, understands me."

"That's not what I asked," he growls.

The breath in my lungs vanishes as he invades my space, my back hitting the wall. Warm fingers trace my jaw, gripping my chin firmly as he tilts my face up to meet his.

Quietly, almost too low to hear, he asks, "Do you love him?"

I can see the physical pain his question elicits. It's mirrored in my own soul, shredding at the very fabric of my being. Nausea churns in my gut at the words that slip from my tongue, "I think I could."

"No, Breyla," he whispers as his fingers fall away from my face. They trail down my neck, squeezing softly as his hand brackets my throat. Warm breath dusts my ear when he leans in to whisper, "You could never love Ayden."

My breath hitches at the surety of his words—the absolute possession.

"Pardon?" I breathe.

"He could be a sinner or the god Saelem in mortal form," Aurelius starts.

Confusion lifts my brow. "I'm fairly certain he's the future king of Prudia," I deadpan.

A frustrated growl reverberates through his chest, and he bands his free hand across my mouth. "He could be your saving grace or your ruinous destruction. A stranger or your oldest friend. I don't care if he married you ten times over or knew every part of your radiant soul."

What's your point? I want to ask, but his hands squeeze tighter.

The air catches in my throat from the pressure as he murmurs, "But he will never love you like I can."

"You can't love me like that," I gasp, fresh oxygen flooding my lungs when he finally eases the pressure around my throat.

"Why not?" he demands.

I close my eyes, squeezing them tightly to combat the burning of the tears that threaten to break free. "Because one or both of us is going to be forced to watch the other walk away. I'm engaged. A fact neither of us can change without risking war."

Aurelius leans his forehead against mine, hand stroking my cheek with aching tenderness. "It never stopped us before."

"Maybe it should have," I say, the words bitter on my tongue. Everything about the statement feels wrong, but I can't take it back now.

He stills, then slowly pulls back, searching my eyes, pleading for something I'm too broken to give.

"Take it back," he whispers.

I remain quiet, biting the inside of my cheek to keep my composure.

My voice is a raspy whisper when I finally utter, "I fucking love you, but I can't."

"No," he grits, his jaw ticking and eyes burning. "You don't get to say those words and break my heart in the same breath." I swear I see the reflection of tears pooling in his eyes as he demands, "Take. It. Back."

Everything in me screams, my heart begging me to comply and take it all back. But I can't. We were doomed from the start, and everything has led to this moment. The moment I break us both.

Silence.

"I see," he says, withdrawing from me. The devastation is plain in his eyes.

He's gone, the light going with him, in the next second.

In the pitch dark, I suck in a rattling breath, fighting the sobs clawing up my throat. Tears stream down my cheeks, soaking the mask still covering my face.

The door bursts open once again, and I gasp in surprise.

"There you are, darling. I've been looking for you," Ayden's smooth accented voice rolls through the space between us.

"Why?" I ask, voice unsteady.

He creates a new Faerie light, illuminating the space. In his outstretched hand is a damp cloth, and in the other are fresh bandages.

Smiling meekly, I hold my hand out to him.

"It looks like it's already stopped bleeding," he says as he gently wipes the dried blood and wine from my palm.

The flesh is tender, but he's right. It's no longer bleeding, thanks to Aurelius.

Once the wound is clean, he wraps it with deft fingers, tying the bandage snugly.

"I'm sorry it took so long to find you. I got stopped in the kitchen when I was looking for supplies." His voice is achingly sincere. "Are you okay?"

I shake my head. "It's fine."

He studies my face, unconvinced.

"I'm just tired," I lie. "Can you make an excuse for me?"

He looks me up and down, seemingly not buying my excuse. "Of course," he says, much to my surprise. "I'll tell them you weren't feeling well from the wine."

He offers his arm.

I take it silently, letting him lead me away from the wreckage of the night, and into another kind of battle altogether.

CHAPTER TWENTY-FOUR

AURELIUS

I flip through the weathered pages of the book in my lap, trying to lose myself in the words in hopes of ignoring the pain in my chest. Breyla's suggestion that we shouldn't have been cut deep.

It felt like something cracked inside of me when she refused to refute it. She was adept at using her words as weapons, but never had she wielded them so precisely against me.

The third time I read the same sentence, and it still makes no more sense than the first, I let out a huff of frustration.

Closing the book gently, I lay it on the bedside table, opting for the glass of spiced rum instead. I take a long sip, tasting each spice as it rushes over my tongue and burns down my throat.

A soft knock sounds from the door. It's so quiet, I wonder if I imagined it.

The ball had ended hours ago, the last of the guests departing before I returned to my room.

Breyla never came back to the celebration after I left her in the dark. Not that I could blame her.

Another knock, this time louder. This time, I know I'm not imagining it.

Shock rattles through me when I open the door to find Breyla standing there.

She's dressed in a white nightgown, a heavy black robe wrapped around her, auburn hair disheveled, bare feet peeking out beneath the hem. She's the single most beautiful creature I've ever seen.

"What are you doing here, Breyla?" I choke out.

Lifting her hand to me in the offering, she says, "It won't stop bleeding."

Sure enough, there's a steady trickle of blood pooling in her palm and dripping onto the floorboards.

I step aside, letting her pass. Closing the door behind her, I take her hand gently to inspect the wound.

"This should have started scabbing over by now," I mutter.

"It did," Breyla confirms.

"What happened?"

"I don't know, it just started bleeding again." She shrugs. "I didn't want to bother the castle surgeon."

I hold it closer, inspecting the wound closely. "Did you pick the scab off this?"

"Why would I do that?" Her voice holds none of the usual snark I would expect from such a question.

"You didn't answer," I say, meeting her gaze.

"No. Of course not."

Lie.

I choose not to call her on it. Instead, I use my Gift, weaving the blood back into order, forcing it to clot. I suck in a deep breath, wondering what she's doing in my room after pushing me away so definitively.

"You meant it earlier," I say quietly, "when you suggested we never should have been."

Her voice is soft, trembling as she says, "It's not a lie."

"That doesn't make it the absolute truth."

"We've always been a bad idea, Aurelius."

I flinch, her words striking as sharply as a slap to the face.

She'd always been off-limits, something I should have never wanted. But I never once considered her a mistake.

Her tone is regretful, but I would *never* regret her.

"I know that, Princess," I rasp. "So then, what are you doing here?"

"You kissed her," she hisses, diverting her gaze to the floor.

I pinch her chin between my thumb and forefinger, forcing her to look at me. "You know damn well *I* didn't kiss *her*. The only female I wanted to kiss is standing right in front of me."

"Wanted?" She asks, emphasizing the past tense.

"Yes, wanted." I let the word hang there between us. "She also happens to be infuriatingly stubborn and determined to shatter my heart. I can't keep wanting the female who has made it painfully clear she belongs to another."

I watch her endless emerald eyes search mine as the blow of my words settles on her. Tears pool at their corners.

"Take it back," she pleads, wrapping her small hand around the one still holding her chin.

The gentle squeeze nearly breaks my resolve.

When I remain quiet, letting her feel the weight of her words the way she made me, she makes a startled choking sound that I feel in my soul.

"Aurelius, please," she chokes. "Take it back."

"Why should I?" I demand. "Give me a reason, Breyla."

"Because every time I close my eyes, I see her kissing you, and it fills me with a rage so poisonous it burns. Because every time I lose that stupid bargain and have to kiss Ayden, I desperately wish it were you." Her tone grows frantic, desperation filling every word. "I would wear dresses every day for the rest of my life if it meant I never had to kiss another who wasn't you."

Her chest heaves, breath coming in short, as her free hand twists into the hair at the back of my neck. The tips of her nails dig into the skin on the back of my hand and neck as she pulls closer.

"Do you hear me, Aurelius?" Her voice teeters on hysteria. "I would give up pants for the remainder of my days if it meant having you. Forget Ayden. Forget this gods-damned marriage. I just want you."

A few tense heartbeats pass before I break.

"You really do hate dresses," I murmur, a rough laugh breaking from my chest. "That's a mighty declaration coming from you."

The sound that breaks from her is somewhere between a sob and a choked laugh. The tears that were pooling in her eyes now freely flow down her cheeks. "I really do," she manages, her voice hitching with relief.

I release her chin, my fingers reaching to caress her cheek and wipe away the rogue tears.

"I'm sorry, Aurelius," she says softly. "I'm sorry I punished you for so long and refused to hear you. I used Ayden to hurt you because I was hurting, and that wasn't fair to either of you."

Her voice trembles, but she doesn't falter. "I still don't know how we fix this. I still don't know how we dissolve this betrothal without risking war. But I want you. I choose you."

"Breyla," I whisper, my heart breaking open inside my chest. "It's always been you."

I run my thumb along her jaw. "I couldn't explain it for years, but that's how long I've been fighting what I feel for you." The confession slips off my tongue like the sweetest honey.

She blinks up at me, confused. "You hated me."

"I've never hated you, little demon." A smile curls my lips. "Found you infuriatingly stubborn and obnoxious at times? Absolutely. But hate you? Never."

I step closer, my voice a rasp of truth. "You have been the source of my greatest frustration and the epitome of my most consuming passion for years."

The words are on the tip of my tongue, but I hesitate to utter that last confession for fear it will shatter the tumultuous peace between us.

"I don't care if we shouldn't be together," she says fiercely. "You feel right. You feel like home."

"You are my home, Breyla." I drop my hand to her waist, pulling her flush against me.

"Where you go, I go. You are mine."

Suddenly, there is far too much clothing between us.

A subtle gasp escapes when I capture her lips with my own. The kiss is an all-consuming representation of every emotion floating between us. It tastes like passion, sorrow, regret, joy, desire, and undeniable familiarity all woven together.

The heavy black robe slides from her shoulders, pooling at her feet. The white nightgown she wears does nothing to hide her body from me, the hardened peaks of her nipples, the curves I know as well as my own skin.

It's too much. And not enough.

She pulls the nightgown over her head in one fluid motion, leaving her gloriously bare before me.

I walk her backward until she hits the bed, the air around us electric.

Her fingers snap, erecting a sound barrier around the room. A wicked gleam dances in her eye.

"We don't need anyone hearing what's about to happen," I murmur approvingly, shoving her down onto the mattress.

She cocks a brow at me. "That's not what you said the last time."

I lean over her, shoving my sleep pants down with one hand, leaving us both completely exposed.

"I had a message to send last time. But now that we know you belong to me, no one else will ever hear those noises from you but me."

"That shouldn't be arousing," she mumbles.

Goose bumps pebble her flesh as I trace a finger down the center of her chest, drawing lazy but intentional patterns over her most sensitive spots.

"Everything you do is arousing to me, little demon," I counter, peppering soft kisses along her jaw.

She gasps as my fingers find the soft flesh of her thighs, then climb higher until I'm perched at her entrance.

"I need you to soak my fingers, beautiful," I warn. "I'm going to use my Gift on you now."

She moans, grasping at the bed sheets. "You don't need your gift to get me wet."

"Oh, I know," I snicker. "But you're going to find release at least twice before I enter you. I'm just helping the process along."

"Confident tonight, are we?" she smirks, breathless.

"Not confident," I say, thrusting two fingers inside her. Her moan is a symphony of pleasure for my ears. "I just need you as relaxed as possible for what I'm going to do to you tonight."

Her inner walls are already tightening from the effect of my power and the slow, deliberate thrust of my fingers. I curl them forward, searching for the spot I know drives her wild.

"What… what is it that you're going to do to me tonight?" The raspy desperation in her voice has me nearly saying fuck it to my plans and taking her now.

But I've waited far too long for this.

"I'm going to give you the one thing we've been dancing around for months—the thing you're too afraid to ask for."

Alarm flashes in her eyes, her body tensing beneath me.

"None of that," I murmur, softening my strokes. "Relax, little demon. I'm going to give you pleasure you've never felt before, but I need you loose."

I take her nipple into my mouth, giving it a soft nip. Her hips buck, rubbing against my palm.

Everything about this female is divine.

My hips roll against her, letting her feel exactly what she does to me.

I thrust my fingers in and out, curling them deep inside her, my thumb gently circling her clit.

She gasps my name, her body shaking below me. Her orgasm hits fast and hard, her back arching, eyes rolling back as she falls apart in my arms.

Pure male satisfaction washes through me at the sight of her lost to bliss at my hands.

"That's my good little demon. That's one," I praise. "Now you're going to do it again on my tongue."

"Or you could just fuck me," she whines.

"All in good time." I wink at her, moving to position my face between her thighs.

Before she can complain again, I swipe my tongue up her center over the already sensitive flesh.

The taste of her arousal is more intoxicating than any liquor I've ever known. I could live the rest of my life only knowing the taste of her.

Long fingers tangle in my hair, pulling sharply, demanding both mercy and more. A desperate mewl escapes her mouth that nearly does me in.

I flick my tongue over her clit and dip my fingers inside her tight cunt, gathering the liquid arousal until my hand is dripping.

Then I trail my fingers lower, down to the tight hole I've been teasing for far too long.

A soft gasp leaves her mouth when I dip one slick finger inside.

"Relax, little demon," I coax from between her thighs, my tongue never slowing. Gently, I push deeper, easing her open.

We've done this much before, but tonight she's strung so tight it makes my heart ache.

My tongue works her clit in slow, deliberate circles, the tension building fast.

Her inner walls tighten, signaling how close she is.

Pulling back from her, I growl, "You're going to come on my tongue, but not before I stretch out this tight little hole. You're not ready for my cock yet."

"Aurelius, please," she moans, her voice a breathy, delicious sound that ignites my primal urge to claim her. "I'm so close."

"And you will *not* come again until I say so. If you fail, I'll keep you on edge for hours, denying you any release."

A frustrated groan is all the response she manages.

"Tell me you understand," I demand, pushing a second finger inside her tight heat.

"Fuck!" she gasps, back arching from the bed. "Fine, yes. I won't come until you say."

Her voice is wrecked with need—and surrender.

With a devilish grin, I return to my ministrations between her thighs, lapping at her core with slow, devastating strokes. I flatten my tongue, tracing from her opening to her clit in long, lazy circles.

Her thighs tremble from the restraint it's taking to obey my command. I smile against her flesh, then slowly add a third finger to her ass.

"Gods," she hisses, eyes fluttering shut.

"There's only one being I'll ever worship," I chuckle softly, watching her teeter on the edge of bliss. "And she's more demon than goddess."

I pump my fingers in and out several more times before determining I've tortured her enough.

"Look at me," I rasp, desperate to see her eyes as she shatters.

Her gaze locks on mine—bright, dazed, desperate.

"Come on my fingers, Princess." The command is soft, but firm, and I feel her immediately shatter around my fingers.

The orgasm tears through her, her body shuddering violently as hot, liquid heat floods my hand.

I stroke her through it, coaxing every last tremor from her body.

"That's my good little demon," I praise, a dark, possessive thrill racing through me.

Slowly, I withdraw my fingers, smirking in pure male satisfaction as her legs tremble violently. I pepper soft kisses to the insides of her thighs before standing.

"Where are you going?" Breyla asks, brow furrowing.

"I'll be back shortly," I say with a wink, striding across the small room.

I shuffle through the belongings in my trunk, looking for the oil I had brought from home on the off chance this moment would arise.

When I return, jar in hand, she watches me with lust-drunk eyes.

I dig out a generous amount of the semi-solid oil, warming it in my palm until it melts into liquid as I spread it over my cock.

Her eyes track the movement of my hand up and down my shaft as I stroke myself until my skin is slick with the oil.

I catch the pink of her tongue darting out to wet her lip and the hunger flaring in her hot gaze.

The bed shifts as I kneel between her parted thighs, hitching them over my shoulders. I rub slow circles into her over-sensitive clit, and she whimpers.

"Please, no," she mumbles, weakly attempting to close her legs to me. "Too sensitive."

"I'm doing it for your benefit," I explain, pushing her legs wider as I align my cock with her tight entrance.

She tenses as the head of my cock presses against her.

"Just do it," she whispers.

"Sorry, darling, that's not how this works." I push a fraction of an inch further inside her, nearly groaning at how slowly I must take this for her sake. "If at any point it's too much for you, you will say the word *king*."

She writhes beneath me, eyes flaring wide, whether from my words or the additional inch of me now inside her, I can't be sure.

Her hands grasp at my arms, nails biting into my skin, drawing blood in tiny pebbled bursts that only make me groan.

"It's so much, *My Lord*," she rasps as I work another inch deeper, the head of my cock breaching the tight ring of her ass.

A dark rumbling laugh escapes me at her defiance with that title, even now, in the midst of being fucked.

"What's so funny?" she pants.

"You, little demon," I smirk. "Your defiance, even in the most intimate of moments, is entirely predictable. I do love your pervasive need to defy me, though."

I can see her actively resisting the urge to roll her eyes as she stares me down.

"Are you in yet, *My Lord*?" she snarks

Looking down between us, I grin. "You're doing so well for me… but you're only halfway there, little demon."

She curses under her breath, but it quickly becomes a garbled moan as I push deeper.

Her lips open as if to reply, but I swear if the next words from her mouth aren't my name as she moans, then I'll bottom out in her just to hear her scream.

As if she senses my thoughts, her mouth snaps shut.

Good girl.

I lean down, taking her nipple into my mouth and swirling my tongue around it until it hardens into a stiff peak.

Inch by slow inch, I work the rest of my length inside her, until I'm fully sheathed in a tightness so euphoric we both groan.

"Fuck, Princess," I rasp, "look at how well you take my cock."

Her eyes burn into mine, full of a web of emotions I work to disentangle. In the corners, shadows swirl in a way that makes her emerald eyes glitter in contrast.

I pepper kisses along her jaw, biting softly at the pulse point of her neck, giving her time to adjust.

"Such a good fucking girl," I praise when she rocks her hips against mine in a clear demand.

Gently, I pull out and thrust back in, short, controlled strokes.

The tightness of her around me nearly unravels me with each slow, deliberate thrust. She was tight before, but this fit has me nearly delusional with pleasure.

There is no doubt in my mind, Breyla Rozaria was made for me.

Her nails bite into the skin of my chest, her shadows breaking free of her control and swirling around us.

At first, they gently cover my skin, filling me with a warmth and familiarity that makes my blood hum. But they quickly grow needy, tightening around my neck and shifting my gaze to hers.

"I'm not fragile, Aurelius." Her voice is a breathy demand. "Now, fuck me in the way I know you're desperate to."

It undoes me, my restraint snapping like a twig.

I pull back nearly to the tip and slam back inside to the hilt. The scream I pull from her is like my own personal siren's call.

I take her in deep, punishing thrusts, rolling my hips into hers until her moans turn incoherent.

Her nails tear through my skin, the sharp bite of pain sending sparks of pleasure through me.

The need to be closer overwhelms me. I drop her legs from my shoulders and crash my mouth onto hers, searing and possessive.

She meets my tongue in a fierce battle for dominance, nipping and sucking as I continue pounding into her.

A symphony of flesh meeting flesh, pants, and needy moans fills the room around us as I fuck us both precariously close to oblivion.

Breaking the kiss, I whisper my claim against her lips.

"You're."

Thrust.

"All."

Thrust.

"Fucking."

Thrust.

"Mine."

"Yours," she agrees, her whisper turning into a gasping moan as my teeth find the flesh of her neck and bite down.

Something primal and innate holds me in its grip, refusing to let me release her. The warm coppery tang of her blood assaults my senses and teases me as it coats my tongue.

The taste is rich, yet bright and crisp, as I let her life force run down my throat.

At the sound of her soft whimper, I release her, laving the spot with my tongue to soothe the sting.

Her eyes are blown wide with desire. The shadows seeping from her skin pulse in the air around us, cocooning us in darkness.

"Fuck me harder," she demands, her voice a shredded rasp.

"Mmm," I hum, obliging without hesitation. I piston my hips into her harder, faster. "You feel divine wrapped around my cock, little demon."

The look of pure devastation on her face tells me everything she's too lost to voice. She's trembling beneath me, right at the edge.

I reach between us, rubbing steady circles over her clit to give her that final push.

"Come for me," I say softly in her ear. It's not a command, but a plea.

A moment later, I feel her spasm around me, waves of pleasure wracking through her. The look on her face is absolute devastation—rapture in the form of this female. It drags me over the edge with her, pulling release from me so quickly it startles even me.

My seed floods her as her name tumbles from my lips in a ragged moan.

For a long moment, the only sound is our heavy breathing, the two of us tangled together in the aftermath.

Finally, I slip out of her, drawing a soft whimper from her lips as the last of the connection breaks.

"That was..." Breyla's voice is breathy and soft, searching for words to describe what just passed between us.

Chuckling, I lean my forehead against hers and steal a gentle, brief kiss. "Yeah, I know what you mean."

Reluctantly, I drag myself from the bed. I hastily rinse myself before returning with a damp rag and doing the same to her.

I drop next to her in bed, pulling her body into mine. Her curves fit perfectly against me, molding to every hard plane of my body.

Perfect.

She's absolutely and unequivocally breathtakingly perfect.

The afterglow takes hold of my tongue, the words flying from my mouth before I even register them, "I never hated you."

Breyla shifts onto her back, my arm still slung around her waist, so she can look me in the eyes. She studies my face, worrying her bottom lip as she assesses what she sees. "You already said that. Though I find it hard to believe, given our history, I trust you're telling the truth."

"I know," I say, my heart soaring at her trust in me restored. "But it bears repeating. I have never, could never, hate you. All the harsh words of our past, cruel tricks and insults—"

"Hey, some of those tricks were highly entertaining. Especially the time when I was the cause of your three-month dry spell," she cuts in, and I slap a hand over her wicked mouth.

"It was six months," I growl. "And you've been the cause of my pent-up… frustration for much, much longer, little demon."

She gives me a look like she wants to say something, but I refuse to move my hand, needing to get these words out. "As I was saying… when you blossomed into adulthood, the pull I felt toward you grew unbearable. Everything I did to push you away, every time I hurt you or insulted you, it was all because I was trying to protect myself, and you, if I'm being honest."

Her auburn brow lifts, urging me to explain. "I knew I couldn't be with you, but I couldn't stand being in your presence, not having you. Your father would have killed me for the things I thought about you. It wouldn't have mattered that you were an adult. The male would have skinned me alive and left me as an offering to the gods."

She licks my palm, grinning in victory when I finally pull my hand from her mouth.

"Did you have something to say, brat?" I drawl.

"I did, actually." She smirks. "I wouldn't have let him skin you alive."

"No," I argue, "You would have helped him."

"I'm not *that* bad."

"Yes." I chuckle. "You were."

"Whatever," she mutters. "I was going to ask if that's why you told him that I was the problem."

My brows furrow, trying to recall what she's referring to. "What do you mean?"

"When I was perhaps fifteen or sixteen, I overheard a conversation you had with my father," she explains. "He asked why you let me get under your skin and why there couldn't be peace between us…"

I had many conversations with Raynor regarding Breyla over the years, but this one comes rushing back with clarity. A long sigh escapes me as I finish her story, "And I said you were the problem."

She nods, the corners of her lips turning down. I see the hurt lingering in her gaze, and it feels like a punch to the solar plexus. Seeing her hurt by something I said makes it difficult to breathe. I never want to see that look on her again.

"How long have you been holding onto that, Breyla?"

Her green eyes break from mine, looking toward the ceiling.

Gripping her chin, I turn her attention back to me and demand, "How long?"

With a heavy sigh, she admits, "Only like ten years." A half-hearted laugh escapes her lips, but the joke lands flat.

My fingers stroke her cheek as I whisper, "I am so very sorry that my words hurt you like that. I had no idea you were carrying that for as long as you have."

"It's okay, Aurelius," she says, trying to shrug me off. "Really, I'm over it."

"But it's not okay," I insist. "I didn't realize you were listening that day, but that's no excuse. They were thoughtless, cruel words that aren't the full truth."

"How so?"

"I hadn't noticed you in that way, yet. But I still felt this force between us that drove me mad. Like I was somehow being both pushed and pulled whenever I was in your orbit. You were so damn bratty at that age, I just couldn't process it all. So while you were part of the problem, the real problem was me. The lack of understanding *I had* about how I was feeling. Instead of facing that, I ran. I avoided you, pushed you away, and made you hurt instead."

"So that's why you volunteered for the position of Royal Emissary, why you were gone so often."

"Yes, Breyla. It was all because of you. But hear me now, you were never the problem."

She nods in understanding, the hurt finally receding from her eyes, and I feel like I can breathe again.

"So what is it that you were feeling?" she asks timidly, like she's afraid of my answer.

"You, Breyla," I breathe. "It has always been you."

She lets her actions speak for her, crashing her mouth into mine. The kiss is somehow both tender and scorching, every emotion threaded into the way her lips move with mine.

I push her back, running a hand down her side to grip her hip. When I kiss a trail along her neck, taking special care to lavish my tongue over the mark, she mewls. Her hips lift, undulating against me in a desperate plea.

"I should return the favor for the years you spent tormenting me," I murmur against her neck as my fingers trace the skin of her inner thigh.

Goddess, how I loved these thighs. How I would spend all day between them.

"Hm?" she hums, her hand searching for my cock.

When she grasps it, I groan, already aching and ready to sink into her heat.

"How would you do that?" she asks, stroking her hand up and down my length, twisting as she goes.

"I would build you up just until you reached the precipice of orgasm and stop," I groan when she fondles my balls, precum leaking from the tip. "And I would do it over and over until you were begging for relief."

Her eyes sparkle, the interest undeniable in the way her gaze heats.

I had edged her before. Nothing like I was describing, though. "I would spend hours," I say, slipping two fingers inside her wet heat. "Working you up just to watch you squirm as I withheld your release."

When I curl my fingers forward, her back lifts from the bed, my name a breathy plea on her lips.

Slowly, I circle my thumb around her clit. Just enough to work her up, but not enough to push her over the edge.

She pumps my cock faster, and I grin. "No, princess. That's not how this game is played," I say, stretching her arms above her head. Rather than hold them in place, because I need both hands for what I plan to do to her, I activate my Hemonia Gift, using it to keep her hands immobile. "When I take you this time, it will be slowly," I whisper in her ear, nipping it as I move away.

"Sadistic bastard," she mutters.

I smirk, slipping my fingers out of her to land a sharp smack to her bare pussy. The moan that spills from her lips confirms my theory. "And that makes you a masochist, my sweet little demon," I chuckle, taking her peaked nipple into my mouth and biting down hard enough to sting.

"Aurelius, please," she whines, rolling her hips against my hand.

I align myself with her center, coating my length in her wetness. Always so ready for me.

"Say it again," I demand, notching my tip at her entrance.

"Aurelius," she breathes, need heavy in her tone. "Please. I need you."

"I need you too badly to stretch this out. We'll play that game later," I promise.

When I slip inside her, it's exactly as I promised.

Slow and reverent.

Between each drawn-out thrust, I murmur the words, "It was you."

Thrust.

"From the beginning."

Thrust.

"Through the darkest times."

Thrust.

"My whole life."

Thrust.

"It's always been you."

I take her so slowly it almost hurts, worshipping every part of her my lips can reach.

When we find release—it's together.

Several moments pass before she finally breaks the silence.

"I really hate to ruin this," she murmurs. "But I can't stay. Ayden will show up at my door for training in a few hours."

Something rattles my chest, disappointment filling me at the thought of not being able to hold her all night.

Instead of voicing that, I say lightly, "Still keeping me our dirty little secret, Princess?"

"You know it's not like that. I wouldn't—"

I silence her defensive rambling with another kiss. "I know, Breyla. I was teasing you."

Her eyes narrow in suspicion. "Who are you and what have you done with my Aurelius?"

Warmth spreads through my chest at her words. "*Your* Aurelius?" I echo, a slow grin tugging at my mouth.

She smiles widely, a rosy blush blooming across her cheeks. "Yes. *My* Aurelius."

"I like the way that sounds." I pepper her throat with soft kisses, taking particular satisfaction in seeing the mark of my teeth still on her skin.

It's already begun to darken into a deep purple, and gods help me, I admire how it looks on her.

She hisses softly, tender beneath my mouth. "Am I going to have to hide that?"

"Unless you want to piss off the prince," I smirk. "Which I'm not entirely against."

She rolls her eyes, an act that, on another day, might have landed her over my knee. As it is, I probably deserve that one.

"I need to go," she says, softer now. "Before the rest of the castle wakes for breakfast."

With a heavy sigh, I pull away, the loss of her warmth like a knife to the ribs.

I reach for the wet cloth again and clean my mess from between her thighs. Seeing my seed wiped away instead of buried deep inside her womb fills me with a disappointment I dare not voice.

Once she's redressed, swallowed again by the poor excuse for a nightgown and robe, I wrap her in my arms.

"Let me hold you for just a minute longer," I nearly beg when she starts to squirm.

Laughing softly, she pushes me back. "I need to go."

"Make me a promise before you go," I blurt, catching her by the hip and pulling her tight against me again.

She raises one brow while cocking her head in curiosity.

"Promise me more stolen moments," I say, tipping her face up to mine with a gentle pinch of her chin. "I can't have you the way I want... so promise me more moments like this. Until we can get you out of this engagement."

My fingers stroke her cheek tenderly while I wait on bated breath for her answer.

When it finally comes, the tightness in my chest dissipates.

"Like we've ever been able to stay away from one another," she whispers. "All my stolen moments are yours, Aurelius."

I kiss her once more before leading her to the door.

When I open it, all I can do is stare in horror.

Well, fuck.

CHAPTER TWENTY-FIVE

"Enjoying yourself, love?" Ayden asks, his tone laced with vitriol. He's leaning against the threshold of my door, pure fury burning in his eyes.

Breyla gulps. "Ayden."

Before I can stop him, Ayden shoves into the room, slamming the door shut behind him.

The sound shield is still in place, so I know he didn't hear anything, but the evidence is undeniable. The look on Breyla's face, her disheveled hair, and the blooming mark on her neck all paint a damning picture. And I'm still naked, so there's not much question about what happened here.

"Put some godsdamned pants on, brother," Ayden spits. "We need to have a discussion."

Begrudgingly, I oblige. This confrontation will likely not end well.

Breyla flinches when Ayden brushes her hair aside to run his fingers over my mark. It's not pain I see on her face, though; it's disgust.

"What was so hard to understand when I said you two couldn't be *this*?" Sighing, he drops his hand and steps back. "Where was the confusion when you read that marriage contract ten times over, Breyla?"

Tears brim in Breyla's eyes, her lip quivering. Breyla, who rarely shows these emotions in front of others, is crying in front of *him*. She's not one to act or manipulate, so I know these are real.

"I'm sorry, Ayden."

"Save your apologies." Ayden rubs his temple, shaking his head. "They mean nothing right now."

"Ayden, Breyla isn't—"

"You do not get to speak," Ayden snarls, ramming his finger into my chest. "I let you into this kingdom because I knew it would be easier than trying to keep you out and because I wanted to know my brother. You have spit in my face at every turn, and if you were anyone else, I would have exiled you ."

I remain silent, letting Ayden spill more of his truths.

"You two have completely fucked plans I have spent years putting in place to keep everyone safe."

"There are other ways to have peace between our kingdoms, Ayden," Breyla says. "We don't have to wed. I know you well enough to know you don't want to be forced into a marriage for the sake of peace. Even if you're the one who orchestrated it."

"That's not—" Ayden sighs defeatedly. "That's not what I mean, love."

Breyla grasps his hand, squeezing it gently, and I choke down a growl.

"I've been trying, Ayden. I swear I have." She swallows hard, her tone resolute as she continues, "But my heart isn't yours. If you force me down that aisle, you will spend your life married to a female constantly pining for your brother. Is that really the queen you pictured for your kingdom?"

"You can't be his." Ayden's shoulders drop, and he pulls her into a hug. "If it comes down to spending my life next to a wife in love with another or watching my kingdom and everyone I care about fall, I will gladly sacrifice both of our happiness."

Every muscle in my body stiffens. It's not just his or her happiness at stake. It's my sanity. I cannot bear the thought of him living out every dream I have with her. It will drive me mad to see her marry him, kiss him, sleep in his bed, and grow heavy with his child.

Breyla belongs to me, and they should fear how far I will go to ensure that.

Something in the way he words his answers catches my attention, though. He's answering her, but saying so much more that I can't decipher.

"What aren't you telling us?" I ask, folding my arms across my chest.

Outwardly, nothing about his posture changes. Internally, however, his heartbeat quickens, telling me I'm on to something.

"Now is not the time to lie." My eyes narrow. "I think there's been enough of that in this family."

His jaw clenches, the moments ticking by in silence.

With a heavy sigh, he admits, "Much like your own court, I suspect, no, I know, there are eyes and ears reporting to an enemy."

"You mean the Fae," I say bluntly.

Ayden gives a curt nod, then continues, "There is far more going on here than either of you realizes, and I'm risking everything by telling you even this. I have valid reasons for wanting to wed you, Breyla."

A low growl vibrates my chest at that admission.

One that he pointedly ignores before adding, "More than just your brilliant mind, beauty, and heart."

"So where do we go from here?" Breyla asks.

Ayden's brow furrows, and his eyes narrow just a sliver. "*You two* don't go anywhere. You," he says, pointing to me, "will be assigned duties to familiarize yourself with the kingdom, its citizens, and politics. It will keep you busy and away from the castle for the foreseeable future."

I swear a molar cracks with how hard I clench my jaw.

"And you, Breyla, will be taking more interest in the kingdom you are to rule from within the castle. You will attend council meetings and war strategy sessions. You will assist my mother and sister with winter solstice preparations, and you will continue your training with me."

"Is that all?" Breyla grits out.

"Oh, and you'll be sleeping in *my* chambers moving forward."

His statement lacks the smug satisfaction I've come to expect from my brother.

"Absolutely not," I growl at the same time that Breyla says, "The fuck I will."

"I'm sorry, Princess, but you've lost your say in the matter," he replies, taking hold of her by the arm to lead her out. "And you never had any say to begin with," he says to me as he opens the door.

I don't bother hiding the ire in my voice when I say, "You're a godsdamned prick, Ayden."

Much to my dismay, he doesn't respond to my goading. "Good night, brother. I will send you your itinerary in the morning."

And with that, they're gone. I'm left standing alone in my room, a sense of dread filling my gut. Dread and longing for the female who has wound herself entirely around my soul.

Smoke fills the air as battle cries ring out around me. The clashing of metal against metal and metal against flesh forms a medley of fear and confusion.

To my right is a canvas tent, soldiers streaming out, weapons raised. On my left, an abandoned campfire, the large kettle still boiling and forgotten.

"Lord Aurelius?" a familiar yet grating voice calls.

General Darian.

"What are you doing here?" he shouts over the roar of battle.

What *am* I doing here? I honestly don't know. The last thing I remember was falling asleep after Ayden dragged Breyla from my arms.

"Actually, I don't care." He shoves a sword into my hand. "We're under attack. Be useful and go kill something."

There's no time to question, so I take his lead, following the stream of soldiers to the heart of the conflict.

An unsettling sense of familiarity washes over me when I glimpse our attackers. They're much larger than the average soldier, though not that much larger than Ayden or me. Their armor is an exact match to the three males that attacked Breyla, Nameah, and me when we retrieved Julian's body.

Crimson eyes glow through the darkness, making it easy to distinguish them from the Prudian army.

If history is any indication, this will be a slaughter.

My sword clashes with the nearest male. I block just in time to avoid a fatal blow, then launch my own attack, one he easily deflects. We trade blows back and forth, both fighting for the upper hand, until I finally remember I have more than just a sword.

I let my Gift flow, willing it to freeze his arm mid-strike. To my horror, it doesn't work. It slows his movement, but doesn't stop them entirely. Still, it's enough. I plunge my blade through his throat, severing his head.

I move on to the next, then the next, and the next.

My limbs grow heavy, exhaustion dragging at me. Finally, the attackers retreat, disappearing before my eyes. Much like before.

I'm not sure what time I arrived, but by the time the battle ends, it's mid-morning.

"Aurelius," Darian calls. "Join me."

I follow him into his tent, dropping the borrowed sword at his feet before collapsing into a chair.

"Did Ayden send you?" he asks, handing me a mug of water.

I take a healthy gulp, then another, swallowing so quickly I almost miss the burn. Choking on the liquid, definitely not water, I clear my throat and wipe the spill from my chin.

"What? No, he didn't." I peer at the mug before setting it aside. "Do you have actual water?"

He throws a water skin at me, letting it hit my chest. "Then what are you doing here?"

"Truth be told, I don't know. The last I knew, I was falling asleep in my bed. At the castle." I pause. "Where exactly are we?"

"Darest, the closest town to the coast. It's the heaviest hit in Prudia and nearly a day and a half's ride from the castle." His brow furrows. "So I'll ask you again: how the hell did you find your way into my camp in the middle of an attack?"

"I. Don't. Know," I reiterate for his gnat-sized brain. "But I do know those soldiers."

"You've come across them before?"

I nod. "They were behind the murder of Breyla's second, Julian. They sent her his head in a velvet-lined box. When we went to retrieve his body, they attacked us. Ended up killing a female Breyla had grown attached to in the process. Until recently, we had believed them to be connected to Ayden, actually."

Darian scoffs. "That's not really the prince's style."

"Oh really? Setting traps, dramatic flare, and leaving cryptic notes doesn't sound like Ayden to you?"

He shrugs, taking a pull of the clear liquor. "You have me there. Tell me about this note."

"It didn't say much, just included a line from that prophecy Ayden showed us. *The Queen of Shadows and Crimson Prince will fall.*"

"Anything else?"

"One of them said *'The prince sends his regards'* just before they disappeared."

Darian grunts, but says nothing more.

"I'm impressed, General." I gulp down another drink of water. "Having fought those soldiers before, I know it is no easy task. I expected a total loss, but your army seems to have held its own."

"You insult me, Prince."

"That was not my intent. It was meant as praise, but I'm clearly out of practice."

"It's fine." He waves me off. "It hasn't always been that way. I've lost many good soldiers to this conflict. My predecessor even more. It is why Ayden fights and schemes so hard to protect what we have." A hint of sadness slips through his tone. Perhaps even a bit of shame.

"I'm a bit fuzzy on the details. What is this conflict, General?"

"Have you truly not figured it out yet?"

I shake my head, though the question feels rhetorical.

"It's the Fae. They toy with us like a cat playing with a mouse before it devours it. Full-blown war is inevitable, and what you witnessed tonight is merely a taste of the devastation to come."

I'm not surprised by his answer. "But why? What conflict do either of our kingdoms have with the Fae?"

"That is the question, isn't it?"

CHAPTER TWENTY-SIX

"**M**y Lord, there is someone here to see you," Lyla says from the doorway of the royal family's private dining room.

This room was the last place that offered even a sliver of peace, outside of Elijah's chambers. And since we're more inclined to partake in *other* activities there, we've taken to eating alone in here.

Elijah and I have been run ragged preparing for the influx. A week after Jade sent the survivors to Ciyoria, we received a missive from Pelanor reporting attacks nearly identical to the ones that decimated Caedel. While Pelanor hasn't been formally evacuated, its residents are arriving in droves. The late King Raynor's and Lord Aurelius' parents were among them. Not long after, Nameah's family arrived, bearing grim news that every farmland between here and the towns south of Pelanor has been burned. All the livestock and crops we rely on for winter... gone.

"Who is it, Lyla?" Elijah asks, smiling. It doesn't quite reach his eyes, though. Deep purple circles rim the brown of his irises.

I squeeze his hand in a sign of silent reassurance.

"He told me he was Rimor's newly appointed guard dog," Lyla says, her tone lifting at the end, like it's a question rather than a statement. "Though he used several vulgar words that I won't repeat."

At her words, Elijah tenses. His fork hovers halfway to his mouth, frozen.

"That sounds about right," Elijah mutters, dropping the forgotten food onto his plate. "Tell *Cillian* we will see him in here. Thank you, Lyla."

"Of course, My Lord." Lyla curtsies before backing out of the room.

"What do you think he wants?" I ask as the door clicks shut.

"It can't be anything good," Elijah sighs.

With a soft hand on his cheek, I turn his face to mine, looking deep into the brown of his irises. A soft afternoon light catches them, illuminating the amber bursts that surround his pupil. My thumb strokes his skin softly, and he leans into the touch, savoring the comfort I wish I could wrap him in.

"Whatever it is, we'll handle it," I whisper, leaning my forehead to rest against his. "The weight on your shoulders is immense, and I wish I could bear it for you."

"You make the load feel like a warm blanket rather than the crushing boulder it is, Ophelia." His lips ghost against mine in the slightest of kisses. "You make everything a little easier to bear."

Though I'm desperate for more of his touch, more of these quiet moments with him, the spell is broken by the crash of the heavy wooden door slamming against the stone wall.

"What a touching moment," Cillian drawls, the lilt in his voice uncharacteristically unmasked.

"It was," Elijah says, drawing back. "Until you graced us with your presence."

"Well, don't stop on my account. I don't mind waiting." A smirk curls the corner of Cillian's lips. "Or watching."

Elijah shakes his head, sighing deeply. "Sometimes I wonder what females see in you."

"I don't," Cillian replies flatly. "I have a massive cock and I use it to make them scream. Loudly. And Frequently."

My eyes flare wide at his vulgar description, the words sparking an image in my mind that I definitely don't need.

"Gods, I forgot how blunt you could be," Elijah says, a hint of reluctant humor slipping through his irritation.

"Says the one who is best friends with Breyla. She is the bluntest female I've ever met." Cillian snorts. "I find it quite refreshing."

"Fair point." Elijah shrugs.

"Why are you here, Cillian?" I ask, steering the conversation back to what matters.

"I do love it when you say my name, darling."

A low sound closely resembling a growl escapes Elijah before he catches himself and clears his throat.

Cillian smirks, clearly pleased with himself, before lifting two fingers to the corner of his mouth and letting out a high-pitched whistle.

Another one of his mercenaries enters the room, dragging a bound form. Dark material covers their face, but the stature tells me they're male.

Elijah's eyebrows shoot up. "Who is this?"

"I don't know his name." Cillian rips the covering from the male's head. "The fucker wouldn't divulge it."

The blood in my veins turns to ice.

Eyes the color of steel stare into mine. Mottled purple skin and swelling distort the face in places, but the eyes are unmistakable because they're *mine*.

Dark brown hair frames the misshapen face of my father.

He can't speak from the gag, but I see the disgust and contempt clear in his face as he eyes me up and down.

A breath catches in my throat at the memory of every time I had seen that look before. It was frequently followed by the burn of his Gift frying every nerve ending in my body.

Elijah and Cillian speak, but their voices dissolve into static. I hear nothing but my own breath and the rush of blood in my ears.

Two strides.

That's all it takes to cross the space and wrap my fingers around his throat.

I squeeze, feeling the way he swallows against my palm, fear filling his eyes.

"Layne is dead because of you," I cry.

His brows furrow, an emotion I'm not accustomed to seeing on his face—confusion.

Before I can second-guess myself, I unleash my Gift. Black light flickers to life around my hand, a dull glow as I press against his windpipe.

He has no time to fight. No time to resist. His life drains beneath my fingers as his skin pales and cracks, shriveling until he's nothing but a husk. His eyes go glassy, and I release him, the breath rattling in my chest more relief than remorse.

"Ophelia," Elijah says softly, stepping forward. His hand wraps around mine, drawing me toward him.

Something like concern flashes in his eyes as he looks from me to the dead male at my feet.

"Yes, Elijah?" I ask after a long moment, my voice soft and empty.

"What are you doing?"

I struggle to understand why he would question me removing the male responsible for so much pain and death in this court. "Dealing with a problem."

"We don't even know his name, Ophelia." His tone is hesitant, cautious. "Much less why Cillian brought him here."

"Who cares what his name was?" Cillian chimes in, tone reverent, as if I were a goddess blessing her chosen or performing a miracle. "That was brilliant."

I shake my head, confused by them both. "Of course, we know his name. That is, or was, my father, Lord Seamus."

Cillian looks puzzled, while Elijah just looks… sullen. He pulls me into his chest, wrapping an arm around my middle and holding me close.

"Ophelia, whatever you just saw…" Elijah says into my hair, running his hand up and down my back. "It wasn't real."

"What do you mean? Of course it is," I argue, heat creeping up my throat. "I know what my own father looks like."

"I know you do, sweetheart. But I need you to look again. Really look. And tell me what you see."

Pushing out of his hold, I turn back towards the lifeless male.

"What color is his hair?" Elijah prompts.

"Brown," I answer without hesitation.

"And his eyes?"

"Gray—just like mine."

"Look again, O."

I look again, blinking several times as the gray shifts, softening into a steely blue rather than gray. "They're not gray," I whisper, my voice trembling.

"What else do you see?"

I study the body again. The face is still misshapen, but the features are clear enough. A strong brow, a thin scar dissecting the left at its arch. His nose was long, but slightly crooked, likely broken at some point. That wasn't right. My father's nose had been perfectly straight. Then I notice the birthmark just above the male's cheek.

My breath catches. "That's not my father."

"No, it's not," Elijah says gently. "We burned him alongside your brother and Queen Genevieve two months ago."

"Oh gods," I gasp, stumbling back a step into Elijah's arms.

"Breathe, Ophelia," he urges.

But I can't. A sob tears through me, jagged and raw. "I killed someone I don't even know."

"Shhh," Elijah soothes, pulling me tighter, trying to quiet the hysteria clawing at my throat.

"Elijah, I killed someone. I killed an innoce—"

"Oh, he was far from innocent," Cillian chimes in, cutting me off. He's standing right behind us now, close enough for me to notice his clove and vanilla scent.

I twist in Elijah's arms and reach for Cillian, my fingers fisting in his tunic. "What do you mean?"

"He was a spy," Cillian replies without hesitation, meeting my gaze head-on.

The tension in my shoulders bleeds away, replaced by a rush of relief. Guilt still lingers, but it no longer threatens to choke me. I can live with this. I can live with ending the life of someone who may have taken others.

"You could have led with that, asshole," Elijah mutters, prying my hand from Cillian's shirt and lacing our fingers together.

"I was getting there." Cillian shrugs. "But the little *goddess of death* kind of interrupted my explanation. Not that I'm complaining, much, because watching you end his life was like watching a piece of art come to life. I'm only slightly annoyed that you stole my job and killed the bastard before I could."

"You can keep your job." I shudder. "It makes my skin crawl."

"That's not how it looked from here, darling."

My cheeks flush, my eyes dropping from his to the spot on the floor that had suddenly become interesting. I can't face the truth in his words.

The thought of ending an innocent life is abhorrent to me, but ending that life didn't feel wrong. I feel the best I have in days. But that isn't a truth I can speak aloud.

"How do you know he was a spy?" Elijah asks.

"Some of your guards are idiots," Cillian says bluntly. "The spy approached them in my brothel, of all places. They were drunk, and I heard them answering questions about sensitive matters of the crown."

Elijah curses under his breath.

"Needless to say, you'll also find yourself short a few guards when you do roll call tomorrow."

"You really should have turned them in for questioning and discipline," Elijah says, jaw tight.

"Not really my style." Cillian shrugs, inspecting his nails and picking at some speck only he could see. "They were guilty of treason, and I passed the sentence."

"Did you happen to catch where the spy was from?" I ask.

"Not exactly, but I know it's not from any of the four kingdoms."

Elijah's brow raises. "How do you know that?"

Cillian crouches next to the body, brushing the hair back away from his ear, revealing an elongated point. "The last time I checked, nobody around here had ears like this."

I gasp. "Was he Fae?"

The spy's elongated canines peek out through parted lips. Other subtle features stand out now, details that had blended in before.

Cilian crosses his arms, leaning casually against the wall. "I'm no expert, but I'd say it's a distinct possibility."

"How was he able to go unnoticed?" Elijah asks, his brow furrowing.

"Oh, that's easy," Cillian says. "He had some type of magical cloak over his features, making him appear like one of us."

Elijah's eyes narrow. "Then how did you know about his ears if they were cloaked?"

"Gods, you're dense." Cillian lets out a frustrated sigh. "I didn't know about them before I arrived here. Whatever magic he had must have died with him. I only noticed *after* Ophelia ended him. Were you even paying attention?"

"My sincerest apologies for being more concerned with Ophelia in that moment," Elijah responds, his voice sharp with sarcasm.

"See, this is why you'd make a terrible mercenary."

I stifle a laugh at Cillian's mildly inappropriate humor in the middle of a serious conversation.

"It's a good thing I have no interest in being a mercenary. I'll leave that to you, *Your Highness*," Elijah says with a dry smile.

"Why, thank you, *Your Majesty*," Cillian drawls, sweeping into a mocking bow.

Elijah throws him a crude gesture, shaking his head at Cillian's jest.

Cillian just grins.

"Dispose of the body," Elijah demands. "Discreetly."

"No problem. My hounds need fresh meat, given the kingdom-wide food shortage."

At the sound of Cillian's sharp whistle, the mercenary from before enters and hoists the body on his shoulder like it were a sack of flour and not a fully grown Fae male.

"Until next time, Elijah." Cillian salutes, turning to leave.

He stops next to me, close enough that I can smell each note of his masculine scent. Spice, vanilla, and something dark.

"Don't worry, Goddess," Cillian whispers. "Your secret is safe with me." His hot breath pebbles the flesh on my neck, turning my stomach at the implication of his words.

Once he's gone, Elijah asks, "What did he whisper to you?"

"Uh—I'd rather—"

"None of your concern, Elijah," Cillian yells from down the hall.

"It doesn't matter," I say, wrapping my arms around him and forcing a smile to hide my inner turmoil.

CHAPTER TWENTY-SEVEN

Despite my protests at sleeping in Ayden's room and the unease I feel lying in bed next to anyone but Aurelius or Elijah, sleep finds me quickly. The emotional and physical exertion of the evening had been enough to let me drift off the instant my head hit the pillow.

But it doesn't last.

Barely two hours later, I jolt awake, the sun just barely peeking over the horizon. My heart races, a surge of adrenaline crackling through my veins as my eyes dart around the dark room. There's no obvious threat, but dread churns in my gut like something is terribly wrong.

Slipping from bed, I find Ayden's sword resting on the chair across the room. Weapon in hand, I creep through the room on silent feet in search of what may have disturbed me.

"Get back in bed, love," Ayden groans, his voice rough with sleep.

"Something's wrong," I whisper.

I check the bathing chamber and the sitting room, finding nothing unusual. Nothing's out of place. The lock on his door is secure.

His sleep-tousled hair sticks up in every direction, and red rims his eyes. "The only thing wrong is that we've only had an hour of sleep and you're trying to fight ghosts."

I huff, dropping the sword back into the chair before settling on the edge of the bed.

An electric current courses through me, my muscles begging to be used, and my mind a whirlwind of thoughts. My whole body hums like it just walked off a battlefield.

I cross my arms in front of my chest. "I can't sleep anymore."

"Why not?" Ayden yawns.

"My body feels…" I pause, trying to find the words. "It feels like I've just come off a fight."

"You're experiencing battle high at six in the morning?"

"Apparently so."

Ayden groans as he lifts himself upright, swinging his legs off the bed. The only thing he'd worn to sleep was a pair of loose gray pants, and getting him to wear even that had been a fight. Apparently, he usually sleeps naked.

I swear I hear him whimper as he drags fleece-lined leathers up his legs. Once he's fully dressed, he turns to me, running a hand over his face in an attempt to wipe the sleep from his face. "Well, come on then. Get dressed and we'll go spar."

"You're going to spar with me half asleep?"

"It's either that or fuck, and even if you'd let me between those creamy thighs, I don't fancy the idea of taking you when my brother's seed is still leaking from your pretty little cunt."

My mouth gapes open, trying to process the words coming out of his mouth.

"Too vulgar for you, Princess?" He yawns, stretching his arms above his head. "Sorry, I get crude when I've only had an hour of sleep."

I refuse to let this male rattle me, so before I can think better of it, I snap back, "Oh my cunt isn't the only place his seed was left."

That wakes him up. His eyes snap wide, the last of the sleep vanishing.

"My, my." A smirk curls his lips. "Aren't you full of surprises?"

"Among other things," I mutter, yanking on my gear.

Ten minutes later, we're circling each other in the training ring. Ayden had given the soldiers the morning off after last night's festivities, so we're alone. It's eerily quiet as I wait for Ayden to make the first move.

"Come on, General," he taunts. "Throw that first punch like I know you want to."

"I don't think so, Prince."

I see the exact moment his patience runs out. His fist is a blur as it flies toward my face. I manage to dodge it easily enough, dipping low and throwing a punch of my own into his solar plexus. My aim is off by an inch, and it doesn't have the impact I was hoping.

Ayden sputters, but recovers quickly, aiming another fist for my stomach. This one lands, stealing the breath from my lungs, and I stumble back.

I snap a roundhouse kick at him, but he catches my leg mid-air and flips me to the ground.

I wasn't born yesterday, though. Before he can pin me, I roll to the side and spring back onto my feet.

Our match continues, we trade blow for blow, neither of us relenting. For a moment, I think I'll drive him outside the boundary line to claim the victory. The excitement is short-lived when he ducks low and drives his shoulder into my stomach.

The move catches me off guard, giving him the opportunity to pin me to the ground.

His arm bands across my chest, pressing into my throat just shy of choking. "Yield?"

After a few more seconds of struggling to free myself, I finally tap his arm twice to signal my yield.

He stands, offering me an outstretched arm. "Good match, let's go again."

An hour later, we're both drenched in sweat, panting heavily, and ready for a break.

I've worked off enough of the battle high to remember that I'm thoroughly irritated by this male.

"Thanks for the distraction." I salute him, turning to leave. "Till next time."

He grabs my arm as I pass. "Not so fast."

"Ayden, let me go," I demand, trying to yank my arm free.

"There's something I want to show you." His grip loosens, but doesn't release me entirely. "And since you're on a short leash right now, it's not a request."

A falsely sweet smile curls my lips. "There's the unpredictable terror I've come to know and love."

"It's worth it. I promise."

Resigning myself to the knowledge I'm not going to win this one, I give in. "Fine. Lead the way."

With a devilish grin, he leads me through a side door in the barracks and into the castle. We duck into a hidden hallway tucked behind a tapestry, winding through corridors I'm not surprised exist.

It's a castle, after all. What kind of castle doesn't have at least a few hidden passages?

When we emerge, my breath catches in my throat.

We're standing on the roof of the eastern wing. The ledge is narrow, maybe three feet wide, with a wrought-iron fence lining the edge that I'm not sure would keep me from falling.

Ayden drops down onto the ledge with practiced ease, legs dangling over the side. He pats the spot beside him, inviting me to sit.

I hesitantly oblige, sitting next to him.

The view is breathtaking. The rising sun casts the land in a warm orange glow, igniting the autumn colors covering every inch of the realm. Reds, yellows, and glimmering golds. It's like the entire kingdom is on fire with color. From here, I can see the sprawl of the city beyond the castle, its homes and shops, and the people beginning to stir, stepping into their morning routines. So small from this height, and yet so significant.

Awe and admiration fill my voice. "The view is beautiful."

"My father used to bring me up here," Ayden says. "Told me no one else knew about it and that it would always be our little secret."

"He didn't show Rowina?"

"Oh, gods no. She's terrified of heights." He chuckles quietly.

I glance sideways at him, then work up the nerve to ask, "What was he like?"

"If you ask my mother, she'd say he was a lot like me."

"And if I ask you?"

He pauses, his smile softening. "I'd say he was a lot like Aurelius, actually."

That catches me off guard. "Really?"

"Way more mischievous, though." Ayden's eyes grow distant for a moment as memory washes over him. "Ro and I definitely got that from him."

"Aurelius has his moments of mischief."

Ayden arches a skeptical brow.

"It's true," I insist. "When I was a teenager, we spent years trying to one-up each other. It started when I created a shadow blind and made him walk into a wall face-first. He broke his nose. It was quite funny."

"I don't know that he'd agree with that sentiment."

I shrug, not really caring whether Aurelius found it funny, because I had. And still did. "Looking back, I think maybe he was only playing along to get my attention. He never pushed things further than I did."

"You don't say," Ayden deadpans.

"Whatever," I mutter. "Do you think that's why Aurelius was appointed emissary to Prudia?"

"Because you tormented him with pranks for years? I hardly think that's why your—"

"That's not what I meant." I nudge his shoulder. "Do you think your father requested Aurelius return to Prudia because he saw himself in Aurelius? Wanted to be close in whatever way he could?"

Ayden goes quiet, face contemplative. "It's possible. He was always treated better than the emissaries from other kingdoms. He definitely spent the most time here."

"I'd always assumed he spent so much time away because he was avoiding me."

Ayden shrugs. "Could be both."

A few minutes pass in silence as we watch the sun climb higher in the morning sky.

"When we lost him, I think I lost a part of myself," Ayden says, voice low.

"I can relate. My father was everything to me."

"They say it gets easier with time, but that's a lie." Ayden pauses, running a hand through his curls still damp with sweat. "It's been seven years and I still miss him."

"It doesn't get easier," I agree quietly. "You just get better at carrying it. You find little moments of joy and cling to them for when the moments of grief threaten to consume you."

He smiles, but it doesn't reach his eyes. "Those are wise words."

"It's just a lesson I'm still learning." I push a loose auburn curl behind my ear, the breeze threatening to tug it free again. "Most nights, when I close my eyes, I see my mother take her last breath, or I see Nameah enjoying her final sunset. Sometimes, it's Julian's blank stare, or the flames of Nolan's pyre."

"That does get better with time," he reassures me. "It may take years, and it will never completely go away, but there will come a day when you close your eyes and just see black."

"I'm not sure I want that."

He glances at me, puzzled. "Why?"

"Because it feels like forgetting them."

"Our ghosts don't want us living in the past, Breyla. Finding peace doesn't mean you love or miss them any less. It just means the grief learns to live beside everything else."

"That sounds exhausting," I joke, but it lands flat.

"It can be."

"What's your moment of joy today?" I ask, needing something lighter.

He smirks. "When I pinned you in the training ring. The sight of such a fierce female submitting is quite beautiful.

"Typical male," I say with a half-hearted eye roll.

"What about yours?"

I don't even need to think. "This. This moment and view right here."

"I told you it would be worth it."

CHAPTER TWENTY-EIGHT

Something aches deep within me.

The last time I saw Aurelius was three weeks ago. True to his word, Ayden kept him busy and out of Elentia. The distance between us sets me on edge in the most uncomfortable way.

Today, I'm attempting to fill the void with sweets.

Technically, Rowina and I are baking them for the people of the capital, but with so many cookies already made, a few won't be missed.

Rowina turns her back to put a tray of ginger snap cookies in the oven, and I stuff another sugar cookie into my mouth. I don't care what anyone says. These are better than chocolate chip.

With her back still to me, she says, "Your joy spikes every time you shove another cookie into your mouth."

"Consider it my moment of joy today." I shrug, crumbs spewing from the half-eaten cookie as I speak.

Since our moment on the roof, Ayden and I had made it a point to share our moment of joy with each other every day. No one else needed to know what we were talking about, because we understood. And that's all that matters.

"Well, you've had *eight* moments of joy today, so you should be set for the next week." Rowina laughs, the sound full and free. "At this rate, there isn't going to be any left for the townspeople."

I'd learned from Ayden that baking sweets for the entire castle and surrounding village was a Mordet family tradition in the months leading up to the Winter Solstice. Generations of Mordets participate. It takes months, given how many people live here.

Today, we're starting with the farthest part of the town and working our way inward. Every week, we'll take a batch leading up to the eve of the solstice. On Solstice Eve, we'll share the last round with the castle staff before letting them enjoy the night off with their loved ones.

"There are dozens of cookies here."

She slaps a fresh bowl down in front of me. "And you're about to actually help me make three more to replace the ones you've stolen."

"What do you mean? I've been helping this whole time."

"No, you've rolled dough balls and eaten almost a dozen cookies by yourself. I've done the rest."

I sweeten my voice, hoping to win her over with flattery. "You're better at it."

"Nice try." Rowina arches a dark brow at me. "I'm just more practiced. Would you prefer chocolate chip or almond?"

I contemplate it for a moment. "Do I get to eat any?"

"No," she says flatly.

"Ugh, fine. Almond, I guess."

"Good choice. That's one of my favorites." She drops a sack of flour next to the bowl and hands me a measuring cup. "Start with one and a half cups of flour. Mix it with a teaspoon of the baking soda."

I follow her instructions, mixing and combining ingredients until a sticky dough forms.

As I begin rolling the balls onto a sheet, she asks, "What are some of the traditions in Rimor?"

"We don't have anything on quite this large scale, but we do have the kitchens prepare food and send it out to those most in need."

"You only do that around the solstice?"

"I never really agreed with it, but yes." I scrunch my nose at how inattentive that makes us sound. "We only ever seemed to help when the solstice came."

Rowina pours batter into a tin baking cup, some of it spilling over the edge. "Don't you think that's a little bit… selfish?"

A few months ago, her comment would have irritated me. But seeing how Prudia operates, how the royal family actually serves its people, has changed my perspective. It opened my eyes to the short-comings in my own kingdom and how willfully ignorant I'd been.

"Yes." I frown. "I suppose you're right."

"Does your family have any traditions?"

"Elijah and I always sneak away for a snowball fight." I smile fondly at the deluge of memories. "Sometimes we let the twins join, but usually it's just us. No matter what, we always end the evening with a card tournament. My family, the twins, and even some of the staff gather in the library for a game, or several, where we bet using candies and baked goods."

"What a wonderful way to honor the goddess Revna." Rowina pauses, scrunching her nose. "So… you love the snow?"

"Hardly," I laugh. "I detest it. But I tolerate it for the chance to kick Elijah's ass. We've done it since we were ten."

Sadness, sharp and sudden, hits me when I realize I'll be missing our snowball fight for the first time in eighteen years.

Rowina must sense the shift in my emotions because she reaches over and takes my hand, rubbing the back of it in gentle reassurance. "Perhaps we can incorporate some of your traditions with our own this year."

"I'd like that." I pause, glancing at her. "It's still so strange how easily you read me."

"It's the Fae blood; it makes our Gifts stronger. Keep training with Ayden, and you'll build stronger mental defenses."

I plop the last cookie onto the sheet. "I think this is ready to go in."

"Perfect timing. These muffins are as well." She swipes her finger through some batter that's spilled over the edge and slips it into her mouth.

"That's not fair. Why do you get to taste test, but I don't?"

"You want a taste?" She gives me a coy grin, then covers her finger in leftover batter and holds it out to me. "Here."

My cheeks warm as I debate whether it's worth it to take her offer. If it were anyone else, I wouldn't think twice. But there is always a double meaning with her, and she lives to rattle me.

Fuck it.

I wrap my lips around her finger, licking off the excess batter. It lasts no more than a few seconds, but the satisfied smirk on her face burns into me.

I retreat, looking for a towel to clean my hands, only for her to catch my wrist.

"My turn," she whispers, pulling my dough-covered hand toward her mouth.

"Absolutely not," I laugh nervously, yanking my hand away.

"What's wrong, Princess?" Rowina lets out a devilish cackle. "Afraid you'll like it?"

"Much like your brother," I murmur, washing my hands in the sink. "You're incorrigible."

She lifts a brow, her honey eyes sparkling. "Which one?"

"Yes," I reply, sending us both into a fit of laughter.

We slide the new batch into the oven, pulling out the last round in the process, and settle into quiet waiting as the scent of almond and cinnamon fills the kitchen.

Once everything is baked and ready, we load it into a carriage and head for the edge of the city.

I admire the scenery as we travel, watching the vibrant reds, golds, and yellows from just a few weeks ago fade into a muted brown. There's a chill to the air that whispers of the first snow.

A phantom ache stirs in my arm at the thought of winter, an old injury Elijah and I earned from an act of pure stupidity. But I count it as joy now. The pain makes me feel closer to him.

We step out into the waiting crowd, warm smiles greeting us from every direction.

"Come and get it!" Rowina yells. It turns into a laugh as children swarm her.

"Can I have an almond cookie?" a small girl with big brown doe eyes asks.

"Of course you can!" Rowina smiles, handing her two.

The little girl gives her a big, toothy grin, hugs Rowina's leg, and dashes off with her prize.

Nearby, a boy asks for a muffin, followed by a toddler shouting, "Chocolate!"

I can't help the smile that spreads across my face from seeing the children so excited. It suddenly makes sense why this tradition has persisted through the generations. Serving others in this capacity creates contentment in my soul.

Once they figure out I have my own basket of goodies, I'm swarmed as well.

"Thank you, Princess," says a boy with blue eyes and freckles, his face lighting up as he bites into the sugar cookie.

Leaning down to his level, I whisper, "They're the best, don't you agree?"

He nods enthusiastically, so I slip him a second for confirming my long-held theory on superior cookie flavors.

As the young ones clear out, the adults approach, curious what the little heathens have left. I glance down and see we still have plenty, so I discreetly slip two more sugar cookies into my cloak pocket.

"I saw that," Rowina chides.

"I don't care, I do what I want!" I exclaim, my words rolling into devious laughter.

We finish dispersing the sugary treats and store the remaining cookies in the carriage.

"And now we shop." Rowina loops her arm through mine and steers us toward a row of nearby businesses.

We stop in front of a shop with a sign reading "Books" above the door. It has a green façade, planter boxes in the windows, and a tiny bell that jingles as we enter the space.

It's instantly warm and comforting, everything I love about libraries.

I begin browsing the shelves, letting the scents of paper and cinnamon settle me. After flipping through a few titles, I find one that catches my eye. From what I can tell, it sounds like something Ophelia might enjoy. A fallen goddess with no memory of who or what she is, fated to two males that are as similar as they are different, and their quest to rebuild a fallen kingdom and restore her memories.

I tuck the book under my arm and move on, searching for something for myself. Ayden said our physical training would lessen once the snow arrived, and I'll have more free time in the coming months.

Eventually, I settle on a book I think I might relate to. The demon king kidnaps the human princess on the day of her wedding and holds her hostage to incite war. Technically, I'm trying to avoid war, but other parts hit a little too close. Plus, the love interest has a filthy mouth from what I skimmed, and that's enough to sell me.

"Well, hello there," says a warm voice as I approach the counter. "You must be our new princess."

He's an older male with salt-and-pepper hair and deep laugh lines framing his ice-blue eyes.

I give him a warm smile. "My name's Breyla."

"Of course it is. Who else would be good enough for our prince other than the beautiful Breyla Rozaria?"

"Are you flirting with my sister, Collin?" Rowina teases, placing her own stack of books beside mine.

"Never, dear! You know Maureen is the only female for me," he says with a wink. "What did you find this time?"

"Mmm, well, these are for me." She gestures to a stack of four books. "But I got this one for Darian. Do you think he'll like it?"

Collin picks up the book, flipping it over briefly before nodding. "I think it's perfect for that son of mine. He'll love it."

"Darian is your son?" I sputter in disbelief. How this kind soul could have fathered the same male that threatened to kill me the first time we met is beyond my comprehension.

"One of them." He smiles proudly. "I've got three."

"It's so nice to meet you, sir. I never would have guessed you two were related."

Rowina giggles beside me. "Darian doesn't much like Breyla. They've come to blows on more than one occasion. It's quite the spectacle."

I shoot Rowina a look of irritation for betraying me.

"You tell that boy of mine that he needs to treat his future queen with respect, or I'll send his ma after him," Collin says sternly, eyes focused on Rowina. "Don't think I won't."

"I'll make sure he knows."

Rowina places entirely too much coin on the counter, which Collin tries to refuse, but ultimately, he fails, taking the money from her when she insists.

He wraps our books in brown paper before handing them back to us.

Rowina places a small package of cookies on the counter before leaning in and planting a kiss on his cheek.

"It was good seeing you," she says sweetly.

"Always a pleasure, my dear." He smiles, the lines around his eyes creasing. "Don't be a stranger. Maureen misses you."

"I'll make sure Darian brings me back for your next family dinner."

"See that you do," he says, patting her on the cheek.

Once we're outside, I say, "I had no idea you were so close to Darian."

It's not entirely truthful. I had seen the way he looked at her when they danced at the ball. It was clear they were friends, but I was still trying to work out the nature of that friendship.

"He's my best friend, has been since we were old enough to walk."

"And he's in love with you," I say, finally voicing the suspicion I've carried.

She blushes, her breath catching on a soft sigh. "I love him."

"But?"

"But I'm just not attracted to males. He's my best friend, but it breaks my heart that I can't love him how he wants me to."

I squeeze her arm gently, my lips turning up in what I hope is a reassuring smile. "Asking us to change who we love would be tantamount to asking the sun to rise in the west and set in the east."

Rowina smiles back, one dark brow quirking. "Speaking from experience, Princess?"

"My track record would suggest so," I admit, for the first time, unashamedly.

"Oh, now you have to give me the details."

I chuckle, feeling lighter than I have in weeks. This moment feels like something I would have Ophelia, and for just a moment, I let Rowina fill the void her absence left in me.

"The first male I ever cared for romantically was the son of the leader of the Midnight Brotherhood, a mercenary guild in Rimor. He enlisted in the castle guard with the sole purpose of spying and recruiting from within."

"Wow, that's a lot to unpack."

"I was the one to figure it out, but I couldn't bring myself to execute him. Or even report it formally."

She tilts her head, her honey-gold eyes assessing me. "Why not?"

"If you'd asked me back then... I'd have said it was pragmatic. His father was a problem, and I knew one day he'd take his place. I figured the devil you know is better than the one you don't and took a chance that Cillian would be a better option than possibly inciting war with the Midnight Brotherhood by killing their heir."

"But that's not the only reason, is it?"

I sigh, deliberating how to explain why I spared Cillian. "Don't get me wrong, having a mercenary king with a life debt to you is very useful. But if that were all it was, I wouldn't have found myself back in his bed so many times over the years."

"Was the sex really that good?"

"That's beside the point," I deflect.

"It so was!" Rowina laughs, bursting into a fit of giggles.

"Calm down, you fiend. Yes, Cillian knows exactly what he's doing when it comes to the female body." I nudge her shoulder. "The point is that I loved him, though I would've never admitted that out loud. And I couldn't stomach the heartbreak of his betrayal and the devastation of ending his life. It would have broken me entirely."

"When did you finally move on?"

Our walk slows outside another storefront, similar to Collin's bookshop, though this one bears no sign. From the outside, it's impossible to tell what it holds.

"Shortly before I realized what I felt Cillian was a fraction of what I feel for…" I trail off, remembering Ayden's warning about there being a traitor in his kingdom, and think better of uttering Aurelius' name out loud.

"My brother?" Rowina offers.

Bless her for saving me, whether she knows which brother I'm referring to or not.

I nod, my cheeks flushing.

She opens the door, ushering me inside.

The shop is stunning. Lavish garments cover every inch of the space. Every color and style of clothing imaginable is available on the racks of rich fabrics, shelves of delicate lace and furs, all bathed in warm light. I bypass the gowns and make for the back, where fur-lined cloaks and trousers hang like forbidden treasure.

A warm brown cloak with gold stitching and a white fur lining catches my eye. Upon further inspection, I find the gold stitches form the pattern of stars along the edges. I run my fingers along the collar, admiring how buttery soft the material feels.

"Find something you fancy, Your Highness?" a soft, feminine voice inquires.

I turn to find the same seamstress responsible for my engagement ballgowns. "It's Emery, right?"

"It is, Princess." She nods, smiling demurely. "You have a sharp memory."

"You are immeasurably gifted," I praise, watching her eyes light. "I'm sorry to report that something tragic happened to the gold gown, but the black one served me well."

Emery blushes. "Ah, well. It would have been a disservice to let anyone else wear that dress. It was made for you, after all."

"This cloak is marvelous. What fur is this?" I ask, stroking the soft inner lining.

"Snow leopard from Meloria, my lady." She gestures to a table nearby. "There is a pair of matching gloves, as well."

A wide grin splits my face. "That would be perfect. Can you wrap it up and have it delivered to the castle, please?"

"It would be my pleasure," she replies, already moving.

I stroll through the rest of the shop, admiring a gown here and there, but find nothing else that truly grasps my interest.

"Are you ready to return to the castle?" Rowina asks when I find her a short while later.

Her arms are full, gowns of deep blue, black, and purple hanging from one arm and fur-lined leggings hanging from the other.

"Do you need any help?"

"No, Emery has it handled," Rowina says, dropping her pile onto the counter, followed by a heavy bag of coin.

My brows furrow. "That seems like a hefty sum for all of that."

Rowina shuffles me out the door, throwing Emery a wave over her shoulder as we step outside.

"That's because I pay her well for the lengths she must go to get those leggings into the castle for me."

My brows raise and my eyes widen in confusion. "You pay for your own leggings?"

Rowina scoffs. "Surely you didn't think you were the only one subjected to my mother's archaic views on female attire."

"Actually, yes," I reply. "I thought it was a personal attack on my comfort, or at the very least an attempt to turn me into the perfect lady-like bride for Ayden."

"Don't hear this the wrong way, but you aren't *that* special, Breyla." She pats my shoulder, laughing softly. "I've been smuggling pants into the castle for over a decade."

"And you haven't shared your secrets with me before now, why?" I ask as we climb into the awaiting carriage.

"What do you think I was doing today? Half those leggings were for you."

"You are officially my favorite Mordet sibling."

A wicked grin tilts the corners of Rowina's plump lips. "Oh, I know. I'm very good at what I do."

Ignoring her innuendo, I dare to voice the question that's been eating at me since we left Collin's shop. "Darian's father said he had three sons. Why haven't I heard about them before?"

Rowina stiffens, but quickly smooths her expression. "His youngest brother, Tiberius, is too young for court. He usually stays at home with their mother."

"And the other?".

"Malcom is…" she pauses, searching for the right words. "He's no longer with us."

"Oh, I'm very sorry." My tone softens, betraying the regret I almost feel for asking these questions. "What happened to him?"

Rowina worries her lip between her teeth, shifting uncomfortably in her seat. "That's really not my story to tell."

Sensing I've treaded in unwelcome territory, I reassure her, "Forget I asked. It was not my place."

Her shoulders relax, the tension in her muscles uncoiling. The rest of the ride back is filled with trivial chatter, but I can't help wondering what piece of the puzzle I'm missing when it comes to Darian.

CHAPTER TWENTY-NINE

BREYLA

Golden patches of sunlight cast shadows through the room, warming my face and every other surface they touch. I've been awake for hours, but haven't mustered the will to extract myself from the comfort of the covers. Ayden had given me the morning off from any training, physical or otherwise, and I had spent all of it in bed.

He claimed it was because we were attending a council meeting today where the topic was the increasing number of attacks, not just within Prudia, but across the entire continent. The countries were tearing themselves apart, and something needed to be done.

But I knew the truth. He left me in this bed because I, the general and princess of Rimor, was moping. We had taken the first batch of cookies out three days ago, and since then, I had grown increasingly irritable.

I am not blind to my own shortcomings. I'm quick-tempered, and yes, I'm impulsive at times. But lately, control over my emotions has become elusive. No matter how desperately I grasp for it.

I lie staring at the ceiling, a small tendril of shadow twirling between my fingers as I recall the incident from yesterday.

"Breyla, would you prefer cream or ivory linens on the wedding banquet tables?" Queen Josephina asked.

"Does it really matter?" I sighed.

They had asked me this and a dozen other questions over the last hour. None of them was of any great importance or interest to me. If I were being forced down an aisle, they could dress me in a potato sack for all I cared.

"Of course it matters," the queen scoffed, indignation sharpening her tone. "You will only wed my son once. It must be perfect."

"The only thing that could make it perfect is if I didn't have to do it," I muttered.

"Excuse me?" She clutched her chest, head rearing back as though I'd physically assaulted her.

"You heard me, Your Majesty," I snapped.

"You will listen to me now, Breyla." Queen Josephina's gilded eyes hardened, her tone dropping low. "In two months' time, you will walk down that aisle, you will marry my son and rule by his side, you will joyfully bear his children—and you will do it all happily."

I shot to my feet, the pitiful excuse for needlework falling to the floor. Anger flooded my veins, a heat scorching through my core at her demands. "I will do no such thing. Your son may control my future, but you do not control my feelings on the matter."

"You are a stupid, impulsive child," she seethed.

My eyes hardened, narrowing into slits. "Impulsive, yes. Stupid? Never."

"What would Raynor and Genevieve think of you now?"

The blow is low, meant to hurt me. It enraged me.

"Fuck you," I snarled, my hand lifting, ready to strike.

Before I could do something punishable by death, strong fingers wrapped around my wrist, stopping it in midair. The grip was firm but not painful.

Ayden.

"Leave us, Mother," his deep voice commanded.

She opened her mouth as if to protest, but he cut her off. "Now."

With an exasperated huff, she turned to go.

I didn't bother to face her, calling over my shoulder, "Keep my parents' names out of your fucking mouth."

"What was that about, darling?" Ayden asked, far calmer than I expected.

With the absence of the queen, my anger receded, replaced by a wave of nausea. Ayden's skin on mine turned my stomach, and I swallowed, resisting the urge to lose my breakfast all over his shoes.

I pulled my hand from his grip, surprised by how easily it slipped free.

"I can handle her opinions of me, her thinking I'm stupid and impulsive, but I cannot tolerate her insulting my parents' memory. Or dictating how she believes I should feel."

Tears stream down my cheeks before I can process the sudden shift in emotion. Ayden didn't even have time to respond before I was full-on sobbing.

Blinking hard, I shake the memory away.

Ayden had carried me to bed, completely unsure of what to do with me. The moment I hit the mattress, every ounce of fight had left me, leaving me so exhausted that I fell asleep almost immediately.

Healers had been in to see me, confirming that I am in perfect physical health, but could not determine why I was acting so irrationally.

Reluctantly, I drag myself from bed and dress. To my delight, Rowina hadn't lied when she said the leggings were for me. Unfortunately, I have to wear them sparingly since they seem to disappear any time they are sent to be laundered.

Since it's unlikely that I will be traveling outside of the castle today, I forgo the leggings, slipping into a warmer dress instead. It's black, long-sleeved, and unremarkable. But it's comfortable.

The hallway is empty, save for the usual guards posted at the far end. I slip past them on silent feet, heading toward the kitchens. I missed breakfast, but there are always leftovers.

I have just enough time before the council meeting to grab something small to hold me over until dinner.

The kitchen is quiet when I arrive. Most of the staff are elsewhere, preparing for the midday meal. On the counter sits a plate of pastries, but none of them appeals to me. I want something fresh to balance the embarrassing number of cookies I've consumed over the last few weeks.

In the corner, I spot the pantry where Rowina and I pulled ingredients for baking.

A Faerie light flickers to life in my palm as I step into the dark space.

The unmistakable sound of a door shutting and a lock turning sends a chill up my spine.

I'm not alone in here.

But I don't even reach for my shadows. I don't need to.

Because I recognize his scent immediately.

"Aurelius." His name escapes me in a rush as my back hits the wall, and I let him pin me there.

"Yes, my little demon?"

In the flickering light, all I can see is the intense look in his eyes as he stares me down.

Hunger.

"You're back."

"For now." A sober look crosses his face. "We've got limited time, so extinguish that light before someone finds us."

Soft lips plant heated kisses along my neck as the light flickers out between us.

"What are you doing?" The breath hitches in my throat as rough hands reach for my skirt.

"Stealing a moment," he whispers between kisses to my clavicle.

Heat pools in my core, body aching for his touch after weeks apart. The constant churn of my stomach settles instantly when his lips land on the spot on my throat where he had last marked me. The scar from his teeth lingers as a sensual reminder.

"Fuck," I whimper when he nips at that same spot again.

He rolls his hips into me, the bulge of his arousal firm against my belly. "I delight in my marks on you," he growls.

My dress is pushed above my waist, leaving me exposed to the chilled air in the pantry. Warm fingers dance over the skin of my thighs, leaving pebbled flesh in their wake.

I raise a hand to cast a silencing shield, but Aurelius' hand wraps around my wrist.

"No silencing," he warns. "I want to see how quiet you can be while I feast on that sweet cunt."

"I thought I was the reckless one in this relationship," I breathe, panic rising in my chest.

But the protest dies on my tongue when he drops to his knees. In the dark, I can barely make out his profile, but I feel his breath, hot against my center.

"I guess it's my turn to be reckless," he says just before burying his face against my heated core.

Tenderly, Aurelius peels the undergarments down my thighs.

His mouth is sin incarnate, tongue sweeping up through my folds in one slow, devastating pass. I throw a hand over my mouth the second he sucks my clit between his lips. My other hand tangles in his inky hair.

A low chuckle vibrates through him. If I could see, I know I'd find that smug look of pure male satisfaction carved into his too-perfect face.

He swirls his tongue around my clit in slow, torturous circles. My hips grind against him of their own accord, greedy and helpless. It's like I lose all bodily autonomy when he's between my legs. What he demands, I readily give.

His tongue alternates between teasing my clit and spearing into me like he's fucking me with his mouth. When two fingers slip inside my dripping entrance, I nearly lose all control, a soft moan escaping.

"Shhh," he hushes me before curling his fingers forward in a motion that makes my legs tremble.

We both still when the soft click of heeled shoes echoes through the kitchen just outside the pantry. It's probably just a servant, but the fear of being caught has my heartbeat racing.

The fear slowly turns into excitement, the possibility of being discovered, despite the consequences, heightening my arousal. I writhe, my hips rocking against his mouth in a desperate plea for more.

Such a naughty princess. The thrill of being caught...

I shake my head, unsure where the thought was coming from.

The footsteps retreat, and Aurelius resumes his slow assault, tongue and fingers pushing me closer and closer to bliss.

My hand tightens in his hair, nails digging into his scalp as my inner walls begin to clench around his fingers.

The need to come apart around him floods my system, a violent tingling warmth growing at the base of my spine.

A new set of footsteps sounds. These are decidedly male, though.

But I'm too close to release to stop now. Just before I find bliss, I throw up a silencing shield.

In a move that's pure punishment for disobeying his order, Aurelius bites down on my clit. The masochist inside me cries in sensual feminine satisfaction when the pain tips into pleasure, sending me flying straight over the edge.

His name erupts from my lips in a moan that never leaves the shield.

He laps at my center softly, soothing the pain his teeth caused. As the last waves of pleasure ebb, he places a soft kiss on the top of my pelvis while pulling my undergarments back into place.

The skirts of my dress fall as he stands. "You will pay for that disobedience later, little demon."

"Breyla?" Ayden calls from the other side of the pantry door.

"I'm going to exit first and distract him. You're going to use those beautiful shadows to hide yourself in here until we're long gone," Aurelius commands, taking a bite of something, an apple from the smell of it.

"Will you be at the council meeting?"

"Unfortunately." Aurelius brushes a knuckle along my cheek, the unexpected tenderness tightening my chest. "Now be a good girl and eat this before you pass out. I can hear your stomach growling."

"Breyla, are you in here?" Ayden calls again, closer this time.

Aurelius drops the apple in my hand, ushering me into the furthest corner of the pantry. Once I'm fully cloaked in shadows, I drop the shield as he summons a Faerie light and opens the door.

"It's just me, brother," he says smoothly as he steps out.

"Oh, it's you," Ayden says flatly. "Have you seen Breyla? The council meeting starts in ten minutes, and I can't find her anywhere."

Aurelius grunts. "I haven't seen her in nearly a month." Bitterness coats the lie that rolls off his tongue.

"An unfortunate consequence of your own actions," Ayden replies coolly.

"That you're conveniently benefiting from," Aurelius bites out.

"And how is that?"

"You smell of honeysuckle, Prince."

"Oh, do I?" I can hear the smirk I know is covering Ayden's lips.

"She may be sleeping in your bed, Ayden," Aurelius drawls, his tone taunting. "But only one of us knows what she tastes like."

The familiar sound of bone meeting flesh rings out, followed by a grunt from Aurelius.

He hit him.

Rage boils through my veins at the thought of Ayden punching Aurelius.

A hysterical laugh bursts from Aurelius. "What's it like to be on the other end of someone getting under your skin, brother? Can't handle a little of your own tactics turned against you?"

"I'll see you in the council meeting, Aurelius," Ayden seethes.

The sound of both males' footsteps slowly fades as they leave the kitchen. I wait several minutes before slipping out of the pantry, shadows clinging to me like smoke.

I enter the council room ten minutes later, last to arrive. Everyone else is already present and seated. Darian sits to Ayden's left, glaring daggers at me the moment I take my seat to Ayden's right.

"Did you get lost, *General*?" Darian sneers.

"I apologize for my tardiness. I was hungry," I say, keeping my voice even.

"Then perhaps you should eat the apple in your hand," Aurelius says casually from down the table.

Charlie sits beside him, her arm brushing his on the table and making my stomach turn sour. I drag my gaze away, sweeping down the rest of Ayden's council.

Three other males occupy the chairs on my side of the table. One is older—his hair more grey than not, and wrinkles creasing his eyes and corners of his mouth. The other two look as if they could be related with their blond hair and moss-green eyes. Another female occupies the last chair. If I were to guess, I would say she's in her middle years. Not young, but not exactly old.

I bite into the apple, savoring the crisp, tangy taste that coats my tongue.

Wait.

This variety of apple isn't tangy—it's always sweet.

Realization hits me, and I choke on the juice. Coughing into my hand, I avoid making eye contact with anyone at the table as my face burns.

He bit into the apple before handing it to me. His mouth had been covered in my arousal. I was tasting myself on the apple.

Ignoring the quizzical looks, I force myself to chew and swallow. *Another bite.*

I take another bite, bracing for the slightly off-taste this time.

"The attacks are growing more frequent," Darian begins, thankfully drawing the room's attention away from me.

From the corner of my eye, I catch Aurelius and the barely-there, insufferably smug smirk that plays at the corner of his lips.

I finish the apple, bite by devious bite, until all that remains is the core, as Darian details the attacks Prudia has suffered over the last month.

"Are they using the poison each time?" one of the blonds, Lord Talon, asks.

"No," Darian answers. "They've only been using it roughly one attack out of every four."

"What are the casualties like?" Charlie asks.

"Minimal when the poison isn't used." Darian's navy eyes dull, and he runs a hand through his short chestnut locks. "But when it is… nearly thirty percent."

My chest deflates. Thirty percent is catastrophic.

"And their casualties?" Ayden asks.

Darian's jaw clenches. "Not nearly enough. As best we can tell, maybe a fifth of our own."

My mind does the calculations, my stomach dropping at the severity of the situation.

Six percent.

For every one of their soldiers that fell, *five* Prudian soldiers fell in their place. This wasn't sustainable.

"Is there any difference in the attacks when the poison is present?" I ask abruptly.

Darian shoots me an irritated look. "Not that I'm aware of."

My brain whirls, trying to puzzle out why they would only be using the poison a quarter of the time. Either the supply was limited, which seems unlikely, or there was something different about the locations they were attacking with the poison.

Charlie starts to ask a question, but I cut her off. "Show me."

Darian cocks a brow at me. "Show you?"

"Yes. Show me on the map where the attacks with poison happened."

"I don't see why the location matt—" Charlie starts.

"I thought you were supposed to be clever, Charlotte."

She rears back as if I had physically struck her.

Shooting to her feet, a look of disbelief covers her face. "Excuse me?"

"You're excused." I turn back to Darian. "Now show me. There *must* be a pattern here somewhere."

"Sit down, Charlotte," Lord Talon chides, shooting me an encouraging look. "Let the generals work this out."

A vexed huff leaves Charlie's lips as she drops back down, refusing to make eye contact with anyone.

Darian unfurls a map across the table in front of me, marking various spots around the kingdom with an X for the attacks where poison was used, an O for those where it wasn't.

"These are the locations of every attack over the last year. Now tell me what pattern I'm not seeing," Darian demands, but it lacks his usual bite.

"What about prior to the last year?"

A darkness swims in Darian's eyes, his fists clenching at his sides. "I don't have records of those," he grits, anger and something far darker lacing his tone.

Ayden clears his throat, drawing my attention to him. "Those records exist only in the memory of my previous general."

I read between the words Ayden is and isn't saying.

The previous general is dead.

It's something I should have known, having been in conflict with Prudia for far longer than the last year, but I had missed something.

"We'll work with what we've got," I concede. Darian's posture relaxes, and I store that information away.

I study the various marks on the map, looking for something, anything at all that will provide a pattern for me to work with.

Darian's calloused fingers trace over the map, the wheels turning in his mind.

Several minutes pass in silence before I release a defeated sigh.

"Godsdammit. There's something here, there *must be*."

"Or perhaps…" Darian says, dropping back into his chair. He rubs his jaw, his brow furrowing. "You aren't as clever as everyone lets you believe."

A low snarl rumbles from Aurelius, but Ayden speaks over him. "That's enough, General."

"Unbelievable," Darian mutters, shaking his head.

"Lady Seris, has there been any progress with the tonic?" Ayden asks, redirecting the conversation.

The older female smiles, the corners of her lips not quite reaching her eyes. "I'm disappointed to report that a cure for the poison still evades us. We were, however, able to formulate a tonic that slows the spread. As far as we can tell, it extends the life expectancy by up to a few days. Just depending on when the tonic is administered."

"You're working on a cure?" I ask, recalling how Aurelius and Ophelia both failed to counter the poison's effects.

"We're *trying*," Lady Seris iterates.

"The results have been less than ideal," Ayden explains.

"It's something, though. Right?" I can't help the traces of hope that linger in my tone.

Ayden squeezes my hand. "It's a start."

The meeting continues, questions and updates flying faster than I can keep up, while I simultaneously fixate on the map still spread on the table. The pattern is there. I just haven't found it yet.

I manage to pay attention enough to learn that the other blond male is named Oren, and he is, in fact, the brother of Talon. They are the ruling lords in the town south of the capital and are responsible for crafting the majority of the weapons used by the Prudian army. Lady Seris is a healer with a family-run apothecary in Andhull. The eldest male with the graying hair is Lord Fenwick. He served on King Ayden I's council and has a knack for battle strategy. His body no longer allows him to train, but his mind remains sharp.

As the meeting draws to a close, there's one absence I can't understand.

"Does your mother not attend these meetings?" I ask Ayden as the council members file out of the room.

"She normally does, but there were matters that took her away from Elentia today."

Our walk down the hall is quiet for several minutes until Ayden finally breaks the silence. "I didn't want to bring it up in the meeting because there's not much we can do for now, but reports are coming in from Rimor. The attacks on your borders have become severe, Princess."

Nails dig crescent moons into the palm of my hand, the frustration at my situation boiling my blood. "How severe?"

"More towns are being evacuated, and food has become scarce." He slips his hands into the pockets of his trousers, tension radiating from him in waves. "Farms and livestock are burning as your people flood the capital."

My footsteps falter, eyes squeezing shut as I fight the injustice and frustration at not understanding why. I struggle to remain in control, my shadows twirling around my fingers and forearm in thin, angry wisps.

A few deep breaths later, I regain composure, recalling the shadows. "There is nothing I can do here," I confirm.

Ayden reaches for me, his hand grasping my shoulder in an attempt to soothe. There is no solace to be found in a situation like this. I don't want to be comforted when I carry the guilt for my kingdom being in the situation to begin with.

Shrugging him off, I sigh. "Those are still *my people*, Ayden." My eyes connect with his. "They're my responsibility, and I am failing them. So, I'm pleading with you, Prince. Do something. Anything."

The corner of his lips quirk in a subtle smirk. "I never thought this would be the first time I'd hear you beg, but fuck, does it sound good coming from you."

"I draw the line at getting on my knees," I retort, crossing my arms. "I bow for no male."

"Very well. You don't have to be dramatic." His tone softens. "I already sent what food and supplies we could to your people. I wish I could spare the soldiers, but we're stretched thin as it is."

It wasn't nearly enough, but it would have to suffice.

"Thank you," I breathe, shoulders sagging in relief.

It's late, but my mind refuses to calm. Sleep has evaded me for the past three hours as I stare at the ceiling while Ayden snores softly beside me.

The restlessness in my limbs draws me from bed, being careful not to disturb him as I slip on a robe and leave his chambers.

I silently curse myself for walking the halls barefoot as the chill from the marble floor numbs my toes. I relish the feeling of my bare feet against the ground, but despise the bite of the cold.

When I reach the council room, the door is already ajar. Guards patrol the hallways, leaving me with little concern for safety, but I form a shadow dagger in my palm just in case.

The door creaks, alerting anyone in the area to my presence, as I push it open. Soft light flickers from Faerie lights scattered throughout the dark room. They illuminate the room, casting a warm glow over the last person I expect to see.

Darian.

Slipping inside the room, I let the door click shut behind me as his blue eyes raise to meet mine.

He's dressed similarly to me, a thick robe hanging open to reveal sleep pants and a bare chest. His disheveled hair further confirms my suspicion that I was not the only one unable to sleep.

"You too?" he grunts.

I lean against the table beside him, taking in the map he's studying. "I've been staring at the ceiling for three hours, wondering what I'm missing."

The map is the same from earlier, the markings still not showing any obvious pattern.

"What *we're* missing," Darian corrects, exhaling a sigh. "It was wrong of me to suggest you were stupid for not finding the pattern that I myself could not identify."

"Careful, General," I tease. "That sounds an awful lot like an apology."

He scoffs. "I said I was wrong, not that I was sorry."

And there it is. Asshole.

My fingers trace over the map, measuring the distance between attack locations and the towns surrounding them.

"Have they ever taken anything in their attacks?"

"Other than my soldiers' lives?" Darian deadpans. "No. They don't loot, pillage, or rape."

Cocking a brow, I ask, "Does that not strike you as odd?"

"Of course, it's strange, but nothing about this enemy is typical. The Fae have never played by the same rules."

"An enemy that attacks with deadly intent, possesses a poison that could end the lives of every opponent, that they utilize only a fraction of the time, but they take nothing? None of this adds up."

He grunts. "I'm well aware."

The number of facts that just don't make sense becomes overwhelming the more I think about it. It's like I have pieces to a puzzle, but they're all for different puzzles.

"What if we're looking at too much?" I ask, worrying my bottom lip.

"How so?"

"Forget the lack of plundering, they're not looking for our resources or weapons. Let's just focus on the attacks with the poison. Do you have a blank map?"

Darian retrieves a fresh map, laying it atop the other. "What are you thinking?"

"Perhaps the pattern isn't in the locations of the attacks. Can you mark where just the attacks with poison occurred in order of occurrence?"

He nods, slowly placing marks on the map, adding the dates beside each one. The earliest attacks start along the border between Prudia and Rimor. About halfway through, they shift towards the top of the map, towards the capital.

Darian continues marking as I read each date.

"They shifted focus… right after we arrived from Rimor."

The realization sits heavily in my stomach.

"They've been tracking one of you," Darian adds, finishing the last of the locations.

"Why did they spend so much time along our border?" I ask, recalling the first time I had encountered the Fae when searching for Julian's body. "How is it possible they only broke through once?"

Darian's jaw ticks. "Ayden has been protecting you far longer than you realize."

"You've been keeping them out of Rimor," I breathe.

He says nothing, his silence answer enough. Ayden had been so much busier than I ever realized.

I turn my attention back to the map. The last several are scattered, nowhere near the others.

"What changed here?" I ask, pointing to the last three.

He eyes the dates before pointing to one. "That's the night Lord Aurelius appeared in the middle of my camp right before we were attacked."

"He appeared?" My heart stumbles, breath catching in my throat. "You mean when Ayden sent him away from the castle?"

"No. I mean, he quite literally appeared in the middle of the camp just before we were attacked."

"That's not possible," I whisper, shaking my head.

"I assure you that is exactly what happened," Darian insists, his tone bordering on impatient. "One moment, he was just standing there, the next, we were being attacked. I didn't exactly have time to ask questions on how he got there."

"That was the night of the engagement ball. He was there with Charlotte. Ayden and I argued, and he sent Aurelius away from the castle as punishment… but that's over a day's ride from the castle. It's not physically possible unless he Traveled with you."

Darian sighs, running a hand through his mussed hair. "Look, I don't know *how* it happened, but it did, Breyla. He's been with me ever since, fighting alongside my soldiers at every attack."

I drop it, deciding this topic was better broached with Aurelius himself. "Was he at the remaining two attack sites?"

He freezes, his gaze slowly sliding to mine. "He was."

Dread fills me at the conclusion we've both come to.

My heart beats so fast, I hear the pounding in my ears like the torrent of a river about to pull you under. The muscles in my chest tighten and constrict as I whisper, "Aurelius is their target."

CHAPTER THIRTY

BREYLA

"If you continue that pacing, you might actually wear a hole in my library floor, sweetheart." Ayden's voice startles me out of my thoughts.

I've been in the royal library all afternoon, looking for answers. I need to understand what is happening between Aurelius and me, but I need to understand why my kingdom is under attack more.

The answer is at my fingertips, but it continues evading me. It's driving me to madness.

I roll my eyes at him and continue my pacing as I read through a scroll I've read a dozen times already.

"My kingdom is under attack, Ayden. What do you expect me to do, needlepoint?" I ask sarcastically. His mother's attempts to mold me into the perfect docile wife for him would continue to fail. Over my dead body would I allow her to dress me in gowns and sit idly by.

Ayden chuckles and steps into my path, plucking the scroll from my hands. Without looking, he tosses it on the nearest desk and threads his fingers through mine. "Come on, we're going somewhere."

I raise a skeptical brow. Ayden's proclivity for mischief makes me weary by default. "Where?" I ask cautiously.

"To take your mind off the things you can't control," he answers, tugging me forward. "I can see them eating at you, and it's not healthy."

I dig my heels in, refusing to take another step. "Where, Ayden?" I demand.

"It's the Winter Solstice festival!" Rowina squeals, coming from around the corner.

Had I really been so consumed, I didn't even realize solstice was upon us?

No, that wasn't right. "Solstice isn't for two days."

"Technically, you're correct," Rowina says. "But here, we celebrate it for three days. Tonight is the festival we throw to let loose before the longest night of the year."

"Exactly," Ayden says with a grin. "We're going into the city to celebrate."

"It's tradition," Rowina sings.

"It's freezing," I scoff and gesture to my clothing. I had lost the battle of clothing today and ended up in a heavy gown. At least it was black. Winter and I were not friends. Not only was it hard to navigate on the battlefield, but it was also just generally miserable. I long for the warmth and sunlight. The winter was dark, cold, and lonely. I hate it.

"That's what these are for." Rowina brandishes a pair of fur-lined leggings like they're sacred treasure. "Put them on under your dress. All the females do."

I sigh in relief at the sight of comfortable clothing. Grabbing them from her, I say, "I'm not giving these back. I'll hide them under my mattress if I must, but your mother can pry them out of my cold, dead hands."

Rowina leans in close and whispers, "I'd expect nothing less."

I throw my arms around her. "My savior!" I say exaggeratedly and kiss her cheek.

"My lips are over here, Breyla." She laughs and throws me a wink as my cheeks heat.

"And I'm still into males," I mumble, not adding specifically *which* male I'm into. I pull the leggings on under my skirt and relish the feeling of the soft fur hugging my legs.

"Are you sure about that?" she teases. "I never see you blush like that for either of my brothers."

"Alright, you two. That's enough of that. Let's go." Ayden holds out his arms. Rowina and I loop our arms through his, letting him lead us out of the library.

As we make our way through the castle to the gates, I work up the nerve to ask, "Is Aurelius joining us?" I try to keep my voice even and not betray the hope I feel fluttering in my chest at seeing him.

"He's meeting us there," Ayden says in an equally unreadable tone to my own. He's no fool. He must know my heart still beats for his brother, but does he know what happens in the dark when no one is looking?

I could easily spend all day worrying over the state of my kingdom and the starving citizens, my impending wedding to Ayden, or the way my heart refused to beat for anyone other than the one person it couldn't have. But it would do no good. So instead, I shove them all to a dark corner of my mind, slam the door closed, and lock it tight. Those problems would all be there later. Right now, I'm choosing to remain in this moment.

When we reach the castle doors, a shiver runs down my back as a cool blast of air hits my skin. "You better be right about these leggings," I grumble and pull on the cloak Ayden hands me.

"I'm right about most things," Rowina says with a grin.

As we make our way into town, Ayden leans over and whispers, "You know, you could have access to all the pants you could ever want. All you have to do is accurately guess all the illusions I cast around you. Or, I'd settle for you just taking your clothing off for me."

I laugh so hard I snort. "I'll figure it out soon. We both know you couldn't handle me, Prince, so I'll keep my clothing on." I'm sure it's not the answer he was expecting, but I would never admit that I've secretly grown to enjoy the games we play. I lean in to whisper, "Though, if I did take my clothes off for you, I'm sure the scene Aurelius would cause would be well worth the price of admission."

"Ewww. I can hear you," Rowina groans. "Can you not talk about *both* of my brothers like that when I'm standing right here?" Rowina complains, faking a disgusted shudder. Damn, Fae hearing.

I arch a brow. "Does it bother you more that it's your brothers I'm talking about or that they're males?"

"Yes," she confirms.

Snow crunches under our boots, and new flakes cling to my

eyelashes. It being the shortest day of the year means that it's already dark, and the moonlight glints off the snow, casting the world in a soft silver hue. My breath clouds in the air in front of me as I take it all in.

The village reminds me of the capital in Rimor in size and layout, but there's a different energy here. It's lively, but peaceful. The homes are well-kept, and there's no harsh dividing line between the wealthy and poor. Faerie lights line the street in gleaming rows, welcoming and warm.

A cold wind hits, and I shiver, my teeth chattering. My legs may be warm, but the rest of me is freezing.

Ayden pulls a silver flask from his cloak and twists off the lid before throwing back a shot of whatever is inside.

"Here, this will help warm you up," he says and hands it to me. Without thinking twice, I take a long pull and let the liquor run down my throat.

It's spicy and harsh, but it does warm me. I cough, my eyes watering as I hand it back to him and ask, "What the hell is that?"

"Prudian spiced whisky. It's made with cinnamon and clove for this time of year, but it's my personal favorite to drink year-round."

"It's disgusting," I say, shaking my head vigorously.

"It is not!" A look of offense plasters his face, and I try not to laugh.

From his other side, I hear his sister agree, "It is pretty disgusting, brother."

"More for me then, since that's the primary drink served at the festival."

"The cinnamon is just so strong…" my voice trails off as I realize why it's familiar to me.

Cinnamon.

Elijah smells like cinnamon and chocolate. While the drink may be horrid, the scent reminds me of Elijah and how much I miss him. I long for my best friend's presence almost as much as I long to have my mother alive again. Nothing feels right without him and Ophelia here.

Sensing my shift in mood, Rowina pulls out her own flask and hands it to me. "Don't worry, I brought my own, and it's much better than that rubbish."

I smile half-heartedly as I take a pull from her flask and relish the burn of her chosen libation. This one is much smoother and sweeter. It tastes of crisp apples and subtle spices.

"This is *much* better." I lick my lips. "Your sister has far superior taste, Ayden. I think perhaps I'll choose her if I am forced to marry into the House of Mordet."

"Very funny, love," Ayden says, smirking. "But the marriage contract was with me, not the House of Mordet. You're still my fiancée, unfortunately," he jests back.

I'm not sure how we reached this tentative peace, but I enjoy how easily I can be around him. Though my heart belongs to Aurelius, a sort of kinship has grown between Ayden and me.

The music becomes noticeable as we approach the festivities, and I bask in the feeling of pure joy I receive as the notes wash over me. Several fiddles and drums play upbeat tunes meant for dancing. The people of Prudia fill the streets as they dance, drink, and laugh like nothing weighs them down. Bright lights are strung around the square, evergreen trees frosted in snow have been placed around the edges, and vendors and merchants fill the spaces in between.

In the center of it all sits a makeshift dance floor, several bodies already filling the space.

"Excuse me, Princess," a small voice says behind me.

I look down to find a girl around the age of ten smiling at me and holding a crown made of evergreen sprigs and red berries.

"Thank you, sweetheart," Ayden says, taking the winter crown from her.

She giggles and skips off.

Turning to me, he lifts the crown and places it on my head.

"Well? How does it look?"

"Perfect," he purrs.

I shake my head, ignoring his flirtations. More bodies have gathered on the dance floor, and I stare on curiously as musicians begin playing.

"The next dance is a group dance." He offers me his arm. "Shall we?"

I take it, and he leads me into formation. Two lines form, and we stand facing each other. Before it begins, he leans over and explains the dance.

"This dance is called Maya's Wedding. We're at the end of the line, so you'll have several rounds to watch the pattern and steps. At the end of our turn, we break off and return to the end of the line. It's pretty simple. I'm sure you'll catch on quickly." He gives me a wink before falling back in line.

As the music picks up and couples begin the dance, I watch intently. The dancing couple weaves figure-eights in a diagonal pattern with two others in the line. They meet in the middle, grasping forearms and spinning each other, before continuing the figure eight pattern with the opposite couples from the first round. The steps and pattern continue, each couple taking their place at the end once their turn is done, effectively progressing us forward.

The dance is lively but simple. When it finally comes to our turn to join, I smile in glee as we begin the familiar pattern. The upbeat lilt of the fiddle, the consistent beat of the drums, and the whistle of the flutes fill my ears, making my body and soul hum in delight.

Around and round, we spin, weaving our way through the other couples until we fall back to the end. The instruments fade as the dance comes to an end, but I'm left wanting more.

When I reach the table our group has chosen, Rowina hands me a glass filled with something that looks like cider. I take a large gulp, savoring the rich spices and fruity tang of the drink.

"This is delicious," I say between drinks. I glance around and notice that everyone else seems to be sipping theirs while mine is nearly gone. "Do you not think so?"

Ayden chuckles before responding, "Oh, I find it quite enjoyable. Just… give it a few minutes."

Rowina pries the empty glass from my hand, setting it on our table. Clearing her throat, she explains, "That particular cider is meant for sipping. It might not taste like it, but you just drank the equivalent of six shots of rum, Breyla."

My eyes widen. "Why didn't you say anything?" I ask in horror.

"You didn't really give me the chance, babe. You'll be okay, though. You'll just get to the drunk stage much faster than the rest of us." She smiles sheepishly at me.

"Why would I need to ask if it was okay to drink cider normally? Most cider doesn't contain enough liquor to get a small child drunk."

"It's solstice," Ayden says by way of explanation, giving me a shrug and trying to hide his amusement.

"Well, shit." I sigh, wondering how long it will take to feel the effects of the alcohol.

Depositing his still mostly full drink on the table, Ayden grips my elbow and gently leads me away. "Come on, love. Let's play a game. I have a feeling you'll excel at this one."

"Does it involve more drinking?" I mumble.

"Yes, but I'll take all your drinks, wild one. You just focus on winning."

"Fine," I relent.

We make it to the other side of the town square, where several long tables are set up. There are groups of cups set up on each end of the table in the shape of a triangle.

"We're up next," Ayden says to the two males standing at one end of the table.

"Come to lose, Prince?" one of the males goads.

"Not today, Jerome."

"I don't see how you stand much of a chance without your usual partner," the other adds with a shrug.

Ayden just grins. "You've never seen the princess here play drinking games, either. She has impeccable hand-eye coordination."

For a brief moment, I'm flattered by his praise until I realize he's never seen me play drinking games, either.

I remain quiet, deciding not to undermine Ayden's confidence in front of these males.

"The premise of this game is pretty simple. You want to throw this ball," he says, holding up a small white ball, "into those cups. We each get one shot per round, and once the cup is made, it's removed from play. The first team to eliminate all its cups wins. For each cup the opposing team makes, we drink. Like I said, I'll drink for you, which means I'm drinking double, so do your best not to miss."

"Seems easy… What's the catch?"

"No catch. There are a few nuances, but I'll explain those as they come up."

I nod my head, trying to decipher the look in his eyes and whether I believe him.

"Are you two ready or not?" Jerome calls from the other end of the table.

"Ready to kick your sorry asses," Ayden fires back.

The game starts quickly with both Jerome and the other male, who I find out is named Shay, making their cups in the first round. I quickly learn that that means they get to take a second shot. Thankfully, they miss those.

Ayden takes four drinks, two for each shot they made.

"Hey now," Jerome protests. "Why isn't she drinking?"

"Because she had already drunk an entire glass of cider. I give it five more minutes before you hold the upper hand against us both."

Jerome and Shay both grin widely, a cocky look gracing their faces.

That look falters slightly when we both land our shots in the same cup. Three cups are pulled, and our balls are returned to us.

When Ayden makes his second shot, Shay narrows his eyes. "Are we being hustled?"

"Nonsense," I reply with a chuckle that leans dangerously close to a giggle. "Your prince would never hustle the loyal citizens of this kingdom."

"Actually," Jerome mutters, "that's exactly what he would do."

The rounds continue, each team playing a close game as it comes down to the final cup. Ayden, having taken all my drinks, has begun missing more shots than he makes. Surprisingly, I make most of mine, despite the amount of liquor I consumed before the start of the game.

I line up my shot, taking a deep breath. Before I release, I feel the gentle, reassuring presence in my mind. It's almost as if I can hear the word *Now* right as I make the shot.

The ball lands directly in the last cup, and I squeal in delight, jumping up and down. Ayden grabs me by the waist, spinning me around as we laugh in glee. "You're a natural, love."

"I'm a natural at all drinking games," I retort.

As he leads me away from the table, he leans into me to whisper, "I have a confession."

"Is it that I am far better at that game than you?" I wink.

He chuckles before admitting, "I am far drunker than you at the moment."

"You only finished two mugs of ale in that game. Surely that's not more than the cider."

"Okay, I have two confessions." Ayden grins sheepishly. "I swapped your cider for the cider we give the children. You're not actually drunk."

"Ayden," I exclaim. "That certainly explains why I don't feel drunk. But why lie?"

"I needed you to believe you were getting drunk so Jerome and Shay would believe it, too. They got cocky, which led them to be sloppy."

"You filthy liar," I accuse, trying to hide the grin curling the corners of my mouth. "You did hustle them."

"Indeed," he agrees, grinning.

"You're not even a little bit sorry."

He smirks. "Not even a little bit."

We fall into a fit of laughter, and I feel lighter than I have in weeks. As we arrive back at the table, I find a full glass of the real cider waiting for me. Aurelius has also arrived and is talking with Rowina.

I take a small sip of the cider, savoring the burn and spices as they drift across my tongue. It is easy to tell that this mix is heavily laced with liquor.

"That was a good game you both played," Aurelius says mildly. "Even if you did lie your way through it."

"Does it get uncomfortable?" Ayden asks.

Aurelius cocks a brow. "Does what get uncomfortable?"

"That stick you have stuck up your ass," he snorts with a roar of laughter.

I stifle a giggle, taking another drink of cider. This time, I actually feel the effects of the alcohol start to take over. A warmth spreads through me, and I smile widely.

"I'm not the one here that likes things up their ass," Aurelius replies smoothly. "And when done properly, I assure you it's anything but uncomfortable."

Ayden's jaw drops, and I blink slowly at the insinuation in Aurelius' words. I probably should be embarrassed by his words, but I can't find it in me to care right now. A full laugh breaks free from me, and I fight a snort.

"Oh, I'm well aware." Ayden quickly recovers, giving us all a cocky smirk. "But that's good to know. I'll keep it in mind for the honeymoon."

"I'm not sure when this turned into a dick-measuring contest, but we're going to dance!" Rowina shouts, grabbing my hand. I quickly take another drink of the cider before I let her lead me into the crowd.

Ignoring both of their protests, Rowina shouts over her shoulder, "Besides, we all know I win that contest!"

She hands me her flask of the apple-flavored liquor, a devilish grin spreading across her beautiful face.

I take a sip, licking my lips. "Are you trying to get me drunk, Princess?"

"I thought that much was obvious," she says with a wink.

"I should warn you, I've been known to make questionable decisions when intoxicated."

"Oh?" she purrs, tracing a delicate finger along my jawline. "Are you saying you'll finally let me have my chance between those pretty thighs?"

"Not *that* questionable." I roll my eyes. "I'm still into males, Ro."

"Only because you don't know what you're missing." She pulls me into the center of the dance floor. "I know I make you curious, darling. Your mental shields aren't completely impenetrable."

I toss back another shot of the sweet liquor as I let the music take me. "You and your brother do like reminding me of that, and it drives me wild. I've never met anyone who was capable of breaking through my mental shield. Not even my own father."

She just shrugs and says, "You'll figure it out eventually."

A pleasant buzz takes over my body as we lose ourselves to the melody. Time slows, and I'm unsure if it's a few minutes or a few hours later that I feel Ayden's presence behind me.

"Can I help you, Prince?" I ask without so much as looking at him.

He takes my hand, twirling me out and back into him. "They need to break down the dance floor."

"I'm not done dancing," I protest.

"Well, you'll have to do it off the dance floor." He tugs me gently away from the center of the space so the villagers can begin dismantling the makeshift dance floor.

Despite its absence, the musicians continue playing.

"In that case, I don't need a dance floor," I say with a grin, eyeing the empty tables.

Before anyone can stop me, I take a running leap and land in the center of one of the long tables. The thud is soft, but the attention is immediate. Out of the corner of my eye, I catch Aurelius watching. His gaze is intense, but he doesn't move toward me.

"The musicians are playing a dance that requires two people, love." Ayden stares up at me, arms crossed, and raises a brow. "Do you plan to dance on your own?"

I laugh, mirroring his posture. "If I must. Or someone could join me up here. There is enough room for two."

"How drunk are you?" he asks, stepping onto a chair.

"Not that drunk," I say, just as Aurelius adds, "She's obliterated."

I flip him off as I giggle, "I don't like you right now, Aurelius."

He's only maybe ten feet from us, so I can see the smirk that covers his face as he says, "You're still a terrible liar, Princess."

Ayden is fully on the table next to me now and leans in to whisper, "Well, if you're obliterated, that makes two of us."

He takes my hand and leads us in a quick-paced two-step dance. With the limited space on top of the table, we have to get creative, but we navigate the steps mostly gracefully. A few missteps and stumbles leave us both laughing in time with the music.

I'm drunk on both the cider and the atmosphere. The world spins around me as Ayden spins me out and back into him.

I laugh, my head thrown back, as I crash into his chest. He stumbles but catches me before we fall, steadying me with a hand on the curve of my hip.

He grins drunkenly at me. "Steady there, wild one."

"I'm fine," I slur. "But thanks for the save," I add before patting his cheek.

With a deep sigh, I say, "This is it, my moment of joy for the day."

His other hand cups my jaw as he stares into my eyes. "We could be happy together, Breyla."

"I'm sorry, Ayden," I whisper.

"Sorry that you don't love me, or sorry that you know I'm right?"

My chest constricts as I realize how right he is. "Another life, another time, I think you'd be right. Against my better judgment, I trust you; hell, I actually really enjoy your company. But I don't love you."

He sighs, his finger gently stroking my cheek. "Your heart was never mine to hold."

"It has a mind of its own. I've stopped questioning why it chose that broody brother of yours."

"Only the gods know the answer to that, love. I'm obviously the better, more attractive choice."

I erupt in laughter, his deep chuckles joining my own.

"You're certainly funnier," I say, smiling at him.

"You know I can't call this marriage off, right?" His face is serious now, almost haunted.

"I think you could if you wanted to." I splay a hand across his chest, meeting his gaze. "You don't really love me, Ayden."

"I would love you if you gave me the chance." His voice is resolute and unwavering.

"And I'm certain you would do it well. But we don't live in that version of the story." I move my hand to squeeze his shoulder in quiet apology. "We live in this one—where my heart belongs to Aurelius."

"There are bigger things at play here, Breyla. I've told you what I can, but I need you to trust me. Everyone must believe our union is genuine, despite what we feel."

"Then you must know that while you have my friendship, Ayden," I sigh, leaning my head against his chest, the weight of it all sinking in. "I will fight you every step of the way to that altar."

"I would expect nothing less from you."

A beat of silence passes as the world keeps spinning around us. As we break apart, the table beneath us wobbles. The unsteady motion combines with the alcohol swimming through my veins, making a dangerous combination.

Just as I think we've gained our balance, a harsh winter wind hits us. I squeal as we both lose our footing and fall backward.

Ayden hits the ground first with a painful thud. I'm a heartbeat behind him, but find myself instead in the arms of Aurelius.

His heat engulfs me as I bask in the spiced bergamot scent I adore. "You caught me," I say in wonder.

"I'll always keep you safe," he says, voice low and certain.

"I'm okay, thanks for asking," Ayden says snarkily from the ground.

We both ignore him as I continue staring into Aurelius' eyes.

"How much of our conversation did you hear?" I ask curiously.

Aurelius' gaze is unreadable. "All of it."

"Oh," I whisper.

"I can't decide whether I want to worship or punish you right now," he growls.

"Maybe a bit of both?" I suggest sheepishly.

"That sounds like us," he whispers as his eyes heat, the crimson flecks blazing to life.

"We're not allowed to do that anymore." I drunkenly giggle. "Ayden says—"

"I don't give a fuck what Ayden says," he cuts me off.

Ayden is standing now and shoving his way between us. Roughly, he pulls me from Aurelius' arms, keeping me cradled in his own, as he bites out, "Thank you, brother, for catching my fiancée. I've got her from here."

Without waiting for a response, Ayden brushes past him, carrying me back toward the castle.

"I can walk, you know," I grumble, kicking my legs in protest.

"Oh, I know. That's not what this is about," he says, smirking.

"Stupid male bullshit," I grumble.

"Stupid male bullshit, indeed."

It takes us a few minutes to reach the castle, but by the time we arrive, I'm already yawning. He sets me down once inside and walks me to his room.

I reach for the door, ready to collapse into bed.

"Sleep well, love. We have training tomorrow," he says with a snicker, stripping down to his night clothes.

I groan. "I'm not coming."

"It's only training with your projection. You don't have to face Darian hungover."

"That's not a reassurance. I'm still not coming," I yawn in protest as I slip into his bathing chamber to change into my nightgown.

When I return, Ayden's already in bed, the soft glow of a Faerie light casting golden shadows over his face.

"I don't recall giving you a choice," he says, brow arched smugly.

"Then you'll have to drag me there," I reply, shrugging as I climb into bed. "Good night, Ayden."

"Good night, Princess."

CHAPTER THIRTY-ONE

"Ophelia," Elijah shudders, my name sounding like both a prayer and damnation.

My tongue swirls around the head of his cock, his length bobbing in and out of my mouth as I hollow my cheeks around him. With a wet pop, I release him, stroking up and down his length slowly.

Lust-filled brown eyes meet mine in a desperate plea for more.

"Please, baby. I need to be inside you," he begs, his voice husky.

I swing a leg over his hips, lifting my nightgown and seating myself just above his length. He palms my breast, slipping the thin material down to expose my heated flesh.

Weeks have passed without the feel of him between my legs, surviving on the sparse kisses as we passed one another in the hall. The number of refugees flooding the capital has grown exponentially, keeping us apart during the day and leaving us too exhausted for anything but sleep once we finally come together at night.

I have had enough of it.

It wasn't just that I wanted him; I *needed* this intimacy and moment of reprieve in his arms. The weight of running a kingdom in peril, facing an entire city of starving citizens, and everything in between has become debilitating.

That was why I had feigned a stomachache at dinner to allow us to retire early for the evening. Unless the city was on fire or under siege, there would be no interruptions.

I slide down his length, sheathing him fully in one smooth, claiming motion. We groan in unison at the connection, and my skin pebbles, nipples hardening to stiff peaks.

"Goddess, you're exquisite." The praise rolls off his tongue as swiftly as I roll my hips against his, making us both gasp.

The feeling of having him after being deprived for so long is like the first breath of air when you've come up from drowning.

"You're soaked for me," he whispers as he rolls his hips beneath me in tandem with mine.

"This is what weeks of not having you feels like," I sigh, rolling my hips in a slow figure-eight motion, feeling as every inch of him hits perfectly within me.

One hand tweaks my nipple, rolling it back and forth between his forefinger and thumb. The other hand grasps my hip, guiding my motions as I continue to rock against him.

The tingling sensation that signals my impending orgasm starts quickly, coming easily after weeks of yearning for him.

Just before I shatter, the door to his room flies open, hitting hard against the stone wall.

Cillian stands, staring at us but seemingly unfazed by what he's walked in on.

"For fucks sake," Elijah curses, throwing a blanket over my exposed form.

It's too late, though.

My eyes connect with Cillian's, and the adrenaline spikes as he watches me come undone.

My hips still as I shatter around Elijah's cock, my orgasm hitting me harder than I care to admit.

I convulse around him, inner walls squeezing tightly and pulling Elijah over the edge into damnation alongside me.

"Fucking hells, I don't have time to comment on what I just witnessed," Cillian says, raking a hand over his face. "Let's do it again sometime when your lives aren't in imminent danger."

He's dressed head to toe in black leathers. They're similar to Breyla's but somehow darker. Two sets of matching leathers are thrust at us as he demands, "You need to get dressed. Now."

I pull myself off Elijah, dropping the nightgown to the floor in favor of the leathers.

"Could you at least turn around, you bastard?" Elijah asks, annoyance filling his tone.

"Modesty seems rather pointless, considering I just watched both of you orgasm," Cillian replies, shrugging.

I don't admit it aloud, but he has a point.

As we dress, Cillian explains the situation. "A mob of starving citizens is headed here as we speak. The people have turned, and they're looking for someone to blame. Most of the nobles have already gone into hiding. If we leave now, I can get you both to safety."

"Why are you doing this?" I ask, trying to understand what could motivate him to care about whether we lived or died.

"I still owe Breyla my life. I'm not about to let her friends die when I can help it," he answers quickly. He drapes a heavy cloak around my shoulders, pulling the hood up to hide my face. "You have three minutes. Pack only what you can carry."

Elijah and I set to shoving the warmest clothes into a pack. From beneath the mattress, Elijah pulls out a bag of gold, several daggers, and his gloves. Cillian tosses him a cloak that he drapes over his shoulders before strapping the pack to his back.

"I've got food and more supplies packed and waiting with the horses. Let's go," Cillian says, but Elijah refuses to move.

"Wait," he says, grabbing my wrist. "Where are we going, Cillian?"

Cillian reaches for the door handle, but Elijah's hand shoots out to stop him from turning the knob. "I'm taking you west to Prudia."

The anxiety churning in my gut is momentarily eclipsed by the excitement of seeing Breyla again. But if we weren't safe here, what made Cillian think we would be safe in Prudia?

"I'll let her know we're coming," Elijah offers.

"There's no time," Cillian argues. "I sent a rider her way already. She'll be expecting us."

"Fine, but there's something else I *must* do before we leave." Elijah's tone shifts, tinged with desperation. "More than just our lives depend on it."

It's enough to make Cillian acquiesce to his request. "You have ninety seconds, then I'm walking out this door with Ophelia, with or without you."

Elijah nods, closing his eyes tightly. A few moments pass before they fly open again, finding Cillian. They take on an eerie quality that I've come to realize is someone else seeing through his eyes.

"General Jade." Elijah's voice is steady and clear. "Consider this your final order to retreat from all fronts. Evacuate what civilians you can, but do not delay. Your only objective is to protect our people by whatever means necessary."

The command strikes me as strangely vague, but Elijah and Jade knew each other far better than I knew either of them. Perhaps they had a code or a language all their own.

"My mercenaries are at your disposal, General," Cillian adds before Elijah severs the connection.

My head tilts, taking in Cillian before I ask, "You knew?"

"It's my job to know, sweetheart. Time to go." Cillian ushers us out of the door.

The halls are eerily quiet as we take back corridors and hidden passages, exiting through the castle's side entrance toward the stables. Except for a few guards, the halls are empty. It's a silence that sets my nerves on edge.

As we step into the night air, the first thing I notice is two figures dressed identically to us. Their faces are obscured by the hoods, but judging by their stature I can tell they're male.

The second thing I notice is the lifeless eyes of the castle guards that stare up at me.

Cillian's hand wraps around my mouth right as a scream erupts from me.

"Shhh," he hushes me, an arm banding around my waist to hold me in place.

Blood pools around the bodies, their throats slit deep for a quick death.

"They were traitors," he explains calmly. "I got to them before they had the opportunity to let in the angry citizens coming for your heads."

I relax enough that he releases his hold on me.

With a firm hand on my lower back, he ushers us forward to the stable. Three horses wait, fully saddled for our journey.

Elijah approaches a sleek chestnut mare, patting her neck lovingly as he murmurs, "Hi, beautiful."

Beside her is a smaller white Arabian that I assume is meant for me. I approach cautiously, laying my hand on his snout. Immediately, he nuzzles into my touch, huffing a warm breath against my hand.

"What's his name?" I ask.

"That's Alanis," Cillian explains. "Most call him Beast, though."

"Beast?" I ask, my brow arching.

"Don't let his smaller stature mislead you." Cillian chuckles. "He came to us wilder than hell and with a penchant for biting his handlers. Well, except for me."

"Why is Ophelia riding him?" Elijah asks, stepping between Alanis and me.

Beast swings his head, smacking Elijah hard enough to make him curse.

With Elijah out of the way, Alanis nuzzles my shoulder. "Hi, Beastie," I coo with a giggle.

"Seems like she's handling him just fine," Cillian says, smirking. "He's also the fastest mount we have."

An all-black destrier horse towers above the others. The animal is massive, standing at least eighteen hands tall if I were to guess.

Cillian's eyes rake up and down my frame. "Do you need help mounting?"

"Don't insult me," I scoff, slipping my foot into the stirrup before swinging my body up and over Alanis.

"My apologies, lady. I should have known you could mount." He swings onto his own horse with ease. "I was, after all, privy to your exquisite riding skills."

An apple smacks him square in the temple, which only makes him laugh. I flip my middle finger up at him, his laughter increasing at the crude gesture.

"Don't waste our food," Cillian chides, shooting a glare at Elijah and rubbing his bruised temple.

"Worth it," Elijah grumbles as he mounts the chestnut mare named Honey.

"Hoods up," Cillian commands, pulling his own low over those sparkling turquoise eyes. "If they believe you're mine, they should let us pass without question."

We comply, letting the dark cloaks blend us with the night sky.

The further from the castle that we ride, the more I hear. Cries of starving children, groans of injured refugees, and yells of the angry citizens blend together in a painful cacophony.

"I thought we were doing what was right," I whisper.

"You did what you could," Cillian replies, his voice low. "But it was an impossible task."

Tears threaten to fall, and I swallow hard against the lump in my throat. "It wasn't enough."

"You were never going to succeed. The odds were stacked against you from the start." His tone is far too nonchalant for my liking.

As we reach the edge of Ciyoria, we pass an overturned carriage.

"Oh, gods," Elijah whispers. I can't see his face, but I can hear the horror in his voice.

Noticing the body lying haphazardly from the shattered door, I swallow back the bile in my throat. Lord Jaeson stares blankly ahead, his neck bent at a grotesque angle.

I shoot an accusatory look at Cillian. "I thought you said they went into hiding."

"I saw them leave. It doesn't appear they all made it."

He kicks Midnight into a faster pace, urging us away from the crumbling city.

Once we've left the carnage behind, I muster the courage to ask, "Why would they do that?"

Elijah shifts in his seat, turning to face me. "Starvation births desperation in otherwise good people. More than that, though, they need someone to blame. So, they look to those that they see as having what they lack as the problem."

We've sent every scrap of extra food out to the people displaced and affected by the attacks on our borders. For weeks, we've been consuming broth and bread, not feasting on meat or sweets. I don't bother voicing that, though, because they both know it. They lived through it just the same as I had. "They're going to be disappointed when they reach the palace food stores," I say instead.

We ride for several more hours until we're a comfortable distance from Ciyoria before we make camp for the night. Avoiding cities for fear of being recognized, we choose a wooded area somewhere between the capital and Caedel. The path we take is an alternate route thanks to reports of looting, attacks, and fires, extending our journey by several days.

As we dismount, I hear Cillian let loose a curse that has my head snapping to him. He steps out from behind a dense grouping of trees, his brow furrowed with annoyance.

I pull the pack from Alanis' saddlebag. "What is it?"

"The messenger I sent ahead of us to Prudia didn't make it."

My brows arch. "How do you know?"

"I found his body about fifty yards east of here just now."

Elijah stiffens. "It's not safe to make camp here."

"Probably not," Cillian admits. "But our options are limited."

"Then what are we going to do?" I ask.

"It'll be dawn in an hour. I'm going to sleep while Elijah keeps watch. Once there's enough light, I'll use my Madilim Gift to shield us while you sleep." Cillian begins laying out his bedroll, Midnight dropping to his knees to sleep next to his rider. "It'll only be a few hours, but it must be enough for now."

Elijah lowers himself to the forest floor, his back against a wide oak tree. It takes only minutes for Cillian's breathing to even out into a rhythm that tells me he's asleep.

I feed Alanis a carrot from the pack before dropping next to Elijah.

His eyes close for several moments before he opens them again and says, "Hey, B."

My heart rate spikes knowing he's connected to Breyla right now. I cup his face in my hands, turning him to face me. "I miss you," I whisper.

Elijah chuckles, brushing a chaste kiss against my lips. "Now that Ophelia has hijacked my message, we should probably let you know you'll be seeing us shortly."

Elijah's shoulders fall, defeat lining every inch of his handsome face. "We'll explain more when we arrive, but Rimor..." He gulps, struggling to get out the words that weigh so heavily on us both.

"Rimor is no longer safe," I finish the words Elijah can't seem to voice. "Cillian is bringing us to you. We're so sorry we failed you."

"Love you, brat," Elijah finishes, ending the connection and dropping his head.

"You should sleep," he says, but wraps an arm around my shoulder, nonetheless.

My fingers trace simple patterns on his thigh as I snuggle into his side, basking in his warmth. "I'll sleep when you sleep," I say, fighting a yawn.

He presses a kiss to the crown of my head and whispers, "I don't deserve you."

I don't bother dignifying that sentiment with a response.

When I wake, I'm still wrapped in his arms, but we're lying down on Elijah's bedroll. I must have fallen asleep at some point and not woken when Elijah relocated us. The mid-morning sun streams down on our faces. It's unusually warm for the season, so I bask in the heat for just a minute longer before moving.

I move slowly so as not to disturb Elijah's still sleeping form behind me.

Cillian's staring at me, his eyes calculating like he's studying something intriguing. "You sleep so soundly," he finally says.

I begin the motions of packing Alanis' saddle in preparation for moving out. "It's only thanks to him."

"How so?"

I pull the cloak around me tighter, a sudden breeze sweeping through and chilling me. "I sleepwalk. Between that and the nightmares, I've nearly ended myself at least once. He keeps them at bay."

Cillian considers my words for a moment. "It's good that you have him, then."

"He's a blessing I didn't know I needed," I say, emotion tightening my throat.

CHAPTER THIRTY-TWO

BREYLA

The palace is quiet. It's the kind of quiet that brings peace rather than unease. As promised, the staff had left breakfast for us this morning, but not a single one of them was anywhere to be seen now.

I trade my normal spiced tea for steamed cocoa in celebration of the Winter Solstice. The liquid chocolate coats my tongue, creating a nostalgia that reminds me of home. Flakey biscuits coated in butter and sweet berry preserves comprise my breakfast as I curl into an overstuffed wing-back chair in front of a fireplace.

A tall, full-bodied pine tree stands in the corner to the side of the fireplace. Strands of tinsel are woven amongst the branches, the light from the fire catching them and sending shards of dancing light across the room.

Elijah's message had awoken me before dawn and left me simmering with nervous anticipation. On the one hand, I was elated at the prospect of seeing two of my closest friends after months apart. On the other hand, their warning about what's become of my kingdom left me sick to my stomach. Grief, guilt, and anxiety form an unpleasant combination in my gut.

With no staff on site today, the rest of the castle's occupants were still tucked cozily in their beds. There are no meetings, no obligations, and no courtly proceedings to attend to today. I relish the tentative silence as I shove another savory and sweet biscuit in my mouth.

"Happy Solstice," Aurelius says, his voice like velvet dragged over gravel from sleep.

I set the cup of cocoa and the plate of biscuits on the table beside the chair and stand to greet him. Still dressed in sleep clothes, with a robe draped over his shoulders, hair mussed from sleep, he looks more beautiful than he has a right to.

"Happy Solstice, Aurelius." I smile and reach for his hand.

He ignores my outstretched arm and grips my waist instead, pulling me flush against him. Our lips meet in a burning, but all too short, kiss that leaves me wanting.

"You're sweet today," he comments as he falls into my chair, tugging me down with him.

"Are you saying I'm not usually sweet?" I ask, batting my lashes with mock innocence.

He levels me with a look that reads something along the lines of *Are you serious?*

"Fine, point taken," I grumble and reach for my cocoa.

Aurelius drags his nose up the curve of my neck, peppering soft kisses behind my ear as he whispers, "What I meant was, you *taste* especially sweet today."

Scandalous shivers run up my spine from his heated breath on my flesh.

"That would be the cocoa," I explain, lifting the mug to my lips.

Before I can swallow, he captures my chin between his fingers, tilting my face toward him. "Let me taste."

I press my lips to his, parting them to let the hot liquid chocolate spill down his throat. He tangles his fingers through the loose strands of hair at the nape of my neck, deepening the kiss.

A soft moan rattles through my throat when I feel him harden beneath me. We've stolen brief moments here and there since our time in the pantry, but in the weeks he's been back at the palace, I haven't gotten him where I really want him, buried deep inside me.

I shift so my legs straddle his hips in the chair, and grind myself against his hard length.

Reaching between us, I grasp his cock through the thin fabric separating us. "I need you," I whimper.

With a pain-filled groan, Aurelius pulls my hand away, settling me back into his lap once more. He buries his face in my loose curls, breathing heavily before he finally says, "As much as I want nothing more than to be buried in your tight, wet heat, that's not why I got out of bed this early."

Reluctantly, I move off his lap and try to will my overheated skin to cool. "Why can't it be both?"

"The castle is waking, and our time alone is coming to an end. I would rather spend these last few minutes of solitude giving you your gift."

He shifts and retrieves a small parcel wrapped in brown paper from the pocket of his robe.

"You didn't need to get me anything. You've showered me with more than enough gifts over the last several months," I try to protest, but I know it will do no good.

I tear open the wrapping, revealing a sheathed dagger. But this isn't just any weapon. The hilt is gold inlaid with three rubies centered on the handle. Unsheathing it, I find the metal is dark and sharpened to a deadly point.

"Turn it over," Aurelius whispers.

On the back are the etched words, *'Until the very end.'*

"Aurelius..." My voice is weak, the sound catching in my throat.

"I found the plans in some of your father's belongings," he explains quietly. "The hilt and pommel were crafted from your mother's crown. There are a few tweaks of my own making, but I wanted you to have something from both of them. I wanted you to have a piece of your parents, no matter where you go. *Until the very end.*"

I don't even try to fight the tears that flow freely down my cheeks as I turn it over and over, savoring the feel of holding something so precious. "Perfect is too simple a word for this gift."

He brushes the tears away from my cheeks, stroking my jaw with aching tenderness. "Perfect doesn't even come close to describing the one it was crafted for."

Setting the dagger aside, I contort myself, searching for the gift I had prepared for him.

He looks puzzled when I place the small wrapped package in his palm. "What's this?"

"You didn't think I wouldn't get something for you, did you?"

"You didn't need to get me anything, Princess." He nuzzles my neck. "I have everything I want right here."

I push him off, fighting a smile. "When did you get so sappy?"

"Don't get it twisted, I'm only soft for you, little demon." He nips the skin at the point where my neck meets my shoulder, and I shudder.

"Open your gift, or I'm leaving," I threaten.

His arm wraps tightly around my midsection, holding me in place while he tears into the wrapping.

The carved wooden pendant rests perfectly in his palm, the dark stain of the wood looking beautiful against the warmth of his skin. On the front is a replica of the tree from my grandparents' estate. The tree my father helped craft into a haven for Aurelius.

"It opens here," I explain, pressing and turning the center of the tree clockwise until it clicks. The top half swings open, revealing a hidden compartment within. Small tendrils of my shadows trail out, coiling around the pendant and my hand.

"You can store what you'd like," I say. "The shadows were just a placeholder."

"No," he commands, his voice gruff. Aurelius grips my wrist before I can recall the shadows. "It's wonderful. Leave them."

I coax them back inside and close the pendant. A lengthy gold chain was a last-minute addition that I don't regret as I loop it over his head. It lies perfectly against his chest, just above his heart.

"Thank you, Breyla. I love it," he murmurs.

Our lips meet in a kiss so innocent yet heated that my toes curl.

A flicker of warning tugs at the back of my mind as I catch sight of Ayden's bedroom door opening. Recalling my astral form, I groan and push myself from Aurelius' lap.

"Our moment of solitude is over, I fear." I straighten my robe, tucking the dagger out of sight in one of the deep pockets.

"I don't hear anyone approaching," Aurelius says.

I find a new chair, this one not nearly as cushioned as the one Aurelius stole from me, and sit down. "Ayden just woke up. He's on his way here."

"How do you know that?"

"My astral projections have been getting better," I reply, winking at him. My astral form appears behind his chair, leaning down to kiss his cheek before disappearing again.

"Impressive," he praises, stroking his fingers over the spot.

"What is?" Ayden asks groggily, shuffling into the room.

"I was just showing how much my Vizie Gift has grown, thanks to your lessons," I say sweetly. And I mean it. My once-impossible Gift has grown significantly thanks to Ayden.

Ayden's eyes narrow, one brow arching subtly in my direction.

Without breaking eye contact, and just to prove a point, I project myself right behind Ayden's back. I smirk when he doesn't notice and launch my astral form onto his back.

The projection passes through him, but the look on his face tells me he feels it.

"Eh, that was mildly intriguing," he says, shrugging. "I'm not sure *impressive* is the word I would use for it."

I shake my head as my astral form flips him off from the floor. "Whatever."

That has both Ayden and Aurelius chuckling.

I recall the projection, crossing my arms.

"Happy Solstice, love," Ayden says, his arms wrapping around me.

Reluctantly, I return the hug. "Why were you out of bed so early?" he whispers.

I don't know why he bothers, seeing as Aurelius' sensitive Fae hearing can easily pick up what he's saying.

"Elijah," I sigh. "Ciyoria has been deemed unsafe. Cillian evacuated them late last night. They're on their way here."

"Cillian is on his way here?" Aurelius growls, possessiveness flaring in his dark eyes.

"Who is Cillian?" Ayden asks as he drops into the chair beside me.

"He's the leader of the Midnight Brotherhood. A mercenary group I've allowed to operate within Rimor," I explain, taking a sip of the cocoa that has now grown tepid.

"You conveniently left out the part where he's your ex and a massive pain in the ass," Aurelius adds.

I shrug. "Both are true. Wait, when did you meet Cillian?"

"Shortly before we left Rimor. Luella kicked me out of her pub, leaving his fine establishment as my only option."

"I'm shocked he let you in."

"He didn't know who I was at the time," Aurelius explains.

An involuntary laugh bursts from me. "Oh, Aurelius. Trust me when I say, Cillian knew *exactly* who you were. It's his job to know."

"Are you suggesting he was—"

"Fucking with you? Without a doubt."

"Is this Cillian someone I need to concern myself over?" Ayden asks.

Before Aurelius can answer, I cut in, "He's harmless."

"Elijah is harmless. Cillian is a menace," Aurelius says, levelling me with a look I am all too familiar with. Cillian is harmless *to me*, but he's far from safe for others. "Actually," he mutters to Ayden, "the two of you might get along swimmingly."

Dark shadows bind themselves around Aurelius' mouth, silencing his whining. "Play nice. It's Solstice," I scold.

Yes, Mommy.

I startle, knowing that thought wasn't my own. Shaking it off, I turn to Ayden. "Cillian owes me his life. Regardless of how dangerous he can be, he's not a threat to anyone here. I'm positive he's just ensuring Elijah and Ophelia make it to safety because he knows I would legitimately murder him if anything happened to them." I twirl a dagger made of shadows for emphasis.

Smirking, Ayden twirls the illusion of a dagger. "You're kind of intimidating when you want to be."

"Nice party trick," I mock.

"You're getting pretty good at identifying illusions," Aurelius notes.

"He wasn't even trying with that one," I scoff.

Ayden shrugs, letting the illusion evaporate.

"Good morning and Happy Solstice," Rowina chimes as she breezes into the room. Out of the four of us, she's the only one dressed, albeit casually, in leggings and a long purple sweater.

Not long after, Charlotte and the queen flow in, both dressed impeccably.

"Is that really what you're wearing?" The queen asks. Though

Ayden, Aurelius, and I are dressed similarly, I somehow know the question and utter disdain in her voice is directed solely at me.

Unbothered by her venom today, I simply shrug and ask, "Would you have preferred I wear less?"

"No," Ayden and Aurelius say in unison, while Rowina blurts out, "Yes."

The queen shakes her head. "Insufferable, the lot of you."

That has the entire room, with the exception of the queen, laughing. It's true, we are insufferable. Eventually, our laughter catches, and the corner of her mouth quirks up in the faintest smile.

Hours later, we're seated around the table when Rowina slaps a deck of playing cards in the center. "I thought we could start a new tradition, or rather incorporate an existing one from our new family members, this year."

My face lights, the corners of my mouth tilting upward into a smile.

"I didn't have time to collect a bunch of sweets like you told me about," she explains, setting two trays of leftover cookies in front of us. "But I figured this would do."

"So, we're playing cards… and wagering cookies?" Charlotte asks.

"Yes," Aurelius and I answer as one, pure joy in our reply. Perhaps he is as desperate for a glimpse of home as I am.

"It seems childish," the queen muses.

"That's the fun of it," I explain. "It's far more entertaining to wager sweets over real coin."

The queen doesn't seem convinced.

"One year, Breyla stole a flask of rum and got so drunk she fell into the middle of the desserts, smearing key lime pie all over her leg." Aurelius' eyes shine with mischief. "That was actually the highlight of the evening."

"First, I was fifteen and had never been drunk before. Second, it was *Elijah* who stole the rum," I say, ticking off the numbers with my fingers. "And third, it was *your* rum. So really, this one's on you."

Baffled faces stare at me until finally, Charlotte says, "That logic doesn't track. If anything, you should blame Elijah."

"Elijah will forever remain blameless in her eyes," Aurelius grumbles.

I shove him playfully. "Hush, that's not true."

Deciding this battle isn't worth fighting, Aurelius changes the topic. "What about the top wager? Usually, we each gather what we think will be the most decadent dessert to use as our 'all in' bet."

"What about a favor?" Rowina suggests.

"A favor could work," I agree.

A wicked glint shines in every eye at the table, even the queen's.

"A favor it is," Ayden declares before dealing the first hand.

Several rounds later, I slam the cards on the table, yelling a triumphant "Ha!" at Ayden, calling him on his bluff.

With a deep chuckle, he says, "What a clever girl you are."

My body stiffens at his words, a rush of familiarity pebbling the skin on my neck.

Aurelius narrows his eyes. "What's wrong, Breyla?"

Ayden gives me a questioning look, gathering the cards to shuffle them. "You okay?"

"You know, there was something that struck me as odd about the conversation I had with my father's ghost," I start.

"Wait," Aurelius interrupts. "You spoke with Ryanor's ghost, too?"

I snap my attention to him, a brow arching. "Are you telling me you also spoke with my father's ghost?"

"Do you have a lot of ghosts in Rimor?" Rowina asks.

"No, not many," I reply, fixing my gaze back on Aurelius. "When was this? What did he tell you?"

"A few weeks after you arrived at court. He asked me to protect you, told me he was murdered, and that he suspected Lord Seamus was behind it. What did he tell you?"

"He told me pretty much that... except that he suspected it was *you* who killed him."

Aurelius' brow furrows. "Why would he tell us..." His voice trails off, his gaze hardening before turning to Ayden.

"You know the curious thing about what he said to me, he called me *clever girl*," I say, my eyes narrowing on Ayden.

The jovial expression has dropped, and he wisely keeps his mouth shut as I continue. "My father never called me that."

"But you've called her that twice now," Aurelius growls at Ayden.

The whole room is so quiet, I'm not even sure they're breathing.

"If you have something to say, just say it," Ayden grits out.

Standing from my chair, I take my time circling the table until I'm next to Ayden. He stands to meet me, and I bring my hand to his cheek, stroking softly as I ask, "Did you use the illusion of my dead father to turn me against Aurelius?"

Ayden takes a deep breath before answering. "That wasn't exactly the intention, but yes. Your father's ghost was my illusion."

I drop my hand from his face, my eyes darting to the side. I can't look at him right now. My gaze meets Aurelius' stare. His expression is pure fury on my behalf as I tremble. He nods ever so slightly, letting me know he's with me.

Curling my hand into a fist, I pull back from Ayden.

"Breyla, I can—" Ayden starts, but is cut off by the punch I throw straight at his nose. Bone crunches beneath my fingers, and I can't tell if my fingers are broken, but his nose definitely is.

"Fuck," Ayden seethes, hands flying to his nose to stop the blood flow.

"Breyla!" The queen shouts, outrage filling her tone as she gets up to rush for Ayden.

Ayden throws up his hand, halting her in her tracks. "No, Mother. I quite deserved that."

Aurelius stands silently behind me, his hand resting supportively on my shoulder. "Do you feel better, little demon?"

"A little. You should give it a try."

His grin is devilish as he rears back, landing a punch on Ayden's jaw.

Ayden groans, rubbing at his aching jaw as blood continues running down his face. "Bloody hell, that hurt. Are we done with the punching?"

"Tell us why you've been fucking with our court," I demand. "Did we not have enough going on already?"

Rowina holds out a napkin to Ayden, and he drops back into his chair with a groan.

"Your own ignorance was going to lead to your death," Ayden

starts, his voice muffled by the bloody napkin. "I had to open your eyes to the corruption in your court without directly involving myself. You wouldn't have even known about the threat of the Fae if it weren't for me."

I hate that he's right. It doesn't excuse his actions, but it does explain them.

"So you thought impersonating my father's ghost was the way to do it? Why not just tell me?"

Ayden sighs. "Again, I couldn't directly involve myself, and be honest, love, would you have actually trusted a word I said?"

Until recently, I believed him to be an enemy seeking vengeance for his father's death. "Probably not," I admit.

"What you did was fucked up," Aurelius says, his lip curling.

"I know," Ayden says, rubbing his temple.

"If you ever pull something like that again, I will make sure your balls are well acquainted with my dagger," I threaten.

"I won't, I promise," Ayden says sincerely.

I grab all the sugar cookies in front of him. "And I'm taking all of these. You don't deserve them."

Ayden stares at his diminished pile of sweets and frowns. "Very well," he sighs.

I fall back into my chair, shoving a cookie into my mouth. "You seem more upset I took your cookies than you were over being punched."

"I really like sugar cookies," he grumbles.

"I could punch you again, if you prefer," Aurelius offers, and I snicker.

"No, no, I'm okay," Ayden says, throwing up his arms placatingly. "She can have whatever cookies she wants from me."

"Deal the next hand," I demand as I lick the sugar crystals off my fingers in an exaggerated motion meant to taunt him.

Ayden deals the cards, doing his best to ignore my childish behavior. "At least you only have one illusion left to identify," he says casually.

"What have you identified so far?" Aurelius asks.

"When I had him arrested in Rimor, he wasn't actually in the room. We arrested an illusion as he watched from elsewhere," I explain.

Aurelius contemplates the answer a moment before saying, "The forest on the way to Prudia."

"Come again?" I ask.

"Think, Princess. What did you see that no one else did?" Aurelius asks, and Ayden stiffens. He's onto something.

I think back to our time in the woods, fighting a blush at the thought of what we did there while Ayden watched. What had I seen that led me there?

"Lord Craylor," I realize. "He was never really there, was he?"

"Lord Craylor was gone long before we left for Prudia, love," Ayden confirms. "I needed to see what you'd do when confronted with your mother's murderer."

"If I ever see him again, I'll slit his damn throat," I growl.

Aurelius slides me a chocolate cupcake and pats my hand gently in reassurance. He pulls his hand back when the queen shoots him a seething glare. I bite off a piece of cupcake and look at my cards. I will not let this information ruin our solstice celebration, even if I have to eat all my cookies by the end of the game.

CHAPTER THIRTY-THREE

OPHELIA

It takes us two days to reach Caedel, or what remains of it. The city had been the first attacked and evacuated by Jade. What was once our most prominent border town is now smoking rubble.

To avoid being seen, we fall into a strange rhythm. Cillian's gift grants us the unique ability to move undetected by day, but since we're in the part of the year with the least amount of sunlight, we opt to sleep during the brightest part of the day. Cillian covers Elijah and me while we rest, and we keep watch over him in the early morning hours before the sun has risen.

Snow falls on our second day, getting heavier as we near the border of Prudia. Thankfully, the mercenary garb is outfitted for any weather condition. The cloaks provide plenty of protection against the biting cold, but I can't shake the dampness that clings to my bones.

We're all running on fumes by the time we reach the empty city walls. There's been no attacks, but we all feel it. It's the sense of anticipation, of someone watching our every move.

The streets are littered with debris, some buildings even still smoking. Occasionally, we pass the fallen soldier, but what's worse is when we pass the bodies of innocent civilians. I shoot up a prayer to the gods for all those that we pass along the way. It's wrong to leave their bodies in the street, and something aches deep inside of me for their souls.

"They should have been burned," I say solemnly.

"There wasn't time," Elijah explains. "Jade couldn't even afford the time to burn her fallen with the effort it took to evacuate the city."

His words don't make me feel any better. They don't assuage the wrongness I feel at seeing the dead neglected so carelessly.

The setting sun casts an amber hue over the city, turning the freshly fallen snow to a golden shade that almost seems beautiful. Eventually, we find a moderately intact inn.

"We'll stay here for the night," Cillian declares.

"You think it's safe to stop here?" Elijah challenges.

"Safe is a relative term. I think if I keep going in this state, I'm of no use to anyone if we're attacked."

Cillian pushes through the door, doing a sweep of the first floor to ensure safety. He motions for Elijah to check the second floor as he moves towards a long hallway of doors, presumably guest rooms.

Elijah draws his sword, taking the stairs to the upper floor. I find the kitchen, searching for food that may have been left behind. Every canister is overturned, the pantry stripped bare, and I sigh. The oven is intact, but it means nothing without food to cook.

"I guess it's another night of hard bread and dried meat," I mumble, turning back for the foyer.

Elijah returns, taking the stairs down two by two. "The upper floors are clear, but most of the rooms have been destroyed, so I'm not sure they'll be of much use."

"There's no food."

"But I found a bottle of whiskey and one intact bed on the first floor," Cillian adds as he returns, cracking open the bottle of liquor and taking a swig.

My brows shoot up, mouth hanging slightly ajar. "Should you really be drinking right now?"

"Relax, sweetheart. One drink won't impair me more than what the sleep deprivation is already doing." Cillian offers me the bottle, a smirk playing at the corner of his lips. "Have a taste. It'll help warm you."

Pushing it away, I say, "No, thank you. The only thing I want right now is a warm bath and a bed."

"Last door at the end of the hall," Cillian says. "But you're not going to find a hot bath here."

"I'd even settle for a cold bath if it meant I got to wash the grime off." I push the door open, taking in the only available room. There's a bed, a fireplace, and not much else. Not even a bathtub in sight.

Sighing, I drop the pack to the floor. Elijah and Cillian file in behind me.

"There's only one bed," I yawn.

"It's a big bed, though," Cillian adds, dropping his own pack next to mine. His cloak drops next, followed by his boots.

"W-What are you doing?" I stammer.

Cillian's scarred brow raises, "Uh, getting ready for bed. You didn't expect me to sleep fully clothed, did you?"

"You've slept fully clothed for the last three days—"

"I was sleeping on the ground, so, yeah. But now there's a bed." His tone is so matter-of-fact, like he can't see why this would be an issue. His shirt comes off next, leaving him in only his leather pants.

Goddess help me.

The muscles of his abdomen are expertly crafted, no doubt honed from years of training. He's no more impressive than Elijah, so why can't I look away?

Cillian catches me staring, his full lips smirking as he shoots me a wink. "Don't worry. I've been told I'm a great cuddler."

Elijah grunts, taking off his own shirt and boots, before pulling me into his chest and slanting his lips over mine. The kiss is a show of pure possession and devotion. I melt into him, letting his tongue explore every part of my mouth.

Cillian clears his throat, breaking the spell between us. "This isn't having the effect you think it is." His tone is heated, eyes molten as he stares at us.

"Ugh," I groan, shoving away from Elijah. I drop my cloak, but decide it's probably best if I remain in my leathers tonight. "I take it you expect us all to share that bed?"

"There's not exactly room on the floor, sweetheart." Cillain slides into bed, patting the empty space beside him.

Elijah smirks, sliding into the middle of the bed. "Do you prefer big or little spoon, *sweetheart?*"

Without missing a beat, Cillian replies, "I'm always big spoon." He throws his arm around Elijah's waist.

I don't hide the giggle that spills out as I join them in bed, curling into Elijah's side. In our exhausted state, it takes us minutes to find sleep.

My eyes flare open when I feel a hand cover my mouth. Cillian stares down at me, fully clothed, weapons strapped to every available space. I'm reminded of just how deadly this male is. He lifts a finger to his lips, signaling for me to remain silent.

Elijah is dressing at the end of the bed, lacing his boots into place. I'm immediately grateful I decided to stay fully clothed last night.

Was it even last night? The moonlight streaming in through the single window suggests it's not yet dawn. I nod my understanding that I know I need to remain quiet, and Cillian removes his hand, handing me a dagger instead.

I wrap my fingers around the hilt, trying to listen for a potential threat, for an answer as to why we're awake already. I'm unsure how to use the dagger, but I get the general idea. Stab with the sharp end.

Sliding my feet over the edge of the bed, I lace up my boots and reach for the cloak. Elijah fastens it in place, pecking my lips before turning to Cillian.

They nod at each other, speaking a language I'm unfamiliar with. Swords drawn, they exit the room, keeping me behind them. I follow, my steps light and dagger gripped tightly in my fist.

A floorboard creaks overhead, the sound echoing in the otherwise silent inn. Cillian points to the upper floor and holds up three fingers. I take that to mean there are three people on the floor above. He holds a hand in front of us, signaling for us to stop.

In the blink of an eye, Cillian disappears into thin air. I have no questions about what is happening when I hear the unmistakable thud of a body hitting the floor, followed by grunts and the sharp clash of steel on steel.

Elijah whips his head toward the foyer just as a figure steps into view. The male is dressed head to toe in black, crimson eyes the only splash of color.

Elijah doesn't stop to ask questions. He charges the attacker, weapon drawn.

Swords clash, the metal ringing and bodies moving faster than I can track. Elijah eventually outmaneuvers his opponent, driving his sword deep through the center of the male's chest.

Cillian rounds the corner, blood dripping from his blade. "Nice work. Sorry, the three upstairs took me longer than normal. These Fae bastards are tough."

"Are you okay?" I ask, wiping away the blood streaking down his face.

"I'm fine," he replies, grinning. "But your concern is adorable. One of the arseholes threw a dagger, but it only skimmed me."

Regardless, I press my palm to the cut and push healing energy into him, watching the skin mend itself instantly. Relief floods my system as the wound disappears, knowing that whatever dagger cut Cillian wasn't poisoned. We walk toward the foyer, trepidation filling every step.

All I hear is the sharp whistle of wind just before arrows shoot through the broken windows and door. We drop to the floor, rolling towards anything that can act as a shield.

I land behind an overturned table, but Elijah and Cillian have found refuge behind the bar. At least six feet separate us as arrows continue to rain down on the room, thudding into walls and furniture like a relentless storm.

My chest heaves as I work to steady my rapid breathing. Across the room, Cillian and Elijah peek out from behind the bar.

"The sun is starting to rise." Cillian waves his hand, gesturing me over. "If you can get over here, I should be able to dispatch the rest of the attackers."

Another volley of arrows streams in, splintering the wall above my head. I let out a shriek, covering my head with my hands. "I don't think I can make it."

"You can do this, sweetheart," Cillian urges.

"You've got this, baby." Elijah stretches out his hand. "On my count."

I worry my lower lip, nodding. "Okay."

"One... two..." Elijah starts, breaking eye contact only long enough to look out toward our attackers. "Three!"

I push off the floor, sprinting across the space between us and diving for safety. Arrows fly past, slamming into the wall behind me.

I startle, turning right as another flies straight for my face, and freeze.

Elijah's hand shoots out, catching the arrow before it can touch me. Cillian pulls me into his chest, tucking me firmly behind the bar.

Wiping his hands on his pants, Elijah throws the arrow down. "Shit, they're tipped with poison."

"Are you okay?" I grab his hand, turning it over and over, searching for any open wounds for the poison to infect.

"I'm fine, doll," Elijah reassures me, tugging his hand from my grasp.

"Just a few more minutes," Cillian says, watching the window for the first rays of light.

The next few minutes feel like an hour as we wait for light. Cillian grins when the morning sun finally stretches across the floor next to him. Winking, he twirls the light around his fingers before disappearing entirely. Surprised grunts and the sound of bodies dropping are all we hear as Cillian makes quick work of the Fae outside the inn.

"It's safe to come out," Cillian yells.

When we step outside, no less than a dozen Fae corpses litter the street. Cillian leans casually against the wall, one foot crossed in front of the other, looking utterly bored.

"You just took out a dozen Fae warriors in a matter of minutes," I say, my eyes flaring wide at all the bodies on the ground.

"It wasn't nepotism that got me the title of King of the Midnight Brotherhood, sweetheart."

"Arrogant, much?" I ask.

Cillian swipes a cloth along his daggers, sheathing them as he goes. "It's not arrogance if it's earned. That's called confidence."

Elijah rolls his eyes and moves to check the horses. Somehow, miraculously, they're untouched.

I breathe a sigh of relief. I've grown quite fond of Beastie in the last few days.

I load his saddle bags, eager to leave Caedel behind.

"If we make good time, we can be in Prudia by nightfall," Elijah says as he mounts Honey.

Cillian mounts Midnight, urging him forward. "We should be able to reach the capital by tomorrow afternoon, just as long as there's no more attacks along the way."

A few minutes pass before Elijah asks, "Are we going to discuss the Gift you've been hiding, or the fact that you haven't used it to transport us closer to Prudia?"

"I'm allowed to have secrets, Elijah." Cillian grunts. "How many people know about *your* second gift?"

"Touche, but you still haven't answered my question."

"I have limitations. I can only move short distances if I'm carrying others," Cillian explains.

"How far?" I ask.

"Perhaps a few miles at most. More than that would require days to recover."

I tilt my head at Cillian. "What family of Gifts does this fall under? I've never met anyone with the ability."

"I've heard it referred to as Travelling," he replies. "But I've never met anyone within Rimor that possessed the power. Others exist, but I'm not sure how the Gift is classified."

"Perhaps it deserves a classification all its own. It doesn't quite fit the existing families of Gifts." I wrap the cloak tighter around my shoulders, the hood falling low across my forehead.

We arrive at the edge of Caedel, the sun high enough to light our way and provide some warmth against the chill of the winter wind.

"Let's pick up the pace," Elijah says, kicking his horse into a brisk trot.

We're all eager to leave this place behind for the safety of Prudia. That's a sentiment I never fathomed until just now.

CHAPTER THIRTY-FOUR

AURELIUS

The scent of saltwater kisses my nose, letting me know I'm no longer in Prudia. Well, no longer in Elentia, at least. I stand on a shoreline, the cliffs behind me both unfamiliar and known. Nowhere in my memory do these cliffs exist, but in my soul and in my dreams, they're home.

For most of my life, I felt like an outsider to some extent. Sure, Raynor and my parents loved me, but I never felt completely at peace. With Breyla was the only other place that I felt this serene, this sense of belonging.

A forest of tall white birch trees looms in the distance; the limbs barren for the winter. My uncovered feet crunch in the freshly fallen snow, the cold nonexistent. I study the landscape. It's difficult to determine where the snow ends and the trees begin.

"It's serene, isn't it?" Gen asks, her arm slipping through mine.

I hadn't noticed her there before, but it feels right. "It seems like somewhere I've been before, yet also the place I've been looking for my entire existence."

Her dimples appear in that way when her smile is most genuine. It's not the smile she gives her people or the smile she gives when sitting for a portrait. It's the smile that lights her face in the midst of full belly laughter or the ones I'd catch her giving Raynor in intimate moments. "That's typically what home feels like."

It reminds me of the peace I feel anytime Breyla is in my arms. It has been far too long since I felt that.

"This isn't the home I know." *We walk along the beach, our feet leaving shallow prints in the snow-dusted shore.*

"Perhaps it's the home you're yet to find, the one that was always meant to be yours," *she suggests, leaning her head against my shoulder.*

"But where is it?"

"You don't need me to answer that," *Gen replies, a knowing smile curving her lips.*

I know her well enough to know that she isn't going to answer my question. "It would be nice if you did, though," *I grunt.*

"Hm, where do you think we are?"

"I'm afraid to say," *I admit. I don't want to say aloud where we are, because I don't want that to be what feels like home.*

"Sometimes, the things that scare us the most are the most rewarding."

The first thing her words bring to mind is the beautiful redhead she calls daughter. My feelings for her were the most terrifying thing I had ever experienced. I spent years fighting them, avoiding being at the palace or anywhere that Breyla might be. Yet, when I finally gave in, finally faced the emotions she evoked in me, that was the most rewarding satisfaction I had ever known.

But that isn't what she's talking about now.

"I'm afraid to face whatever this place is. This half of me, it's cruel. This part of my heritage is responsible for the death and suffering of so many. It's what took you," *I whisper.*

She stops, turns to face me, and runs her hand over my jaw. "A Fae may have laced that wine with the poison that took my life, but I died the day I slipped an ice dagger in Raynor's head."

My chest tightens, feeling the pain of losing her and Raynor all over again. The memory Elijah shared with us flashes through my mind as we both relive the moment Gen realized she had to end the life of the male she loved.

"I don't know how to reconcile this part of me that feels responsible for the pain of so many," *I admit.*

"Perhaps you're blaming the actions of the few on a population of many," *Gen suggests.*

"What are you saying?"

"That perhaps you are making a judgment without all the information."

"Are the dead always this vague?" I tease.

"Only when we're really trying to get a message across," she laughs.

Her form wavers, the feel of her arm in mine beginning to fade. "I think it's time to go."

"One last thing, Aurelius," she says, placing her semi-translucent hand on my chest. "If you ever keep things from my daughter again, I'll find a way to help her end you, whether you're my dearest friend or not."

I release a hearty laugh, kissing her on the cheek. "There's the terror I know and love."

She smiles, her form fading. "Goodbye, Aurelius."

"Goodbye, Gen," I reply as my vision starts to fade.

The shoreline and salty air fade first, the birch trees and cliff fading next, until all I'm left with is darkness.

When I open my eyes again, I'm staring at the ceiling of the bedroom I've been calling home in Prudia. My toes are freezing.

A book in the far corner of the library calls for me when I enter the library. With nothing else to occupy my day, I decide research might be exactly what I need. Gen's dream message left me uneasy and hungry for answers, for a truth other than what I already knew. If Gen were right, and she normally was, then I need all the facts. I'm missing a large piece of my history.

The pulling sensation guides me to a shelf in the back corner, undisturbed dust leading me to believe this section had been forgotten over the years. Running my fingers over the spines, I land on one particularly ancient-looking text. It's leatherbound, the pages yellowed, and I flip it open.

No title.

I scan the first few pages, the words reading more like a journal entry or research notes than a finished book.

A few more pages reveal that I'm reading the diary entries of my grandmother, Elythia. The story of how she met Myer engrosses me, their love story unfolding in the entries on the pages before me. To my surprise, it wasn't love at first sight. They hated one another.

"Reading something enthralling?" Breyla asks, her voice a breathy whisper in my ear.

I startle, having not realized she was that close. My head snaps to her, taking in her emerald eyes and auburn braid. A few strands remain loose around her temples, and it takes everything in me not to unravel that braid and sink my fingers into the chaos of her curls.

A quick check with my Hemonia Gift tells me we're alone in the library. My fingers wrap around the slender column of her throat, pulling her lips to mine in a tantalizing kiss.

A soft pant leaves her mouth when I finally release her. Pulling out a chair, I motion for her to join me.

"I'm reading about how Elythia fell in love with Myer," I explain.

Her head tilts, eyes roaming over my face. "I didn't take you for a romance reader," she teases.

I chuckle deeply. "I've read my fair share of... scandalous novels, Princess."

Intrigue flares in her eyes.

"But that's not what this is," I continue, nudging the book between us.

She scans the book, sharp eyes taking in each detail on the page like it's battle strategy. "This is her diary?"

"Mhm," I confirm, moving to flip the page. Before I can, several pages turn over on their own, until we're left at an entry dated several months after the previous.

"Whoa," Breyla breathes, mouth hanging open.

Thanks, Gen, I think, somehow knowing her spirit had something to do with it.

We read in silence.

Today I am certain Myer is my mate. Not just a soul mate, but my twin flame. Something I didn't even realize was possible between a Fae and a human. I don't know how to tell him.

I hear snippets of his thoughts when we are apart, the words almost sounding like my own when I know they're not. I caught him staring at me from across the ballroom when I suddenly had the thought of what I'd look like underneath my gown.

When his emotions run hot, as they often do, I will feel them as if they're my feelings.

Last week, another human woman trained with him. He overpowered her easily, pinning her to the ground in minutes. I had to restrain myself from removing every piece of skin that touched his from her body.

I hated this male mere months ago, but now I can't bear the thought of another touching him. He doesn't just balance me as a soul mate would; he fuels my fire so we both burn brighter.

When we're intimate, I battle the unrelenting urge to sink my canines into his skin and mark him as mine. My body yearns to forge our mate bond, but my mind refuses to relent.

I swallow hard, waiting for any indication that Breyla has finished the passage.

"Are there any more books on this topic?" Breyla asks, her voice unsteady.

"I haven't looked."

Finally, she peers up from the book to face me. "Perhaps we should."

The suggestion has my full attention. I've understood the depth of my feelings for her for months, but it's been something she's struggled to accept. I know she's come to terms with them now, but it appears she may be keeping secrets from me. "Now, why would we do that? Is there something you wish to tell me, little demon?"

"Is there something you wish to tell me, Aurelius?"

I huff a laugh, willing to play along. "Tell me again, how did you feel when it was suggested that I marry Lady Charlotte?"

"Like I wanted to shove my shadows down her throat and watch her choke," Breyla says viciously. There's no hint of shame or remorse in her answer. "How does it make you feel when Ayden kisses me?"

"Like, brother or not, I would delight in ripping his lips from his face," I say with perfect calm. "I never shied away from how possessive I am over you."

"What happened to you the night Ayden caught us and sent you away from the castle?" Breyla asks.

Odd question, but I'll bite. "I went to bed. When I awoke, I was in a war camp along the western border of Prudia."

"Yes, then what?" she urges.

"I was immediately thrown into battle when Fae warriors attacked."

Her brow furrows, that beautiful mind working through something pivotal. "The battle high," she gasps.

A knock interrupts that train of thought just before Ryder pushes his head through the door. "Apologies, General. Word has just arrived that Lord Elijah and Lady Ophelia have entered the city."

All talk of mates and what may or may not be between us is instantly forgotten.

I trail Breyla as she rushes through the palace halls for the front gate. A trip that should take us ten minutes takes us five.

Elijah has barely dismounted when Breyla throws herself at him. With a grunt, he catches her mid-air, spinning in a full circle. Breyla's cry is muffled as she buries her face in the crook of his neck.

"Gods, I've missed you," she breathes as Elijah brings her feet back to the ground.

Rowina saunters up beside Ayden and me. "Has she ever greeted either of you that way?" she asks, her lips quirking in a smirk.

"No," Ayden grunts.

"That enthusiasm is reserved solely for Elijah," I explain. And it's true. I may hold her heart, but he's always been the other half of her soul.

With a kiss on her cheek, Elijah releases her, and she turns to Ophelia.

They exchange radiant smiles before embracing in a hug that lasts an eternity. "The gods knew I needed you," Breyla whispers, squeezing Ophelia tightly before finally letting go.

Elijah laughs. "We've been apart for far longer than this before. What's all the emotion for?"

Breyla punches him playfully in the shoulder, and he winces. "Yes, but you've never been in imminent danger."

"Being friends with you has always been a hazard to my health," Elijah teases.

"And I'd like to think my expertise has contributed to their continued vitality," a deep, lilted voice adds.

Cillian.

"Are you expecting a thank you, *My King?*" Breyla taunts, a fierce look hardening her features.

Cillian's eyes catch mine for just a brief moment before he replies, "I wouldn't protest a thank you kiss, *little general.*" He trails a gloved hand along Breyla's jaw, tipping it up to meet his gaze.

My chest vibrates in a warning growl, Ayden tensing beside me. But Breyla doesn't need either of us to handle her battles for her. Shadows constrict around Cillian's hand, effectively halting it in place. The ruby-hilted dagger I had crafted for her is poised at his throat. Watching her threaten another male using the weapon I gifted her has my cock stirring.

"Not a chance, Cillian."

A deep laugh erupts from the male, his freckled cheeks lifting in amusement. Streams of light dissolve the shadows keeping him immobile before caressing her cheek. "Oh, little general. I've missed that fire."

She grins, dropping the dagger and sheathing it along her thigh. "Thank you for keeping my friends safe."

"This is the former lover you mentioned?" Ayden asks, keeping his voice low so only I can hear.

I grunt in confirmation. "Does he seem *harmless* to you?"

Ayden's eyes sweep over Cillian slowly. "That's not the word I would use to describe him."

"What are we whispering about?" Rowina whisper-yells, inserting herself between us.

"Just how incredibly annoying you are, sister," Ayden responds, playfully shoving her away.

"Can you read him?" I ask, gesturing to Cillian.

"Hmm, let me see," Rowina hums, narrowing her gaze. "He's conflicting. A mix of amusement, curiosity, and I think that's arousal, but I can't discern who it's for."

"Harmless, my ass," Ayden huffs, striding toward Breyla. Taking her arm in his, he smiles at Elijah and Ophelia. "Come, love. Let's show your guests to their rooms."

"Please!" Ophelia squeals. "I'm dying for a warm bath."

Rowina links her arm in Ophelia's. "Well, you're in luck. We happen to have a few bathtubs in the castle. Let's get you clean."

Elijah trails behind, and I fall into step beside him. "It's good to see you, Elijah. She's been… chaos without you."

He smiles, but it doesn't reach his eyes, falling swiftly. Sweat lines his forehead, and his heart rate is unusually high. He almost appears sickly.

My Hemonia Gift reaches out unbidden, exploring his blood for any signs of infection. While not common, thanks to our enhanced rate of healing, it is possible to fall victim to infection.

My heart nearly stops beating at what I find. I stop moving, grasping his shoulder to turn him in my direction. I wait until the others are out of earshot before confronting him.

"Elijah," I start, voice catching in my throat. "Tell me I'm wrong, and that's not the Fae poison in your veins."

"Ophelia doesn't know," is all he says, a desperate, pleading look on his face.

"Fuck," I say, running a hand through my hair. "How long ago did it happen?"

"Nearly three days back," he says, swallowing hard.

My jaw goes slack. "You should be dead."

"I know." His voice cracks. "I don't know why I'm not, but I understand I'm living on borrowed time."

Tears pool in his deep brown eyes.

My Gift reaches out again, trying to gain an understanding of how far the poison has progressed. "It's hard to say, but based on my limited experience, I'd say you have until sunrise tomorrow."

He nods, a grim acceptance in his eyes. My arms wrap around him before I can process what I'm doing. I'm not a hugger. I can count on one hand the number of people I've ever hugged, but I'm hugging Elijah, and it feels right.

"Fuck you, Elijah," I mutter against his shoulder as he finally returns my hug. "Fucking hells, what am I supposed to do? This will destroy her. How do you expect me to pick up the pieces of the female I love when you leave her shattered?"

"You're the only one who can, Aurelius," Elijah replies, breaking from my embrace. "I tried to warn you months ago that you two would need one another. I just pray someone is there to hold Ophelia together when I'm gone."

"Why wouldn't you tell her, Elijah? You can't ask me to keep this from Breyla. If she finds out I knew and didn't tell her, it will destroy the progress I've made in regaining her trust."

A panicked look fills Elijah's eyes. "You can't tell either of them. If they knew…" he sighs, "they would spend my last hours trying to change the fate we both know can't be undone."

In this moment, I truly understand why he's kept this secret. Breyla would undoubtedly spend what time he had left trying to fight the God of fate.

"I hate that you're right."

"So what are you going to do?" Elijah asks, wiping at the sweat pooling along his hairline.

An idea forms. "I can't change your fate, but I might be able to buy you more time."

Confusion scrunches his brow. "That's not what I meant."

"I know," I say, urging him toward the castle. "I won't say anything. But if Breyla hates me for this, I will find a way to resurrect you, just to kill you myself."

"She hasn't truly hated you for longer than you realize," Elijah reassures me.

"I'd like to keep it that way." I hold the door open for him, watching him disappear inside.

Rowina is turning the corner, and I gesture for him to follow her. "Go bathe and settle in. I'll find you in an hour."

I knock on Ayden's door ten minutes later, my eyes scanning for a flash of red hair as he opens. My voice is low as I ask, "Is Breyla inside?"

"No, she's helping Rowina get our guests settled in."

"Good, let me in. We need to talk."

Ayden's brow furrows in confusion, but he steps aside, letting me into his chambers. I lock the door, throwing up a silencing shield as I pace.

"What's wrong?" Ayden asks when I fail to find the words after several moments.

"Elijah is dying."

His entire posture stills. "Pardon?"

"He was poisoned on their way here. He hasn't told anyone."

"And your Gift detected the poison in his blood," Ayden surmises, and I nod.

He curses. "How long?"

"It's not behaving like previous cases. He should already be dead, but my best estimate is twelve hours."

"How is it different?"

"He was poisoned three days ago."

Ayden rubs his jaw. "That's… interesting."

"It's not enough time," I say tightly. "That's why I'm here."

"You've come to ask for the tonic." It's not a question; he's already put together why I came to him.

I nod, tacking on a "Please." Asking him for anything feels like swallowing glass, but if it means delaying Breyla's heartache, then I would get on my knees if that's what he asked of me.

He crosses the sitting room to a desk stacked high with orderly papers. "I have to stress, we don't know how long this will give him, and there could be side effects."

"I understand."

He nods, opening the bottom drawer. "For whatever it's worth, brother, my heart breaks for you." Sympathy flits through his golden eyes, the corners of his lips turning down.

The glass vial feels small and precious in the palm of my hand. The liquid represents everything and not nearly enough in this moment. Gently, I squeeze the vial before slipping it into my pocket. "I'm not the one you should concern yourself over. I don't think you grasp what this will do to her."

Ayden's lips turn slightly in a bittersweet smile. "Actually… I know exactly what this will do to her."

Elijah's time is limited, and I have none to spare for examining that answer.

I find the room he's been assigned with Ophelia and knock on the door. Thankfully, it's Elijah who answers, sparing me from having to make a reason to speak with him if Ophelia had answered. I peek over his shoulder, looking to see if she's close by.

"She's in the bath," he explains.

"Drink this," I command, slipping the vile into his hand.

He studies it, but slips the cork out, tipping the concoction back. "What is it?" he asks, wiping his mouth.

"A tonic to slow the spread."

"That exists?"

"It's new and experimental. Congratulations on being one of the first test subjects," I say dryly.

"How long?"

I shuffle restlessly, wishing I had a firm answer. "We don't know for sure. A day? Maybe less?"

Elijah swallows hard, his Adam's apple bobbing. "Thank you," he whispers.

"Use your time well."

"I intend to," he says with a nod, then closes the door, returning to Ophelia.

CHAPTER THIRTY-FIVE

Elijah's warm tongue circles my clit in slow, maddening spirals that drag a moan from my throat. The last traces of sleep vanish the moment he thrusts a finger inside my center, curling it. In and out, he pumps his fingers as his tongue continues lapping at my sex.

My fingers thread through his loose curls, hips arching off the mattress. A whimper escapes me as he sucks my clit, his fingers continuing their deliciously torturous ministrations. That familiar warmth builds low in my core, a tingling sensation growing at the base of my spine.

"Elijah." His name comes out as a breathy plea.

"Come for me, my dark goddess," he demands, a devilish grin spreading his sinful lips.

With a few more strokes of his fingers, I'm tipping over the edge as release courses through me. Pleasure electrifies every nerve ending, stealing the breath from my lungs.

Before the orgasm can subside, I feel Elijah's length aligning with my entrance. He thrusts in to the hilt in one swift motion. Giving me no time to adjust to him, he moves in and out in long, punishing strokes.

His lips find mine, swallowing my scream as his strokes perpetuate my pleasure. My fingers dig into his scalp, eliciting a delightful hiss from his lips. Deft fingers massage my butt as he guides one leg up, placing my ankle on his shoulder. The new angle leaves me panting from how much deeper he feels inside me.

"Gods, Ophelia. I would gladly lose myself in the feel of you," Elijah reverently whispers against my mouth.

Ecstasy-filled gasps escape me as goosebumps cover my flesh. He continues rocking into me, trailing reverent kisses over every piece of skin he can. My nails drag over the skin of his back, leaving red marks in their wake.

"Then lose yourself, Eli. Just come back to me in the end," I say, my words a raspy demand.

Something flashes in his eyes, but is gone before I can decipher it. His thrusts increase in tempo, stealing the breath from my lungs. Our bodies writhing together creates a symphony of pure carnal bliss.

The familiar tingling of impending bliss starts low in my belly, intensifying rapidly at Elijah's long, smooth strokes.

"Fuck, baby," he groans. "I can feel how close you are. I need to feel you shatter around me."

His words heighten my arousal, pushing me ever closer to the edge of orgasm. My inner walls clench in response, dragging a deep moan from his lips.

I reach for a pillow to stifle the scream I'm useless to stop.

"No," Elijah snarls.

"Breyla is two doors down," I protest, albeit weakly.

"I don't fucking care. When you come all over my cock, I want to hear you scream my name." His tone is demanding and borderline possessive. The gleam in his eyes is intense and unrelenting. I've never seen him like this before, and it does inexplicable things to me.

I nod in understanding and drop the pillow.

"Now fucking come for me, Ophelia," he demands, his words throwing me over the edge into utter oblivion.

I shatter around him, his name a scream as I do so. Wave after rapturous wave crashes into me, my body trembling with pleasure as his thrusts continue, growing frantic.

Elijah's lips find mine, taking my mouth in a brutal kiss full of teeth and tongues as he shudders and spills inside of me. I groan into the kiss at the sensation of him pulsing inside my core.

After a few more moments, he breaks the kiss and pulls out, dropping next to me on the bed. Our breathing takes a few more seconds to even out as the high from our release finally fades.

I roll to my side, facing him with a satiated smile. "That was certainly one way to wake a girl," I tease.

He strokes my face softly, hand cupping my jaw. "I should have been waking you up that way every morning since the first."

"You'll just have to do it for the rest of our days, then," I suggest, giving him a flirty smile.

That same haunted look crosses his face, disappearing as quickly as it arrives. "Deal. For the rest of our days together."

"Good. I'll hold you to it."

His eyes lock on mine, searching for something momentarily before he whispers, "I love you, Ophelia."

A startled gasp escapes me. I hadn't been expecting him to say that, but as I read the sincerity in his gaze, a feeling of rightness settles in my chest.

"Elijah, I—"

He raises a hand to my lips, cutting off my words.

"I didn't tell you because I want you to say it back. I just needed you to know."

"But what if I feel it too?"

"Then tell me at the end of the day," he says, smiling softly.

A strange request, but one I oblige. I nod and show him how I feel, the only way I can. I press my lips to his in a kiss, soft, reverent, and laced with every feeling he won't let me speak.

Our tender kiss quickly turns heated as I push him back, straddling his hips. He hardens beneath me, and I slide down his length. We let out a collective sigh once I'm fully seated. Then I roll my hips and use my body to say all the things he won't allow me to speak.

When we finally emerge later in the afternoon, we head to the private library in the royal wing. Hand-in-hand, we enter to find Aurelius,

Breyla, Ayden, his sister Rowina, and, surprisingly, his general, Darian.

Breyla greets us by wrapping us both in a tight embrace. "I've missed you both so much," she whispers, her body relaxing in our hold.

"You know I can't stay away from you, B," Elijah jests.

"These last few months have been inexplicably difficult without you. I'm so happy you're safe now."

She releases us, stepping back and handing me a plate of food. My stomach growls at the sight, and she gives me a knowing smile.

I shove a piece of chocolate pastry in my mouth, moaning at the explosion of sweetness on my tongue. Elijah's eyes heat as he reaches for a piece of food on my plate.

I yank the plate away from him as he lays his fingers on my chocolate delicacy. "Mine," I say, giving him a side-eye.

He furrows his brows at me. "Ophelia, share."

"Get your own." I shove the rest of the chocolate delicacy into my mouth. It was too much for one bite. I have no regrets, even though I struggle to chew.

"You and your chocolate," he says, rolling his eyes.

I just shrug and mumble around my food, "You should know better by now."

Breyla chuckles and hands him his own plate, complete with a chocolate pastry.

He takes it, nodding his thanks. "At least one of you cares about me."

Finally managing to swallow, I pat him on the cheek and say, "I think I showed you just how much I care about you this morning."

Elijah's nostrils flare, his eyes dancing with heat as he looks me up and down.

"Oh, we know," Breyla says dramatically, taking a seat on one of the couches surrounding the fireplace.

We take a seat on the empty couch, and I tuck my feet under me as Elijah wraps an arm around my shoulders.

"So, tell me more of what's going on in Rimor," Breyla says.

Before Elijah can respond, Aurelius cuts in. "I think that can wait a day, Princess. Let's just relax and enjoy this time together."

She raises an inquisitive brow before Ayden adds, "Elijah already briefed me. Aurelius is right. Let's just enjoy the day."

AYDEN

I lean against the bookshelf nearest the group currently playing cards. The pure joy I see in Breyla's face nearly breaks my own heart. A piece of her has been missing all these months away from Elijah. Seeing her now is bittersweet.

"You're hiding something, brother," Ro accuses. I hadn't even noticed her approach.

Discreetly, I cast a sound shield around us. "Use your Gift, Ro. What do you feel from Elijah right now?"

Her honey-gold eyes slide to him, focusing intently. "I feel joy and love. Something that tastes an awful lot like acceptance and regret tangled together..." Her voice trails off before a startled gasp leaves her lips. "Oh gods." Tears gather in her eyes as she stumbles from the intensity. Rubbing at her chest, she croaks, "Pain, so much pain."

Her gaze turns to me. "What's going on?"

"He stopped a poisoned arrow meant for Ophelia on their journey here. She doesn't know he's dying."

"How the hell does she not know?" she all but demands.

"He kept the cut hidden from her and Cillian, and he's a master at masking his pain. He wants neither Breyla nor Ophelia to know."

"Why would he keep this from them?"

"Is it not obvious?"

"Explain it to me."

"He wanted this." I gesture to the laughing group. "He wanted to enjoy his last moments without them fussing or trying to change the fates."

She nods in understanding, her lips thinning. "Then I shall help him enjoy it pain-free."

With smooth strides, she crosses the room to where Elijah sits. A delicate hand runs across his shoulders as she leans down between him and Ophelia.

I see Elijah's shoulders relax, his pain fading away at the touch of Ro's Empath Gift.

"What do you say to us escaping this stuffy castle to go dancing?" Rowina suggests, grinning and wrapping her arms around the couple.

"Dancing?" Breyla perks up at the mention of her favorite activity.

"Yes, Princess." I grin. "There's a tavern in town that local musicians frequent. There's music playing nearly every night of the week."

Aurelius' eyes narrow at the use of his pet name for Breyla, making me stifle a laugh.

"And you're just now telling me about it?" Breyla asks, voice dripping in disbelief.

I shrug. "I didn't know you enjoyed dancing so much until recently, so why would I have told you?"

Breyla scrunches her nose in confusion.

"Are we going or not?" I ask, trying to move this conversation along. "We haven't got all day."

Elijah's eyes meet mine, and a look of understanding passes between us at just how true those words are.

He jumps to his feet, pulling Ophelia with him. Breyla is up next and already striding for the door. The rest of our group joins them, pulling fur-lined cloaks around their shoulders as they go.

"Go ahead with Breyla, doll," Elijah tells Ophelia. "I need to grab something first."

I stop beside him as the others disappear into the corridor. He turns to me, all traces of playfulness gone.

"A word, prince."

"Of course."

When the door clicks shut behind the others, he turns to me. "I want to thank you."

I raise a curious brow at him. "Whatever for?"

"For everything you've done and will do to protect them."

I stiffen at his words, not fully understanding his meaning. "I don't follow."

"I know, but you will," he says with a half-smirk.

"And they call me cryptic," I say sarcastically.

His smirk fades, voice dropping into something quieter. "Take care of her. Or so help me, I will find a way to haunt your ass."

"She's my fiancée. Of course, I will take care of her."

"That's not the she I was referring to."

Oh.

"What aren't you saying?"

"A great many things, Prince. But I leave you with this: there is room enough in her heart for two great loves. Don't be the one to stifle that."

"You have grown frustratingly vague in your old age," I try to joke, but it falls flat.

"Come on, let's go catch up with them. I don't want to miss a thing." He clasps my shoulder, ushering us forward and out the door.

CHAPTER THIRTY-SIX

BREYLA

By the time we reach the tavern, my cheeks are flushed from the biting winter wind. It's all worth it, though, if it provides a night of dancing with the people that mean the most to me. I hadn't realized how deeply I'd missed Elijah and Ophelia until they arrived yesterday.

The tavern is warm and lively when the eight of us enter. I was surprised to see Darian relaxing with us today, considering the stick that seemed to be permanently present in his ass. When he followed us out to the tavern, my jaw nearly hit the floor.

Darian trails Rowina, a hand on her lower back, to the bar to order drinks as we settle in a booth along the wall. It's warm enough that we can comfortably peel off the fur-lined cloaks and gloves. Dark wood paneling lines the walls, but paired with the gentle gleam of Faerie lights, it creates a very cozy environment.

I slide in next to Elijah, Ayden taking the seat on my right side, followed by Aurelius. As promised, a group of musicians occupies a raised area in the corner.

"They must be taking a break. Have a drink, darling, then we'll dance," Ayden says, seemingly reading my mind.

Not a minute later, Rowina and Darian return, their arms holding mugs for each of us. As I lift the drink to my lips, I realize it's not ale but mead. The strong, semi-sweet honey liquor slides down my throat smoothly, filling me with a heat that leaves me grinning.

We sip in companionable quiet until Darian breaks the silence. "Mykel is playing tonight," he says. "He always chooses the best melodies for dancing."

I should know better when it comes to him, but I can't help the question that slips from my lips. "You dance?" I scoff disbelievingly. "You are the antithesis of fun."

His fingers curl around his mug at my words. "It's not *fun* I dislike."

I bristle at his insinuation. "Yes, *General*, you've made your distaste for me abundantly clear."

Sensing the rising tension, Ayden cuts in smoothly. "You'll find that Darian is actually quite the skilled dancer."

I consider his words for a moment before shrugging. "Doubtful."

Darian stands abruptly, and I expect him to storm away from the table in irritation. When he holds his hand out to me, I lift a brow.

He rolls his eyes. "Dance with me, General."

I stare at his hand. "Is that a request or a command?"

"Why are you always this obstinate?" He sighs, thoroughly exasperated.

Elijah snickers beside me, and both Aurelius and Ayden stifle a chuckle. Cillian doesn't even bother; his laugh bursts out unrestrained.

"Some find that my most endearing trait," I say sweetly.

"I assure you, they don't. Now dance with me so I can wipe that smug look off your face."

"He really is a talented dancer," Rowina assures me.

"Fine," I grumble, standing from the table.

I place my hand in his, letting him lead me to the dance floor. He leans down to the male, whom I assume is Mykel. The male nods and chuckles.

Returning to me, Darian smirks and says, "Try to keep up, General."

His large hand finds my hip, pulling me close while still keeping space between our bodies.

A moment later, the music begins, and a moderate-paced melody fills the tavern. Several couples join us on the floor, but not nearly as many as still stand along the fringes.

"Why aren't more joining us?" I ask as we spin across the floor.

This isn't some ballroom dance, and it isn't one I'm familiar with, but I'm an adept learner.

His grin turns sinister. "You'll see why shortly."

I must admit, he is a skilled partner, leading me effortlessly through an unfamiliar dance. He spins me out and back under his arm in a twirl that has my hair whipping around my face.

The song increases its tempo suddenly, our pace increasing with it. He continues gracefully guiding me through the spins and twirls as we move across the dance floor.

I give up the fight, letting a wide smile grace my face from the pure joy I feel in this moment. A laugh bubbles up my throat as our tempo increases once more, the rest of the tavern blurring around us.

"You ready for this next part, General?" Darian asks.

"Bring it, General."

"Keep your hands on mine and trust me," he commands.

His blue eyes sparkle just before he circles one arm around my head, his hand coming to rest on my throat. Effortlessly, he lifts me from the ground above his head and holds me there a moment before letting my body swing back into his. Instinctively, I wrap my legs around his hips as he dips us both until my hair brushes the floor. I keep my eyes on his as he brings us upright. He slowly releases the hand around my neck but keeps his eyes on mine.

Holy. Shit.

I've danced with many talented partners in my life. All the males currently sitting at our table are fantastic dancers, but then there is Darian. I was absolutely going to eat my words about his ability.

As my legs slide back to the floor, the song comes to an end. Our chests heave, heartbeats erratic as we come down from the high of the dance.

"How did you learn to dance like that?" I ask, still stunned.

He grins triumphantly at me. "How did you?"

"My father encouraged it when I started showing interest in swordplay. He said it would make me more fluid and graceful in fights."

"Your father is a wise male, and of a similar mind to my own."

I'm not sure how I feel about sharing something so unexpectedly... personal with him.

"Can we do that again?" I ask, grinning despite myself.

"Maybe later." His gaze darts behind me. "I believe you have another hoping for a dance right now."

Darian releases me, turning to Rowina, waiting for her turn to dance. A bright smile creeps across his face as he pulls her into his arms.

I turn around to find Elijah waiting patiently for me. Behind him are three sets of heated eyes. Aurelius, Cillian, and even Ayden stare as if they wish they were Darian right now. I throw them all a wink as I step into Elijah's arms and tease, "Are you sure you want to dance with me? My last partner is a lot to live up to."

"I would never say no to dancing with my best friend."

We fall into step alongside the other dancing couples, many more for this dance than the last.

"Do you remember our first dance lesson?" Elijah asks after a few beats.

I groan. "How could I forget? I insisted on leading because I thought it made me weak to follow. I stepped all over your feet."

He chuckles at the memory. "You also got so caught up in watching your steps that you led us into a wall."

"I have no idea why you would continue being my partner after that. I would have quit if I were you."

"I considered it," he admits. "But I also realized that even though you clearly were not meant to lead in a waltz, you would one day be an incredible leader. I recognized that you needed me then, but you wouldn't always. So I made a decision to always be what you needed for as long as you still needed me."

"Elijah, I will *always* need you. There will never be a time when my soul does not need yours. I love you, Eli."

"I love you, too, B." He smiles before spinning me out. As I return to him, he continues, "But you're wrong. You're stronger than you believe. And one day, you'll trust your own strength."

I open my mouth to tell him he's wrong, but he cuts me off. "Do you remember being afraid of thunderstorms?"

"Of course," I say, a memory bubbling up like a dream I hadn't realized I'd forgotten.

"Eli, wake up," I said impatiently.

His snoring continued, clearly not having heard my pleas. I shoved his shoulder, trying to rouse him, just as lightning struck and thunder sounded through his room.

I let out a startled scream, jumping slightly.

Elijah's eyes flew open as he sat straight up in bed. His eyes settled on me, mind piecing together why I'm standing in his chambers.

"Again, B?"

"I can't sleep, Eli. Please, let me sleep with you," I begged. Tears welled in my eyes as another round of thunder shook the walls.

He was quiet for several moments before his eyes lit. "Fine, but only after you try something with me first."

"What do I have to do?" I questioned softly.

Elijah got out of bed, pulling on his boots and a cloak. "You have to trust me."

He handed me a pair of slippers and wrapped a spare cloak around my shoulders.

"I trust you, E, but you've got to give me more than that."

Tugging me out of his room and down the hall, he said, "I'm going to teach you to associate a positive emotion with what you fear."

"Okay," I said, my voice unsteady as we approached the servants' exit.

Turning to me, Elijah asked, "Do you really trust me, Breyla?"

I took a deep breath before responding, "Yes."

He gripped both of my hands in his, keeping his eyes on me as he opened the door. "You can do this."

I nodded, never taking my eyes from his.

Walking backward, he took a step outside. Behind him, lightning struck, freezing me in place.

"You are stronger than the storm, Breyla." His voice was reassuring and full of confidence.

"I am stronger than the storm," I repeated back, taking a step with him.

One step at a time, we worked our way outside into the onslaught of rain until we stood ten feet from the castle door.

Thunder rolled again, and I cried out, clinging to him.

Without hesitation, Elijah pulled me into his arms, whispering, "Shhh, I've got you, B. You're okay."

Tears streamed down my face, mixing with the rain covering every inch of me.

Elijah's hand came to rest on my hip, his other clasping with mine as he held them out to the side. "Dance with me."

"There's no music," I protested.

"We don't need music," he responded, dragging me into the steps we had memorized.

Muscle memory took over, my body moving with his, despite the paralyzing fear. The more we danced and swayed, the more I felt my body relax.

Thunder sounded again, causing me to jump and look around in panic.

"Eyes on me, B. Ignore everything else. Just feel the dance, feel the safety of my arms, the cool touch of rain on your skin."

My eyes found his brown ones and stayed there. We continued dancing, my eyes locked with his as we swayed.

After several more minutes, I no longer even noticed when thunder sounded. All I knew was the comfort of Eli's arms, the joy of doing something I loved, and the feel of the rain on my skin.

Throwing my arms out to the side, my head flung back, I savored the moment.

"Never forget to dance in the rain," Elijah whispered.

Returning to the present, I say, "You told me I was stronger than the storm."

He smiles at me. "I also told you to never forget to dance in the rain."

I tilt my head, trying to read him. "Why the sudden trip down memory lane?"

"I thought you could use the reminder right about now."

The song comes to an end, and Ayden steps forward, tapping Elijah's shoulder. "May I steal your partner?"

"Of course, Prince," Elijah says, smiling warmly. "She's all yours."

OPHELIA

"Your turn, darling," Elijah whispers, taking my hips in his hands from behind. He nips at my earlobe, sending a shiver down my spine.

He turns me so we're face to face, his grip firm as we sway in time with the music. This tune is slower, meant for lovers.

I wind my arms around the back of his neck, pressing close. He leans his forehead against mine, whispering softly, "You are so beautiful, Ophelia. The gods have truly blessed me."

I soak in his words, trying to find something to measure up to that declaration. "It is I who has been blessed."

He kisses me tenderly before speaking again, "When you ran into me in that hallway, the only thing I could think was, 'This looks like someone I could spend my life with.'"

I lift a brow. "We had barely spoken before then."

"Ah, but you forget, I saw into your soul that day. I saw your memory of healing Lyla and countless others. Your memories showed me who you were, and I knew then that I could fall in love with you."

"I was only doing what I knew to be right. I've also taken life..." My voice trails off, memories of my father and that male's final breath clouding my mind.

"Because that is who you are at your core. You may have lost yourself along the way, but your soul was created for love. The darkness in you isn't evil. There's darkness and light in us all. You just have to remember where to look for the light when the darkness feels like too much."

"Is it the end of the day yet?" I ask, wishing to utter the words I felt in my soul.

"Not quite." He grins. "Tell me, what do you think forever would look like together?"

"With you?" I sigh contentedly. "I think it would look like joy."

"And what does joy look like, Ophelia?"

"A summer wedding, so we could honeymoon in Amala. I think Layne would want you to take me there in his place." A bittersweet smile crosses my face at the thought of going without my brother, but instead with my love.

"Tell me more," he urges.

"It looks like two beautiful children with my hair and your eyes."

"Boys or girls?"

"One of each."

"What else?"

"Story time with hot chocolate around the fireplace on Winter Solstice. Slow dances to no music when we're alone. Falling asleep next to you every evening."

"And waking you up every morning with my tongue," he adds in a low rasp.

"You did promise that," I say with a giggle.

"I like the sound of that, Ophelia. It would be a perfect life."

"It *will* be our life, Elijah. I want nothing more than that life with you."

"Of course." The smile doesn't quite reach his eyes.

Rowina's scream slices through the tavern. I snap my head to her right as I see her punch a male in the jaw.

"We should go see—"

Elijah groans, a sharp, broken sound, and collapses at my feet.

CHAPTER THIRTY-SEVEN

"Find Rowina," I command Darian the moment I see Elijah drop to the floor. She'd been getting drinks when I heard her scream. Heaven knows why she punched the male, but he probably deserved it. Her grasp on her Gift must have slipped, letting Elijah's pain return and overwhelm him.

In two strides, I'm at his side. Kneeling, I place a hand on his shoulder. Sweat clings to his brow, the color draining from his golden skin. I'd been carefully monitoring the poison's progression all day, and it destroys me to say, "It's time, my friend."

Our group gathers around us, looks of confusion and sorrow lining every face.

"Time for what?" Ophelia asks.

"What's going on?" Breyla asks next.

"I'm so sorry!" Rowina bursts between us, her hand flying to Elijah's cheek. "I got distracted by the asshole at the bar, and my power slipped."

A relieved sigh leaves Elijah as my sister's Gift goes to work, blocking his pain once again. But it's only able to do so much. I catch the way his breath catches when he moves too quickly, and the slow jerking foot steps he takes.

"How much time do I have left?" he asks.

"Left for what?" Breyla screams, panic filling her voice.

Ophelia's tears spill over as recognition flashes across her face. She knows what Rowina's Gift looks like. "You lied to me," she whispers.

"I'm sorry, my love," he says softly.

"When we were attacked on the way here…" Cillian mumbles, putting the pieces together.

Ophelia sucks in an unsteady breath. "The arrow you stopped from hitting me, it actually did cut you." It's not a question. It's a realization.

"No." Breyla shakes her head, clutching at her chest as if *she's* the one with poison running through her veins. Her lip trembles, moisture glistening in the corners of her emerald eyes.

"Can we continue this conversation outside?" Elijah asks gently. "I'd like to see the stars."

We quickly gather our cloaks and step into the cold.

"How did you hide this from us all day?" Breyla demands, tears streaming down her cheeks. "*Why* would you?"

Elijah looks to me for the answer I haven't given yet. "You have maybe ten minutes left," I say solemnly.

Choked sobs emanate from Breyla and Ophelia.

"In that case, they can explain it when I'm gone. I have things I need to say with the time I have."

Elijah wraps his arms around Breyla's trembling body, whispering, "I love you, B."

"You fucking asshole," she sobs, her legs shaking so violently she struggles to hold herself up. "You can't die. I still need you."

"I've tried to tell you in so many ways already, you don't. You can and will do this without me."

"I refuse to do this without you," she stammers.

"Don't you dare," he warns, voice firm. "You will do great and wondrous things. Don't you dare deprive the world of the impact you're meant to have."

"H-how do I do this without you?"

Elijah presses a kiss to her forehead. "You are stronger than the storm. Never forget to dance in the rain."

He releases her, turning to Ophelia. "Come here, my love."

She crashes into his arms, unable to stop the trembling in her limbs. "You promised me forever."

"I had you for my forever, just not yours."

Ophelia pulls in a deep breath, fighting to calm herself and savor her last few minutes with Elijah. "The sun has set," she remarks, looking up at the stars.

"Indeed, it has."

"It's the end of the day."

"That it is," he says with a smile.

"I fucking love you, Elijah Mara."

"I fucking love you too, Ophelia Dabria Delencort." His lips crash into hers in a heated kiss that she returns in equal measure.

"How fucking dare you," she says meekly between kisses. "How dare you promise me forever and draw a picture of what our life will be, only to leave me."

"Oh, my love. You will have that future, and it will be beautiful. Those two kids will have your hair. You will get your summer wedding and honeymoon in Amala. You will tell them stories and drink hot chocolate. You'll slow dance to no music when no one is around."

"I don't want it if it's not with you!" she screams.

"Shhh," he soothes. "The truth is, I've known for much longer than today that your forever didn't include me. And I knew that the only way that was possible was if I no longer walked this plane. Because nothing could ever stop me from loving you, Ophelia. Maybe it makes me selfish, but I don't care. I chose to love you, knowing I wasn't your forever. But you were *mine*. I don't regret a single moment spent loving you."

Somewhere between the hushed words and desperate kisses, they simultaneously lose the fight to stand. Dropping to the snow-covered ground, Ophelia continues peppering him with soft kisses as Elijah whispers inaudible words into her midnight hair.

Pained sobs choke her at his words, her body trembling as she begs and pleads with the gods to spare him. Those same cries are echoed by Breyla, who barely manages to stand. Cillian wraps a steadying arm around her, letting her lean into him. I bite back the possessive growl, sensing his intentions are pure.

Elijah leans in to whisper something inaudible to the rest of us. Ophelia vehemently shakes her head, denying his words, her hands glowing white as she pushes her healing Gift into his body.

It does nothing.

"Aurelius," he says, his voice a soft plea. I don't need him to finish his request, knowing exactly what he's asking.

Darian and Rowina step back, giving us privacy, while Ayden hovers nearby, trepidation filling his gaze.

I kneel beside Elijah, Breyla dropping with me. He keeps one hand locked around Ophelia and takes Breyla's hand in the other.

"I'm ready."

Nodding, I lay a hand on his shoulder. "Just like falling asleep," I say softly.

I hesitate for just a moment, knowing what this will do to the female who holds my heart. It'll be my hand that severs part of her soul from her. Merciful death or not, I know I will bear this scar eternally. I will carry this burden because he asked me to, for her.

My Gift winds through Elijah's chest, wrapping softly around his heart. Slowly, I stop it. As his eyes drift shut and his body goes limp, both females before me shatter.

Their pained screams fill the night, and I swear I sense a part of each of their souls leave with his. I'm not sure either will ever recover from this loss.

Breyla slumps beside me, and I pull her into my embrace. I hold her close as her cries echo into the darkness. Next to me, Ayden pulls Ophelia from Elijah's limp grasp, tucking her into his chest as she breaks.

Cillian and Darian lift Elijah, preparing to take him back to the castle. But as he moves, Ophelia flies from Ayden's arms.

"No!" she screams. "You can't take him."

"They have to, little one," Ayden says softly, trying to pull her back. "Elijah must be prepared for his last rites."

"They can't," she sobs. "Elijah promised me forever."

"He gave you his forever, Ophelia," Ayden says softly. At his words, Ophelia goes lax, allowing Ayden to pull her away from Elijah's body.

Cillian's sorrow-filled gaze lingers on Ophelia for a brief moment before Darian quickly Travels the body back to the castle, leaving the rest of us to walk back.

Breyla says nothing as I stand with her in my arms, Ayden joining me, Ophelia in his. Together, we trek through the capital's snow-covered streets as I try to figure out how the female in my arms is supposed to recover from this.

An answer never comes.

CHAPTER THIRTY-EIGHT

Much like when my mother died, I see Elijah's face every time I close my eyes. In the two days since Aurelius stopped his heart, I have not eaten, nor have I slept. The overwhelming sense of wrongness weighs on me. How I can feel so heavy when such an integral part of my soul has been ripped from me is beyond my understanding.

Anxiety churns in my gut as I think about what today is.

A soft knock at my door reveals Aurelius. I say nothing but let him enter my room. In his arms is a dress, a familiar one at that. It's the dress from my mother's funeral. The one that made me feel like I was wearing armor instead of a mourning gown. It was everything I needed at that moment and everything I would need today. I didn't realize it had made the journey with us to Prudia.

"Where did you get that?" I ask, my voice hoarse.

"Elijah had it packed with your things. I simply located it for you," he replies quietly, stepping inside and closing the door behind him.

"You mean you stole it from wherever your brother had it hidden."

"Fuck my brother." His words hold no venom, and silently, I wonder when that changed.

Aurelius lays the dress across the bed and pulls me into his arms.

He presses a kiss to my hair, and I sigh, searching for any emotion, trying to find anything to feel aside from numb.

Tears well in my eyes, and I whisper, "I don't think I can do this."

"I know you can. But even if you can't, even if you fall and shatter, I will be there to gather every broken piece."

"But what if you can't find them all? What if some are just… gone?"

"Then we will be beautifully broken together."

We stand there, still and quiet, until I finally whisper the words I had uttered only once before, "I love you."

He pulls back just enough to see my face, his eyes searching mine as he processes my words.

"You mean it?"

"I mean it," I confirm. Technically, I had meant it the first time I said it, but I can understand why he would question it.

"Why now?" His hand brushes down my jaw, gently cupping my cheek.

"Because I don't want the first time you hear that to be as you lay dying. I just thought you should know."

Aurelius' eyes flutter shut, a relieved breath escaping him, just before he takes my mouth in a kiss like no other. It's tender yet scorching as he pours every emotion he's feeling into it. I meet his passion with fire of my own, our tongues dancing, teeth clashing and nipping as we fight for control. Little does he know, I would give it all to him. The kiss is soul-searching, and as we break for breath at last, something deep inside my chest settles.

He rests his forehead against mine, his hand still caressing my jaw. His touch chases away the numbness for just a moment, and I relish in his warmth.

"It would seem we are finally on the same page, Princess." He exhales a heavy breath, something relaxing in him for the first time in a very long time. "I love you. With everything I am, I love you. My brother can get fucked, because you are mine." The last of his words comes out with a possessive growl.

"Yours," I agree.

His hand wraps around my neck as he whispers, "I am so very mad at you right now, little demon."

My head tilts back slightly, relishing in the slight pressure he applies to my throat. "Why?" I rasp.

"Because you waited until we're minutes away from needing to leave for your soul mate's funeral pyre to tell me you love me. The last thing I should be thinking about is bending you over and fucking my claim into you so you never forget who you belong to."

My breath comes in soft pants, heat blooming in my core. "All you need is thirty-seven seconds."

A dark chuckle erupts from him as he smirks. "All *you* need is thirty-seven seconds. I'm going to need hours after what you just professed." He runs his thumb along my bottom lip, pulling it down softly. "I'm going to draw those words out of your pretty lips again and again while I fuck you raw. Then you'll beg me for more."

Reluctantly, he releases me before I can reply. "Time to get dressed, Princess."

He spins me so I'm facing away from him. Teasing fingers graze the length of my neck, then down my shoulder, pulling my nightshirt away and leaving my skin bare. Honeyed kisses pepper my neck as he pulls the shirt off, letting it fall to the floor.

I grunt in frustration when I feel his body heat desert me, leaving me naked and cold.

He returns a moment later, my dress in hand.

"Arms up."

I oblige, letting him maneuver my limbs into the dress. The leather-like material slides on like a second skin, hugging me tightly. Sighing, I smooth the skirt as Aurelius gathers my hair and pulls it over one shoulder.

Featherlight touches trail along my skin, leaving goosebumps in their wake. His fingers trace my spine slowly, coming to a stop at my hips. The touch leaves me desperate for more—more of his hands, kisses, and skin all over my body. I'm silently begging him to keep touching me, to chase the numbness from my veins.

"You look just as fierce," he murmurs, pressing a kiss just below my ear, "and absolutely fucking edible, as you did the first time you wore my dress." Another kiss lower along my jaw.

I turn my head to look him in the eyes. "Your dress?"

His lips curl in a smug smile, dark irises sparkling. "Who did you think had this dress designed for you?"

"Ophelia said it looked like it was *made for me*. It was exactly what I needed to face my kingdom at my mother's funeral. It made me feel strong when I was utterly broken."

"It *was* made for you, Breyla." Aurelius tucks a stray tendril behind my ear, his thumb tenderly stroking my cheek. "Only you."

Tears well in the corner of my eyes as my hands clench his tunic, pulling him closer. "You knew what I needed even when I didn't. You made sure I had it when you were just as hurting and broken. Even when you thought I hated you, you still put me first."

Gently, he strokes my hair before pulling me in for a soft kiss.

"You will always be my highest priority. I promised both your parents I would keep you safe, and I'm vowing to you now that I will always take care of you, whether you want me to or not."

"I don't deserve you," I whisper, and the tears finally spill down my cheeks.

"Probably not," he says with a faint smile, "but there's no returning me now, Princess."

I laugh through my tears, because it's such an Elijah thing to say. But the laughter twists into sobs as pain wracks through me in waves. For several moments, he says nothing. He just holds me while I break.

"I know you feel guilty for finding a moment of joy right now, but he would've wanted you to laugh."

"I know," I whisper.

"Your capacity for love is why you feel this loss so deeply. It's one of my favorite things about you."

"What do you mean?"

"You feel the pain of loss so viscerally because you love just as deeply. The more you hurt, the more you love just as fiercely. It's a trait you inherited from your mother."

My smile is bittersweet, and I let the pain and simultaneous joy seep inside my bones.

"We need to leave," Aurelius says after a few minutes.

"It's cold as shit." I squeeze him to me tighter, hoping it will keep him from moving.

"Then I guess it's a good thing I also stole you some of Rowina's fur-lined leggings."

"Have I mentioned I love you?"

"No. I think I need reminding."

"I fucking love you, Aurelius."

"I fucking love you, Breyla. Now get dressed."

Reluctantly, I release him and reach for the leggings. Slipping them on, I sigh in sweet, warm relief. Without needing to be asked, Aurelius drops to one knee, a pair of thick wool socks in hand. I brace against the dresser and lift my foot. He rolls one sock on, followed by my boot, then repeats the process with my other foot.

Lastly, he drapes a fur-lined cloak across my shoulders and ties it snugly in place.

"No matter what," he says as we head for the door, "I'm with you, Princess. Always."

We stand in the courtyard, waiting for the others to arrive. Cold winter wind nips at my skin, painting it pink. I should feel cold, but the overwhelming emptiness is all I notice. The warmth recently conjured by Aurelius' presence has fled as he stands beside me, not touching any part of me.

There are still traitors in this court, just as there were in my own. Though Ayden hasn't explained entirely, I knew we were being watched and they needed to believe the farce that was our engagement. Which is why I lean into his heat when he steps up behind me.

It was comforting, but he didn't chase away the gnawing emptiness like Aurelius had. His handsome face is solemn as he pulls me close, his fingers curling gently around my shoulder.

I glance around at the attending faces. There were so few, and even fewer who truly knew Elijah. Queen Josephina is here, but I suspect it's out of royal obligation. There should be more. In Rimor, he was well-loved by everyone at court, but this kingdom did not know the male resting on the funeral pyre.

Rowina and Darian stand on the other side of Aurelius. Cillian and Ophelia are the last to join. With no regard for the prince, Cillian shoves his way between us, pulling me into a tight embrace.

After my initial shock wears off, I wrap my arms around him, returning the gesture.

"I'm so sorry, Breyla," is all he whispers before releasing me and returning to Ophelia's side.

He guides her to stand beside Ayden, her face unreadable. Her eyes are red and swollen but vacant. They're somehow filled with immeasurable pain, yet nothing at all. It's a haunted look that I don't recall ever seeing on her before. Not even when she lost Layne.

Something is irrevocably broken in her. My soul echoes the sentiment.

"Love," Ayden says, offering me a flower, "we have a slightly different ceremony here than in Rimor."

To call it beautiful would be an insult; there were no words to describe it. Deep burgundy petals that fade into the darkest of black tips surrounded a gilded center. Iridescent gold specks covered the flower, giving it an ethereal glow. I had never seen a flower like it before.

"We call it the La Crencia flower," he explains. "It's believed to be a product of the faeries of old, made of pure magic. It only grows here as far as we know."

I lift the gorgeous flora to my nose, inhaling deeply. "It smells like…"

"Citrus and honeysuckle," Aurelius says, his nose buried deeply in his own flower.

"It smells different to every individual, but the scent should mean something to you."

That explains why it doesn't smell at all like honeysuckle or citrus to me.

"Mine is… spicy and earthy," I say, trying to avoid outright saying it smells exactly like Aurelius.

"To me, it smells like honey," Ayden muses. "That's new."

"Lilacs," Cillian mutters.

Ophelia tips the flower to her nose, her brows furrowing. "It doesn't matter," she whispers.

"What do we do with them?" I ask.

Ayden twirls his stem, gaze distant as he contemplates something. "You place them on his body just before we light the pyre."

I nod in understanding, then turn my stare to the unlit pyre. Heavy sorrow blankets me as the group waits for me to deliver the hardest goodbye of my life.

"Truthfully, I never imagined I'd be giving this eulogy." My chest constricts at the weight of each word. "Elijah and I would joke that when the gods came to take us home, I would undoubtedly go first due to some reckless mistake on my part. I always believed that would be the case."

My voice breaks, and I fight to continue.

"How does one say goodbye to the other half of their soul? How do I say goodbye to the one who made me laugh when I wanted to cry? Who supported me through every single mistake, and who held me through every storm?"

Tears flow freely down my face. "Furthermore, how do I pick up the pieces and move on after I've figured out how to let you go? Because I never wish to forget. Even if I piece myself together with crucial parts missing, I refuse to leave behind the first male who taught me that family isn't just blood. The one who knew exactly when to push me and exactly when to hold me back. The boy who broke his arm with me and suffered every consequence alongside me. The person who taught me how to dance in the rain." My voice wavers, the memory playing out in my mind.

"You will be forever with me, my brother, my best friend, my soul mate."

The last of the words catches in my throat. I'm trembling, though I can't tell if it's from the cold or something else entirely.

On shaking legs, I force myself toward the pyre. I place the La Crencia flower atop Elijah's chest, resting my hand against his for a brief moment.

His face is peaceful but unmistakably lifeless.

Stepping back, I turn my attention to Ophelia.

When she speaks, her voice is raw with grief. "Elijah taught me so many things. He taught me to love and how to be loved properly. He showed me what it was to trust another, after having spent so long trusting no one. I quite literally owe my life to him several times over, and that is a debt I can never repay nor ever forget."

Her tiny fist clenches tightly around the stem of the La Crencia. "He was everything to me. He made me so many promises, and I'm so godsdamned fucking pissed at him for breaking those promises." Her broken words drip with anger.

"Damnit, Eli. We didn't have the life you promised me. We will never get to grow old or find out what our kids look like. There will be no slow dances and no hot chocolate by the fire. There will be nothing because, without you, nothing has any meaning. It should be me on that pyre and fuck you for taking my place," she sobs.

"But for all that it's worth, thank you. Thank you for teaching me to love and for loving me. I will never, not for a single breath, regret loving you. Thank you for showing me how to trust, for showing me so much passion and devotion. Thank you for dragging me out of the dark and reminding me what light feels like. Thank you… for it all."

Her voice breaks as she lays her flower beside mine.

One by one, the rest of those in attendance walk up to leave their flower atop his pyre. When the last flower is placed, I step forward, my arm outstretched to Ophelia.

She meets me, her hand slipping into mine.

"Together?" I ask.

"Together."

As his pyre is set ablaze, together we sing the Rimorian death hymn one more time.

May the mother keep you close
And the father protect you now
The tears that once were shed
Make the flowers grow
When the night is darkest
And the sun has ceased its shining
May you remember
My love for you is eternal
From your first breath
Until your very last
May the gods grant you peace

The flames crawl higher, fully engulfing his body as the second round begins and the remaining voices join. When the fire reaches the flowers atop his body, something breathtaking occurs. Simultaneously, they burst into flames, golden sparks dancing around him and high into the sky. The scent of chocolate and cinnamon fills the courtyard.

I catch Ophelia from the corner of my eye and see the bitter acceptance flash in her silver eyes.

It's Elijah's scent.

And this is the last time we'll ever smell it.

I make it through the third round before my voice fails me, pained cries taking its place. Waves of sorrow wash over me as every memory I have with Elijah floods my mind. Each one is a beautiful juxtaposition of joy tinged with sadness.

Desolate, piercing screams reverberate through the too-empty courtyard as my chest cleaves open, leaving me exposed and even emptier. My knees hit the ground, but I don't even notice the cold of the snow below me. All I feel is the void in my chest growing wider with each passing breath.

I release the hold on my shadows, letting them flow freely and react to what I'm feeling. Wave after wave of emotion tears through me. Grief, anger, regret, denial, joy, guilt, and finally acceptance all tangle inside me simultaneously.

I feel it all, then nothing else.

The numbness creeping back in takes root and leaves me empty once more.

CHAPTER THIRTY-NINE

BREYLA

Thunder cracks overhead, making me jump and scream.

Elijah pulls me into his arms, his voice a soft murmur. *"Shhh, I've got you, B. You're okay."*

Rain plasters my face, tears joining them as I cry softly.

His palm settles on my hip, the other clasping my hand, our fingers weaving together.

"Dance with me," he whispers.

"There's no music," I protest.

"We don't need music." He pulls me into familiar steps.

Muscle memory takes over, my body moving with his despite the paralyzing fear. The more we dance and sway, the more the tension in my limbs eases.

Thunder roars again, and I jump, looking around in panic.

"Eyes on me, B. Ignore everything else." Elijah squeezes my hand in gentle reassurance. "Just feel the dance, the safety of my arms, the cool touch of rain on your skin."

My eyes find his and stay there. We continue dancing, my gaze never leaving his as we sway.

I throw my head back, feeling the cool rain pelt my face, a tentative smile forming.

The unmistakable whistle of an arrow slices through the night.

My head snaps forward.

Wide-eyed shock plays across Elijah's face as he looks down at the arrow protruding from his chest.

I scream, Eli's body dropping to the ground.

I fall to my knees beside him, hands cradling his cheeks.

Blood pulses steadily from the wound, the smell coppery and sour. I know enough of battle wounds to know he'll bleed out before anyone reaches us. Rivulets of crimson pool and drip out of his mouth, his chest rising shallowly as he fights to pull in air.

"No, no, no," I murmur, my head shaking in denial.

"I love you, B," he chokes on his words, blood splattering across my face.

"I love you, E," I cry, but he's gone before the words pass my lips.

I scream again, my cheeks already wet with the tears shed in my sleep. Chest heaving, I sit up in bed, fighting to pull in oxygen between sobs.

Strong arms pull me against a solid chest, cradling my trembling form. Ayden's fingers comb through my hair, rubbing soothing circles as he rocks me gently. He pulls my legs over his lap, resting his free hand loosely on my hip.

These aren't the arms I want. His scent is similar, but somehow all wrong.

The nausea that usually accompanies being touched by anyone other than Aurelius is blessedly absent. I continue crying, the tremors becoming less severe as his fingers maintain their soothing motion along my skin.

Even though it's not the embrace I want, I savor its comfort regardless.

"I'm sorry I didn't catch the nightmare," Ayden says softly.

"Don't be," I mumble. "I need to feel the pain."

It's the only thing I've felt since he died.

"I disagree. You've endured enough pain for a lifetime."

I don't reply.

"Sleep," he urges, laying me back down. "You won't dream anymore tonight."

It's not the reassurance he believes it to be. I want to hurt. Removing the pain feels like removing Elijah. The pain reminds me that he lived and that I love him.

Eventually, I drift back into a dreamless sleep.

Snow flurries coat the windowpane with a fresh layer of white misery. The arm that never healed properly aches, and I rub it absent-mindedly. That twinge of pain is all I feel, all I've felt in over a week. At least, I think it's been a week.

Breakfast sits untouched beside my chair, the oatmeal a cold, congealed paste that holds no appeal. I recognize that I need to eat, but I can't bring myself to care.

My toes curl in the cushion where they're tucked underneath me, my arms wrapped around both knees as I stare out the window.

Inside my mind, a symphony plays. It's a mixture of thunder crashing in violent crescendos and the gentle melodies of the violin and piano. The tempest harmonizes, complementing the deep beats of the thunder.

Closing my eyes, I lose myself in the musical masterpiece of my mind.

Elijah dancing with me in the rain.

Crash.

Ophelia twirling in his arms at the palace ball.

Crash.

Elijah's laugh.

A *soft violin trill.*

Five-year-old Elijah clutching my hand in front of his parents' funeral pyre.

Piano chords in a gentle melody.

Elijah's eyes glazing over as Aurelius stops his heart.

The closing notes bring together the orchestra of thunder, rain, piano, and violin.

The symphony in my mind quiets, leaving me with a numbing silence.

Somewhere beyond the silence, I recognize the sound of male voices. They're heated. An argument.

"I heard her scream last night," a deep voice says. Aurelius, I think.

"The whole bloody castle heard her scream, brother," Ayden drawls.

"I thought you had the nightmares under control."

"I've spent three weeks handling her, and Opheliah's, nightmares. Forgive me if I slipped."

Aurelius sighs. "I'm concerned. For them both."

"It's been three weeks, Aurelius. What did you expect?"

Three weeks. Had it really been three weeks since we burned Elijah?

"I expect you to take care of her," Aurelius snarls.

"Watch your tone, brother."

"Then do your fucking job since you won't allow me to care for her," Aurelius grits out.

"She is not your concern," Ayden growls.

A humorless laugh. "She will *always* be my concern."

Silence stretches between them.

"Tell me of the errand I sent you on," Ayden says, abruptly changing the subject.

"Another body was found. The throat was slit, but there were no witnesses."

Did he say *another* body?

I should feel something. Concern, sadness, intrigue. But I can't even manage to summon mild surprise.

Nothing.

I lose interest, turning my attention back to the window and watching the snow fall.

My eyes slip closed, and the symphony starts again in my mind. The memories of Elijah flash behind my eyelids, my brain conjuring every moment of joy I had with him.

I lose myself in the vision of a Winter Solstice snowball fight, one of the few where Jade and Julian had joined us.

I'm shaken from it by Aurelius. He's crouched in front of me, crimson-flecked eyes scanning my face with cool precision. Assessing.

Whatever he sees, he doesn't like.

"You're freezing." Concern is etched on his face, wariness and exhaustion clear in the purple that paints his under eyes.

"Am I?"

Without warning, he scoops me up from the window seat and carries me to a chair near the fire. A heavy blanket is draped across my shoulders and wrapped tightly, cocooning me in the softest furs.

"When did you last eat?"

I shrug. I don't even remember the last time I drank.

"She's refused every meal," Ayden says. I don't see him, so he must be standing behind us. He doesn't sound pleased.

"Breyla," Aurelius urges, his voice taking on a tender quality. "You must eat."

I don't respond, opting to watch the flames instead.

He reaches out, gently gripping my chin between his thumb and forefinger, and turns me to face him. His strong jaw is dusted in dark stubble. Prominent cheekbones. That sun-warmed skin he shares with Rowina and Ayden, no doubt from their father.

He's not just beautiful. He's breathtaking.

Even in this worn-down state.

His full lips twitch into a smirk, a huff of laughter escaping. "Stop ogling me, Princess, and eat."

I don't bother to deny his accusation. I just stare blankly at him.

Aurelius holds a scone to my lips. "Eat."

Where did he get a scone?

I have no desire to eat, but I do have the sudden desire to appease him. He slides the pastry past my lips when I open my mouth, and I bite down.

The buttery sweetness is cut with a tartness.

Is that cranberry?

I chew slowly, my tongue delighting at the mix of sweet and tart.

Once I finish, Aurelius smiles. "That's a good girl."

The words should spark arousal, satisfaction at pleasing him, but still, I feel nothing.

Aurelius' eyes shift to Ayden behind me. "Next time, call for me when you need her to eat instead of letting her starve."

"How was I to know she would eat for you?" Ayden scoffs.

"I'm not going to dignify that with a response," Aurelius replies flatly.

"Fine, I will call for you next time," Ayden begrudgingly agrees.

Aurelius returns the next day with roast chicken.

I reluctantly eat it, my stomach clenching in pain when I'm finished. I throw it up right after he leaves.

When he brings me the next meal, I tell him to get fucked.

The following day, he tries again, opting for a sliced apple instead. I try to refuse again, but he threatens to use his Hemonia Gift to force my jaw to chew.

With my middle finger raised, I eat the damn apple.

The next time I see Aurelius, Ophelia is with him, and he has warm broth and crusty bread. The look in her eyes is haunting, her cheeks gaunt as she reluctantly sips on her own broth at Ayden's request. She reaches for me, but I turn away.

Aurelius returns daily, food in hand, for the next two weeks.

Still, blistering cold numbness is all I know.

CHAPTER FORTY

BREYLA

"**G**et up," a gruff voice commands.

I turn my head to find Darian standing in the doorway, an annoyed look plastered across his face.

"I don't answer to you, General," I say flatly.

He huffs in irritation, crossing the room to where I sit by the fireplace. Dressed in full leathers, winter cloak, and strapped with weapons, he looks ready to face battle.

"You do today." Darian folds his arms, eyeing me up and down. No doubt he's assessing my pathetic appearance. "Prince's orders, you're helping me with an investigation."

Ayden had *ordered* me to assist this prick?

"Whatever," I mumble, turning back to the fire.

The chair tips forward unexpectedly, dropping me on my ass on the hard marble floor.

Pain spikes through my hip as I cast a scowl his direction. "What's wrong with you?"

"You mean other than the fact that I'm being forced to include an invalid in official court business?"

"Fuck you," I hiss, throwing him a crude gesture for good measure. "I'm not an invalid."

He shrugs, not even bothering to meet my eyes. "Could've fooled me."

I move to my feet, rubbing my hip to assuage the sore flesh. "Was dropping me on the floor necessary?"

"Yes."

Infuriating male.

"It hurt."

He levels me with a look of utter boredom. "Your feelings are not my concern."

"Obviously," I deadpan.

"Get changed."

"Or what?"

He lets out an exasperated sigh. "You're sorely mistaken if you think I won't drag you outside in your nightgown."

"I detest you," I say, glowering at him.

"The feeling is mutual."

I finally relent, turning for the door that leads to the bedroom, only to find an outfit already laid out on the bed.

Black leathers folded neatly beside a fur-lined cloak and matching gloves. They're black with gold stitching running along the seams. They remind me of the cloak I'd purchased as a Solstice gift for Elijah. The one that now sits untouched in a chest at the foot of my bed.

When I return, dressed and sullen, Darian is waiting exactly where I left him.

"Let's go," I grunt.

Outside the castle doors, horses wait, along with Ryder and Zion.

"Good morning, General," Ryder says.

"Morning," Darian and I reply at the same time.

Our eyes connect, a look of mutual irritation on each of our faces.

Zion chuckles, and Ryder shakes his head.

"What investigation does Ayden deem above your expertise?" I ask, fighting a smirk, as I swing into the saddle.

Ignoring my insult, Darian replies, "Four bodies have turned up over the last month. All male, all with their throats slit."

"Is there anything linking them?"

"Other than their proximity to the castle? No."

"Where are we headed now?"

"The fourth body was only discovered this morning." Darian swings into his own saddle and adjusts the reins. "We're on our way to speak with his widow."

I nod in understanding, and we fall into a comfortable silence as we make our way through town.

Twenty minutes later, we arrive at a modest home located in the middle of the city. Two stories overlooking the square, painted deep green with white shutters.

The door opens to reveal a pretty female with blonde hair and mossy green eyes. She distantly reminds me of the brothers, Oren and Talon, from Ayden's counsel.

"Greetings, General," she says politely to Darian before turning to me. "Princess. How may I help you?"

"Good afternoon, Mariel. We're here about Holt." He smiles grimly. "May we come in?"

She nods, stepping aside to let us inside.

Two small heads peek from around a corner as we enter the home. Sandy blonde hair and green eyes stare up at us.

"Children, go to your rooms, please."

Reluctantly, they disappear down the hall, doors slamming behind them.

Mariel gestures toward the sitting room. "Would you like to sit?"

"Thank you," I say, settling into the chair closest to the fire. "Your children seem to be handling things well, all things considered."

Mariel stiffens, taking a deep breath before answering, "Yes, well, it's hard to miss someone you barely know."

I nod in sad understanding.

Darian clears his throat. "When was the last time you saw Holt?"

"Three days ago."

"Is it normal for him to be away for several days at a time?"

Mariel offers us tea, taking a sip of her own. "Business usually takes him away from home for weeks at a time. He is, was, a textiles merchant."

I remain quiet, studying the female as Darian continues questioning her. She's well put together, her eyes holding a certain sadness, but not the grief I expect. Her cream dress is perfectly pressed, not a wrinkle to be seen. Golden hair is twisted neatly in a bun, not a single lock out of place.

This female is more composed on the day her husband was found dead than I've been since Elijah died.

Grief is a fickle mistress.

"Do you know of anyone who would want your husband dead?" Darian asks.

"I'm sure any number of his business rivals would love to see him gone. But dead?" She shakes her head, taking another sip of tea. "No, I can't think of anyone who would have a reason for wanting him dead."

There's a yellow tint to the skin beneath her eyes and a strange stiffness to her posture. Her breaths are shallow and more rapid than most.

It could be a looming panic attack.

"Do you know what your husband was doing at the pub last night?" Darian continues.

"Not the faintest idea," Mariel replies airily, her voice cold and indifferent. "I just hope he settled the tab before he died."

I get the notion that she might have an idea why he was there, but I doubt it has any relevance to solving his murder.

"Thank you, Mariel. We'll let you know what we discover. If you think of anything else that might be of importance, please don't hesitate to find me." Darian stands, the rest of us following suit. "My condolences to you and your children."

Mariel nods curtly, her lips pressed in a thin line.

Once we're back on our horses, Darian turns to me. "Did you notice anything?"

"She was rather calm for a grieving widow," I muse.

"Indeed. What are your thoughts?"

My brows shoot up. "You're asking for my opinion?"

"Despite my personal feelings toward you, I cannot overlook the way your mind works." Darian kicks his horse into a slow trot. "You proved yourself when you spotted the pattern in the poison attacks."

"Ryder, Zion, did you hear that?" I lift my voice. "I need witnesses for the first time Darian has complimented me."

"I assure you it will never happen again," Darian says, rolling his eyes. They're such a piercing shade of blue, I find it hard to look away.

"To answer your question, he beats her," I say bluntly. "She doesn't look like a grieving widow, because she's not one. She's a relieved widow."

"That's a bold assumption to make," he challenges.

"There was a healing bruise under her left eye. It was faint, but there. Her posture was too rigid. I know a cracked rib when I see one." I explain, pulling my hood tightly around my head to keep out the winter wind. "Then there was her overall demeanor and her comment about the kids."

He lifts an eyebrow, urging me to continue.

"I don't know that he hurt them, but he certainly never loved them as a father should. No one in that home was particularly sad about his loss, and I think that says a lot more about him than it does them."

The edge of Darian's mouth twitches, like he's fighting a smile. "How astute of you."

"You already know all of this?" I ask in disbelief.

She's a cousin of Oren and Talon. Their parents are friends with mine and like to give them updates about anything to do with their family," he explains, pulling his hood up to block out a gust of wind. "She hides it well, but yes, he was a violent male."

"Good riddance," I mutter. My brow furrows. "Why did you bring me if you already knew all that?"

We've already made it back to the castle walls when he answers, "It wasn't my idea, remember? That was all Ayden."

"Then why did he?"

He shrugs. "My guess? He was tired of seeing the ghost of you and knew that I'd provoke you out of whatever stupor you were in."

"My best friend *died*," I say quietly. "I'm allowed to grieve."

"You're right. You are allowed to grieve. But you aren't permitted to just give up on living." He holds my gaze, challenging me to disagree.

"Well, I'm still living, aren't I?"

For the first time in weeks, I feel the acidic burn of anger rising in my throat. It's painfully scorching in comparison to the emptiness that has consumed me until today.

"No, Breyla." Darian shakes his head. "Until now, you were simply existing. It's up to you to decide what you do from here."

And with that, he leaves me standing in the courtyard, debating whether to return to my chambers or follow him just so I can punch him in the face.

CHAPTER FORTY-ONE

Breyla's pain-filled moans ring through the empty hallway, echoing off marble floors and walls. Her cries increase, and the emotion in them tastes just like my own. I push open the door to Ayden's chambers, the lock shockingly not in place.

I'm surprised to find Breyla alone in bed, Ayden nowhere to be found. Her body thrashes, her mind caught in a nightmare. I see tears coating her cheeks as I approach the bed. I have no idea how to chase the demons from her sleep, but I can't bear to leave her like this. So, I do the only thing I can think of. I slip into the bed beside her.

"Breyla," I whisper, shaking her shoulder gently. "Wake up."

Her eyes flare wide, surprise filling them at seeing me in bed next to her. "Ophelia," she pants, her breathing still heavy. "What are you doing here?"

"You were screaming." I run my hand over her damp cheek, stroking softly. "I'm not sure where Ayden went, but I needed to make sure you were alright."

Her hand comes to rest on top of my own, squeezing gently. "Thank you, Ophelia. It was just a nightmare."

"I get them, too."

A beat of silence passes between us.

"Do you want to talk about them?" she asks, voice barely above a whisper.

I almost tell her no. But these last six weeks without her have been harder than the months without her in Rimor. Maybe talking about it will help.

"Some are just memories. They make me sad, no matter what the memory is," I whisper, and she nods. "Other times, I watch him die over and over anytime I close my eyes."

"That happens to me, too."

We lie there for a while, not saying a word, just enjoying each other's presence.

"Tell me a story about him," I request.

"Did you know I taught him how to swim?"

I shake my head.

"When we were seven, my father fashioned a rope swing over the river that runs behind the palace. Elijah adamantly refused to go anywhere near it, preferring to watch the other kids swim while he sat on the banks." She readjusts in bed, flipping onto her back with her head still turned toward me. "For a while, I just believed he didn't like the water, like he was a cat or something."

I giggle at the image of Elijah with cat ears and a tail. "A cat?"

"I was seven. Give me a break."

"Please, continue."

"I realized eventually that he didn't dislike the water because he loved storms. He would dance in them, saying it appeased the Goddess of Life and Death."

"It most certainly does," I agree, playing along.

Her lips tilt in a half smile. "When I finally put it together that he didn't know how to swim, I made it my mission to change that."

"How?"

"I asked him to play a game with me on one of the cliffs overlooking the river."

I adjust in bed, mirroring her position. "What game?"

She grins widely. "Truth or dare."

"You dared him to jump off the cliff?"

"I did, and when he refused, I shoved him off instead." She smirks. "Then I followed him in."

I gasp. "Was he mad?"

"He was livid, but once I showed him how to tread water and swim to shore, he was fine."

"Remind me never to ask you for lessons on… well, anything," I tease.

Breyla laughs. "I like to think of myself as a particularly effective teacher."

"You're scary, is what you are," I say, faking a shudder.

She bumps my shoulder with hers. "Tell me something about Layne."

"He's the one who taught me to love reading." Fondness fills my tone. It had been a long time since I could recall something about him that didn't make me immediately cry.

"Tell me more."

"I struggled to read. My mother showed me the basics, but she died when I was young. My father let my education slip, never bringing in a tutor after she was gone."

"He's always been a piece of shit, then?"

"Pretty much," I agree. "Layne refused to let that stand. He was only two years older, but he taught me everything he learned. Since my reading skills were so basic, I often gave up on books before I'd even tried."

"That's a shame."

"Layne thought so, too. That's why he started reading to me every night. He would pick the most captivating stories, read them out loud to me, and act out each part. Every character had their own voice, and he would make sound effects that went along with the story. The whole thing was a production."

I smile fondly at the memory. "Eventually, I became so enamored with the story, or rather the way he was telling it, that I would want to find out what happened next. I couldn't wait for the next night's reading, so I would force myself to read ahead."

"That's amazing," Breyla says.

"Yeah, it really was." I sigh wistfully. "It was hard at first, but over time, it got easier and easier until reading became like breathing."

She smiles softly. "I love that."

"The last gift he gave me was a first-edition copy of my favorite book. It was signed by the author and had gilded edges. It's stunning."

I frown, remembering that the book had been left in Rimor, and I would likely never see it again.

Breyla's brows shoot up, her eyes flaring wide. "That reminds me!"

She jumps up, going to the trunk at the foot of the bed. Flipping it open, she rummages through before pulling something free and climbing back into bed.

"I picked this up for you for Winter Solstice," she says, handing me a book. "But I forgot I had it with… everything that happened."

"Thank you, Breyla." I open it, brushing my fingers across the pages. "I feel bad that I didn't bring you anything."

She brushes me off. "Don't. Your presence is all I need."

I hold the book close to my chest, my arms curling tightly around it. "I can't wait to read it."

"I expect a full report once you've finished it. It sounded intriguing when I skimmed it in Collin's bookshop."

"Of course," I say, smiling softly. "Tell me something else about Elijah."

"Hm," she hums. "When his Gift first developed, he had absolutely no control over it. He became the court's biggest gossip because he kept accidentally reading people's memories."

I gasp. "Oh no."

"Oh yes. It was the most entertaining time. I'm surprised you don't remember it. Weren't you living at court by then?"

"I was… but father kept me incredibly secluded. No one would've dared gossip with me."

"Probably for the best that you weren't subjected to that chaos. He nearly ended three different marriages."

"Yikes," I say, chuckling lightly.

"On the other hand, it was how he discovered Julian was attracted to him. So, I suppose there was some positive that came from it."

"And his slip in control was also how he knew I could be trusted," I add.

"Very true. You tell me something now."

"He saved my life, and not just on our way here."

"Tell me."

"I started sleepwalking after Layne died. One night, I ended up in the river behind the palace and nearly drowned. Jade was the one to pull me out, but it wasn't the last time. Elijah found me in the garden, sleeping on the ground. I had lost time and had no memory of the previous day. He slept with me every night after that, never letting me wander into danger."

"Yeah, that sounds like him."

"I broke, Breyla. My mind still isn't…" I pause, searching for the right word. "Whole. It feels fractured. But each time I found myself consumed by the darkness, he pulled me back. He was my sun in the dead of night."

Breyla weaves her fingers with mine, squeezing gently. "Broken or not, your mind is a beautiful thing."

A few beats of silence pass before Breyla says, "I need to apologize, Ophelia."

"For what?"

"Recently, I haven't been the friend you deserve. I shut you out, shut everyone out, after Elijah died. I know you were hurting just as much as I was, and all I did was hide. You needed me, but I was too selfish to see it."

My first instinct is to tell her it's alright, but I stop myself. "I'm not going to lie just to save your feelings. Losing Elijah was the hardest thing I've ever experienced, but being disconnected from you these last few weeks? That hurt, too. I love you. And I forgive you. But it did hurt."

"I know," she whispers. "I'm so sorry."

"Just don't do it again."

"Never again."

We continue exchanging stories until we're both yawning, sleep clawing at the edges of our minds. Just as unconsciousness threatens to overtake me, I hear the bedroom door open and shut.

"Two beautiful females in my bed and I wasn't even invited?" Ayden says quietly.

My eyes crack open just enough to see him leaning against the wall beside the bed, a rakish smile tugging at his lips.

He looks exhausted. Mud cakes his boots, his tunic and pants are wrinkled, and his curls lie messily on his head. They look like he's run his hands through them too many times.

"Where did you go?" Breyla yawns, not bothering to open her eyes.

"A fifth body was found late last night," Ayden replies. "It was fresh, and I wanted to be there to inspect the scene myself. I'm sorry for leaving you."

My gut churns with anxiety. Another body was found already?

"So soon?" I croak.

"This victim was discovered faster than the others thanks to a civilian stumbling upon the body by accident."

I worry my lower lip between my teeth. "That must have been terrifying for them."

"They were quite disturbed." Ayden's gaze settles on me, and something in his expression shifts; his eyes soften. "You have nothing to worry about, little one. You are safe within my walls."

I nod, turning away from him. His promise does nothing to assuage the anxiety building in my gut.

"Now," he drawls, "are you two going to make room for me in *my* bed or will I be forced to sleep elsewhere?"

"I'll go," I yawn.

"Good night," Breyla mumbles. She's snoring softly before I even make it out of bed.

Ayden offers me a hand up that I gladly take. He squeezes my hand tightly, holding on for longer than is comfortable.

The walk back to my chambers is short. I undress, too tired to search for a nightgown, and crawl into bed.

When sleep claims me, it's deep and dreamless.

CHAPTER FORTY-TWO

It takes another week for me to voluntarily leave Ayden's chambers, but I no longer shut out Ophelia. We sit together every day, telling stories and reminiscing over the ones we've lost. There are tears. There is laughter. There is grief. And finally, there's a small semblance of peace.

When I finally venture out, I find myself drawn to the library. Something about the smell of parchment, the feel of the leather tomes, and the soft crackle of logs in the fireplace calms me. I curl my feet under me, settling into the chair closest to the fire.

Elythia's journal lies sprawled across my lap, but before I can lose myself in her story, I sense Ayden approaching from the left.

"It's good to see you out of the bedroom," he says, surprise coloring his tone. "You're even wearing real clothing."

I resist the urge to make a crude gesture or curse him because I deserve that. I've been a shell of myself, incapable of even the most basic self-care, for almost two months.

"I figured if I want to train with you, I should probably be dressed appropriately."

One dark brow arches. "You want to train?"

"I need to do something."

"What's changed?"

"Darian said I had given up on living, that I was simply existing. I haven't been able to get those words out of my head," I explain.

Pity flashes across his face, softening his expression. "Darian was—"

"Right," I interrupt before he can justify my behavior. "His words wouldn't have hurt so much if they weren't true."

He nods, choosing not to argue.

"So… training? I thought maybe we could work on my projections," I suggest.

"As much as I love that you are feeling more yourself," he says, "I don't have any time today. There's a council meeting in ten minutes."

"What are you discussing?"

"Primarily, the murders still plaguing the kingdom."

"I'll join you."

"Are you certain?" he asks cautiously, as if a council meeting might break me. Bore me to death, perhaps, but it wouldn't break me.

"I'm sure."

That earns me a small smile. "Then, I'll see you there."

Eight minutes later, I find myself outside the council chamber, inhaling a deep, steadying breath.

"Breyla?" a familiar voice asks, thick with disbelief.

Aurelius.

My eyes meet his as he halts a step away from me.

It's too much space.

I practically throw myself into his arms, wrapping tightly around his torso and burying my face against his chest. His scent floods my senses, calming the rapid beat of my heart and releasing every taut muscle in my body.

His arms lock around me instantly, one at my back, the other threading gently through my hair. I feel the sigh ripple through him as he melts into me, matching the release in my own chest.

In my numb, grief-consumed state, I hadn't realized how much I had missed him. I needed Aurelius, and I had kept him away for months, torturing us both.

"We should go in," I whisper, but I don't make any effort to move.

He breathes in deep, his chest shuddering against mine. "Let me steal just one more minute."

We stay like that longer than propriety allows, but all it feels is *right*.

"I'm sorry I shut you out," I breathe.

"Don't be." His hand strokes up and down my back. "I'm just relieved to see you."

"We should probably go in."

"I'll find you later, and we can talk," he says, stepping back.

My lips curl in a tentative half-smile. "I'll hold you to it."

Inside the chamber, I'm surprised to find every seat is filled. The one I sat in last time is occupied by Queen Josephina, who is currently casting her critical gaze on Aurelius.

Leaning into Ayden, I ask, "Where would you like me?"

He turns his head, speaking low enough for only me to hear, "On my lap would work just fine."

Gods help me, some things never change. Despite my entire world being turned upside down, he's still the flirtatious, arrogant male who strolled through Rimor's gates like he owned them.

I give him my best unamused look, making him chuckle.

He pushes back from the table, leaving the chair empty and gesturing for me to take it.

The look on my face must portray how confused I feel.

"Take it," he says. "I will never allow my queen to stand while I sit."

The violent switch back to the compassionate and respectable male gives me whiplash. I never quite know what to expect of him, and I fully believe that's intentional.

Darian's assessing gaze lingers on me as I take the seat. "Finally decided to leave your rooms, *General?*" Even though he says my title with his normal disdain, his question's tone doesn't match.

His words from our last conversation ring in my ears: *"Until now, you were simply existing. It's up to you to decide what you do from here."*

"I decided to start living again, General," I reply.

The look on his face can't exactly be described as happy, but I see the slightest bit of respect cross his features as he nods to me in understanding.

"Now that everyone is present," Ayden says, voice steady. "Let's begin."

Fifteen minutes in, and my head is already pounding.

The amount that I had missed during my mourning is over-whelming.

The total death count was five. No more bodies had appeared since Ayden had been called away in the middle of the night a week ago.

But people are scared, and fear is never rational. That's what worries me most.

"I'm only familiar with one of the victims." I glance toward Darian. "Can someone please give me a brief accounting of the others?"

Darian rattles off the details of each victim, noting their age, gender, name, profession, and whether the victims were married.

"They were all found within the city walls?" I ask.

"They were," Ayden confirms.

I consider all the information for a moment, recalling what I had learned about Holt from his widow and children. "Aside from Holt, did any of you actually know the victims?"

"Most certainly not," Queen Josephina answers tersely, speaking for the first time this meeting.

Lady Seris shifts, folding her hands in front of her before clearing her throat. "I knew of one of the victims, or rather, how he was known."

"How was he known?" I ask.

"Not favorably," she replies. "He was fond of the drink and a brute. A few of the taverns refused to serve him because of the fighting and his treatment of female patrons. A year ago, a serving girl died tragi-cally. It was suspected he was to blame, as she had turned down his advances quite publicly earlier that evening, but there was no proof."

Disgust churns my gut, my upper lip curling. "It sounds like someone did the kingdom a service with that one."

The queen gasps, her eyes flaring wide. "Pardon me?"

I drag my gaze to her, quirking a brow. "What part of my state-ment was unclear?"

"The future queen of this kingdom cannot be found condoning the cold-blooded murder of one of its citizens."

I laugh, the sound completely humorless. "I'm not condoning murder, Your

Majesty. I simply do not tolerate the mistreatment of females or threats against those under my protection. Make no mistake, had I caught him in the act, I would have taken care of the bastard myself."

"Your hands are stained red with the blood of your actions," the queen accuses.

"I never pretended otherwise." I shrug. "I'm not the delusional one at this table trying to make me something I'm not."

The queen seethes in silence, her rage simmering beneath her polished exterior.

And then, shockingly, Darian speaks. "Her hands are no more blood-stained than my own."

Darian does not defend *me*, of all people. My mouth actually drops open, unsure what to say.

"Breyla and I may not agree on much," he says, voice even. "But had I been there when Piper was attacked, it would be his body we burned. Not hers. And I wouldn't have lost a single night of sleep over it."

His calm delivery only underscores the conviction in his words. There's a fierce loyalty in him, one I hadn't truly recognized before.

"We're getting off-topic," Ayden steps in, trying to diffuse the situation.

"I digress," I say. "This feels like vigilante justice at best, and hired mercenary attacks at worst."

"What brings you to that conclusion?" Lord Oren asks.

"I think we can agree that the victims were all killed by the same person. The pattern suggests either they were being watched, or someone knew them and sent someone else to do the work."

Darian rubs at his jaw, his sapphire eyes cold and calculating. "You're assuming all the victims were similar in their nature."

"I am," I agree, "but I would wager it's a correct assumption."

Ayden leans forward slightly, resting his hands on the table. "How do you propose we find the killer?"

"We start by figuring out if these murders are isolated to Elentia or if the problem is wider spread," I say confidently. "Have any of you spoken to the ruling lords in any of the other cities?"

Darian rubs the back of his neck, offering me a regretful expression. "Admittedly, I have not had the time. There have been no messages received from them, but that does not mean they aren't happening."

"Then that's where we begin," I conclude.

Darian eyes me. "Should I expect you to accompany me for that?"

"I think that's an excellent idea," Ayden cuts in before I can respond otherwise. I hadn't been planning on it, but apparently, I am now.

"What do you plan on doing with them once you find the one responsible?" Aurelius asks.

I glance over my shoulder to Ayden, knowing that's not my decision to make.

"I think…" he pauses, trying to determine what feels right. "That depends entirely on what we find when we do."

There are a few murmurs from the council members, but no one has anything to say against the proposed plan.

"Have there been any further attacks along our borders?" Lord Talon asks.

"No," Darian answers tightly.

"That's good news," Charlotte offers.

"Maybe," he mutters. "But…"

"The sudden silence makes you nervous," Aurelius concludes.

Darian nods. "It's like we're waiting for something worse to hit."

"When was the last attack?" I ask.

"Just before Ophelia, Elijah, and Cillian arrived," Ayden answers quickly. Too quickly.

My head snaps to him. "What am I missing?"

"Noth—"

"The last known attack *was* Lord Elijah," Darian cuts in, leveling Ayden with a sharp look. Some silent battle passes between them.

"Quit trying to protect her, Ayden," Darian snaps. "She's capable of hearing this. She *deserves* the truth."

"It's my job to protect her." Ayden sighs, exasperated. "I simply thought it better to wait until the wound wasn't so… fresh."

Aurelius smirks. "Take it from me, brother, keeping information from Breyla for the sake of protecting her only makes her resent you."

Ayden looks like he wants to strangle them both.

"I am not fragile, Ayden." I fight to keep my voice level and emotions in check. "Tell me."

Ayden sighs, turning back to me. "I have a theory that the attack on Elijah was not a coincidence, but meant to punish you."

"What makes you believe that?"

"Three people you care for were traveling to Prudia, and they were attacked just before crossing into the city closest to our border. I think it was meant to hurt you. Or to send a message."

My heart nearly ceases beating in my chest at his theory. At how much it makes sense that I could be responsible for Elijah's death. But there's one problem.

"I'm not their target. Or... I haven't been lately."

"Then who is?" Aurelius asks.

I swallow, my throat tightening as I meet his gaze. With everything that happened since Darian and I pieced it together, I hadn't gotten the opportunity to tell him.

"You," I say, the word catching painfully in my throat. "Darian and I figured it out, but with everything that happened... I didn't get the chance—"

"It's okay, Breyla," Aurelius says calmly. "I can tell you didn't mean to hide it from me."

Relief floods my chest. The peace between us was something I didn't want to risk breaking. I hadn't meant to betray his trust, and he seems to know that.

"How did you figure it out?" Charlotte asks.

"When considering just the attacks involving poison, the pattern formed around Aurelius," Darian explains. "The moment he joined me on the front, they followed him."

"Assuming you are correct, why switch targets?" Lord Talon asks.

"Who says they have?" Lady Seris offers. "Princess Breyla hasn't left the capital. Perhaps they're both targets. Lord Aurelius has simply been more accessible."

"I hadn't considered that, but you're right," Darian agrees.

Silence settles over the table.

"You two have brought death to our kingdom," the queen says, vitriol lacing every word.

"Might I remind you," Aurelius drawls, "that it was not our decision to come here."

"What's done is done," Ayden interjects, his tone flat with warning. "Mother, if you cannot contribute without spitting venom at my fiancée and brother, then perhaps you should find somewhere else to be." Ayden levels her with a look that says it all. He's as tired of her shit as the rest of us.

The queen wisely falls silent.

"Darian and Breyla will visit Prudia's major cities," Ayden announces. "They'll investigate whether similar murders have been reported."

"You just said she is a target, but you still think sending her outside the safety of the walls is wise?" Aurelius asks in disbelief.

"They will travel with extra protection," Ayden says, clearly trying to appease him.

Darian and I scoff in unison.

"That is a command, General," Ayden says, his eyes narrowing on us both.

"Fine," Darian mutters. "But you know it will only slow us down."

"So be it. That's all for today."

The room clears quickly until only Ayden and I remain.

I tilt my head, studying the prince. "You were rather quiet today."

"I wanted to see how you handled it." He pauses. "And frankly, I'm thrilled at your interest in the kingdom's affairs."

We exit the room, and I turn toward the guest wing.

"Where are you headed?" Ayden's brows furrow. "I thought we were training."

I stop, turning back to him. "I didn't want to say anything in front of the council or your mother, but you're overlooking a massive resource in this investigation."

"And what is that?"

I smile coyly. "The mercenary king living under your roof."

Ayden curses under his breath. I can't tell if he's frustrated that I want to talk to Cillian… or because he didn't think of it first.

"You're not talking to him alone," Ayden warns.

I roll my eyes. "Cillian's not going to hurt me."

"It doesn't mean I trust him."

"Good. You shouldn't."

He curses again but falls into place behind me.

Cillian's massive figure fills the doorway as he leans against the frame, looking me over with that familiar glint in his eye. "It's good to see you, Breyla." His teal eyes flit to Ayden. "And you, princeling."

"I have a name," Ayden says, irritation filling his voice.

"Congratulations," Cillian replies with mock enthusiasm.

Ayden shoves his way into the room, a frustrated growl on his lips.

I catch the amused smirk tugging at Cillian's mouth and realize he's antagonizing the prince. It would appear Ayden isn't accustomed to someone ruffling his feathers in the way he's used to doing himself.

"Play nice," I whisper as I shuffle past him.

Cillian closes the door, leaning in to whisper back, "You know I don't take orders well."

"He's the prince and you're in his kingdom, not mine."

"That's where you're wrong." He chuckles. "Everywhere is *my* kingdom."

I sigh, shaking my head. There was a reason I had been attracted to this male for most of my adult life, and the devil-may-care attitude was definitely part of it.

"We need your assistance, Cillian," I say, standing against the wall nearest Ayden.

Cillian drops into a chair in the corner, his legs spread wide in pure male arrogance. "Are we killing something or fucking something?"

"Why would you assume we need you to kill or fuck something?" Ayden retorts, already on edge.

"Princeling, there are only three reasons someone seeks my help," Cillian says, holding up a finger. "One, they need someone dead." He puts up a second finger, then continues, "They need to fuck, or they need me to fuck someone. It's a win-win on that one."

Ayden scoffs. "What's number three?"

Cillian grins wide enough to show teeth. "My personal favorite, a little bit of both. So… which is it?"

They lock eyes, and the tension crackling in the room becomes something palpable. These two should not be left alone together. I can't tell whether they'd end up naked or dead.

I take a leisurely stroll across the room, stopping in front of Cillian's chair, right between his spread legs. He drags his gaze over me, but doesn't speak as I lean down and place my hands on the armrests.

"How about reason number four?" I ask, voice low. "We need information. Your expert opinion, if you will."

He raises his scarred brow. "And how exactly are you paying for that?"

"How does *you're staying in my kingdom, in my castle, and I'm the godsdamned prince* sound?" Ayden bites back.

"Say the word and I'm gone, princeling." Cillian's lilt thickens, a tell-tale sign of his rising temper. "I've only stayed this long for Breyla."

"Ignore him," I tell Cillian, dragging his gaze back to me. "Answer my questions and I'll pay twice your normal fee."

"No."

"No?" I ask, dumbfounded. "Then what do you want?"

Cillian smirks, his eyes flicking over my shoulder to Ayden. "I'll answer your questions, Breyla, but I'm not interested in coin." His voice drops lower. "I want the prince to get on his knees and ask me himself."

Ayden bristles. "You mean you want me to beg."

Cillian shrugs. "I prefer asking nicely. I usually reserve begging for those at the end of my sword—or my cock."

With a sigh, I step aside, looking at Ayden. "The only way he'll answer our questions is if you do what he's asking."

Ayden's jaw ticks. "I do not beg, Breyla."

"Is your pride worth your people's lives?"

A long beat of silence stretches. Then, finally, Ayden grits, "Fine, but you tell *no one.*"

"Understood," I say softly. "Thank you."

Ayden kneels slowly, several feet away from Cillian.

Cillian's eyes spark with amusement as Ayden shifts uncomfortably, crossing and uncrossing his arms.

"Cillian, will you—"

"Ah, ah, ah," Cillian purrs, beckoning Ayden forward with the curl of his finger. "Closer."

With a deep growl, Ayden crawls forward until he's nearly between Cillian's spread knees.

"Better," Cillian murmurs, utterly delighted. "Proceed."

Ayden exhales a sharp breath. "Cillian, will you please answer our questions?"

Cillian pretends to consider the request for a moment, mischief practically glowing in his teal eyes. "Why yes, princeling, I will."

Ayden starts to stand, but Cillian catches his shoulder, keeping him in place. "One more thing."

"What?" Ayden grits out, glaring up at him.

"You look exceptional on your knees." Cillian's grin is slow, wicked. "Perhaps next time you'll try my version of begging, hm?"

Ayden jerks to his feet, rage simmering just beneath his skin as Cillian bursts into raucous laughter.

"Now that we have that confusing display out of the way," I say, stepping between them. "We have questions about a string of murders that occurred here over the last six weeks."

"I have heard something about that," Cillian says, shifting into a more serious posture. "Do you have any suspects?"

"None," Ayden says tersely.

"We believe them to be related," I explain, "but we can't determine if it's a vigilante or a mercenary."

"Walk me through it. Every detail—how they were killed, where they were found, everything."

We spend the next several minutes laying out everything we know. Cillian listens, asking sharp, efficient questions.

Once he's satisfied, he says, "It's difficult to say for sure without seeing the bodies and the scene for myself," he admits. "But it sounds like a vigilante exacting their own version of justice."

"Fantastic. How do we catch them?" Ayden asks.

"Let me look into it," Cillian says. Then, to both our surprise, he offers, "I'll see if I can catch them in the act."

Ayden narrows his eyes. "And what is that going to cost me?"

"Nothing." Cillian shrugs. "This sight of you on your knees was payment enough."

"Fuck me," Ayden mutters, already heading for the door. "Are we done here?"

"Unless you want to explore that begging option, then yes, we're done here," Cillian drawls seductively.

"Good. Let's go, Princess," Ayden grits, grabbing my wrist and yanking me from the room.

Cillian's laughter follows us down the hallway, low and rich and thoroughly entertained.

CHAPTER FORTY-THREE

Blood… warm and sticky runs down my hands as I watch the life leave the male's unremarkable eyes. He begged like all the others before him, calling out for the gods to shine mercy upon him. The gods had ignored my every plea to show mercy to Elijah, to save him from his fate. If not for him, why would they give such a gift to the filth before me?

Like all the others, I had carefully picked this male. I watched him for hours before deciding his fate. He was no innocent. I had seen the bruises that covered his young wife's skin, the fear in her eyes a distant echo of the fear that once lived in mine.

I wipe the blood off my dagger using his tunic before letting his lifeless body drop to the ground. The guards would find him in the morning, and I would be sleeping safely in my bed at the castle. One more useless bastard is off the streets, bringing my total to six.

"Hello, little assassin," Cillian's lilted voice echoes around me.

Spinning to face him, I slide the dagger behind my back. Caught up in the high of my kill, I hadn't even noticed his presence. No one had caught on to me yet, but I'd gotten careless.

"Cillian," I say, my voice coming out as a breathy whisper.

He saunters forward, forcing my back against the wall. Invading the space around me, he leans against the brick wall behind me and braces an arm above my head. Everyone is tall compared to me, but Cillian's height forces me to crane my neck up to maintain eye contact. He's not touching me, but I still feel his presence everywhere.

"This isn't what it looks like," I say, doing my absolute best to keep my voice even.

He quirks a brow at me. "And what does it look like?"

I'm at a loss for words, not having expected that question.

"Because to me, it looks like you're making good use of that dagger I gave you." He swipes a thumb down my cheek before pulling it away, stained with blood. "To me, it looks like you are absolutely stunning, covered in blood. A breathtaking, murderous creature."

His words spark a warmth in me I haven't felt since Elijah died.

"He deserved it," is all I can come up with in response.

"Did he, now?"

"He beats his wife." The words rush out of me, my chest heaving as he closes the space between our bodies. His broad frame presses firmly against mine, his spicy and sweet scent wrapping around me like a cloak. My head spins as I breathe out the rest of my reasoning. "Nearly killed her last week."

Understanding flashes through his teal eyes. "You don't have to justify anything to me, little assassin. I quite literally kill people for a living."

He tucks a stray lock of hair behind my ear, his fingers slowly trailing down my throat, leaving goosebumps in their wake.

"Do they deserve it?" I ask, not sure if I really want the answer.

"Some of them."

"But not all of them?"

"No one is truly innocent, Ophelia."

"Elijah was," I whisper. Pain dances in his eyes, my chest constricting at the sight of it.

"Why are you doing this?" he asks, changing the subject.

"Since Elijah died, I have felt one of two things: violent, burning rage or nothing at all. I tire of having no control over my feelings. I *need* to feel something other than that, Cillian. That moment when I see their life fading away gives me a reprieve."

He nods in clear understanding. "Sooner or later, the prince will catch on. If you need to feel, Ophelia, if you crave that control, there are much better ways." His tone is suggestive, heating my blood even further.

I reach a tentative hand out to cup his jaw. Desperate to feel more of this, more than just the anger of the last weeks, I whisper, "Show me."

A devilish grin spreads across his handsome face. Leaning close so our lips are nearly touching, he murmurs, "I'm going to give you that control you crave, darling. But I'm going to take away all illusions of control in the process." His breath ghosts my lips, hot and dangerous. "You will do exactly as I say. *No* and *stop* have no place between us. If you want this to end, you will say *lilac*. Am I understood?"

I nod, silently begging him to close the distance between our lips.

"I need verbal confirmation, Ophelia."

"Yes, sir. I understand."

"What's your word?"

"Lilac," I say, my voice breathy.

His nostrils flare at my response. "One last thing, this can't mean anything. I'll give you what you need, but I can't be anything more."

"I don't want this to mean anything," I confirm. I need to feel something. "I just want you to fuck me, Cillian."

"Good. Now close your eyes."

I feel his lips brush faintly against mine and a slight tugging sensation before the scrape of the brick behind me disappears.

With my eyes still closed, Cillian takes the dagger from my hand, tossing it somewhere behind us.

"Open your eyes."

When I do, I find us not in the alley but in a bedroom, presumably his.

"Why—"

"No questions," he growls as he unfastens my cloak, letting it drop to the floor.

A moment later, his lips finally meet mine, taking my mouth in a scorching kiss. He wastes no time deepening it, demanding entrance with his tongue.

I give in, parting my lips for him and meeting his tongue with my own. His scent invades my nostrils, a rich mixture of clove and vanilla. Everything about him is intoxicating.

With every kiss and lash of his tongue, the anger and pain in me fade, overrun by the heat blossoming in my core.

Long fingers make quick work of my corset, unlacing and pulling it from my body. It drops to the floor, leaving me in nothing but a shift. It does nothing to hide my peaked nipples, and he takes notice.

He rips the thin cotton down the middle without breaking our kiss, leaving me entirely bare as the ruined fabric falls.

A whimper escapes me with the combination of pain and pleasure erupting as he bites my lip and pinches the delicate peak of my breast.

With one hand, he unbuckles and removes his belt. I reach for the button of his leathers, but he swats my hand away, instead grabbing both my wrists and bringing them together in front of me.

He binds my wrists tightly together using the belt and grins wildly. Something sparks in his eyes at having me bound and helpless before him. Something equally as dangerous fires inside of me at the same thought.

His left hand threads through my dark waves, fingers tugging tightly, leaving me groaning from the sting.

"On your knees," he demands before shoving me down. Thankfully, I land on my discarded cloak, lessening the impact with the stone floor.

Using his right hand, he flicks open the button of his leathers, dragging them down until his length springs free, a drip of pre-come glistening the tip.

"Shit," I mumble. Elijah was my only point of comparison, but while he had been impressive, Cillian legitimately scares me.

"It'll fit, I promise," he says with a chuckle. "Now open those pretty lips for me, Ophelia."

I do as he says, opening as wide as possible to allow him entry. Groaning at the taste of him in my mouth, I circle my tongue around the crown. I repeat the action before hollowing my cheeks and sucking him in further.

A loud moan leaves as he pants, "I'm going to fuck that heavenly mouth of yours."

His grip in my hair tightens just before he thrusts hard, making me choke when he hits the back of my throat. But he doesn't relent. He viciously thrusts in and out of my mouth, using me for his pleasure. Over and over, I choke around his length while tears stream down my cheeks.

Unable to move or control any of this has me more aroused than I care to admit. Wetness pools between my legs as his thrusts increase, and I'm forced to do nothing but take it from him.

Cillian abruptly pulls out, his chest heaving. He wipes away a tear as he growls, "Fuck, you look gorgeous choking on my cock."

I bite my lip, unsure what to say to that.

He yanks me up with the hand still fisted in my hair and directs me to his bed. I lay back, letting my legs fall open for him. Teal eyes roam my body like a predator eyeing its prey. And that's exactly what he is, a predator.

He shoves my still-bound wrists above my head as he kneels over me on the bed. His remaining clothing is removed next, and he drags his fingers up my inner thigh.

"You're dripping for me, little goddess." He smirks, biting seductively on his lower lip. "I'm going to fuck you so hard you beg me to stop. But I won't. I'm not stopping until you're thoroughly spent, with my cum dripping down your thighs."

I groan, "Then why are you still—" I'm cut off mid-sentence as he sheaths himself inside me.

I scream, partly at the pleasure erupting under my flesh and partly from the burn as I stretch to accommodate him.

"You were saying?" he asks with a wink.

"Fuck me," I pant.

"I'm trying to, love." He brushes his thumb over my other nipple, trailing his hand down to my navel. "I need you to relax for me so I can bury myself fully."

My eyes widen, looking down to where we're connected. "There's more?" I ask in disbelief at how full I already feel.

"Not even half of it," he growls, pushing forward another inch.

His lips find my breast, sucking the hardened peak into his mouth. At the same time, his thumb finds my clit, working it in tight circles. It's enough to distract me as he pushes the rest of the way in one smooth stroke.

A moan rips free from my lips, my back arching off the bed as he bottoms out. He continues his ministrations on my clit and nipple for several seconds before whispering, "Enough adjusting."

The way Cillian fucks is animalistic and raw. There is absolutely nothing soft or gentle about the way he ruts into me, his hips snapping against mine, as soft growls resonate in his throat.

His hands grip my hips so hard I know I'll see bruises in the morning. I whimper when he tilts my hips up slightly to hit that spot inside me that has me delirious with pleasure. I clench the sheet above my head, grasping for something to hold onto.

The pressure threatens to break me, my body still fighting to handle the size of him, combined with how brutal his thrusts are.

"Cillian, please," I gasp as tears prick in my eyes. "It's too much."

"No," he snarls, leaning down and biting the space where my neck meets my shoulder.

Something wet trickles down my throat, and I realize he's broken skin. My blood runs down my neck, pooling on the pillow beneath me. Cillian runs his tongue along my throat, collecting every drop of blood on his tongue before taking my mouth in another bruising kiss.

The coppery taste mixed with his kiss sets my nerve endings aflame. A feral energy stirs inside me, driving me to bite down on his lip. I bite hard, eliciting a moan from him, until I taste the tang of his blood on my tongue.

"Vicious little thing," he mumbles against my mouth before flipping me onto my stomach. He does it with such ease, like turning his pillow over to the cold side.

His thrusts resume, the new angle even more delicious, leaving me gasping for breath.

Just as I feel myself relaxing, he circles his finger around my puckered hole. Warning bells sound in my head as we enter unknown territory.

"Cillian, what—"

"Shhh, Ophelia," he says right before slipping his finger inside.

I scream again at the burn from the finger inside a place previously untouched.

"This isn't what I agreed to," I whimper, trying to crawl away from him.

He pulls me back to him, slamming his finger the rest of the way in.

"This is *exactly* what you agreed to, Ophelia," he snarls. "But please do keep running from me. I love the chase."

After several more thrusts of his hips and finger, I find myself actually enjoying the way I stretch and burn for him. The pain only heightens my pleasure, and I start thrusting my hips back to meet his.

He chuckles lowly and asks, "Should I replace this finger with my cock? I absolutely love the way you take me. I think you'd quite enjoy it."

"Gods no," I beg. As much as I enjoy this, I can't imagine taking him *there*.

The sharp sting of his palm hitting my ass makes me gasp. "Tell me no one more time, Ophelia. I dare you."

I keep my mouth shut as he continues thrusting into me, driving me closer and closer to release. My inner walls tremor as I dance closer to ruin.

"Fuck, you're squeezing me so tightly..." Cillian pants, the sound desperate and tortured. "Come for me, Ophelia."

And just like that, I explode. But when I expect him to come with me, he continues fucking me, his pace increasing. He pushes me through my orgasm, never relenting.

I cry out, once again trying to pull away from him. My over-sensitized flesh screams at his continued thrusts, and tears flow freely at the overwhelming pleasure that borders on pain.

His hand grips my throat, pulling me up so my back is flush with him as he drives into me. Still caught in the waves of orgasm, I cry out again when his fingers find my clit and begin circling.

I reach for his hand, digging my nails into his flesh. "No more. I can't take it."

I'm trembling against him and know that it's only his strength keeping me upright.

"You can, and you will." He pinches my clit. "I'm not done until you come around my cock again."

Without warning, a second orgasm hits me even stronger than the first.

This time, when I scream, it's his name on my lips. A few thrusts later, he joins me, calling out my name in reverence as he fills me.

We're both panting, fighting to catch our breath as the world slowly tilts back into focus. Cillian pulls out and disappears for a moment, then returns with a damp washcloth. Gently, he flips me onto my back and runs it up my thighs, wiping away the evidence of our sex. He tosses the cloth aside and unfastens the belt binding my wrists.

His touches are tender, almost worshipful, as he rubs the red marks left on my skin. The soft kisses he places there serve as a beautiful juxtaposition to the brutal way he just took me.

Those kisses continue, slow and unhurried, traveling up my arms, over my shoulders, until they reach my jaw. His fingers trace the forming bruises on my hips, feather-light. He tugs gently at my hair, massaging my scalp.

"Why did I like that so much?" I whisper.

"I already told you, no one is truly innocent. There are dark parts to your soul, just as there are bright parts of mine. Your darkness is a part of you, and it's beautiful. Watching you embrace it? It's intoxicating." His lips brush my jaw. "You crave control. But giving up control like that… that's the most powerful act there is. You held all the power tonight, little goddess. If you'd said the word, I'd have stopped. No questions. You never did."

His kisses continue along my jaw until he reaches my lips. He places a chaste kiss there, whispering, "But for the record, I'm really glad you didn't. You're so beautifully vicious."

His fingers continue softly caressing my side.

"I'm a broken little thing," I choke out the words.

"Broken doesn't mean less than. There will come a day when you put yourself back together, and I pity anyone who stands in your way when that day comes."

I fall silent, letting the weight of his words settle in my chest. I want to believe him. I hope he's right.

"Thank you, Cillian," I say softly.

"For what?"

"For embracing the part of myself that I fear."

"I rather like that part of you," he says with a wink. "You should let her out to play more often."

"My friends wouldn't understand," I sigh.

He cocks his head at me. "Wouldn't they?"

"No, they wouldn't."

"You're wrong, just so you know."

I don't have the energy to argue, so I don't. Instead, I begin to shift out of bed.

"Stay," he demands softly, pulling me back toward him.

"I can't. This can't mean anything."

"Then it won't. It's just sleeping."

I push myself up and fight the tears forming behind my eyes. "I can't, Cillian. I've only ever shared a bed with *him*. If I stay, it will mean something. It can't mean anything because then it feels like everything I shared with him means nothing."

The admission has pain creeping back in, and Cillian gives me a sad look. With one last kiss, he lets me go. "I don't agree, but I understand. Good night, Ophelia."

I dress quickly and wrap my cloak around me, stepping into the hallway as quietly as possible.

My shoulders fall as I fight the pain creeping further under my skin. As it turns out, Cillian's room isn't far from my own.

Looking down the hall, I startle when I notice a figure across from me. As they step away from the wall, I find Ayden staring at me. My cheeks flush at what he must have heard if he'd been outside the door for long.

"Good evening, Ophelia."

"Good evening, Prince." My voice is soft as I ask, "How long have you been standing there?"

His chest rises as he inhales a deep breath before answering, "Long enough."

"Why?"

"I went to your room looking for you. I was going to offer to quiet your dreams. When you weren't there, I went in search of you. It didn't take long to find you."

I'm not sure how to read the emotions on his face right now. His words are neutral, but he sounds uncomfortable or upset by something.

"You came to help me sleep?" I ask, dumbfounded. "Why would you do that?"

"I could say it's because I gave my word to Elijah. But the truth?" He pauses. "I can't stand to see you in this much pain. If I can help, even just a little, I want to."

His explanation leaves me speechless.

Without thinking, I step forward and wrap my arms around him. He holds me tightly for several long, quiet moments.

When I finally pull back, my cloak slips. The edge of the hood falls, baring my neck.

Ayden stiffens.

His amber eyes turn molten as he eyes the angry red mark left by Cillian's teeth. I know it looks much worse than any love bites, but truthfully, I delighted in it.

"He did this to you," Ayden hisses as his fingers trace over the mark.

I flinch slightly at the sting of having him touch the wound.

"Yes," I say softly, reaching for his hand and squeezing it. "But it wasn't anything I didn't want."

His eyes turn from venomous to curious in an instant.

"Intriguing," he says, dropping his hand from my neck.

We walk the rest of the way to my room in silence. But it's not uncomfortable.

After I shut the door behind us and drop my cloak to the floor, I turn to him. "Ayden, I'm sorry."

"Whatever for?"

"For whatever you overheard between Cillian and me. It seems to have upset you, and I just— "

"Stop, Ophelia." He places a hand over my mouth, silencing me. Once he's satisfied I'm done talking, he lowers it.

"You are responsible for your own self-rescue," he says. "How you decide to heal is up to you, and I don't ever want to hear you apologize for it again. You are not responsible for my feelings."

I nod, heart thudding in my chest.

"Now go get dressed for bed."

I slip into the bathing chambers and quickly discard my dress and ruined shift in one swift motion. Pulling a nightdress over my chilled skin, I fight back the tears pressing behind my eyes.

I had worn Elijah's shirt to bed every night since his death, soaking in the last remaining bits of his scent that lingered. The faint scent of cinnamon and chocolate clinging to the fabric was all I had left of him, and it was nearly gone. But it felt wrong wearing his shirt to bed when I was covered in Cillian's scent.

A fresh wave of grief rolls through me as I realize I will never again be covered in the smell of cocoa and cinnamon. It would never again be his love marks that marred my skin. I would never wake up next to him again.

It was all… gone.

I sink to the floor, the weight of it pressing me down as the sobs take over, raw and unrelenting. I don't know how long I sit there, knees drawn to my chest, tears soaking my nightdress.

When Ayden finds me, I barely hear the door open. But then his arms are around me, lifting me from the cold tile without a word. He carries me to my bed and lays me down gently, pulling the covers up to my shoulders like I'm something fragile.

My body still trembles, but the tears eventually slow. I feel the warmth of his magic press gently against my temple, soothing, quieting the edges of my mind.

Between his Gift and the exhaustion Cillian left in his wake, I know I'll sleep deeply tonight.

A thought occurs as he pulls away. "Why do you have to kiss Breyla's forehead for your Gift to work?"

A soft smile tugs at his lips. "I don't. I just really enjoy pissing off Aurelius."

"That sounds about right," I mumble through a yawn.

"Sweet dreams, Ophelia."

"Good night, Ayden."

CHAPTER FORTY-FOUR

BREYLA

Darian pants heavily, bent at the waist as he fights to catch his breath. He'd just jumped Ryder, Zion, and me from Andhull to the Rimor border, a distance that would normally take a full day's ride. While his Gift allowed him to make that distance on his own, taking others with him took a much heavier toll on his energy. He'd explained as much during our travels the week prior.

An urgent missive had arrived from the city's ruling lord. A group of Rimorian refugees was crossing the border just as the Fae had launched an attack on the town.

"For the record, I still think this is a trap," Darian huffs.

"For the record, I'm pretty sure you're right. That knowledge doesn't change my decision."

We had argued for five straight minutes over the decision to come here. There hadn't been an attack since Elijah's death, just complete, unnerving silence. The attack, happening just as Rimorian citizens crossed the border, was no coincidence. He argued that Ayden would kill him for endangering me so recklessly. I argued that I would kill him myself if he refused to help those in need.

We stand in the middle of a deserted courtyard, a small stone keep looming in front of us, but not a single soul in sight.

A heavy wooden door creaks open, revealing a burly, gray-haired male. "General, this way."

We step inside the fortress, my eyes trailing over the souls inside. Mostly females and children, all displaying terrified looks on their faces.

"I had hoped you would bring more reinforcements," the male says, disappointment filling his weary eyes.

"Lord Renfer, the nearest troops are stationed over a day's ride away. My options were limited," Darian replies. "You've got two generals and General Breyla's personal guards. Now tell us what's happening."

"The females, children, and those unable to fight are within the walls. The refugees arrived at dawn, and the bastards attacking us showed up not ten minutes later. There was no warning, just mass carnage as they volleyed wave after wave of poisoned arrows at us," Lord Renfer explains, his eyes glazing as he recalls the destruction. "There were mass casualties initially. The males I have left are fighting to escort the refugees to safety and find any remaining citizens not inside the walls."

I draw my sword as shadows ripple across my hands, itching to strike. "It sounds like we have two objectives, then."

Darian nods. "Get the refugees to safety first, stop the attack, kill every Fae bastard we find along the way."

"Okay, three objectives. Do you have enough strength to jump us to the edge of town?"

His teeth worry at his bottom lip. "I'd rather save my energy for the return trip."

"Fair enough. I'll cover us with shadows as much as I'm able. Ryder and Zion," I say, turning to them. "You slaughter anything that moves against us, but keep an eye out for potential survivors."

"Understood, General," Ryder replies. Zion just huffs.

Darian turns back to Lord Renfer. "Do you have any horses we can reach?"

"If any remain, they'll be in the stable out back."

"Take us there," Darian demands.

Lord Renfer nods curtly, turning to lead us to the stables.

We wade through several halls filled with terrified wives, crying children, and grieving widows. A few elderly and disabled mingle, but there are far too few souls here for a town this size.

When we reach the stables, they're empty. All the horses are either in use by those fighting or ran off when the stalls were left open.

"Shit," Darian curses, running a hand through his brown tresses as he takes in the empty stalls.

"Guess we're running," I say as I lean down to double-check the laces on my boots are tied properly. All my weapons are in place, save the sword in my hand.

Ryder and Zion both draw their blades, ready to leave at my command.

We stare out at the walls and the gate looming before us. The wind picks up, howling and rustling the trees around us. I know it's thanks to Ryder's Kaminari Gift, and that it should help deter any arrows from hitting their target. Hopefully.

"On my count," Darian says, his own sword drawn as he hunches down, body poised to sprint through the city streets.

We mirror his stance as he begins counting, "Three... two..." He pauses, looking around to verify the coast is clear.

"One!" I whisper-shout, trying not to draw any unwanted attention our way.

We sprint for the gates, and they open a fraction of a second before we arrive, just wide enough for us to slip through in single-file order.

The wind continues to whip around us unnaturally and I throw up a shield of shadows to obscure their vision and deflect any arrows that come within a foot of us.

Three arrows zing past, embedding themselves in the buildings behind us as we run east for the refugees. The clash of steel grows louder as we find our way through the city streets.

It feels like we pass the body of a fallen one every hundred yards. Lord Renfer wasn't exaggerating when he said the casualties had been massive.

We round a corner and skid to a halt.

Three Fae warriors block our path, swords dripping with the blood of innocents as they smile wickedly, their crimson eyes sparkling with sadistic glee.

They don't speak. They don't make any noise as they launch their attack.

It's three of them against four of us, but I'd be a fool to consider those odds in our favor.

Darian meets the first warrior, blocking his attack and returning one of his own. I lose sight of him as a second male charges me.

With a flick of my left hand, three shadow-daggers manifest in the air and launch toward his chest.

He dodges the first two with ease, but the third sinks deep into his shoulder.

He snarls and reaches for the dagger, but his hand passes right through the shadow because they respond to me and me alone.

I use the moment of distraction to swing my sword at him. At the last second, he raises his own to block.

In my peripherals, I see Darian's opponent hit the ground, and I release a shaky breath of relief.

My sword arches in another drive towards my foe, but my arm stops, suspended in mid-air. Roots have shot up from the ground below, wrapping my arms so tightly I can't move them.

Searing pain shoots through my hand as my thumb dislocates with a sickening pop. I grunt, trying to summon my shadows, but nothing happens.

The male just stares at me, a pleased look gleaming in his eyes.

What is he doing? He could have killed me by now. He *should* have killed me.

His mouth opens like he means to speak, but all that comes out is a strangled gasp as he looks down to find the tip of a blade protruding from his chest.

The Fae's body drops, and the roots fall away.

Darian steps up to me after pushing the body aside and takes my injured hand in his.

"This is going to hurt," he warns.

"Just do it."

I cry out as he pops the digit back into place, the pain nearly as sharp as when it dislocated.

Ryder and Zion appear beside me, their chests heaving as they stare down at the third dead Fae at their feet. I must have missed the kill, but I'm grateful just the same.

My hand throbs, but I know it would be so much worse if not for the adrenaline fueling me right now.

"Let's go," Darian says, motioning for us to continue east toward the edge of town.

We make it there with minimal issues.

The number of bodies grows as we near the border. It's not just males and soldiers now. We've found the earliest victims of the attack. I send up a prayer to the Goddess of Life and Death that there are no children amongst the fallen.

Ahead lies an expanse of open field separating the town from the forest that lines this section of the border.

"If they're still alive, they're in the forest," Darian says confidently.

From what we had seen on our way here, the majority of their forces seemed to be focused in the north of the city. I don't dare let hope rise in me that I haven't seen any Fae in the last ten minutes. I just beg the gods to bless us long enough to find the refugees.

We dart across the field, attempting to keep low so as not to be seen. Cillian would be incredibly useful right now.

Somehow, we make it across safely, not a single arrow in sight. We throw ourselves behind a cluster of trees, letting them shield us from view just long enough for us to catch our breath.

I cocoon us in darkness well enough to keep us hidden amongst the trees. "Stick close to me."

Stealthily, we creep, being careful to make as little sound as possible.

We find the refugees, but we're too late. They lay piled in a heap of what must be at least fifteen people.

I bite back my emotions, distancing myself from the pain in the way I must to get through this battle, and drop the shadows around us.

"I'm sorry, Breyla," Darian says.

Gently, I move the bodies on top, searching the faces for those I might know.

I don't immediately recognize any of them, meaning they most likely weren't from Ciyoria. It doesn't make it any easier seeing the bodies of my people, innocents, piled high in a mass grave.

I will mourn them later.

Just as I move to close the eyes of one brown-eyed female, a hand shoots out from beneath her, grasping my wrist.

I jump back with a scream as the bodies begin to shift. The obviously dead ones fall to the side, revealing several very alive faces.

Faces I know.

"Breyla?" Nameah's mother asks as she crawls from the pile of bodies.

I nearly cry in relief that not all my people are dead today. "What are you doing here?"

"We came seeking refuge," she explains. "Rimor has crumbled, and the people are starving."

The rest of her remaining children, with the exception of the eldest son, crawl out from beneath bodies. They're blood-stained, covered in dirt, and more than half-starved, but they're *alive.*

"I know," I say, guilt dropping my shoulders. "We've been sending food, but everything gets burned before it reaches the people who need it. I'm so sorry."

"Just as I don't blame you for Nameah's death, nor do I blame you for this." She takes my hand, squeezing it firmly. "But I do request your aid."

"Of course. We're here to help."

"How many of you are there?" Darian asks, eyeing the pile of remaining bodies like one of them might start walking.

"Including my family, seven total," she replies. "When they attacked, we fell back, deciding it wasn't worth it to cross the valley."

"We used the bodies of the fallen to hide," one of Nameah's sisters says with a shudder. "Gross, I know."

"It was smart thinking," I reassure her, turning back to her mother. "Where's your eldest son?"

Her face darkens. "He enlisted in the army shortly after you left Rimor. We have not heard from him in several months."

Pain lances through me for her, for the possibility of another child lost.

"Let's get you to safety," Darian says, taking inventory of who we have to protect.

"Can any of you fight?" I ask.

Nameah's other brother nods along with two others in the group.

I craft shadow blades and hand them out, willing them to stay solid in their grip.

We pass out daggers to the rest as I explain, "Those with swords stay on the outside of the group. If any of you see crimson eyes, stab first, think second. If you hesitate, you die."

"If any of you possess offensive Gifts, use them," Darian pants. His normal mask of cold indifference has slipped, revealing the sweat-drenched brow and heaving chest of a truly exhausted male.

Our group begins the trek out of the forest, my shadows swirling around us, Ryder's wind howling as we head for the city gate. It's a slower trip back than it was out here, but we maintain a jog to get us across the field.

It takes all of two minutes inside the city for us to encounter our first attack. Thankfully, it's only a group of three, and we're able to dispatch them with no casualties to our group.

It's when we reach the halfway mark that all hell breaks loose.

I turn a corner, and the rest of the group follows me into a narrow alley. My feet come to a halt, the breath leaving my lungs.

What appears to be their entire force stands less than three hundred feet away. Their weapons are pointed straight at me, eyes glowing as they stare us down.

"Queen of Shadows, how lovely to finally make your acquaintance," the one in front bellows, and my gods is his voice melodic. I'm nearly brought to my knees listening to him speak.

I turn back down the alley, facing the group as dread rises in me.

In a hushed voice, I say, "You are going to turn around and take the long way back to the stronghold. Once you get out of this alley, you are going to run like hell and not stop. Don't look back, don't cry out, just run. Ryder, Zion, Darian, and I will hold them off as long as we're able."

Nameah's mother shakes her head, trying to refuse my command.

"There is no time for arguing. I may not have been able to save Nameah, but I will not let her family suffer the same fate. You must live," I command.

Tears fill her eyes as she nods, turning the group around. My shadows follow them; their protection should last until they reach the stronghold, but they'll weaken the further they get from me.

"Why don't you tell your friends to join us?" the Fae male, their General, I assume, yells.

"Breyla, this is suicide," Darian argues, fear flashing in his navy-blue eyes.

"It's our only option, and you know it," I reply. "Something tells me they want me alive."

"And something tells me you shouldn't be listening to whatever voice is telling you that."

I ignore him, turning to Ryder and Zion. "You've been with me from the very start. Thank you."

"We're with you," Ryder says.

"From our first breath," Zion adds.

"Until our very last," I finish, pulling them into a tight hug.

I step back into the street, facing the General and the army behind him.

Darian and I stand center, flanked by Ryder and Zion, as I call out, "What are your demands?"

The front line stands with arrows notched and aimed directly at us, awaiting his command.

I have no way of knowing if the others made it to safety, but I feel my shadows snap, my connection severed as they pass out of range. The moment it happens, more shadows start to gather at my feet, forming into arrows of my own making, as the general speaks.

"My demand is simple." He grins, the expression sinister and dark. "I want you, Queen of Shadows."

"I have a name and that isn't it," I snap.

"Oh, but it is. It's the only one that matters, anyway."

"My name is Breyla. Come on, you can say it," I taunt, trying to keep him talking. "Brey-luh." I exaggerate the syllables like I'm talking to a toddler.

He chuckles. "It matters not what you call yourself as long as you come quietly."

"Yeah..." I hesitate, raising the shadow arrows from the ground and pointing them at the army. "I won't be doing that," I grunt, unleashing them in one swift strike.

Several hit their targets, but most are blocked.

The general tuts. "You should not have done that." He whistles a high, sharp note, and their arrows fly.

I duck, throwing up a shield of shadow at the last minute. When I'm sure the last arrow has flown, I survey the damage.

"No," I gasp when my eyes find Zion to my left.

An arrow is lodged dead center of his torso. Poisoned or not, it doesn't matter. Where the arrow has punctured, he will bleed out in minutes.

"I'm so sorry, my friend," I cry, dropping to my knees by Zion's head. I wrap his hand in mine, squeezing tightly as I look into his eyes for the last time.

Blood bubbles in from the corner of his lips, and he just shakes his head, giving me a soft smile.

"May the gods grant you peace," I whisper as his eyes lose focus, glazing over as his soul finally slips away.

"I grow impatient with your games, Queen of Shadows. Consider that a warning for disobeying my request," the Fae general sneers.

I wipe the tears off my cheeks, smearing Zion's blood across my face in the process.

"Hasn't anyone told you?" I snarl as I stand, my sword raised and ready for attack. "I'm terrible at following orders."

The general's voice softens, almost coaxing. "Then how about I make you a deal instead?" the general purrs. Something in his tone sets me on high alert. "I won't kill your companions if you come peacefully."

It sounds good in theory, but somehow, I know he's lying.

"Sorry," Darian shouts, stepping forward. "If you want Breyla, you'll have to go through us."

"Very well." The general shrugs, falling back into line.

"Can you Travel us?" I whisper to Darian as the enemy advances.

"Not all of us. And not far. I'm nearly drained."

"Fuck."

We can't run, or we risk them following and slaughtering the rest of the city.

"Together we fight," Ryder says.

"Together we die," Darian agrees.

"But we take as many with us as we can on our way out," I finish.

Together, the three of us charge the line of Fae, knowing we won't walk out of here again.

We manage to cut down five of them before someone drives a

sword through Ryder's chest. My shadows retaliate instantly, slicing through his killer's neck and severing his head from his body. There's no time to respond to his loss before the next attacker is on me.

Darian and I fall into rhythm, fighting back-to-back as bodies drop around us. Until it's just us, surrounded by a circle of corpses

"Well, this has been entertaining," the general drawls, a mixture of boredom and annoyance plastered across his too-perfect face. "But we're done appeasing your tantrum."

The strangest thing about this entire fight is that it felt like the enemy was holding back. They were fighting to subdue, not to kill. Like a cat playing with a mouse before it's eaten.

Several archers aim arrows at Darian, and the general snaps his fingers. "Kill him."

I make a reckless decision that I pray is right, that my instincts were correct in believing they have orders to bring me back alive.

I throw myself in front of Darian. I'm smaller than he is, but I cover enough of him that they don't have a clear shot. "If you want to kill him, you'll have to kill me first."

"What are you doing, Breyla?" Darian hisses under his breath.

"Saving your life."

He curses, wrapping his arm around me.

The general tilts his head, contemplating his response before he finally says, "Hm, I suppose we could make use of the Prudian general."

I barely hear the words as I feel the tug of Darian's magic. He's preparing to jump.

"Take them both," the general commands.

The searing pain is all I register as I look down to find an arrow protruding from my gut. Another has struck the arm Darian wrapped around me.

It must be poisoned with something because my vision begins to fade, blackness creeping in around the edges. I try to scream, to call for help, but I'm not sure I actually make any noise. I think of Aurelius, wishing I could see him one last time, but grateful that it's not him with me now.

Something snaps in my chest.

The last thing I hear before the darkness claims me is Aurelius screaming my name.

CHAPTER FORTY-FIVE

Blinding rage consumes me as Breyla's screams echo in my mind, raw and desperate, crying for me. She's in pain, and she's terrified.

Then it goes quiet.

I'd suspected for quite some time that we were able to hear each other's thoughts, but we never had the chance to discuss or confirm it. Now, there was no doubt in my mind.

But it's the silence that terrifies me more than hearing her screams.

Something primal and foreign builds in my chest, ripping out in the form of a viscous snarl. The thought of something happening to her, that she could be in pain or worse, is unbearable.

Dropping Elythia's journal, I tear out of the library in search of Ayden. Whatever happened, whatever this is, it's because of him. Because he sent her out on a godsdamned suicide mission with Darian.

I barely register the guards and staff I pass in the hall as door after door flies open in my attempt to locate the prince. All I see is red. All I feel is terror and fury. I will find her, and those responsible for her pain will suffer.

When I find Ayden, any shred of control deserts me.

I slam him against the wall, the glass in a nearby window rattling from the impact. A pained grunt leaves his lips as I wrap my fingers around his throat.

The queen screams, calling for the guards.

Ignoring her, I snarl, "Where the fuck did you send Breyla?"

"I—" Ayden gasps, clawing for breath. "The border, with Rimor."

A delicate hand wraps around my bicep, and the queen speaks, "You will release the prince's throat. Now."

In my heightened state, her Anima Gift slips through my mental defenses. My grip eases slightly, and Ayden greedily sucks in air. "What is this about?"

I growl, realizing the queen has coerced my actions, and shake off her hold.

She isn't shaken in the least, though. "Release my son before I have you executed for treason," she says calmly, power lacing every word.

Reluctantly, I drop my hand from Ayden's throat, but I don't retreat.

"Breyla… she's been hurt," I stammer.

His brow narrows in confusion. "How do you know that?"

I rake a hand through my disheveled hair, pacing back and forth as I try to make sense of what I felt earlier.

"I heard her scream," I pant. "I heard her scream, and I think she's injured."

"Breyla is miles away," the queen scoffs.

I narrow my eyes at her, not sure why she's still part of this conversation.

"I don't know how, but I know she's in danger," I insist, my hands tugging at the strands of my hair.

"Breyla's with Darian, Zion, and Ryder. I'm certain she's fine," Ayden says.

"She's not fucking fine!" I roar. My hand clenches tightly at my side as my Hemonia Gift fights to lash out.

Guards begin to flood the room, looking between the prince, queen, and me to ascertain where the threat is coming from. Their response time is disturbingly lacking.

"Guards, restrain Lord Aurelius," the queen commands.

They close in, moving slowly as if I'm an animal that might spook and lash out.

"Guards, halt," Ayden commands, contradicting his mother's order.

They don't listen. Because, despite Ayden running this kingdom, his mother still outranks him.

One places their hand on my bicep, and I see red. My barely there restraint snaps, my Gift lashing out and seizing control of every guard's body in the room.

Everybody moves back at once, save for me and Ayden. Their limbs are frozen in place, bodies levitating an inch off the floor.

"Where. The. Fuck. Is. She." I growl, low and lethal.

"Let me check on them." Ayden finally seems to grasp how serious I am, nodding his head. "I'll speak with the lord in charge of that stronghold."

He goes quiet, projecting an illusion to wherever he's sent Breyla. After a few minutes, he shakes his head, letting out a string of curses.

"Lord Renfer says they arrived at Inasvine, successfully escorted refugees to the stronghold, but then the attack suddenly stopped."

"And…"

Ayden sighs, his shoulders sagging. "They found Ryder and Zion dead in the street, but there's been no sign of Breyla or Darian."

My heart stutters, breath catching in my throat. "She's gone."

"We don't know that."

The room spins, my grip on the guards faltering. "I can't hear her," I whisper.

"I need to visit the city," Ayden continues.

Queen Josephina scoffs. "Honestly, I'm not sure why you're surprised. Actions have consequences, and these are clearly yours."

Fury burns like acid inside my veins. Turning my attention to the viper they call queen, I grit, "What did you do?"

"What makes you think she has anything to do with this?" Ayden asks defensively.

"Tell me you don't know what's going on," I demand, eyes fixed on the queen.

"Of course I don't," she replies, too quickly.

The Anima Gift flares in me like wildfire. "She's lying."

Hesitantly, Ayden turns his attention to his mother, suspicion sparking in his eyes. "Tell me you don't know what happened to Breyla and Darian."

She remains quiet, her honey eyes narrowing on me.

"Mother..." Ayden warns.

"I will always do whatever is required to protect my son. And my kingdom."

"That's rich," I hiss, "coming from the same female who chastised Breyla for the same thing."

"No," she argues, "what she was condoning was cold-blooded murder."

"There are two dead guards, males Breyla considered friends. You may not get your hands dirty, but your actions leave you guilty all the same."

"Mother, tell me you aren't responsible for the disappearance of my fiancée and general," Ayden says, his eyes begging her to deny it.

"I don't—" She pauses, sighing heavily. "I don't know why they took Darian."

"Who?" I demand.

"Who else? The Fae." The queen rings her hands together, the nervousness leeching through her normally collected tone. "He assured me the attacks would cease."

"We do not bargain with the Fae," Ayden roars.

She flinches, drawing backward.

Manic energy pulses inside me, begging to be released. I want to hurt this poor excuse for a queen.

"You're the spy..." Ayden realizes, his face contorting in pain at the betrayal. "My own fucking mother is the reason the information was being leaked to the Fae."

"Ayden, I did it to protect you." Her voice softens as she tries to reason with him, to rationalize her betrayal. "To protect the kingdom."

"Just stop. I will deal with you later," Ayden spits. Turning back to me, regret fills his eyes. "If the Fae have them, they're no longer on this continent."

Panic claws up my throat. "How do you know?"

Ayden's face falls into a deep frown. "This isn't the first person they've taken from me," he admits softly.

My voice turns hysterical as I demand, "Tell me you got them back."

Ayden nods, his eyes refusing to meet mine. "In pieces."

My chest cracks, and I gasp. Fear, pain, and anger mix in a deadly maelstrom inside me, but all I hear is the deafening silence of Breyla's absence. "I can't hear her," I nearly sob.

Pained groans echo through the room, the sound of bodies hitting the floor somewhere in the background. I lose the battle to stand, falling to my knees with them.

"I can't hear her," I cry.

Ayden grasps my shoulder, and for the first time, I notice the blood streaming down from his eyes and nose. "Aurelius, you must stop. You're killing everyone in this room."

A quick glance around proves his words true. Every guard is doubled over in pain, blood draining out from every orifice.

Icy indifference settles over me. "Good."

"Aurelius, I know you don't mean that," Ayden tries to reason, the whites of his eyes now fully red. "These are good people. They don't deserve to die."

"Nothing matters if she's dead," I mumble.

"She's not dead, she's just not on the same continent. We can still find her. We'll bring her back," Ayden pleads. "You would know if she were truly gone."

Somewhere behind me, a female screams. It's not the queen. Ayden turns his gaze to the sound, horror crossing his face. There's a conversation between them, but I don't understand any of the words said.

The world around me blurs in and out of focus, the power in my veins growing steadily stronger.

It's still silent, so silent where I should hear Breyla.

Delicate fingers splay across my temples, and the female, Rowina, I realize now, leans into my ear and whispers, "Sleep, brother."

Exhaustion, drowsiness like I've never known, wraps around me. I lose the fight to stay conscious, darkness overtaking me in a matter of seconds.

CHAPTER FORTY-SIX

"**G**uard this door closely. Lord Aurelius is not to leave under any circumstances," I instruct the guards carrying his unconscious body to the bed. Dried blood cakes all our faces, but by the grace of the gods, we're all alive. Rowina arrived at precisely the right moment.

"What should we do if he wakes and becomes violent again?" one of the guards asks.

"Princess Rowina will remain close by. If she needs to, she can put him back to sleep."

The guard nods but doesn't look confident in my plan. It was the best we had at the moment.

The door clicks shut, the lock sliding into place. Two of our strongest palace guards post themselves on either side of the door, with three more stationed farther down the hall. Fear and uncertainty linger in every face that was present for his outburst.

I've watched Aurelius for years, but never has he lost complete and utter control like that. It was as terrifying as it was impressive.

What have you done, brother?

"He belongs in the dungeon," my mother says, her jaw ticking.

"And the same could be argued for you, Mother."

"I'm the queen," she says like it's some explanation that justifies her actions. "I acted in defense of your life and the kingdom's well-being."

I rub my temples, trying to lessen the ache growing behind my eyes. "Keep telling yourself what you must to rationalize the havoc you have brought upon Prudia."

She huffs. "I'm not rationalizing anything, son. It's the truth."

"No. The truth is that you withheld pertinent information from me, and it has cost countless people their lives." I meet her eyes, my gaze hardening. "Over half of Inasvine lies dead, waiting to burn."

Her throat bobs as she gulps, the gravity of her actions finally sinking in. "I never intended for that to happen, I had no way of knowing—"

"Your intentions don't mean shit. They're *dead*. Breyla and Darian are missing, likely next to lose their lives, or have you forgotten what they did to Malcom?"

"I haven't forgotten," she says, shrinking back. "I'm sorry for the pain this has caused you."

"Enough of your empty words. Guards," I call, feeling only a tinge of remorse for what I'm about to do. "The queen is not to leave her quarters. I will have meals brought to her. She is allowed no letters, and no contact with anyone outside of me or the princess."

Shock settles over her blood-splattered face. "You can't be serious."

"I am entirely serious. You are a liability to this kingdom and will remain under lock and key until I have assessed the damage done and can deal with you properly."

"I'm their queen," she argues, resisting my hold on her arm. "My orders overrule yours."

I laugh mirthlessly. "I doubt any of the guards here will take your side after hearing your admission in the great hall. Consider this a kindness. I could've had you thrown in the dungeon."

Gods know I'm angry enough to do so, but I'm not entirely heartless.

We reach her chambers, and I shove her inside.

"Oh, and don't let her touch you skin-to-skin," I warn the guards. "That's how her coercion works."

Pure ire burns in her eyes, the same eyes I see in my own reflection. I've just exposed one of her greatest secrets.

Unlike most with the coercion Gift, hers requires touch. A well-kept secret until this moment. Thanks to our father's Fae lineage, Rowina and I were the only ones capable of fighting the strength of her Gift. On any other day, Aurelius would have too, but his heightened emotional distress must have weakened his defenses, allowing her influence to slip through.

"Just tell me one thing," I say, raking my hand through my wild curls.

"What do you want to know?"

There's a lot about this situation that bothers me, but one thing I can't make sense of. "How did you even come in contact with the Fae?"

She wrings her hands, worry darkening her delicate features. "You aren't going to understand."

"Try me."

"Before your father… there was another."

My brows shoot up. This information is nothing I've heard before. As far as I was aware, my father was my mother's first and only love.

"He was a bastard born half-Fae, much like Aurelius. Only he turned his back on us in favor of the Fae." She begins to pace, slowly gathering her courage. "He was my mate. The Fae call them fated, or twin flames. A soul so perfectly mirrored to your own, it's said to be blessed by the gods."

"I've heard of such bonds," I admit. "But I never imagined you would…"

"He claimed me. Initiated the mate bond." Her voice cracks. "I rejected him, and the bond, though, and it nearly destroyed us both."

"What happened?"

"Physically, the pain is akin to childbirth. But emotionally, it's even worse," she explains. "Imagine yearning for someone so violently it hurts. I couldn't breathe and didn't sleep for weeks. The further I got from him, the sharper the pain grew. Since my half of the bond was never initiated, he could still hear my thoughts, sense my emotions, and physically locate me for years after."

"When did it stop?" I ask, chilled to the bone.

"I don't know exactly. His letters stopped arriving once you were born. But they started again after your father died."

True, violent horror washes over me. "You've been feeding information to your ex-lover for years?"

She nods, tears glistening in her eyes. "You don't understand, Ayden. He promised safety for you and Ro, for the kingdom."

"You're right; I don't understand," I bite out. "I don't understand how you could betray your people like this, how you could send Breyla and Darian straight into enemy hands. You know what they did to Malcom."

My voice shakes with every emotion crashing through me: anger, betrayal, horror, fear, and devastation all fill me, fighting for dominance.

The door slams shut between us, and I turn to make my way back toward the guest wing. I find Rowina standing at the end of the hall; her brow scrunched in worry.

"Where are you going now?" Rowina calls, rushing to keep pace with me down the corridor.

"I'm going to Inasvine to assess the damage and appoint an interim general," I say, jaw clenched. "But first..." I grit my teeth, dreading the thought of what I'm about to say. "I'm going to ask Cillian for help."

Surprise, then disbelief, flits across Ro's face. "What am I to do?"

"You're to watch Mother and Aurelius," I instruct. "I need you to keep them sequestered so they don't kill one another."

"I'm *babysitting?*" she asks, indignation clear in her tone.

I shrug. "If that's how you want to look at it, then yes."

"Unbelievable," she mutters, stalking off in the opposite direction.

I hesitate briefly, my fist hovering an inch from Cillian's door. All I can think about is the scent of him on Ophelia's freshly fucked skin, the marks he left behind that she seemed to have no qualms with.

She'd felt obligated to apologize to me for sleeping with him. I told her she didn't owe anyone an apology for how she chose to heal. That had been true, but so was the fact that my control almost slipped in that moment. Caught between wanting to punch him for leaving marks on her and wanting to replace them with my own, I did nothing.

Ophelia wasn't mine.

But I had promised Elijah I would protect her, and I meant it.

I shove the memory aside and knock hard.

He takes too damn long to answer.

When he finally opens the door, my jaw ticks.

Sweat drips down his bare chest, running in rivulets down his well-defined muscles to the waistband of his sleep pants.

"My, my," Cillian says, folding his arms and leaning into the door frame. "You are not who I expected knocking at my door," he purrs.

I shake my head, ignoring the confusion in his tone. "I need your help."

He lifts a scarred brow. "Oh?"

"Breyla has been taken by the Fae."

The playful smirk he's sporting falls. "What do you need?"

"How far can you travel with more than just yourself?"

Much to my chagrin, it takes us an entire day to reach Inasvine.

This isn't Cillian's primary Gift, so his range is shorter than Darian's. The first jump takes us only a third of the way. We ride horseback the next stretch while his magic recharges. That portion takes us most of the day until he's able to Travel us the remaining distance.

It's nearly midnight by the time we arrive. The guard post at the gate stands empty, no doubt due to the staggering number of dead.

At the stronghold, Lord Renfer greets us at the walls.

"Good evening, Prince," Lord Renfer says, motioning us inside. "Through here."

"Can you show us the bodies?" I ask, eager for answers. "Where you found them?"

The lord cringes. "Which bodies, Your Highness?"

"The two guards that accompanied Breyla," Cillian drawls like it should be obvious.

"This way," the lord says, guiding us deeper into the city.

Most of the bodies have been cleared, but blood still stains the stone and dirt, turning the streets into silent graveyards.

"How many did we lose?" I ask.

"It would be easier to tell you what we have left," Lord Renfer says stiffly.

"Go on, then."

"Thirty-three children and two hundred or so grown females remain. We have thirteen guards and soldiers, and ninety-six males."

Three hundred and forty-two souls remain. This had been a city that once held over a thousand.

The loss is catastrophic, the bitter taste of failure filling my mouth.

Cillian lets out a low whistle. "They sure did a number on you," he says as his eyes dart around the carnage.

"I have never seen such devastation," Lord Renfer remarks.

Cillian laughs dryly. "You should see Rimor."

We walk a few more minutes before the lord stops. "This is it."

I can see where the bodies once lay, the blood still soaked into the earth below. My fingers brush the cold ground, my heart clenching for Breyla. I had once told her that I didn't wish to see her hurt, that I wasn't her enemy.

But when had I started hurting for her?

"What happened?" I ask quietly.

"I don't know, no one here saw—" Lord Renfer begins, but a familiar voice interrupts.

A female passes by, cradling a squirming child in her arms.

"Breyla and your general, along with the other two, sacrificed themselves to save my family," Nameah's mother explains.

"It's good to see you again..." I pause, realizing I never got her name.

"Calliah," she offers. "They found us in the forest in the midst of the attack. Led us here, then held off the Fae while we took a different path to the stronghold."

"How recklessly noble," Cillian sighs.

"They're the only reason my family is alive," Calliah says reverently.

"Thank you, Calliah."

"I only wish I could tell you what happened after that. We heard her scream just as we reached the walls, but I don't know what happened after we split ways."

"It's okay," I say, jaw tight. "I have a pretty good idea."

"What's next, Prin—" Cillian starts, then abruptly cuts off. "Lord Aurelius?" he asks in confusion.

I whip around to find Aurelius standing behind us, wearing the same clothes he passed out in. His hair is disheveled. His eyes were dark and rimmed in red.

How the hell did he get past the guards?

There's no time to ask as someone shouts, "We're under attack!"

Arrows fly, narrowly missing civilians in the street. There aren't many people out, thank the gods.

I'm thrown inside the nearest building, Cillian's body covering mine. We're the same size, though, so it doesn't do much good. Half of me is still exposed.

Breathing heavily, we peek around the corner, looking for the assailants. I see none, but Aurelius is on his knees, an arrow protruding from his thigh.

I push against Cillian, fighting to break free of his hold.

"Let me—" I'm cut off by Cillian's hand covering my mouth.

"Shhh, princeling," he whispers, his breath hot against my ear. "My magic is only shielding us from sight, not sound."

He moves our bodies sideways to get a better view.

In horror, I watch half a dozen Fae soldiers circle Aurelius, weapons drawn. I can smell the tang of the poison on the tip of the arrow.

Aurelius thrashes, snarling at them. He's unarmed. If he's using his Hemonia Gift, they aren't susceptible to its effects, since none of them so much as hesitate.

"Dose him again," one of them commands.

A dart sinks into his neck, and his movements grow sluggish.

Just before he collapses, I hear him snarl, "Where is my mate?"

The Fae vanish, taking Aurelius's limp body with them.

The city falls silent.

EPILOGUE

OPHELIA

The light glints off the blade as I twirl it between my fingers. I had grown quite nimble with it since Cillian first gave it to me.

The castle is unnervingly quiet. And I'm bored.

Breyla had been sent away with Darian on some urgent mission, and I hadn't heard a word in days.

I was in town when Aurelius attacked Ayden, his mother, and half the palace guards. Everything I knew was learned second-hand from gossiping staff.

Some things never change at court, it seems.

That incident happened two days ago. The only familiar face still in the palace is Rowina, and I barely know her.

I just wish someone would tell me what the hell is going on.

I consider heading back to town. Maybe find a new target to watch. But the blood lust hasn't stirred since my… encounter with Cillian. And damn him for being right about it. His solution, infuriatingly, had worked.

Just as I decide to leave the palace, Ayden and Cillian appear in front of me. Looking utterly depleted and sleep-deprived, they pant hard, falling into me. Somehow, I manage to keep us all upright.

After several heartbeats, their breathing evens out and they straighten themselves.

Crossing my arms, I arch a brow. "Did you remember I still exist?"

"Breyla and Aurelius are gone," Ayden says, voice ragged.

"W-what?" I stammer.

"Kidnapped by the Fae," Cillian explains.

"I think," Ayden starts. "Aurelius might be dead."

I stumble, one hand reaching for the nearest wall to steady myself. "What are we going to do?"

Cillian grins as if the thought of imminent danger excites him. "We're going to get them back, of course."

You okay there? I know that ending was a bit of a wild ride. What did you think of the little twist at the end? If you want to vent, theorize, or perhaps cry with other readers, I invite you to join Morgana's Little Masochists reader group on Facebook. You'll also get sneak peeks and writing updates, plus access to giveaways and incentives.

https://www.facebook.com/groups/808677844456576/

ACKNOWLEDGMENTS

Well, we made it. This one definitely took an army to get across the finish line, but I'm so grateful to every one of you. First off, this book would not have been possible without the help of Chloe I. Miller. Technically, I'm supposed to say you did a thorough beta read and not an edit, but what you did to make The Call of Crimson possible was so much more. From the bottom of my heart, thank you. Your guidance made this a better book and me a stronger writer.

Thank you to all of my amazing beta and ARC readers. Everything you do is important to me. To my friends, both in real life and virtually, your unwavering, sometimes feral, support of me means the world.

To my street team, you all are amazing! Thank you for every post, share, and comment. You truly keep me going at times.

To Jenn, my amazing PA, you're amazing. Thank you for helping me at events, always promoting my book, and listening to every wild idea I have for how to torture my readers.

A huge thanks to M.A. Kilpatrick for proofreading and formatting the ARCs in 72 hours. Not sure how you do it, but you're magical. I know you're proud of me for managing to include beer pong in a high fantasy novel and unintentionally quoting *The Princess Bride* twenty-seven times. That is all thanks to my phenomenal upbringing. I'm being serious, I have great parents.

Last, but never least, to my husband, Johnathan. You've been with me through everything, listened to every rant and breakdown, supported every crazy idea, and helped me cart my books around to all the events. You may never read my books, but I know you're still my number one fan. I love you from the bottom of my incredibly sadistic heart.